Rogues' Gallery

Watch for these future murder mystery novels
by Daniel Eller

In the Interest of Justice
In Search of a Reasonable Doubt
A Case of Felony Murder
In the Heat of Passion

Rogues' Gallery

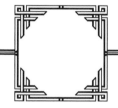

Daniel Eller

NORTH STAR PRESS OF ST. CLOUD, INC.

First Edition, September 1, 2003

Printed in the United States of America by Versa Press, Inc.,
East Peoria, Illinois

Published by
North Star Press of St. Cloud, Inc.
P.O. Box 451
St. Cloud, Minnesota 56302
nspress@cloudnet.com

Dedication

To Max,
my constant and silent companion.

Acknowledgements

This is the third in a series of five novels I have completed—the first to be published. I have imposed upon many family members, friends, and colleagues to read my stories, and their thoughts and critiques have made, I believe, better stories. To name them all would take another chapter. They know who they are and I thank them for their help.

I must, however, single out certain people. First is my legal assistant, Kay Lahr. I firmly believe that if it was not for her encouragement (and constant prodding), I would still be rewriting that first paragraph.

Then I must thank Ann Grunke. I took my first novel to her because of her expertise, and she gave me her time and knowledge to make my stories and my writing better.

Next I thank Corinne Dwyer and the people of North Star Press for their help, and patience, in finalizing this story.

Finally, my family—my wife, Pam, and the girls, Nicole, Nadine, and Natalie—for their many years of telling me to stop talking about writing a book and just do it. I thank them for their persistance, their critiques, and their support.

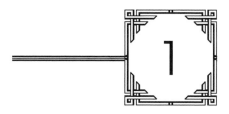

"What are we going to do with all that money?" Kate asked.

"God, I don't know," I replied. "Think about it. Eighteen million! It's like winning the lottery."

"We won't end up with eighteen million dollars, though. What about taxes? And this attorney friend of yours, what's his name again?"

"John Spokes," I replied.

"He'll wanna get paid, right?"

"Well, most attorneys take a third," I said.

"Six million dollars! For just a little advice?"

"If he can put this together for us, Kate, he'll have earned it."

"Okay," she replied. "Easy come, easy go. That leaves twelve million. What about taxes?"

"Taxes! I forgot about that. Normally about forty, forty-five percent." I hesitated. Knowing I could get her dander up, I added, "Maybe we don't have to pay taxes. How's the IRS ever going to find out anyway?"

"Yeah, that'll be good," she replied, grinning. "We finally get enough money we can do the things we want, and you want to take the chance of going to prison for tax evasion . . . makes sense to me."

"Okay, so we pay Uncle Sam. Then we have about seven million left."

"Well, the first thing I'm gonna do is pay all of Carol's bills," she said.

"That can't be more than fifty, sixty thousand," I replied.

"That's right, but at least she won't have to worry about them. Then I want to buy her a new car," she said.

"That's just like you," I replied. "Worry about Carol first. What about us?"

"I've thought about that," she said. "I think we should let Carol have our house, and we'll buy one of the homes in Florida, on Sanibel Island, for a million or so. We'll live there in the winter, and we'll visit here in the summer. We'll have the best of both worlds."

"I could do that," I said. "Maybe I could open an office on Sanibel, do a little estate planning, wills, that kind of thing, nothing major, just enough money to get by on."

"But, Bob," she said, "say we invest a couple million, can't we make enough off that so we don't have to worry about work?"

"Conservatively, we should be able to make a couple hundred thousand a year without touching the principal, but I don't want to just sit around, walk the beach every day, become a beach bum. I have to keep busy."

"Maybe you could open a little shop," she said.

"Nah, that's not for me," I replied.

It was a hot, muggy day in late August. My wife, Kate, and I drove Interstate 94 on our way to Minneapolis. I had a two o'clock appointment to meet with another attorney, a friend of mine, about a business proposition. That proposition, if everything went well, would net me eighteen million dollars, less expenses, of course. On the drive we were fantasizing about what we would do with our new found wealth.

After practicing criminal law in Central Minnesota for over twenty-five years, I had managed to accumulate one house, still mortgaged, one relatively new car, still pledged, and a little in savings. I don't know why, but money and I never managed to keep company very long. Kate, a homemaker, had no desire to find a career; we both preferred it that way. Our only child, Carol, was in her last year of veterinarian school at the University of Minnesota. Now, in our early fifties, an opportunity had come in the mail that was almost unimaginable.

"I still don't understand how you got into this. Who's this Matthew guy?" she asked.

"That's not his real name, that's his American name. His real name is Yakubo Ajayi."

"He's African?" she interjected.

"I was getting to that," I replied. "Remember I had this case several years ago where this Nigerian was suppose to have touched the breasts

2

and made moves on a young lady, the daughter of the president of the bank?"

"I remember you talking about it, sure."

"Well that's the guy. He was a graduate student at the State University at the time, working on a master's degree in international finance. Anyway, one night he's sitting at the Press Bar with a bunch of his friends. There's this girl that he thinks is flirting with him, she's a sophomore in college. They end up sitting at the same table talking about classes, and he finds out she's also a finance major. She thinks he's just a nice guy. It ends up she invites him to her apartment. She thinks it's to keep talking about classes, he thinks it's for a little hanky panky. It's one of these small one-room apartments over by the campus. They end up sitting on the bed. He takes it as an invite, leans over, pulls her down and starts feeling her up. She starts screaming and kicking, actually goes hysterical. One of the neighbors comes over, this girl claims she's being raped, the police are called, he gets charged with attempted rape."

"Well, it was," Kate said.

I hedged. "Well, it was and it wasn't. He said he didn't intend to rape her. When she made a fuss, he started to back off. He assumed this was why she invited him to her apartment. Anyway, I got appointed his attorney. The prosecutor was being kind of hard nosed. He wanted to see him do some jail time, six months I think. Matthew almost went crazy when I told him. He said no way in hell. This was his last year in the master's program. If he got convicted of a crime like that, they would probably yank his student visa, and he'd be sent back to Nigeria. You know what he told me? I don't know if it's true or not, but in Nigeria, if he was charged and found guilty of touching a woman's breasts without her consent, as punishment they'd cut his hand off. Can you imagine that?"

"I think it sounds appropriate," she said. "He probably deserved it."

"You don't mean that," I said, as I took my eyes off the road to glance at her face.

She just shrugged her shoulders, acknowledged my glance with a smug smile.

"I talked to her father, the banker," I continued. "I had met him before. He was embarrassed about the whole thing. He didn't want to make his daughter go into court and have to testify, so he eventually phoned the prosecutor and told him to make us a deal we couldn't turn down. What ended up happening is he pled guilty to a lesser offense, sexual contact. The judge agreed to take it under advisement for a year and then dismiss it if he had no further charges. Matthew got a chance to keep his record clear, there was actually no conviction. It never got back to his family. I didn't see him again until I got a notice of his graduation. All I knew was that he got his degree and went back to Nigeria."

"So that's where he contacted you from?" she asked.

"A couple weeks ago, I got a big envelope, and the return address just said Lagos, Nigeria. I had no idea who it was from. I opened it, and it was a big thank-you card signed 'Matthew.' It just said, 'Thank you for the help.' But then inside was a letter. A copy of it's in the file. Why don't you grab it."

She reached to the back seat, brought the file up front and started to page through it.

"There it is," I said.

She looked at it, read to herself.

Dr. Marshal U. Umah
Plot 23, Badagry Expressway
Maza – Maza
Lagos, Nigeria
Fax/Phone: 243-1-218822
July 26, 1994

STRICTLY PRIVATE AND CONFIDENTIAL.

Dear Mr. Williams:

Let me introduce myself. I am Dr. Marshal U. Umah, Director of Finance, Central Bank of Nigeria. I obtained your name in confidence from my assistant, Matthew Ajayi, who you met while at the University and were so kind to assist. He tells me you are a man of intelligence and integrity, and a person to whom we may make a business proposition which will be mutually beneficial to both parties.

I am a member of the Federal Government Contract Award Committee (FGCAC) on Crude Oil and Natural Gas with the Nigerian National Petroleum Corporation. The Committee recently completed a contract with a foreign oil and gas exploration corporation that included an agreement upon retention fee of $75,000,000.00. (Seventy-five million U.S. Dollars). You can understand, the fee was intended to insure favorable approval of the corporation's proposal by the Committee.

The contract has been completed and the retention fee duly certified and held by the Central Bank of Nigeria. The only parties with knowledge of the fee are the members of the Committee.

In view of the sudden Military take-over of leadership from the Interim National Government on or about November 17, 1993, last year, the GOVERNOR of the Central Bank of Nigeria and I have reached a concrete agreement to transfer and lodge this amount in overseas accounts. On the advice of Matthew, we are seeking your assistance in providing us with the necessary help to lodge the U.S. $75M in your account.

Furthermore, it was unanimously agreed among the members of this Committee that the money would be distributed as follows:

   * 25% of the total sum or US$18,750,000.00 is payable to your account for assistance and co-operation in the transfer of the funds.

   * 55% to be shared by the Committee members.

   * 15% for the Minister of Finance and the Governor of the Central Bank of Nigeria.

   * 5% will be set aside to cover any and all anticipated expenses which may be incurred by both parties during the course of the transaction.

THEREFORE, to enable us to put up claims for and to urgently effect the transfer of this US$75,000,000.00 into your personal or company account, within thirty (30) working days, we simply require the following:

   (a)   Your personal and confidential advice on arrangements to be made to transfer the funds from Central Bank to your personal account or as you advise.

   (b)   Your Private Phone/Fax number where you can receive urgent and confidential messages.

   (c)   Any other information, instructions or questions from you regarding this transaction.

Finally, once this fund is successfully transferred and lodged into your personal or company account, and upon the completion of other administrative and/or ministerial formalities, we will proceed to MEET YOU PERSONALLY in your Country to collect our shares of the fund and to invest part of it in your line of business or according to your noble advice. Thus, all we need from you is simply your assistance in providing us with your advice and co-operation on your part or otherwise a promise that you will not betray the very trust we have for you.

My Phone/Fax number is as listed above and I am looking forward to hearing about your acceptance of this offer by fax sooner.

Sincerely yours,

Dr. Marshal O. Umah, PhD.

When she finished, she folded it and put it back in the file. "I don't know," she said. "This doesn't seem right. That money belongs to the people of Nigeria. It was somehow skimmed off the top."

"I went to the library and did some research. That country's been in political turmoil for years. They're sitting on big oil reserves. There's all kinds of speculators from all over the world going in. There's so much graft and corruption going on it's unbelievable. So, it only makes sense somebody in the government was putting money aside, building themselves a little nest egg. Christ, it happens all the time. Look at Marcos in the Philippines, Suharto in Indonesia. They became multi-billionaires on graft and foreign payments. It's all sitting in banks someplace. This is peanuts compared to some of that stuff."

"Seventy-five million dollars is a lot of money, Bob," she said. "And it seems strange that they're willing to pay you twenty-five percent of that just to get you to help them get it out of their country."

"I agree, but it's sitting there, hidden in a bank. Nobody from the present government knows it's there. It sounds like Matthew works with this guy, Dr. Umah. That was his field, international finance. I suppose they were talking about how they could get this money out of the country, discreetly, and since Matthew had some connections over here, they turned to him. When he called, he told me he was working directly with the committee. He must've worked his way up rather quickly. I would guess a master's degree from an American university would do that for you over there. Anyway, it sounds as if they're anxious to get it done. There's probably a danger that the longer the money sits there, the more likely the military will discover it. That's probably why they're willing to give such a big cut for the help."

"What do you think this attorney's gonna be able to do?" she asked.

"Well, I'm hoping he can help us figure out how we can get the money from a bank in Lagos to a bank in Minneapolis. That's why I need him. I talked to a banker in St. Cloud, I gave him a hypothetical. He said if seventy-five million dollars hit any bank in St. Cloud, the news would go through the city's banking community like a firestorm. We could never hide that kind of deposit. But the big Twin Cities banks, the ones that deal with international finance, transfer that kind of money all the time. So, he said, if it looked like a legitimate business, set up legally with a federal I.D. number, everything else, he didn't see why it would be much of a problem."

"There's got to be more to it than that," she said.

"I suspect there is, that's why I got a hold of Spokes. So if he can put this all together, I guess I'm not going to feel bad about letting him take a third. We wouldn't have anything without his help."

"You think this is dangerous?"

"I don't know. I suppose if somebody in the military regime finds out the Minister of Finance somehow left the country with seventy-five million dollars . . . well. That's why it has to be done right, so they'll never find out."

She let that hang in the air for a few miles. I glanced to the side to catch her reaction. She knew what I was doing, and she gave me a slight smile that, over the years, had never failed to give me goosebumps. Unlike me, the years had been kind to her. She wore her hair back, swept over her ears, the same color it was the day we were married. Her eyes were a chocolate-brown, large and soft, with natural lashes other women would kill for.

She let out a sigh and said. "It worries me."

"Well, if I'm not comfortable with the whole thing after we talk to Spokes, we don't have to do it . . . but you don't get many chances to make millions. It should be worth a little risk."

7

I snuck another glance. The smile she had when dreaming about how we could spend our windfall had turned to a grim stare.

"Don't worry. I'm not going to do anything that would put us in danger. It won't do us much good to have all that money if we have to be looking over our shoulder all the time. But I don't know why that should be. If I understand right, it's just a matter of a couple of bank transfers, everybody gets paid, and it's over."

"You make it sound pretty simple," she said.

"Well, it should be."

Forty-five minutes later I was hopelessly lost in south Minneapolis, looking for an address on Park Avenue.

"Who in the hell would think they would make Park Avenue one way," I said.

"You know, you could've asked for directions," Kate replied.

"When he told me the address, on Park Avenue, I thought, how can you get lost, you just find Park Avenue. How'd I know Park Avenue was one way?"

"You could've asked," she said.

"I did."

"Yeah, after driving around for thirty minutes. Well, it's right up ahead," she said.

"Anyway, it wasn't thirty minutes, it was only ten," I said as I pulled into the parking lot of a two-story building off a shady boulevard.

"How do you know this attorney?" she asked.

"He's pretty well known. A couple years ago I had a drug case in Federal Court in Minneapolis where we had co-defendants. I hadn't been in Federal Court for a while, he helped me work my way through it. I've referred a few other cases to him. So we've kinda kept in contact."

"I expected to be going to one of the big firms, you know, like at the IDS Center or something like that," she said.

"He used to be with one of the big firms. He split away a couple years ago. He's a sole practitioner now."

We parked in back and made our way to the front entry. I looked at the directory: John Spokes, Law Office, Suite 107. I opened the door for Kate, and we walked down the hall.

The decor of the office caught me by surprise. I did a quick glance around. I figured his budget for artwork outdid my annual revenues. The receptionist looked up with a smile, the name plaque said her name was Amy. "Can I help you?" she asked.

"Yes, we're here to see Mr. Spokes."

"Are you Mr. Williams?" she asked as she looked at his appointment book.

"Yes, I am."

She was about to say something when a tall, thin brunette, probably in her middle thirties, came out the side door. "Mr. Williams?" she asked.

"Yes."

"I'm Pam Weber, Mr. Spokes assistant. He just took a long distance call. He'll be with you in just a moment. Can I get you a cup of coffee or a soda?"

"Nothing for me."

I looked at Kate. "I'm fine," she said.

"Just have a seat," she said. "I'll come out and get you when he's free."

We took a seat on a dark maroon leather couch. As we sat down Kate slugged me on the shoulder. "What's that for?" I asked.

"I saw you look at her."

"She just caught me by surprise."

"Yeah, I know what caught you by surprise." She slugged me again.

I just smiled. "No harm in looking."

I glanced around the room. The walls were hung with photos of John Spokes and various celebrities, politicians, people in the news.

"It looks like he's well connected," she said, also looking about.

He's been around for a while," I replied. "He's handled some pretty big cases, some with quite a bit of notoriety."

"I wonder if that's really his assistant," she said. "Is he married?"

"I don't know. I've seen him at various seminars with some blonde lady. I assumed she was his wife."

"I bet she wasn't his wife," Kate replied.

"What difference does it make to you anyway?" I asked.

"I just like to know what kind of person I'm dealing with."

I picked up a *Twin Cities Reader*. I always enjoyed going to the back pages to find out who was looking for romance. The ad would read: "Divorced, white female, 42, looking for a companion, 40 to 50 years old, who likes country western music, long walks, and romance," with a number to call. I was always curious what a call would produce. The next page had the ads for the massage parlors, gay bars, escort services. I figured there was an underside to the city I knew nothing about.

I was going through the last several pages when Pam Weber came back out. "Mr. Spokes is free, please come in."

The office was large and impeccably decorated. He sat behind a dark walnut desk, files neatly placed in front of him. He stood up. "Bob, how ya doin'?" he said, and extended his arm across the polished desk.

He was tall, over six feet, trim, in his late forties. He wore a dark blue suit, blue shirt and maroon tie. It appeared to me he had dyed his hair since I had last seen him, all hint of gray was gone. His eyes were narrow, giving one the impression that he was squinting at you. He had grown a thin mustache, which appeared to be tinted the same color as his hair. It was apparent he noticed I was a little surprised by the change in his appearance.

"Thanks for seeing us," I said quickly to ease his tension. "I don't think you've met my wife, Kate."

He clasped her hand. "No wonder we could never get Bob out to the bars after the seminars. He was always in such a hurry to get home, now I understand why."

Kate blushed a little. "Nice to meet you," she said.

He got down to business quickly. "Well I went over everything you faxed me, Bob. I don't think I'd touch it with a ten-foot pole."

The comment deflated me immediately. Spokes could see the disappointment. "Don't get me wrong," he continued. "If there was any way I could put this together, I certainly would. Eighteen million dollars? A guy would be crazy not to give it a try, so I did a little checking. I have a friend from high school at the State Department. From the information he gave me, Marshal Umah is legitimate, he was the Finance Minister under the provisional government. Apparently he was the only one who managed to keep lines of communication open with the military. When the military coup took place, they couldn't get rid of him. There wasn't anybody else smart enough to operate the finance system, who knew how the banks operated. So it may well be that he and the Contract Committee under the old regime put away millions of dollars in retention fees from foreign contractors, and it may be that the military regime doesn't know about it—I would suspect they don't—but our problem is, it's a federal crime to help him. In fact, it could violate a half dozen federal statutes. First, it's a felony offense to assist anybody in bringing illegally obtained money or property into the States."

He turned around. "I had it here somewhere." After shuffling some papers, he said, "I'll make a copy and get it to you. Although the statutes are generally intended to cover laundering of drug money, I believe they've been applied to importing any illegally obtained funds."

"But we don't know this is illegally obtained money," I said. "The letter indicated that this was a contract retention."

"Well that may be true, Bob, but the point is, it doesn't belong to these people. Either it's suppose to go to the government or be used on government projects, or it's suppose to go back to the contractor, who overpaid. The law simply makes it a crime to engage in a monetary transaction in criminally obtained property, property obtained from an unlawful activity. Seems to me that's exactly what we've got. If your friend doesn't turn this money over to the government, regardless of his feelings about the military coup, it's stealing. That's a felony offense, either here or in Nigeria. And if the money is transferred from a bank there to a bank here, in any manner, it's a monetary transaction."

"He's right," said Kate. "It seemed too easy. I knew there had to be something illegal about it."

"Bob, there are more statutes, other prohibitions. For this to work, you have to conceal or disguise the nature of the transaction. You're trying to hide the fact that stolen money is coming into the country—that's the crime.

I believe the sentence, if you get caught, is up to thirty years in prison and a fine, which can be as high as twice the value of the property involved. Do you have a hundred and fifty million dollars?" he added, glancing at Kate with a smile.

"Well, I'm not ready to give up on it that quickly," I said. "There must be some way of legitimizing the whole thing."

"Really, Bob, I've talked to everybody I can think of. I have a couple friends who do legal work for international corporations, they deal in international finance all the time. They tell me this kind of a transaction is going to be noticed. No bank can take it without a federal I.D. number. Just as important, how are you going to explain taking eighteen million dollars for simply setting up a bank account. There's definitely an ethical dilemma there as well, don't you think?"

As if to realize defeat, I relaxed my body and sunk into the chair. I let out a deep sigh.

"Believe me, Bob, if there was any way we could pull this off, I'd certainly do it. I'd like the money too, but we wouldn't have much fun trying to spend it from a federal prison."

I managed a grin, looked up. "Maybe they'd just give us probation."

"Two shysters, not likely," he said.

"I've heard enough," said Kate. "I don't want you to be any part of this."

I wasn't about to give up. "Look, guys, I've researched it. All we have to do is get one of the big brokerage firms in town to set up an account. International bank transfers happen all the time, why should this be any different."

"That may be true," said Spokes, "but those transfers are being done between United States and Israel, United States and Argentina, United States and France. How many seventy-five-million-dollar transfers do you think go between United States and Nigeria? I'll bet none."

"Bob," said Kate, a little perturbed, "I told you, it's over. It was fun dreaming about it, but I think we both knew things like that don't happen." She grinned. "You better go back to buying lottery tickets."

"She's right," said Spokes. "I think we even have to be careful about who knows about this. Did you tell anybody else?"

"I don't remember," I said, hesitating, hoping I could come up with some idea to keep the plan going. "I did talk to a banker . . . a business attorney in St. Cloud . . . but I didn't give them any particulars. They wouldn't be able to put anything together."

"How about your secretary?" he asked.

"She saw the thank-you card from Matthew when she opened the mail. I don't think she read the letter. I'm pretty sure she didn't. But she did fax this stuff to you. I would expect she knows some things. But I haven't talked to anyone else."

"Keep it that way," he said. "I'd deep six it all. I guess you and I will just have ta keep practicing law."

I still hadn't given up. We sat and talked for a while. It was obvious Spokes wasn't going to change his mind. "I know Matthew," I said. "He's legitimate, a degree in international finance from St. Cloud State University. He called me one night, a week or so ago."

"What do you mean he called you?" asked Spokes.

"I think it was last Thursday night. Probably three, four in the morning. He called me at home. He said they were desperate to get this done. He said I was embarrassing him with the Committee because he had assured them I was their man. I told him I needed more time, that I was meeting with you."

"You mentioned my name?" he asked.

"I think so."

He stood up, looking a little upset. "I have to get to the Hennepin County Courthouse," he said, rather dismissively. "It was nice seeing you again. Nice meeting you, Mrs. Williams." He looked at me. "I would tell your Nigerian friend you can't do anything for him."

"I know you're right," I said. "I just kept picturing me, sitting on the deck overlooking the Gulf of Mexico."

"Just practice a little harder," he replied.

"With my clients?" I replied. "Lots of luck."

By the time Kate and I stood up, Spokes was on the phone to Pam Weber. She was coming in a side door as we walked out the back. She gave me the slightest smile, a warm, expressive look. Kate took my arm and gently tugged me through the door.

Walking to the parking lot, I looked at her. "You don't even seem upset," I said.

"I'm not. I'm not going to lose any sleep over something I never had."

"What about our big plans?" I asked, as I opened the car door.

"We can still have our plans, we just have to scale them down a little."

"Yeah, like ninety-nine and a half percent." I replied.

I pulled onto Park Avenue. "What a bummer," I said.

"It was fun while it lasted," Kate replied. "I'm glad we didn't tell Carol we were gonna pay off her loans. Can you imagine how bummed she'd be? By the way, you're going the wrong way again."

"I know that," I said. "I don't know about you, but I'm keeping this to myself. It was pretty naive to think a guy could do something like this without any repercussions. That's why I better stick to criminal law, keep my nose out of international finance. As they say, a little knowledge can be dangerous. But the banker made it sound so simple, get an account open with a bank under a new business name and have the money transferred from one national bank to another—that easy."

"Yeah, but he was talking about a legitimate transaction. Anyway, I think we're better off just putting it out of our mind."

"You're right," I replied.

I had a hard time putting it out of my mind, though. I went to work the next day with every intention of throwing away the file. I looked at the letter from Marshal Umah . . . so simple, I thought. I wondered what that federal statute really said. I went to my fax machine, nothing from attorney Spokes. I decided I would go to the law library and look for myself.

A few minutes later I was paging through the United States Code. I found it. It was there, pretty much in the same language quoted by Spokes. One statute made it a federal offense to launder monetary instruments, another to engage in monetary transactions in property derived from various unlawful activities. It would probably be impossible to ever determine to whom the money belonged, what foreign companies kicked into the pot, but it didn't belong to Marshall Umah and his gang. For them to leave the country with cash would certainly qualify as an unlawful activity. I closed the book and walked back to my office. Kate's right, it's not worth going to prison over.

I never tossed the file, but as the days turned into weeks, the whole episode seldom crossed my mind. I never sent any response back to Marshal Umah or to Matthew. Any correspondence from them stopped. I was curious why, but not enough to pursue it.

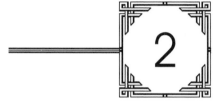

I'm a sole practitioner. I returned to St. Cloud from law school in 1970. Rather than join any firm, I decided I wanted to be my own boss. The first years were slim, but I would take any case that came in the door. Basically because nobody else wanted to do it, I started taking criminal cases as a court appointed public defender. As I developed a reputation over the years, the judges started to rely on me more and more to take every ugly case that came along. After doing that for close to twenty-five years, I was getting burnt out. But I was too young to retire; plus, I had never saved a dime in my life. At times I thought about hiring somebody to help, but then I decided it would just make life even more complicated. There were only two people I relied on, my legal assistant, Faye, and my investigator, Tony. Faye Carlson had been with me for fifteen years, she started right out of vocational school. Tony O'Donnell was a retired cop who took an early retirement. When he got bored with retirement, he started to hire out as a private detective. He had worked on cases with me for close to ten years.

It was eight o'clock on Saturday morning. I met Tony at Jimmy's Café for coffee. Our plan was to talk to a witness on a case coming up shortly. "Hey, grab that *Minneapolis Tribune*," I said.

"How do you know it doesn't belong to somebody?" Tony asked.

"Because it's sitting there all by itself. Somebody left it behind."

"I'm not going to steal somebody's newspaper for you."

"You can be a jerk," I said jokingly as I got up, went a few feet to the next table and grabbed the paper. "Just for that, you're not going to get to read it either."

"That's okay. There's never anything good in there anyway."

We sat there quietly sipping coffee as I slowly went over the first page and then turned to the State and Metro section. The headline caught my eye, "Legal assistant murdered." The article read:

> Authorities have identified the body of a young woman found stuffed in a dumpster behind Park Dale Apartments in South Minneapolis. The police have identified her as 31-year-old Pam Weber of Inver Grove Heights. She was the legal assistant of prominent Minneapolis attorney John Spokes. She was last seen on Thursday evening leaving work at about 6:30 P.M. Her body has been taken to the Hennepin County Medical Examiner's Office for autopsy. Kent Moore from the Homicide Division of the Minneapolis Police Department told reporters that it appeared that she had been sexually molested. According to the police, they have no suspects.

"Jesus Christ, look at this," and I shoved the paper across the table. "I just met her in August. She was the legal assistant to John Spokes. I was meeting with him."

Tony glanced over the article. "What were you talking to him about?" he asked casually.

"It was nothing important. Just a case I wanted some advice on. Can you believe that shit. Somebody must've grabbed her when she left work. You only have to be a block or two off Park to get into some pretty rough neighborhoods. At that time of night . . . Jesus Christ, I can't believe it. It looked to me like she was . . . I don't know. I have to give him a call."

The two of us went silent as Tony finished the article.

"That really bothers me," I said. "How can somebody do that? How can they take a young lady out, rape her and murder her?"

"That's a strange question," said Tony. "How many murder cases have you handled in the last twenty years?"

16

"More than I care to count."

"That's my point. Why should another murder bother you?"

"Well I knew this lady."

"You didn't know her. You met her."

"Yes, I met her and she was a live, vivacious, beautiful young lady."

I hesitated. "I know, I've seen a lot of victims, shot, stabbed, beaten to death, but when you don't know them, or haven't met them, you don't have a point of reference. You don't know what they looked like alive, animated. You don't know if they had a soft smile. She had a soft smile, Tony. I don't know, it's just different."

"Well, if she was a looker," said Tony, "there's probably your motive. There's a lot of creepy bastards on the streets who'd grab a pretty girl and then make sure they leave no witness."

"You still have any connections with the detectives from homicide in Minneapolis?" I asked.

"Yeah, I worked with a number of guys years ago. I would think one of them would still be there. Why?"

"I'd really like to see the police reports on this case."

"You've got your own murder case, remember? We're meeting witnesses today."

"This bothers me, Tony. I want to know what happened."

"I'll see what I can do. What do you hope to accomplish today?" asked Tony.

"We have to find out if anything happened at the bar."

"That's a rough place you know," said Tony. "Stubby's is a biker bar. A lot of shit happens there."

"I know. I've been there," I said. "That's why I've got you along. If one of those biker babes attacks me, I'm hoping you can pull her off."

"No way," said Tony. "I'd love to see you get molested."

I wasn't worried about getting molested as long as I had Tony along. Although nearing sixty, he had managed to keep himself in great shape. He told me he was normally in the gym every morning by six. He still had all his hair, a steel-silver color, had a ruddy complexion and dark-brown eyes. After years of consciously trying to hide his feelings, his face was difficult to read. His expression very seldom changed. When he managed to smile, it was a broad, warm smile. I would call it endearing.

Fifteen minutes later we pulled up to Stubby's Bar. Stubby referred to the owner, a diminutive man with excess poundage. This wasn't a new experience for me. Since Stubby's became a biker bar five years or so before, many cases I handled had their origin at Stubby's—the majority of them drunk driving offenses.

I had met Stubby before. Some of my clients told me that the name also referred to another part of Stubby's anatomy.

It was about 10:30 in the morning when we walked in. Stubby was behind the bar. He was always behind the bar. The night before, Friday night, was a big night at Stubby's. The place reeked of stale beer and smoke. The ceiling tile, once white, was permeated with the smoke of tens of thousands of cigarettes and hung a putrid tan, casting an almost amber light to the room.

Tony and I walked up to the bar, took a stool. Stubby looked at me. "Mr. Williams, how ya doin'? You must be here on Kevin. I'm sure you're not here of your own free will."

"Stubby, how do you know we're not here just to have a Saturday morning shot and enjoy your company?"

"If you told me that, Mr. Williams, I'd tell ya you're full of shit."

"Well you're right on both counts," I said. "I am and we're not."

"I figured that," said Stubby. "I heard you're representing Kevin. That's a bum rap. That fuckin' trucker was gonna kill him, he didn't have any choice."

"How long have you known Kevin?" I asked.

"He started coming in here a couple years ago, right after he got back from Colorado."

"What kind of guy is he?"

"A gem," he said. "I know bikers get a certain reputation. He always tried to make a conscious effort to change that. Remember the bike-a-thon? Where they were out trying to get people signed up, pledging money for their trip for the children's ward at the hospital? That was his idea. He put it all together. I think he probably raised over ten grand. He said there was a lot of good people riding bikes. No more Hell's Angels. We have to change that image. That's what he wanted to do."

"Well, he could've cut his hair," I said.

"Yeah, he could've," said Stubby, "but that isn't the way he is. He wasn't gonna try and portray an image of somebody he wasn't. He liked to wear his hair long, keep it in a pony tail, wear that black leather jacket and chaps, the black glasses. That's the biker image, and he liked it. But that isn't what a biker is, at least that's not what he is."

"Do you remember seeing him here that night? The night of the killing?"

"I remember the night because I was shocked the next day when I heard it on the radio. We were packed. I did see him here. I just don't remember anything out of the ordinary."

"Do you remember how much he might've had to drink?"

"He wasn't a boozer, Mr. Williams. I think I probably saw him get a little high several times. You know, happy, but I never saw him what I would consider drunk, and I never saw him mean or obnoxious. Some of these guys, they get a couple beers in 'em, they're gonna take on the whole fuckin' world. He was never like that."

"How about the young lady, Josie? Did you ever see her?"

"He used to bring her in all the time. He had one bad case on her, but you know, I think she was just using him."

"What makes you say that?"

Stubby looked down the bar. "Just a second." He walked to the end, somebody needed a refill.

Tony looked at me. "That's what I told you, Bob. That's what I've seen in this guy. I haven't found anybody who's willing to say one bad word about him. His dad's an invalid, his mother's in her sixties, he provides for both of them, and the guy does all kinds of volunteer work. He's just not a killer."

I shrugged my shoulders.

"You guys want anything to drink?" asked Stubby. "Or is this all gonna be free?"

"I don't suppose you have any coffee."

19

"What does this look like, a café?"

"I'll take a 7up," I said.

"Make that two," said Tony.

Stubby turned around, retrieved two cans from the cooler and set them on the bar. "That'll be two bucks," he said.

"Jesus Christ, Stubby, I can get it outside in the pop machine for fifty cents," I said.

"Then go out and get it. But you can't drink it in here. You fuckin' attorneys are all alike. You can hand it out, but you can't take it. What are you charging Kevin to be here talking to me?"

"I'm court appointed."

"Then what are you charging the county?"

"None of your damn business. Here's your two bucks."

"You asked me about Josie," Stubby continued. "I would see her flirtin' with other guys, not just teasing flirt but sexual flirt—there's a difference."

"Like what?" asked Tony.

"If I have to explain it to you, you're too old to know the difference."

"Did you ever see her with other guys?" I asked, trying to keep a straight face.

"Once," he said. "I know she and Kevin had an argument about it. It was several months ago. Have you seen her daughter?" he asked. "She's got the cutest little daughter. Six, seven years old. Kevin adored that kid. He'd do anything for her. "

"We were talking about that night," I said. "It's my understanding she wasn't here that night, right?"

"I don't remember seeing her," said Stubby. "If she would've been here, she would've been with Kevin. I didn't see her. You know who you have to talk to? His friend Chris. He was with him most of the night. He could probably tell you exactly what kind of shape he was in."

I looked at Tony.

"Yeah, it's Chris Younger," said Tony. "Several other people mentioned his name. I've tried calling him, but he's been either working . . . or purposely ignoring me."

20

"Well, they were here a lot," said Stubby. "They took a lot of trips together. I think they did some double dating. Chris has got a real nice girl-friend."

Stubby looked past me and Tony. "Oh, no, here they come," he said. "These two are nothing but trouble."

Tony and I tried to turn around without being too conspicuous. Coming through the door was a couple, probably in their early forties, both of them dressed in black leather. The guy had long, stringy hair and a full beard. He still had his sun glasses on. I could barely see a face behind all the hair. The woman wore black leather pants so tight they might prevent her from bending her knees. Broad shouldered, she had a Dolly Parton chest, barely tucked in a black, v-cut t-shirt. Before they got to the stools, the guy hollered out, "Stubby, you asshole, two McMaster cokes."

Stubby looked at us. "I have to go back to makin' a living."

Tony leaned over to me, "I think we better get out of here," he whispered. "I stared at her boobs a little too long. I think I've got him pissed off."

We slowly stood up and quietly exited.

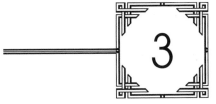

On the drive back to the office, it was agreed that Tony would try to find Chris Younger, see what he could tell him about that evening. I dropped Tony off at his car and went to the office. At my desk I took out the *Minneapolis Tribune* to read over the article about Pam Weber one more time. I flipped my telephone directory and found John Spoke's number. I called. To my surprise a young lady answered.

"Is Mr. Spokes in?" I asked.

"I'm sorry," she said, "Mr. Spokes is out of the office."

"My name is Bob Williams, an attorney in St. Cloud. I just wanted to give him my condolences about Ms. Weber, see if I could be of any help."

"I remember you, Mr. Williams," she said. "I talked to John earlier this morning . . . he's devastated. He's out of the country. He's cutting his trip short. He said he'll be back tomorrow afternoon. I will certainly leave him a message you called."

I leaned back in my chair, staring at the pictures on the wall. I had handled many murder cases over the years, but I never knew anybody who was murdered. If the guy who killed Pam Weber came in right now and said, "I murdered her. I want you to defend me," I wondered if I would do it. What if somebody I knew more than just casually was murdered, would that make a difference? When does a lawyer say, I'm too close to this, I won't, or can't, do it?

I picked up a folder in front of me, walked across the office and took a comfortable chair. I opened the file. The first document was titled, "Indictment—*State of Minnesota v. Kevin Murphy.*" I looked at the page. "We, the Grand Jury, empanelled in the above referenced matter, find that there is probable cause to believe that the above named defendant committed the offense of Murder in the First Degree; Felony Murder – Intentional."

Kevin Murphy was my latest murder case. Forty-two years old, he was divorced from a wife he left in Colorado. No children. A jack-of-all-trades biker who lived in a little apartment in the northeast side of St. Cloud. He was probably five-eight, a hundred and fifty-five pounds. He had long light brown hair, a goatee and mustache.

It was less than a couple weeks after Kate and I had returned from our visit with attorney John Spokes, less than a couple weeks after I had reluctantly given up my dream to be a multimillionaire, that the district court judge called me to see if I would take an appointment to represent Kevin Murphy. I was glad to do it. In fact, I was eager to do it. I needed something to take my mind off my lost fortune. I hung up the phone with the district judge and walked over to the jail to meet my newest client. All I knew about the case was the little bit I had read in the paper. The story was that he was burglarizing the home of an ex-girlfriend, a Josie Klein, when her male companion surprised him. There was a struggle. Murphy stabbed him and ran.

The indictment for first-degree felony murder didn't require that Kevin pre-meditated the killing, only that it was done intentionally in the course of a felony, in this case burglary.

I remembered that on my first visit to the jail, I expected to see some bulging hulk. I was sitting in the professional visitor room, the only decor being a four-by-six vinyl top table with two wooden chairs. There was one barred sliver of a window to the outside. I heard the latch open on the door at the end of the hallway. I walked out of the visiting room to the hall and looked down the corridor. At first I figured this couldn't be my defendant; except for the baggy jail clothes, the guy could've passed for an English professor at the university.

"Mr. Williams," he said, "I'm Kevin Murphy," and he stuck out his hand.

There was no brisk hand shake. It was like I was taking the hand of a lady, about to ask her to waltz. He had a quiet voice. Behind bushy eyebrows, his eyes were expressive. He appeared relaxed. I sensed no fear or anxiety. We took seats across from each other in the little room.

"I've been hoping you'd come to see me," he said. "A friend of mine suggested I give you a call, but I can't hire you."

"Well, the court's going to appoint me as a public defender," I said.

"Really?" he said. "I didn't know that. I thought maybe my mother had contacted you."

"You must've filled out an application for a public defender," I said.

"Yeah I did, ah, quite a while ago. I didn't hear anything."

"Well, right now you're stuck with me."

"That's fine," he said. He looked away, like he was embarrassed to be in a position where he needed a court-appointed attorney. He stared through the thin window. The daylight caught his face, giving his complexion a harsher cast than the muted lights of the hallway. He looked older.

He turned back towards me, lowered his head and in a voice barely audible, he said, "I didn't murder him, you know."

"What?" I asked, not sure of what I heard.

He looked up. In a strong voice, he repeated, "I didn't murder him."

"Have you talked to anyone about this?" I asked.

"No. Look, when you hang around with the people that I hang around with, you know better than to start talkin' to cops. When I heard they were lookin' for me, I went and found Chris. He agreed to drive me to the police station. The first thing he said is, 'You keep your mouth shut until we get an attorney,' so I did."

"Did you tell Chris?"

"I had to. That was the first thing he asked. He wouldn't help me if he thought I murdered the guy."

"Tell me what happened."

"Where do you want me to start?"

"What were you doing at the house?"

His eyes opened wide, he peered at me through round, small glasses. "I was leaving a present for Josie's kid, Lisa. It was her birthday on Sunday. Weeks before we had planned a party. I was gonna take 'em to the Renaissance Festival. Then, for no reason at all, Josie got distant. Last week she called it off. I'd already bought this little music box. I talked to her a day or so earlier, told her I wanted to drop it off for Lisa. She said 'no'. I had it in my car. I had a little bit too much to drink, and I felt bad, neglected, abused, betrayed. It's easy to use it as an excuse now, but Mr. Williams, it was the beer. I would've never gone over there if I'd been sober."

"How drunk were you?"

"I wasn't drunk," he said. "I knew what I was doing. I knew I shouldn't be going over there. I just didn't give a shit. I suppose in the back of my mind, I was hoping she was there, that she would invite me in, would tell me she had made a mistake. My life would get back to where it was. I think that was probably in the back of my mind."

"What happened when you got there?"

"I pulled up. There was a light on in the kitchen. I thought maybe she was still up. I went to the door. I used to have a key, but I gave it back to her a couple weeks ago. I stood on the porch and looked through the window. I couldn't see anybody, I thought she was in bed. I wasn't gonna knock, if they were sleeping, I wasn't gonna to wake 'em. I tried the knob, it was open. I walked in and listened. It was quiet. I walked back to the kitchen, placed the gift on the kitchen table. I had a card along, and I noticed I hadn't written anything in it, so I started writing a little note to Lisa, telling her how much I love her. I remember I just wrote 'Love Kevin,' when I heard some creaking of the steps going upstairs. I thought it was Josie. I turned around, and a man came through the door, a big guy, blond hair, beard, he was in just his underwear. First I was gonna laugh . . . he looked so funny. His face was tan. He had this dark-blond hair and beard and his left arm was real tan up to his shoulder. His right arm was tan but not like the left. And then the rest of his body was white as milk, like it had never seen the sun. He had these god-awful bikini briefs on, like a royal blue. Before I had a chance to say anything, he shouted, 'What the fuck are you doing here?' and he came at me. I'll tell ya, he scared the shit out of me. He was a big guy, much bigger than me. He grabbed me, threw me up against the wall. He was strong. He came over, slugged me in the face. See I still have a bruise here."

"Did the cops take a picture of that?" I asked.

"No, they didn't."

"I'll send my investigator over to do it right away."

He paused for a second. "Where was I?"

"He just slugged you."

"Oh, yeah. Anyway, I had my back to the wall. I said, 'Take it easy man'. He looked at me for a couple seconds. We stared at each other. He said something about me harassing Josie. Then he said, 'I'm gonna break your fucking neck!' He came at me again, got me in a bear hug, I thought he was gonna break all my ribs. He threw me across the room, I flew over the table. He landed on top of me, and we wrestled. I could hear things breaking. He must've rolled over something 'cause I heard him moan, and he let me go."

Kevin started to tense up. He had his hands on his thighs and as he continued with his story, his fingers started to tighten, his knuckles turning white.

"We both stood up. He was in front of the door to the living room, the only door out. All I wanted to do was get out. I said, 'Hey man, I don't want this. Let's just call it even. I want out of here before someone gets hurt'. He said, 'You fuckin' right somebody's gonna get hurt'. It's hard to explain the look on his face. I mean, he wanted to kill me. I could see it in his eyes. In the fall he hurt his back, maybe that's what pissed him off."

Kevin looked up at me. "I know it makes no sense, but honest to God, I thought he really was gonna break my neck."

Kevin let out a deep sigh and leaned back into his chair, relaxed his hands. "Anyway, I had on my black leather jacket. In my belt I had this leather case with a knife, a buck knife. Most bikers carry one for an emergency, like a tool. I thought I could scare him with it. I took it out, flashed it at 'im. In frustration, I said, 'Man, just let me out'. He said, 'In a fuckin' casket.'"

Kevin sat there shaking his head. "I didn't know what to do. It was a nightmare. I tried to make a dash for the door. I remember hitting his arm, he grabbed me, we both spun around. The next thing he's on the floor, the knife stuck in his chest, looking at me, breathing heavy. I heard Josie holler out, 'What's going on down there? You better get out of here. I've called the cops.'

I looked at him for a second. I was gonna help him, and then I just panicked. He wasn't dead. I had to step over his body to get out. I ran to the car and I took off. I didn't go home."

Kevin hesitated for a moment. I could tell he was fighting back emotions. He wanted to cry, but bikers don't cry. I tried to make an assessment: was he telling the truth? I thought so. I watched Kevin's eyes as the story unfolded, and it was like I was watching it on TV. Kevin had a VHS tape in his brain, and he was playing it frame by frame for me. The young man put his hands on the table in front of him. I could see them shaking. I reached over and grasped one. "You'll be okay," I said. "Tell me what you did after that."

He rolled his eyes back as if to start the projector again, leaned his head back, closed his eyes. He let out a sigh and then looked at me. "I just drove around. I couldn't believe what had happened. You know, people were telling me that Josie had a new boyfriend. And I thought to myself, why did she end up with this guy, and why was he there that night, and why did I have to go there to drop off a present? And I wondered how the guy was doing. It never dawned on me he would die. How could he die from a little puncture wound? I assumed the ambulance was there, and they had taken him to the hospital."

He hesitated again and let out another sigh. "That all changed with the 6:00 a.m. news. I was parked at the boat landing on Pelican Lake, sipping a cup of coffee. The news guy says that this man was pronounced dead at the St. Cloud Hospital. They didn't give his name, they didn't give the circumstances. He just said the police were asking for assistance in locating Kevin Murphy. God, my heart sunk. I was just sick. I went outside the car and threw up. No one can imagine how I felt. I have never hurt a thing in my life and then to have your name on the radio because you killed somebody, a man I didn't know, a man I'd never seen before. I wondered whether he had a family, how much pain I had caused . . . then I thought about Lisa, how scared she must have been with the cops and the ambulance and everybody there."

His eyes started to squint, his head went down. "My first thought," he continued, "was to just go jump off the bridge. I wanted to kill myself. I really did. Now when I look back, I wish I would've. I had the resolve then. Now I'm gonna to ride this out."

The comment took me by surprise. "If it happened the way you said it happened, why would you want to kill yourself. It wasn't intentional, it was an accident."

"I didn't think that way," he said. "I just thought about all the misery I had caused, how people were going to blame me, how Josie was going to blame me. It was selfish. It was to end my own pain."

"If you need help coping with this," I said, "I mean psychologically, I can get help. I can get somebody over here who can deal with this, who can help you through this."

"Don't worry, Mr. Williams. I'm fine. The first time I looked at my mother through that Plexiglas in the room next door, I could see the pain on her face. I can't imagine how she could've handled it if I had killed myself."

"I gave Chris a call. I woke him up. He agreed to meet me out in the country. Chris is my best friend. I told him what happened. He said I had to turn myself in. He said he'd go with, but he told me not to talk to the cops.

He's got a couple brothers that have been in and out of trouble. He told me if they had kept their mouths shut until they talked to an attorney, they would've been okay. So he said he'd get me an attorney right away."

"Did he try to get you an attorney?" I asked.

"Yeah, he called a couple of 'em. They wanted huge retainers before they would come over to talk to me. Everybody tried to raise some money, we couldn't get anywhere near what they wanted. That's when I told the judge I needed a public defender. I'm glad he talked to you. I've heard good things about you. Am I going to prison, Mr. Williams?"

That was more than a month ago. I remembered telling him I didn't think he was going to go to prison. Now I was sorry I had opened my big mouth. The prosecutor had a whole different theory on how it happened. To him it was real simple. Kevin was totally obsessed with Josie. He had witnesses who would say that at Stubby's that night, before he went to her house, Josie was all he would talk about, that he kept trying to corner her friends to find out what she was doing, who she might be seeing. One of the witnesses told the prosecutor she had told Kevin that Josie had been going out with another man, she was no longer interested in patching things up with Kevin. She said Josie had complained that Kevin had become suffocating in their relationship, that he was always worried about where she was, what she was doing, kept too tight a rein. Josie had told her she didn't have this problem with the new guy.

I leaned back and stared at the ceiling. Woven in and out of my thoughts of Kevin and his case, the face of Pam Weber would appear, sending a tingle down my spine. I thought of the fear and terror she must have gone through. I drifted in my thoughts for a while until the phone rang. It was Tony. He was waiting for me at the Log Lodge.

The Log Lodge was a bar and restaurant on the edge of town, off the road, back in the trees, skirting the Sauk River. Mainly because it was on my way home, it was a frequent stop, a place with friendly faces. It was nothing fancy, just a comfortable place to meet and have a drink. Tony and I were two of the regulars. We had been going there so long that everybody left our favorite table open. It was in the corner, in front of a big window overlooking the lawn, with a panoramic view of the river. It seemed there was always something to watch. In the spring, before the frozen lakes of northern Minnesota thawed, thousands of ducks used the river as a stopover. For weeks you could watch them floating with the current, diving or dabbling for food, wood ducks, pintails, goldeneyes, mergansers, almost anything. In early summer the geese would move in with their young, sometimes ten or more goslings following their parents around the yard as they hissed or squawked at any perceived danger. It was always a little added entertainment.

I parked my car and started toward the front door. I was going into the bar when I heard the familiar honking sound. I turned and walked to the river. It was a welcome diversion. There were probably twenty, thirty geese sitting in a little eddy. It was the Monday following the opening Saturday of hunting season and the geese had already figured out where they would be safe. All summer long they would come in tree-top high, from every direction, to rest on the river and pick up scraps the patrons of the bar and restaurant would toss out. After the opening day of hunting season, though, they started to come in high overhead, setting their wings and gliding down to sit on the river, out of harm's way. It was just after sunset, and the western sky was bright red, dotted with the v-shaped black dots of geese. It was one of those days you felt good to be alive. I wished I could fast freeze the scene, put it in my pocket and bring it out anytime I needed a lift. Just recalling it never seemed sufficient.

I was standing there when Tony walked up behind me. "Get your gun out," he said.

"I know they can be a nuisance," I replied, "but I don't think I could shoot 'em."

"This time of year," said Tony, "when they're all flying, the colors are so bright, they're pretty. Come summer when they're crapping all over my golf course, I think I could shoot them real easy."

"What did you find out?" I asked.

"Let's go have a drink," he said.

We took our table by the front window overlooking the river. I could just see the edge of the western sky, it was already losing its color. The geese started to make their way up from the river, nipping at the green grass. Two kids from the restaurant ran out with bread in their hands. When they got within a few feet of the geese, the adults stood up straight and hissed at them. The kids screamed, throwing the bread into the air as they darted back to safety. Everybody laughed.

"What do you want to know first?" asked Tony.

Just as I was about to say something, the waitress came up, and we each ordered a beer. As she walked away, I looked at Tony. "Did you hear something about Miss Weber?" I asked.

"Yeah," Tony replied. "My friend from the Homicide Squad called me. He said he'd do me a favor and send up what he could . . . it sounds like it was a real brutal slaying. According to the medical examiner's report, she was raped both before and after she was killed. Can you imagine that? That has to be one sick S.O.B. Based on the semen, they suspect maybe more than one guy was involved. The ME said her throat was cut, almost from ear to ear, with a very sharp knife. Her body was put in a garbage bag and tossed in a dumpster. They suspect it was done someplace other than where they found the body. They didn't find any blood near the dumpster. They don't have all the tests back yet. They're doing a DNA. that's going to take a little while. He said a strange thing, though. He said for a rape and murder, it was awful clean. I didn't think about it at the time. I didn't ask him what he meant. Doesn't it seem like a strange thing to say?" asked Tony.

"I don't know," I told him. "I suppose when you've seen as many homicides as they have, you start making those kinds of comparisons."

I took a swallow of my beer and looked out the window, deep in thought. Without turning back to Tony, I said, "I wonder what a person going through what she was, you know, the terror of it all, what she thinks about while it's happening, before the last breath leaves."

"That's an awful thought," Tony said.

"You know, ever since I heard she was murdered, I've been thinking about those kinds of things. I don't know why, I'll just be driving along and . . . there it is. Just like the case we're working on. That guy's just out getting laid. Think about it. They finished some drinks, probably screwed around on the floor, fell asleep. Later they wake up and go up to the bedroom. She sends him down because she hears some noise, minutes later, he's lying on the floor bleeding from his heart. He was awake, he had to wonder if he was going to die. In those last moments, was he thinking about his wife and children or about what a fun night he'd had?"

Tony gave me the strangest look, shook his head slightly. "God, you are just getting too macabre," he said. "What's your problem?"

"We've both been dealing with this shit for so long it's become just words on a page. I read the autopsy, 'Cause of Death: Exsanquination as a result of a stab wound to the left ventricle.' You know what that means? The poor bastard bled to death. You know how long it takes to bleed to death? I'm just wondering, what do you think he thought during that period of time? You think his life flashed in front of him? You think he had regrets? Remorse? You think he felt sorry for his wife and kids? That they would have to explain to everybody that he died after being shacked up with some strange broad in St. Cloud, killed in a fight with a jealous boyfriend."

Tony was silent. I think he was getting worried about me. I took another swig of the beer. "That's all I'm saying. We've always looked at these cases from the viewpoint of the defendant. They can always tell us what they thought, what was going through their mind just before it happened. Most of the time we know it's bullshit . . . they're lying through their teeth."

"It's not your job to worry about the dead person," said Tony. "Your job is to defend the accused, whether he's guilty or not."

"I don't know," I said looking back towards the river. "My problem is, I can't get her face out of my mind. She just glowed. She had a beautiful neck, long and thin. She could've been a model. And to think, some sick bastard took a knife and slit it. I don't understand that, Tony."

I ordered another beer. "Get me those reports as soon as you can. I want to follow-up . . . for whatever reason. What about Kevin?" I asked.

"It's pretty much what we talked about," said Tony. "I talked to Chris. He's just another nice young guy. He pulls up on his Harley, and he's got his leather jacket and the whole bit, but he's no hard ass, he's just a nice young man. He said that Kevin was obsessed with Josie, but he can't see him killing anybody, not in cold blood."

"What about that morning when he saw him?" I asked.

"Chris said Kevin was devastated. He said Kevin fell to his knees crying. He told me you'd get a half a dozen people or more to come in and vouch for Kevin's good character."

"What about Josie?" I asked. "What did he know about her?"

"He said he started to suspect quite a while ago that she was burning out on Kevin. Nothing specific, just that he thought she wanted more freedom than Kevin was giving her. I think he had heard that from his own girlfriend, Sara. She came in just about the time I was leaving, very attractive young lady. She said that Josie had told her months ago that Kevin was suffocating her, no matter what she said to get him to ease up, he didn't understand the concept."

I mulled everything over. Finally I looked at Tony. "You know everything you've told me cuts right down the middle. It could support what Kevin's saying, it could support what the State's saying. I mean, you look at that, there's a motive. That's exactly what the State will argue. He's obsessed with her, finds out she's got a new boyfriend, and he goes over there with a knife expecting to see him, and then he kills him."

Silence settled in. There was a clinking of dishes and a little laughter in the background. The waitress came up with menus. Tony told her we weren't going to eat. He ordered us each another beer. I continued in thought. "That's the problem," I finally said. "He may have had a motive, but murder's not in his character. I don't think motive is enough. I think it takes a special kind of person, in a special kind of circumstance, to form the decision that he's going to kill somebody. I don't see that in Kevin. There's nothing in him, either thought or deed, that would convince me that he was capable of murdering somebody, even under those circumstances.

"Do you remember, Tony, years ago I had that murder case where that young boy blew that lady's head off with a 30.06? A shrink told me at the time that we all have a mechanism in our head that sets off our conscience. If you're going to do something terrible, your conscience says you can't do it . . . most of us respond to that. He thought some people don't have that mechanism, it simply doesn't work. When they're put in a position to do evil, they can do it and quietly walk away, like nothing happened. I don't see that in Kevin. He has a conscience. In fact, his problem may be that he has too much of a conscience, that's why he's struggling so badly with what happened."

"Maybe that's guilt," said Tony. "How can you tell the difference?"

"I don't know," I said. "Maybe it's a sum of a person's life. You look and see what they've been in their past to decide what they may be now." I shook my head as if to clear a fog. "It's a good thing lawyers don't have to deal with that kind of crap," I said, "we only have to look at the proof beyond a reasonable doubt. Leave moral issues to theologians."

"Well, it's sure been fun talkin' to you," Tony said sarcastically. "I think maybe the next time we should meet at the morgue . . . or we could always go to one of the cemeteries." He grinned at me.

I grinned back. "I'm not through with this," I said. Tony put his glass of beer down and put his elbows on the table, rested his head in his hands and stared out the window. By then, one of the geese had made its way so that it was standing right out the window, gazing in, glued to its own reflection. We both stared through the glass at the goose, momentarily oblivious to each other. Without taking his eyes off the bird, Tony said, "Maybe we've both been doing this too long, maybe we've become callused to the human drama played out in each one of these cases . . . to us it's just a job."

"That's right," I said. "And for some inexplicable reason, the death of Pam Weber," and I hesitated, "not just the death, but the manner of death, has spun my mind around . . ." My voice trailed off.

I knew where I was going. Tony was one of the few people in this world I felt comfortable to have this kind of a discussion with, but I hesitated, not knowing whether I should continue, or let it go for another time.

"I know it sounds strange, Tony," I finally said, "but I've been thinking about last thoughts, what must go through a person's mind. When those animals cut her throat, it wasn't instant death for her. I had a case quite a number of years ago where a young man's throat was cut, ear to ear. He bled to death. The coroner in that case said he probably lived for three to five minutes before he lost consciousness. He had walked around most of the house. It was covered with blood. Ms. Weber had to know she was dying. What do you think went through her mind?"

I looked at Tony. He and the goose were having a stare down. "I don't know," he said. "After being brutally raped, she probably welcomed death."

"I don't believe that," I said. "I can envision situations where death may be welcomed. I think she had too much to live for to despair that way, even in her last moments."

Tony won, the goose finally started eating grass. "This isn't any good for you, you know," he said. "If you're gonna start thinking about the victims, reliving the anguish of their last moments on earth, you're never gonna be able to honestly represent another person charged with murder. When I say honestly, you know, I mean whole heartedly. To give them the type of defense they're entitled to regardless of the kind of scumbag they may be."

I didn't answer him. I knew he was right. Over the last several weeks, I had thought about it. Through all the ugly cases I'd handled over the years, I had never put myself in the place of the victim. Now, thinking back, I couldn't understand why. I considered myself a sympathetic, considerate, sensitive person. It affected the way I dealt with my clients. I wondered why I never transferred the sensitivity to the victims of the crimes. No matter how terrible a crime was committed, no matter how much of an animal the defendant may have been, I was always able to come up with one good thing about them, either real or imaginary, that would allow me to deal with them with some modicum of dignity. I never tried to decide whether that was just being me or whether that was what a criminal defense attorney had to do.

We had been sitting there silently watching the activity outside as dark settled in. A flock of mallards had landed on the river. Some children ran out to throw the ducks bread scraps, but the ducks had already become suspicious of human intentions. They leapt from the water with one slap of their wings to disappear as black dots over the silhouette of a big elm tree hanging over the water. We were both watching when Tony said, "Who's handling Kevin's case?"

"Spencer," I said. "Spencer Moore."

"Oh, Christ," he said, "we have to deal with that asshole again? Have you talked to him already?"

"No, I was planning on doing that tomorrow."

"Has he made any offer?" he asked.

"That's what I intended to find out," I replied. "We do have some problems, you know. They haven't found any of the decedent's fingerprints on the knife. Kevin said he thought the guy may have grabbed the knife in the struggle. The coroner also describes some wounds on his body, some cuts and bruises as defensive wounds. You don't think our kid could be lying, do you?"

"Anything's possible. But, geeze, I don't see how. Everybody I talk to says he's a straight shooter."

"Well, that's how I'm proceeding," I said.

We finished our beers and left.

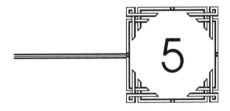

The drive from the bar to my house was about ten minutes. I always made sure I took back roads. Over the last couple years, it appeared there was a contest among every young cop on the police force to write the most DWI tickets. I didn't know where the beer would put me on the alcohol scale, and I didn't want to find out the hard way. When I got home, Kate was watching the evening news, dressed in blue jeans and a flannel shirt that hung loosely. Her face was wind burnt, her hair wrapped in a bandana.

"What have you been doing?" I asked.

"Cleaning out the garden, getting it ready for winter. I've been watching the news, they say it's going to get cold. They're predicting an early snow."

Every fall she loved to worry about whether we would get everything done before the snow would fly. We always managed to, many times with weeks to spare, but it never changed her disposition. The only fall we didn't make it was several years back when it snowed on Halloween. I remember being out, hanging precariously onto the end of a ladder, picking the last of the Haralson apples by flashlight as the snowflakes started and the temperature dipped into the twenties. In retrospect, it was a dumb thing to do. The apples ended up sitting in our basement most of the winter. We had so many, people were getting sick of me showing up with boxes to give away. Since then I just let them sit on the tree, the deer would come and eat them over the winter as they fell off.

"You look awful tasty," I said. And she did. She could've been a young gal.

"You've been drinking!" she said.

"It's that obvious?"

"After almost twenty-five years, it certainly is. The only time you're amorous when you walk in the door is if you've stopped and had a few drinks on the way home."

"That's not true," I said.

"Well, it may not be the only time, but it's a good share of the time."

"Okay," I said, conceding, "but this is one of the times."

"I'm too grubby," she replied. "Later, after I take a shower."

"It'll have worn off by then," I said.

"That's your problem. What were you doing anyway?"

"I was talking to Tony about this case we have. He also gave me an update on the Weber girl."

She sat up in her chair. "What did he find out?"

I told her about the Hennepin County report.

"Oh, that poor girl," she said when I finished. "I told Carol that we had met this young lady at the law office. I told her that's why we worry, that's why she has to be careful."

Carol lived with a friend in an apartment above a store right off the university campus. Every time there was a murder of a young girl, every time there was an assault or rape, Kate would say the same thing, "That could be Carol." She was right, of course. Even though the odds were astronomical, nobody ever believes it could be their child. It still happens. I'm sure Pam Weber's parents never thought something like that would happen to her. They had to be proud of their daughter. An important job with a prominent attorney, making a good salary, living in the big city, everything to live for, and she ends up raped, her throat cut, put in a garbage bag and thrown in the dumpster. I cringed at the thought: How can parents deal with that?

"Tony's suppose to be getting copies of some of the police reports shortly. I told him I wanted to watch what happened with this."

"Why?" she asked.

"It's just something I want to do."

"Have you talked to the lawyer?" she asked.

"I tried calling, but he was out of town. Then I got busy. I feel bad that I didn't go to the wake or funeral."

"There's no reason for you to feel bad. You only met her that one time."

I couldn't tell Kate how much my mind had been occupied with Pam Weber's face and her death. She got up and went to the kitchen to check on the oven. I mixed myself a drink and tried to nonchalantly inch my way towards her. I pulled on the flannel shirt enough to expose her neck and I nuzzled in and kissed her on the neck's curve into the shoulder. She tasted salty. She jerked a little. "It won't do you any good," she said, "not unless I take a shower."

"You taste good," I said.

She turned her head to look at me and laugh. "You're never going to change," she said.

I took her hand and led her into the bedroom.

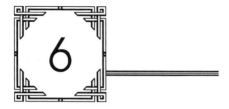

The next morning at ten o'clock, I was driving the fifteen miles to Foley, the county seat of Benton County to meet with Spencer Moore, to talk to him about Kevin. Over the years I had worked with many prosecutors, and most of them I considered friends. Spencer was different. Spencer, to my knowledge, never made friends with anybody. He was a prosecutor, first and last. He loved his work. I truly believe that it was his mission in life, as far as he was concerned, to get every dirt bag he could off the street and into prison for the longest time possible. So in every case, from a misdemeanor traffic to homicide, he started out unreasonable and got worse from there.

He had a military attitude about him from his years in the service. I heard he was a helicopter pilot in Vietnam during the last years of the war; he was involved in the evacuation of Saigon as the North Vietnamese were deploying their tanks at the outskirts of the city. I don't remember ever having, what I would consider, a civil conversation with him. Every time we met, he spent the first five minutes telling me what a dirt bag I had for a client, how he was going to lock the son-of-a-bitch up, and it went downhill from there. Every once in a while, though, he would see the handwriting on the wall, that he didn't have the kind of case he thought he had, and at the last minute would fold, make a reasonable offer and a plea would be entered. I knew better, but I was hoping I could do something like that for Kevin. Some plea that would give him credit for the time he had already served and then get him out.

The prosecutor's quarters were squished into the corner of the third floor of the old courthouse that had long ago outlived its function. Set in a conservative farm community, the commissioners had concluded that a new jail was more important than new court facilities. The county attorney and his two assistants were jammed into one small corner where it was almost impossible to have a confidential discussion. That's why I often thought Spencer discussed everything with such a bravado, to make sure that all the assistants heard what a hardass he was being. I truly believe he thought that his stature in the legal community was based on the number of notches on his gun; or else he viewed his position as prosecutor not that much different from a helicopter pilot in Vietnam. The mission: to search and destroy.

His secretary told me he was busy, told me to have a seat. I knew that was bullshit. He made everybody wait. I'm sure in his mind, he thought it gave him some psychological edge. I picked up a newspaper put out by some association of insurance fraud investigators. It had articles about schemes going on all around the country to cheat insurance companies. The lead article was about a scam in Miami where the clients, the lawyers, the doctors and several insurance adjusters were all in on bilking the company out of millions of dollars on fake accidents. As a result of the investigation, three lawyers, two doctors, and two insurance adjusters and a half a dozen clients had been indicted and were awaiting trial. I wondered how long it would be before the clients would agree to turn state's evidence to hang the lawyers and doctors. Greed, I thought, gets people in trouble every time.

I just finished the article when Spencer walked into the waiting room. In his mid forties, thin and fit, he had black hair, never a strand out of place. With dark eyes and a narrow face, he was actually handsome in his own way. He looked at me. "Bob," he said and nodded, indicating I had his permission to come in.

I'd barely sat down when he said, "You know, you end up with such scumbags all the time. I mean a fuckin' biker. What's he thinking going over there at two thirty in the morning? He's only got one thing in mind. He wants to whack that son-of-a-bitch for dickin' his girl. Isn't that right?" And he looked at me like I should acknowledge everything he said was true.

From my prior cases with him, I knew I had to just give him the opportunity to run my client into the ground before we could talk seriously. After a couple minutes, he finally took a pause. I grabbed the opportunity. "What're you willing to offer?" I asked.

"I think I can get him on first degree felony murder. Actually, I think he went over there with the idea of a showdown with this guy and that's what happened, so it should be premeditated murder, he should be sitting for life. The grand jury didn't see it that way. But I'll tell ya what I'll do (I knew that's what he always said when he thought he had some problems with his case), I'll let him plead to second-degree felony murder. That'll save him a few years in prison."

"I can't let him do that. He didn't go over there with the idea of confronting anybody. He just wanted to leave a present for her little girl. He didn't even know the guy was there. He would've been out and gone if the guy hadn't jumped him. He was only defending himself."

At that point the only advantage I had was that I knew what Kevin was going to testify to; Spencer did not. Because Kevin never talked, Spencer would never know what his testimony would be until he was on the stand. Based on everything, he had to know we would claim self-defense. But there was no way he could know what the scenario was—so he was fishing, and I knew it. I wasn't giving up any part of my defense.

A silence fell over the room. We could hear the secretary typing right outside. Spencer was turning the pages in his file. He looked up. "You know the only fingerprints we found on the knife belong to your client."

"That shouldn't be surprising, it was my client's knife."

"Well," he said, displaying the proper amount of disgust, "I'm not gonna spend any time talking about the merits of this case with you. I made the offer, what did you have in mind?"

"I thought maybe you'd let him plead to a trespass, something like that, credit for time served, let him get back out on the street."

He looked at me, a grin crossed his face, he shook his head. "You never cease to fuckin' amaze me. You think I'm going to let this dirtbag biker back on the street with a misdemeanor trespass? You're outta your fuckin' mind."

"Maybe you're right," I said, getting up. "We'll see what a jury thinks."

"You goddamn right we will," he said, "and don't come crying to me when the judge sends him to prison for life . . . then it's too fuckin' late."

I didn't acknowledge his comment, I just walked out. That was pretty much what I'd expected.

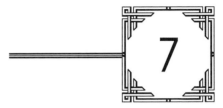

On the way back to my office, I tried to analyze my meeting. There were prosecutors I dealt with who made reasonable offers, who made it difficult for you not to tell your clients that they should plead, take the benefit of the bargain. Spencer wasn't one of those. To some extent, that made life easier. There was no arguing with your client as to what was in his best interest. You just presented it to the jury and crossed your fingers. That's what I had to do in Kevin's case. There was no way he would plead to murder.

I stopped at the jail to talk to Kevin. He agreed. He'd taken quickly to his new environment. He already decided he would have to make amends for the terrible deed committed out of his stupidity. He told me he knew if he had stayed away, that man would still be alive, his children would still have a father. Regardless of how it happened, he felt responsible, and he felt guilty.

A lady had been coming in, ministering to the inmates. Kevin threw himself into religion and before long he was ministering to other inmates, conducting prayer services, counseling, having discussion groups. He was now a trustee, with free run of the jail. He would help deliver meals, work in the library, do small jobs for the guards. Everybody liked him. He became a student of the Bible, and in every conversation with me, he would quote scriptures. I liked Kevin, and I started to believe, regardless of what happened that night, society was better off with him on the street than in prison. His talents would be wasted behind bars.

The court had given us a trial date: the Monday after Thanksgiving. It was further off than Kevin had been hoping, but it gave Tony and me enough time to keep digging to find just the right witnesses. In the meantime, other cases came in, not of the same importance, but enough to keep me busy. I got a copy of the investigative report on Pam Weber. It was heart-wrenching stuff. Many times when I was sitting there, working on other matters, my mind wondering, she would walk into my thoughts and greet me like she did that day, and I would relive the tragedy. They were no further in the investigation, they had no clues, they had no suspects. It appeared to be just a senseless crime, a life taken just because somebody wanted to get off.

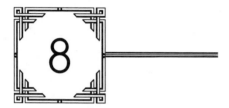

My daughter, Carol, came home for Thanksgiving break. With the trial starting on Monday, I spent most of the holiday reviewing my file, preparing for jury selection, things I knew had to be done. Saturday evening I was sitting at the table, the file spread out in front of me, when she came and sat down.

"Do you think he's guilty?" she asked.

"You know better than to ask that kind of question," I said. "I never make those kinds of judgments."

"Yeah, right," she said.

"You forget, it's not my job to determine whether he's guilty or innocent, just what the state can prove." I continued reading. She picked up the medical examiner's report, started paging through. When she was through, she put it down and looked at me. "You know," she said, "you told me that he claimed the fatal wound was inflicted accidentally, while the two of them were struggling over a knife."

"That's the way it happened."

"I don't know, Dad, that wound is kind of high, and it's also very deep to puncture the heart that way. It had to be done with some force."

"I didn't know you studied human anatomy in vet school," I said.

"I know what kind of force it takes to pierce a body, whether it be animal or human. All I'm saying, to produce a wound that deep through tissue and ribs took quite a bit of force. It's up to you whether that could've been done accidentally or intentionally."

"I wish to believe it was done accidentally. You know, that isn't the whole case, there's more to it than just that autopsy report."

"That's fine," she said smugly. "I just thought I should point that out."

I didn't take it personally, it was just a continuation of many conversations we had regarding my cases. Carol was never fond of the fact that I practiced criminal law. She had a hard time seeing me deal one-on-one with people who could rob, rape, maim and murder other people, sometimes with no remorse whatsoever. She had an even harder time when I got somebody off, knowing they were guilty. Like so many other people, she would ask me, "How can you do that?" I'd tell her what I told everybody else: "It's my job." With her, though, I added with a grin, "Just like you have a job, or will have, hopefully, and in the very near future."

"But in my job," she replied, "I cut the bad part out to make the patient feel good. In your job, you're hoping to put the bad part back in."

On a very pragmatic level, she was right. My only response was, "That's why people like vets better than lawyers."

By Sunday, I was sick of the case, and I put away the file. Carol had to leave about three, she was on call that night at the animal hospital. It was a cool, crisp, sunny day, the temperature in the low thirties. There had been a dusting of snow earlier that the sun had melted. It was fun having Carol home. She would make us do things Kate and I normally didn't do by ourselves, like take long walks in the woods. After lunch we put on our coats and started down the path. There was just small talk. Carol was already trying to plan for what she could do when she graduated, whether she wanted to go in private practice or stay in academia, teach at a vet school someplace. In the distance, we could hear a shotgun blast every so often. This was the last weekend of pheasant season. We got to about the edge of our property, and I quickly motioned them to quiet down. Across the fence, in the field of corn stubble, stood a doe and twin fawns, survivors of the hunting season, rummaging for ears of corn on the ground. We watched for a while, and then Kate moved, stepped on a branch, and it broke. All three heads snapped in

43

our direction, their ears pointing high, tails up in the air. They all sniffed loudly, snorting into the wind. Suddenly the doe turned and loped through the field, the two fawns following; then effortlessly, all three jumped the fence on the far side and disappeared into the woods.

"They're so pretty," said Carol. "I don't know how anybody can shoot them."

"We haven't come that far from the dark ages," I said, "when we lived in caves and ate raw flesh to survive. Killing defenseless things is in our genes."

"What got into you?" asked Kate. "I thought hunting was just to keep the population down so they didn't starve to death over winter."

"I think he's down on all humanity," said Carol.

"Maybe you're right," I replied. "Maybe I'm tired of seeing things killed."

We sent Carol off, and Kate and I went back into the house. As we were standing in the foyer removing our jackets, I had the strangest urge to lean over and kiss her, which I did. Her cheek was cold. She turned and looked at me, kissed me on the lips, full-bodied. With no apparent mental foreplay, there was a meeting of the minds, and we ended up in bed in bright daylight. As we lay there later, she said, "You know, you're getting better in your old age."

For some reason it made me think of something I'd heard years earlier when I was still in college and worked part time on a painting crew. I told her, "Yeah, I worked with this guy back in college who was probably in his fifties at the time. His saying was: 'There was a time I could do it all night, now it takes me all night to do it'." I hesitated. "I think I prefer the latter," I said.

Kate laughed, slapped me on the arm as I crawled out of bed.

She pulled herself up from under the covers, leaned against the backboard of the bed, wrapped a sheet around her and sat watching me dress. As I tightened my belt buckle, I looked at her. She smiled. "I'm glad we didn't get that money," she said.

"The millions?" I asked.

"Yeah."

"Why?"

"We don't need it. I think it would've spoiled our life. Really, think about it, we've had twenty-five happy years here. Sure, we've had a few spats but nothing that ever lasted. We've got everything we need. If we can hang in there for a while, we'll even have this place paid for."

I knew she was right. We never lived extravagantly, a trip here and there. We liked to visit Carol at school, but we'd made ourselves a comfortable spot that was always difficult to leave.

Back in 1971, an older attorney I'd rented an office from had taken in this little farm as part of an estate. Twenty miles out of town, at the time it seemed like the edge of the universe. On a sunny Sunday afternoon, Kate and I and three-year-old Carol tramped sixty acres of hills, woods, and swamp. The house was gone, just a field-stone basement where it once stood. There was a collapsed pig barn and a grain shed. We walked the fields, turned for spring planting. It was gravelly, clay and rocks. It was hard to believe that at one time, only years earlier, the farmer and his wife had raised thirteen kids on this plot of land. For us it was love at first sight. We walked the hills, pointing out home sites, where the driveway would go. I looked at the swamp, it was filled with spring runoff. I could see pairs of blue-winged teal picking nesting sites. The willows popping out of the slough were filled with red-winged blackbirds. As I walked closer, I saw a yellow-headed blackbird across the pond. I put Carol on my shoulders, and we walked almost every inch of it. Neither Kate nor I could believe we had gotten that lucky.

Years later, we built a spreading rambler on the highest hill of the property. Our friends thought we were nuts, but I told them that at least when I was working in my garden and had to take a leak, I didn't have to go into the house to do it. From our front steps we had watched literally thousands of sunsets. When we first moved in, our nearest neighbor was over a mile away. The roads were gravel and, with the spring thaw, many times impassible. That had somewhat changed. Now, in the fall, when the leaves were gone, I could see the nearest home a little over a quarter mile away. The road had been tarred, and the city kids would come out and see how much rubber they could lay.

Although it should have been paid for years ago, we used our equity in the house to pay for other things, including Carol's education. Kate was right, though. Given another four, five years, and barring unforeseen circumstances, it would actually be paid for.

"Do you think the money would have spoiled us?" I asked.

"It has to, Bob," she said. "You can't come into that kind of money that quickly without it having some adverse effect on your life. It's not possible. But more importantly, what would we do with it that would make life any better? We've always had what we wanted . . . and we've always had this place to come back to."

"Yeah, but, remember you said we would give this to Carol and come back in the summer when it's green and beautiful; get out of here in the winter when the snow is past your butt and it's thirty below zero."

"But even with all that, Bob, you know what I've been thinking? We've never had to argue about how we were going to spend money. We've never had enough to argue about. We both quietly accepted who we were and what we were doing . . . I don't know about you, but I was always content. We risked the money spoiling that. Why would we want that?"

"Maybe you're right," I said. "Luckily we don't have to worry about it anyway."

I took her out for dinner. When we got home, I opened my file and started to review my questions for jury selection.

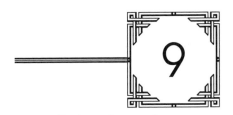

9

The next morning at quarter to nine, I walked up the wooden steps to the top floor of the courthouse, to the area where I would probably be spending the next several weeks. The hall was crowded with bailiffs, clerks and deputies, other people I had never seen before. Kevin's mother was there, three of his brothers, and two of his sisters-in-law. They intended to sit through the entire trial. I walked by a small room labeled "Victim's Assistance." Sitting inside was a young lady with long black hair, a thin face, dark, gentle eyes that appeared to be anxiously darting about the room. I assumed, from the description Kevin gave me, it was Josie. At the end of the hall were two rooms filled with people milling about, nervous chatter, all potential jurors. In a small room, on the side, sat my defendant with one of the jailers. His mother had brought him a suit. He had cut his ponytail, his hair was combed neatly. He wore his small spectacles and he still had his mustache and goatee. He looked every bit the part of a college professor. There was an instant smile as I walked in. The jailer took the clue and left us alone.

"This is what we've been waiting for," he said.

I was glad to see he appeared relaxed. We had spent many hours going over the entire procedure. What I expected the testimony to be, what I expected his role to be. He was a good student, I never had to tell him anything twice.

"How long do you think it'll take to pick a jury?" he asked.

"I suspect probably most of the week," I said.

"I still can't believe you have to ask each one of those people the same questions over and over," he said. "Seems to me there should be a quicker way of doing it."

"I don't know," I said. "Some people believe you end up having just as good a jury not asking any questions at all. Myself, I prefer having voir dire. I would just as soon know what kind of people I have on my jury."

There was a knock on the door; it was the clerk. She told me the judge would like to see both attorneys before we got started. I walked from the visiting room through the courtroom to the chambers. The courtroom was small. Over years of remodeling, they had slowly whittled away at what was once a stately courtroom until they had ended up with a little room with a table for the attorneys, a slightly elevated bench for the judge and his clerk and twelve chairs along the wall. It was an uncomfortable place to try a case, way too compact, way too intimate, as far as I was concerned. I wanted space where nobody could read my thoughts, where nobody could read my client's thoughts and, more importantly, where nobody could see me doodle when I got bored.

I knocked on the door. The judge's law clerk let me in. The presiding judge was Kenneth Morris. The district administrator had brought him in from another county because none of the local judges had two weeks free on their judicial calendar. That was fine with me. I liked Judge Morris. He had been a trial attorney for many years, was well respected as a judge. He bent over backwards to make sure a defendant got a fair trial. The only thing he was lacking was a sense of humor, although I'd heard, after he had a few shots of Schnapps, that changed.

From a trial attorney's perspective, he was a little too prompt. He expected to start every morning at nine, took recesses and lunch like clockwork and ended at exactly four o'clock, regardless of where the case was. But those were minor considerations, things I could live with. The other thing I liked about him, he never took any shit from Spencer.

"Well gentlemen," said the judge, "I hope we're not going to make a career out of picking a jury. I'd like to have testimony start at least by Wednesday, if not tomorrow afternoon."

The judge was looking right at me. Prosecutors very seldom take long picking a jury. With all the politicians talking law and order, most people sided with the state, there wasn't much credence given to the principle of the presumption of innocence. But I had a history of taking a long time picking jurors, and the judge knew it, so the comment was really directed at me.

I grinned. "I'll try, your honor."

I knew he wouldn't give me a hard time if it took longer than that.

"Is there anything we can resolve at this time?" continued the judge. "Any possible plea agreement?"

"No way your honor," the prosecutor broke in. "This guy's dangerous, I'm gonna put 'im away."

The judge looked at me, I shrugged my shoulders. "That's where we're at," I said.

"Then lets get it moving," said the judge. He stood up and reached for his robe, standing behind his desk to slip it on. He wasn't an imposing figure, but there was something about the robe and his demeanor that gave him instant respect. He looked intelligent, I think. You wanted to give him deference. He let the prosecutor and me get out of his chambers first. He came out, led by the deputy sheriff acting as bailiff, who rapped the gavel.

"The District Court for Benton County, Minnesota, is now in session, the Honorable Kenneth Morris presiding."

Everybody stood as the judge took the two steps from his chamber door to the back of the bench. I snuck a glance at the jury panel. There were probably fifty people jammed into that small courtroom, many of them standing. The judge explained to them the voir dire process. He told them that we would be doing what is called a sequestered jury selection, where each potential juror is questioned individually without the other jurors present. The rules called for that in a case of first-degree murder. He then read them the indictment. He looked around the courtroom. "The attorneys will ask you a series of questions to determine your qualifications to sit on this jury. You're all going to take an oath to answer those questions honestly. I want to give you a few opening instructions to keep in mind during the course of this trial."

Judge Morris had a habit of giving the jury some of the legal instructions, normally kept for the end of the trial, prior to jury selection. If you were lucky enough to get a conscientious jury, I believe it helped the defense. The judge gave them the basic instructions: The fact that there had been an indictment was not to be considered as any evidence of guilt; that the defendant was presumed innocent and the State had the burden of proving him guilty beyond a reasonable doubt. Just enough to make the jurors think that this was a contest, that they weren't here to just rubber stamp what the prosecutor wanted.

I had always found the jury selection process interesting. Literally dozens of books and hundreds of seminars deal with the art of jury selection. Jury experts hire out at hundreds of dollars an hour to help select what they consider just the right jury. I had tried to use some of the concepts preached in past jury selections; I never knew if it worked or not. But the theories were always in the back of my mind.

One of the theories was that the defense in a criminal case should look for a person who is anti-authoritarian, somebody who thumbs his nose at the system. That person can be identified by the way he looks and acts, the answers he gives to questions. Once in a while, somebody fits that mold, but the prosecutor always manages to get rid of him or her. It happened that day. The second prospective juror called was a huge man, grossly overweight, with his shirt tucked in loosely over a big belly. He wore wrinkled trousers, had a day or two growth of stubble on his face and unkept hair. There was nothing neat about him. According to all the studies, this should be a good juror for the defendant. His attitude and dress were anti-establishment. Nothing about sitting in court, being in front of a judge had gotten him to clean up; the system wasn't going to dictate what he was going to do. I kept him on after just two short questions, the prosecutor dismissed him without any questions.

A later juror was a woman in her early sixties. Again, through her answers and demeanor, she appeared the kind a defense attorney would want to keep—open, honest, willing to listen, sympathetic. Then I asked her if she ever had any experience with the court system. She told us about a son-in-law who was physically abusing her daughter. She had to bring her daughter to court twice. Not knowing what her real experience was, I had to let her go.

That's how jury selection proceeded, very seldom ending up with somebody pro-prosecution or pro-defense; they're all lumped in the middle somewhere. By the end of the day, we had six jurors, not what the judge hoped for, but better than I'd expected.

I drove back to St. Cloud, stopped at my office to check my messages and drove home. A cold front had moved in; it was jacket weather. The sky threatened snow. My mind wandered while I drove, recalling each juror, their answers to the question, whether I had made a mistake leaving a particular juror on or not. I turned off the highway to the township road, the last mile and a half to my house. Everything wore the bleak look of early winter. The trees all stood like skeletons against the dull, gray background. The farmers had already plowed all of the fields, and the clay soil lay rough and dark, a corn stalk sticking up here and there. The only color to contrast the drab grays, browns, and tans of the fields were the rows of bright green pines and spruce planted years ago as windbreaks. As I pulled into my driveway, I glanced at the pond. Not a duck or goose visible. I suspected that a combination of being shot at and the weather had triggered the little mechanism within their heads that told them to leave for a warmer climate.

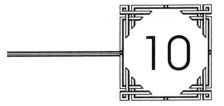

Kate and I had always lived a rather isolated existence in the country. After Carol left, for days, sometimes weeks, she would not see anybody but me. Our weekends were spent around the home doing things we enjoyed. We didn't need a lot of activity, at least outside activity, to be happy. She liked it that way. She never complained.

I pulled up to the garage, and I realized something was different. Dusk had set in, and the house was dark, and then I saw the garage door was closed—it was never closed, it hadn't been closed in years. I got out of my car, looked around. Nothing out of the ordinary. I stood in my driveway staring at the closed door momentarily. It didn't make sense. Kate must have left, I thought. But then why would she close the overhead door? It was always a struggle for her.

I walked to the service door and opened it. The smell hit me first. It was like walking into a service station where years of exhaust, grease and oil had accumulated. Kate's car was inside. It was dark in the garage. I never had a light installed. I quickly went to the overhead door and threw it open. A rush of cool, fresh air entered. I turned around, my whole body froze. Somebody was in the front seat, just a shadow of a head slumped over the steering wheel. I quickly got to the car and opened the door. "Oh, God, no," I said. It started as a murmur, expressing an incredulous moment, and then rose to a scream: "Oh, God, no! Oh, GOD, NO!"

I reached in to move her back from the steering wheel, and Kate's head plopped over like a rag doll. She fell across the middle console, her head on the seat looking at me. Her eyes were wide open, lifeless, her face a cherry red. I reached in to pull her up. She was already cold, stiff. She had been dead for hours. The cold touch of her face caught me by surprise. I let her go, she fell back across the seat. My whole body was shaking. My knees felt as if they were going to give, as though a tremendous weight had suddenly been placed on me. I went to the other side and opened the door, I knelt on the concrete floor. I put my hands on her face trying to feel any sign of life. It wasn't there. Pure grief went through my entire body. I screamed at the top of my lungs, as loud as I could, "No!"

The whole scene was incomprehensible. This couldn't be happening. How could it be happening? How could she have died in her car, in our garage? Something must have happened; maybe she had a heart attack. My mind was cluttered with thoughts—what should I do, what must I do? I had been like a window peeper to so many death scenes over the years, but, now that I was living one, I had no idea what I should do.

My instinct was to pick her up, carry her into the house. All she need-ed was to be warm, a little warmth, and she would come back to life. I reached in again and grabbed her hands. I stopped, I looked at her and the realization set in: She's not just sleeping. I can't move her. I have to get somebody here. I have to get somebody to be a witness to this. I dropped her hands, they fell across her body. I closed the door. I went around the other side of the car and closed that door. I ran towards the house. The door was locked. My hands were shaking so badly I struggled to get the key in the lock. It seemed to take forever. My fingers were stiff from the cold. I rushed to the phone and dialed 911. I told the young lady I wanted to report a death.

I knew it would take at least half an hour for an ambulance to get to my house. My first inclination was to go back to the garage. I started towards the door and stopped midstep. I asked myself, why? I can't do anything. What should I do? There are people I have to notify. How am I going to tell Carol? I couldn't bear the thought of calling her. What would I say? How would I start? Your mother's dead? Nothing made sense. How could she die that way? I realized I was afraid to ask myself the real question: could she have committed suicide? Why would she commit suicide? I couldn't think of one thing that had happened that would lead her to do such a thing. Yesterday was as pleasant a day as we'd ever had together. She had made love like she enjoyed it. Why, less than twenty-four hours later, would she go in the garage, close the door and start the car to die. She would've never done that. I knew that.

I didn't know what to do. I finally called Tony. He answered after a couple rings. "Tony," I said, "can you come out to my house?"

"What's wrong?" he asked.

"Kate's dead."

There was a silence. "What are you talking about?"

"I came home and found her dead in the garage."

Again, silence. "If you think you're funny, that's not much of a joke."

"Would I joke about something like that?"

"In the mood you've been in, I don't know what you're capable of."

Again, silence. "You're not kidding," he said.

"No, I've called the sheriff, please come out."

"I'll be right there."

I had barely put the receiver down when I could hear the sirens in the distance. They were coming off the county road, within minutes they'd be in my driveway. I quickly put on a heavier coat and walked to the driveway to wait. I felt a terrible guilt, but I couldn't bear to go back in the garage, to look at her lifeless body again.

The sirens got closer, and I finally saw the flashing lights turn the curve about a quarter of a mile away. A slight breeze was coming out of the north. I pulled up my collar, involuntarily shivered. I stood there as the squad car screeched to a halt. A deputy I knew, Mike Collins, got out.

"When I got the call, I looked it up on the map. I knew it was your residence," he said.

I pointed to the garage. "It's my wife."

He went into the squad car and got out his flashlight, and I followed him to the garage.

"She's on the front seat," I said. "When I got home the door was closed, I opened it. The garage was filled with a smell." My voice was shaking, my hands trembled.

He opened the car door, the beam of light crossed her face. I squealed. The pain buckled me over. Her eyes were glassy; they reflected the light. He flashed the light to the dash, stretched his neck to see the key in the ignition and then flashed up at the panel. "The ignition is in on, and the gas tank is empty," he said. "I don't know, Bob. Was she depressed about anything? Would she have, you know, killed herself over anything?"

That's all I had thought about since I'd found her. Here I was, an attorney who tried criminal cases, a trained observer, one who studied facts, and everything pointed to suicide—except why? The why was unanswerable; given a thousand years, I believed, I couldn't come up with the why.

I looked at the deputy. "I don't know," I said. "There was nothing I noticed."

"Have you had any arguments or fights, anything like that?"

"Nothing, everything's been good."

"Did you look around the house?" he asked. "Was there any note?"

"I didn't see anything."

"How about in the car, did she have anything on her lap, on the seat?"

"Nothing. Nothing I found."

By then more sirens were coming up the driveway. The ambulance appeared first, two paramedics got out and quickly ran to the garage.

"There's no reason to rush guys," said Mike.

They stopped, peered through the door; neither one said a thing. Finally Mike said, "We'll have to get the coroner here. It's gonna take a while. I suppose if you guys have something else to do, you might as well do it and come back later . . . or, you're free to wait."

"We'll wait," they said.

Another deputy pulled up and then Tony. I met Tony on the apron to the garage. I don't know why I said it, it just spurted out before I had a chance to think: "They believe it was suicide."

"Oh, bullshit! Why would she commit suicide?"

I led him to the car. He looked in. He let out a sigh that included an, "Oh, Christ."

By then I couldn't hold back my emotions. My knees buckled, and I placed my hands on the side of the car to steady myself. I slowly sunk to my knees, my head bowed, tears gushing, my whole body shook in gut-wrenching pain. Tony put his hand on my shoulder.

"Why don't you take him inside," said Mike.

Tony tugged my arm. He helped me up and led me towards the house.

"I don't know what I can tell Carol," I said in a sob. "I should've called her already. I can't."

"Do you want me to call?" he asked.

"No, I have to do it. I will, I will," I mumbled. "I need a drink," I said as we sat down at the table.

Tony poured us each a shot of whiskey.

The evening became just a foggy memory. The deputies kept coming in and out. The coroner showed up. He gave them permission to remove the body. I never went back out. Tony and I sat at the table sipping whiskey, trying to make some sense out of the senseless.

By close to ten I got the courage from the bottle to call Carol. She screamed, and the pain I heard was so intense it cut my heart. I told her she couldn't drive from St. Paul, I would send Tony to pick her up.

I'd never experienced the sudden, unexpected death of someone I loved so dearly. Even after years of dealing with death as an attorney, many times in totally unimaginable circumstances, it had in no way prepared me for the pain, the sense of loss, the despair that quickly settled over me like a black cloak. I became a robot. I functioned because people pushed the right button.

Tony went to pick up Carol. They got home after midnight. By then all the deputies, the medical examiner, the paramedics were gone. I was sitting in the dark when they walked in, my mind washed in liquor. I had decided I didn't care, had no reason to care. Everything planned for the future, all the things Kate and I were going to do, had ended. I could tell Carol was cried out. She had no tears left. We hugged and then we sat and talked until sunrise. No matter how many times we went over it, no matter how many theories we explored, it didn't help.

As daylight crept up, Carol made coffee, eggs, and toast. Like three zombies, we made our way around the kitchen collecting what we wanted and then sat quietly staring ahead, too numb to communicate.

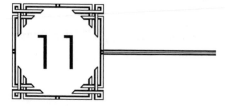

The judge declared a mistrial in Kevin's case. He told me he would reset the matter for a conference in a week or so, that he would give me an opportunity to withdraw as counsel if I felt it was necessary.

That afternoon I met with an investigator from the sheriff's department. He wanted a recorded statement. Carol and I had talked over funeral arrangements, but we couldn't make any plans, not until the medical examiner released the body. She stayed home to pick out a nice suit Kate could wear in the casket. I really don't remember much of what happened. Carol and I spent many hours walking in the woods, trying to make some sense out of it. We analyzed the previous Sunday, minute by minute, word by word, for something we might have missed in Kate's behavior, something that would give us a clue to why she might have done this. By the end of the day, we were as mystified as when we started.

The next day I received word from the deputy sheriff that the medical examiner had released a preliminary report. The cause of death was carbon monoxide poisoning. There were no signs of trauma. His preliminary ruling as to means was suicide. When I told Carol, she collapsed on the couch, covered her face sobbing. We kept believing that something had happened to her; a heart attack, a stroke, something that was disabling, and something that prevented her from getting out of the car. Now, any hope of that was gone. We were faced with the reality that this lovely woman, in some state of despair, consciously closed the doors, started the car and sat there until she lost consciousness. No matter how many times I pictured it, it wouldn't register. My mind wouldn't believe it was true.

Carol and I went to the funeral home. We had already decided two things: First, it would be a small private wake, and, second, Kate would be cremated. That was something all three of us had discussed years before, and there was no argument. The only question was, whether we would have an open coffin. We met with the funeral director and made all the rest of the arrangements, leaving for later the question of whether the casket would be open. The wake was set for the following night.

That evening Carol and I sat at home. Tony called and offered his help. I told him there were things Carol and I needed to resolve. But unfortunately, we didn't resolve anything—we couldn't. One of us would come up with an idea of why she had done this and the other one would slowly take it apart. I told Carol about the conversation I had with Kate after Carol left Sunday afternoon; how Kate told me she was content with our lives. I had thought about it, I wondered whether she had used the word "content" as a recognition this was all she was going to get out of life, a resignation to her position; she wasn't happy just being content, that she needed something more. I was grasping for straws, but it was all I had.

"Dad," Carol replied, "that's just the way Mom thought. When she said 'content,' that was exactly what she meant, content, happy with who she was and where she was. Believe me, Dad, she didn't need a lot of things to make her happy. Realistically, the two of us were all she needed. She told me that many times. You know what I've been thinking, did she do it to spare us pain? I know that sounds silly but what if she had some incurable disease? What if she had cancer and only a short time to live? She would do that, Dad. Rather than make us suffer through her illness, she would prefer to go out with a bang and not a whimper. Had she been to the doctor lately?"

"Nothing I know," I said. "She's had way too much energy to have something like that. That I would have a hard time believing."

That's the way it went for hours. Neither of us being able to grasp the why of what happened. Neither of us had slept for a couple days. It was taking its toll. Our minds were foggy. I finally told her, "I have to get some sleep. We have to face people tomorrow, I don't want to be any more of a physical and mental wreck than I already am."

"I've got some sleeping pills," she said.

"I didn't know you needed sleeping pills."

"When I get home from the vet hospital at two, three in the morning, after some emergency surgery or something like that, I'm in the same shape, I need to get some sleep, it's the only thing that works."

She got them out, and we both popped a couple. I didn't even try to go to bed. I just laid back in my chair, my mind drifted, focused on nothing. Within minutes, I was out.

It was close to eleven the next morning when I was finally able to open my eyes. I know I'd been laying there for hours, drifting in and out of sleep. It was actually the phone that brought me to reality. It was Tony. He wanted to know what the arrangements were. I told him that the wake was from five until eight. We'd be at the funeral home about four-thirty. He said he would meet us.

I walked to the back of the house. Carol was still sleeping. I went into the shower, my body sapped of any energy. Every bone ached. My brain was heavy, the effects of the sleeping pills. I turned on the water and stood there, letting it pound off my back for the longest time. I was truly unable to focus on anything. I felt a pain so deep my knees weakened, I slid down the side of the shower stall, the water pounding on my head. I bowed my head and cried, curled up, almost in a fetal position. My whole body shook. Suddenly there was a knock on the door, "Dad, are you all right? You've been in there a long time."

I tried to regain my composure. I didn't want Carol to know what I had done. I shook my head, got to my knees and finally said, "Yeah, the water just feels good. I'll be out in a little bit."

The afternoon dragged. I couldn't make it around the house without tearing up. Every time I saw a picture of Kate, it was like somebody punched me in the stomach, and I became nauseated. I would have to sit down. I didn't know how I was going to make it through the evening. The tears had finally stopped, but a sick feeling set in, at times overwhelming me. I just wanted to lie in my bed and forget it all.

Carol came home from delivering the dress to the mortician. As soon as she walked in the door, we looked at each other. No words had to be said. The pain was etched on our faces. We hugged and sobbed, clinging to each other for the longest time.

There was no sense talking about it; it only added to the pain. Carol went to her room and closed the door. I heard her crying. I walked about the house aimlessly, looking at my watch, wondering if time was finally standing still.

We drove to the mortuary without saying a word. I was trying to picture who might be at the wake, what I would have to face. I was trying to fortify myself so that I could act the part of a grieving husband without collapsing in tears every time somebody took my hand and said they were sorry. Reflecting back, it was strange that such thoughts didn't bring on tears. I was cried out.

The mortician led us into the back room. He opened the casket. Carol and I both gasped at the sight The mortician said, "I'll let you two alone," in an uneasy tone.

I don't know what I had expected to see, I guess my lovely Kate, looking serene, peaceful. What I saw was a painted lady, rouge cheeks, red lips, a department store mannequin.

Carol looked at me. "That's not Mom. We can't let people see her like that. Remember what she used to say, Dad? She told me, 'I don't want people looking at me saying, "Oh, doesn't she look lovely," and you know they don't mean it.'"

I looked at her, then back at the body. I blinked a couple times, trying to hold back the tears. They escaped, made tracks down my cheeks. I wiped them aside with my hand. I reached up and grabbed the door of the casket and closed it. I took Carol's hand, and we turned and walked out. We told the mortician we didn't want it open. They rolled the casket into the viewing room, and Carol and I sat, waiting for people to show up.

It was a terrible night. I remember shaking hands, hugging. I remember seeing tears, not mine but many tears. I remember hearing condolences, offers of help. Once people started to show up, the hours shot by like minutes. All of a sudden we were standing there, Carol, Tony and I, by ourselves, the mortician waiting in the hall, waiting to lock up. Tony turned to me. "I'd like to see her, Bob."

"No you wouldn't, believe me you wouldn't."

He looked at Carol, she just shook her head.

"You're not going to see Kate," I said. "You're going to see the mortician's rendition of her. If you want a memory, remember her as she was."

He seemed to understand. We left.

Early the next morning, Carol and I went in and picked up a little oak box, inside a brass urn. We took it home and placed it in a separate room. We planned to have our own little ceremony, sometime later.

Carol went back to school. I couldn't face the office. I spent several days at home, alone, alternating between screaming, "Why?" and blankly staring at the ceiling. Tony called me several times to go out, to get away, to get drunk. I couldn't do it. I sat there wallowing in my own pity, wondering how Kate could do this to me.

Saturday developed into a beautiful day, unseasonably warm for the end of November. Dressed in jeans and sweatshirt, I walked to the edge of the pond. On the side of the hill, I found my favorite huge oak and sat there leaning against the furrows of the bark with the sun in my face. My mind wandered. The judge had set the conference on Kevin's case for Monday morning. I would be dragged back into the real world whether I wanted to or not. He said he would let me resign from the case if I told him there was no way I could do it. But I couldn't sit at home by myself in misery, living the nightmare over and over. Carol told me when she left that I had to get on with my life. I knew she was right. Now sitting on the hillside, warmed by the sun, in a spot Kate and I had spent many hours, I realized I needed a purpose in my life to keep me going, and the only expertise I had was defending criminals.

I walked back to the house and called Tony and made arrangements to meet him at the bar at eight o'clock.

I got to the bar early. It was intentional. I had a couple drinks before Tony showed up.

"Where's Carol?" he asked.

"She had to get back to school. She wanted me to thank you for all your help."

"That was a nice service," he said.

"Kate would've liked it," I replied.

He looked at me, tears welling up. "You know, Bob, the more I think if it, the more convinced I am, it makes no goddamn sense."

"Tony," I said, "I've racked my brain every waking moment since I found her body. I have to put it away. It's driving me crazy. I have to get back to work. That's the only way to retain my sanity. That's the reason for the call."

He put his hand across the table, on top of mine. "You're right," he said. "I'm sorry, we've gone over it too many times."

"I'm going to keep Kevin's case," I said. "The sooner we get back at it, the better off I'm going to be. So I'm going to meet with the judge Monday, and, depending on what he says, I may need your help in rounding up our witnesses again."

"How fast do you think he'll put it back on the calendar?"

"I don't know," I replied. "Hopefully within the next week or so."

"God, Bob, " he said, "you need more time than that."

"No, I'm okay," I said. "I need this."

"By the way," said Tony, "I got the reports from Hennepin County Homicide on Pam Weber. Nothing more than I've already told you. But after reading the reports, I was curious enough that I did call him back and ask him about his comment. Remember, I told you he said something like, 'for a rape and homicide, it was awful clean'. That was my impression as well, so I asked him what he meant. He said he had investigated several on-the-spur-of-the-moment rapes where the victim was then killed, which they assumed happened here, and in his experience when it's unplanned that way, the killer, or killers, always leave something behind, some clue. But there was nothing here. It was like it was planned. Anything that would be of any help, neatly disposed of."

"What does he think it means?" I asked.

"He thinks there's a possibility that whoever did it probably had their eye on her for a while, that it wasn't some spontaneous jack off who saw this pretty woman and couldn't control himself, maybe even a serial killer."

"A serial killer?" I asked. "Why in the hell would they believe it was a serial killer?"

"I don't know," he replied. "The MO, I guess. Apparently there's a similar unsolved case from several years ago, might be the same guy or guys. Who knows. Just has to be one sick son-of-a-bitch."

We talked for a while. It was the first time I was able to really get Kate and the events of the past week off my mind.

A little after eleven o'clock, I walked into my house. There was a message on the telephone. It was Carol. I called her. She was glad I finally got out of the house. I told her my decision to go back to work. She believed it was the best thing I could do.

"You know, Dad," she said, "it's occupied my mind almost every moment since I left. There's no way she would've killed herself."

"I know," I said.

"What do you mean, you know? What could've happened? What are we going to do about it?" she asked, in rapid succession, almost a scream.

"I'm working on it," I said. I hoped that would satisfy her for the time being. To Carol and Kate, I had always been the fixer, the one they could come to with any problem, and either I, or somebody I knew, would solve it. So, I knew when I told Carol I was going to do something, she would take me at my word. She always had.

But tonight was different. She wanted answers, now. I finally calmed her down. She said she would give me a chance. The truth is, though, I didn't have any idea what I was going to do. Rather than a man with a purpose, I stumbled around the house. Everything there was Kate. There wasn't a picture or piece of furniture that she hadn't hung or placed. In the bathroom, it was the smell of her shampoo; in the closet, it was the lingering hint of her perfume; in the kitchen, it was the fact that there was no smell at all. I was accustomed to seeing her standing there in a whirl of activity, aromas emanating from steaming pots and pans. Tonight, there was nothing. I sat in the dark listening for any sound. It surprised me how loud silence can be. I ached so deep within me that I believed the pain could never be retrieved.

My mind wandered again to all of the family members I had seen in court over the many years—the families of the victims of crimes, all victims themselves. I had never felt their pain. Now I was ashamed of myself. God, I felt so terrible. I imagined myself sitting, alone, with nothing but my thoughts for the rest of my life. I leaned back in my chair and looked up at the skylight, a little peep hole into the expanse of the night. The moonlight streamed in, bouncing off the silver wings of the little hummingbird mobile Kate had hung from the window sill. I sucked air and blew as hard as I could. The little wings fluttered in the moonlight. I felt like I couldn't move from my chair. I pictured myself lying there for days, not moving, until I rotted away. Somebody would come looking for me, and all they would find would be my bones, lying there, staring toward the ceiling. Somewhere in my thoughts, God put me to sleep.

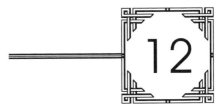

It seemed strange walking into my office the next morning. It had been the same all week. Nobody knew what to say to me. It wasn't like Kate had died in a car accident or of an illness where people felt they could openly offer their condolences. Everyone knew, or had heard, that the report was she committed suicide. So I interpreted every glance, every stare, as an inquisition: "What did he do to cause her to kill herself?"

Everybody was surprised to see me. They expected I would be gone for weeks. Faye came back to my office with a cup of coffee. "I'm sorry, Bob," she said. "I really feel terrible."

"I know," I said.

"There's so much crap going around," she said. "What really happened?"

"What kind of crap?" I asked.

"Oh, that she had been really despondent for a long time, or that she had some incurable disease, things like that. Trying to give some reason for what happened."

"She wasn't sick," I replied, "and she certainly hadn't been depressed, at least nothing that I had seen."

Silence engulfed the room, both of us felt uneasy, as if something was being left unsaid. I looked at her. I could tell she had taken it hard. She had been at the office every day taking calls, making explanations. It had worn on her. "I appreciate your help through this," I finally said. "It doesn't make sense to me, I need some time to sort things out. I need you to help me through this."

"Anything to help," she said.

She stood up, gave me a sympathetic smile and walked to her own office.

I looked at my desk top. A week's mail had been piled high. I paged through it. I could tell most of it was sympathy cards. I didn't want to look at them. I put them in a neat bundle, secured by a rubber band and put them in a file drawer.

A little before ten, I was in my car on the drive to the county seat to talk to the judge and the prosecutor about resetting Kevin's murder trial. I was eager to start again. I needed something concrete in my life, something with a beginning, a middle, and an end. A trial would do that. My mind had been shooting in every direction, like errant darts, sticking here and there but never on target. One minute I wanted to sell the house, I never wanted to go back. I thought if I could distance myself from everything familiar, from everything that brought up an image of Kate, I could survive. Then I would realize it would not be survival but isolation, just me and my thoughts, which would be worse. I thought about quitting my law practice, just sitting at home, rotting away in my misery and grief. In the end I knew that if I really wished to make it through, if I wished to continue life for me and my daughter, I had to go back to what I knew.

I walked into the courthouse and waited by the elevator. I heard footsteps down the hall and turned. Another attorney, Jim Turner, came around the corner. He saw me and for a split second, he hesitated, as if his mind had told him to do an about face but the next step had already proceeded in my direction. I had become used to it. That's how most of the people reacted when they first saw me. I knew they felt obligated to say something, but in their mind they believed it was better not to bring it up. It was one of those awkward moments we all try to avoid.

"Morning Bob," he said. "I'm sorry to hear what happened. How are you doin'?"

"Fine. What've you got today?" I asked to ease his anxiety by changing direction.

"I've got a couple first appearances on some criminal files. How 'bout you?"

The elevator doors opened, we stepped in. I didn't bother responding. We stood there, trying to avoid eye contact, feeling the uneasiness of the closeness of an elevator in a forced, uncomfortable encounter. If you don't look at each other, it's like it doesn't exist.

We both hurried from the elevator and went our separate ways. The judge's clerk was the first person I saw. She said the judge was expecting me. I could go right into his chambers. I made my way down the hall at a fast pace, past the deputy sheriff, past the clerk, the other attorneys, simply acknowledging them with a nod. I thought I could see the relief on their faces that I didn't stop to talk. I knocked on the chamber's door. The judge responded, "Come in."

As I walked in, he stood up from his chair, reached his hand across his desk. "I'm sorry, Bob," he said. "I know how devastating it can be."

I recalled at that moment that he had lost his wife just two years earlier to cancer. "Thanks, Judge," I responded. "It's going to take a while to recover, as I'm sure you know."

We were sitting there commiserating when the prosecutor walked in.

"Good morning, Spencer," said the judge.

He didn't acknowledge either of us. He took a seat across the table. The judge looked at me, shrugged his shoulders a little. "I thought it would be best," the judge said, "if we got together to discuss how we're going to proceed with the homicide trial."

There was a slight pause, and I took the opportunity. "Well, Judge, as far as I'm concerned, I was hoping we could get started on it as quickly as possible for a number of reasons. It's been tough on my client as well, getting it started and then having to put it on hold."

"I can accommodate that," replied the judge.

"Yeah, I know why you wantta get started," replied the prosecutor. "Everybody in this county knows what happened. We won't find a juror who hasn't heard about your wife. Everybody's gonna feel sorry for you. Who could vote guilty, dump on you, after what happened?"

I stared at him coldly. I couldn't believe what I was hearing. "Are you out of your mind or what?" I said.

He pointed a finger at me from across the table. He was about to respond when the judge broke in. "Gentlemen," he said, "that's enough," with such authority that Spencer quickly retrieved his hand and hid it under the table.

The judge immediately turned his stare to the prosecutor. "Spencer," he said, "over the years I've heard you say some awfully dumb things. This one takes the cake."

Spencer was going to respond, "Your honor . . ."

The judge snapped at him, "Don't open your mouth! Not one word!"

Spencer leaned back in his chair with a sour countenance.

"I'm telling you, Spencer," the judge continued, "I was willing to let Bob out of this. Then I think you'd have a real mess. He's willing to stay in, and for you to even think that it would be some advantage to him, simply because his wife died, I can't imagine where you'd come up with something that stupid. I've told the clerk to call a jury. We're starting next Monday morning."

The judge stood up. I followed suit. He reached his hand across the desk. "Again, Bob, you have my condolences. We'll see you here a week from today at nine o'clock."

Spencer didn't say a word. He got up, walked out the door, slamming it loudly as he left. The judge looked at me. "He should've stayed in the military," he said with a slight grin.

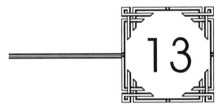

I spent the rest of the day reviewing Kevin's file. I was amazed at how much detail I had already put out of my mind. Maybe the brain cells can only stand so much clutter. Faye kept popping her head into my office all day wondering whether there were things she could help me with. A little over solicitous, I thought, but I knew it was well-intentioned.

For my part, everything was done with a purpose—to keep my mind occupied. I knew I didn't have to review my file again, at least not that day, but I hoped it would keep my mind off of Kate. For the most part it worked, but I struggled.

I had made plans with Tony to meet him at the Log Lodge at about five o'clock. By two o'clock, I was already looking at my watch, wondering if I could leave. I grew up in a predominantly German community, which meant I acquired the central Minnesota German work ethic, the belief that somehow you're lazy if you don't put in eight or more hours a day. Many times in my career that tug kept me in the office long after I wanted to leave. It was doing it again that day. What are you going to do, my conscience asked, waste the afternoon?

It took me until four o'clock to overcome it. Four o'clock seemed to be a reasonable compromise. Over the years when I couldn't wait, I used the ploy of inviting somebody from the office along, that way I could rationalize it as work related. Today I asked Faye if she wished to come along to have a drink with Tony. She seemed almost pleased to be invited into my misery.

We got to the bar a little before five. With daylight-saving time over, it was already dusk. Tony's car wasn't there, so we walked around the front and stood by the river. There was a cool breeze coming out of the northwest, hitting us in the face, making our eyes water. Just a touch of ice was forming along the edges of the river, in little nooks and crannies protected from the current. Out of the dark came a sound, like a jet airplane on a low glide, its wings whistling. There was a gush of air in front of us as a flock of ducks crossed the horizon, just above the water, almost faster than the eye could focus.

Faye flinched. "Geeze, what was that?" she asked.

"A flock of goldeneyes," I said, "on their way south, looking for a safe place for the night."

"I've never heard anything like that," she said.

"It's beautiful, isn't it? If you think that's something, you ought to be on a quiet lake in the morning when a flock of a hundred or so bluebills come in. You'd think you're standing under a 747."

I turned to look at her, she was looking toward the bar. She obviously didn't have the same affinity for ducks I had. A wisp of her warm breath met the cool air, flitted skyward. She shivered.

"Let's go in," I said.

She eagerly agreed.

It was quiet in the bar, a little early for the evening dinner crowd. I directed Faye to the table in the corner, the one Tony and I normally occupied. The waitress followed. I ordered a red label scotch and soda. Faye ordered a glass of wine, Merlot. We both stared out the window, past our reflections, in a comfortable silence waiting for our drinks. I slowly turned my head. My eyes fixed on him. She had brunette hair in long tight curls swept back from her face. She had delicate features with dark brown eyes. She wore no make-up. Just the slightest hint of lipstick. She caught my gaze and blushed slightly.

"You think they have any cigars here?" she asked.

"What?" I said. "What do you want with a cigar?"

"To smoke it, what else?" she said. "I bet you think I'm terrible."

I shrugged my shoulders, a little surprised.

"My husband had some along this summer on a couple camping trips. I tried one, and I just kind of enjoyed it. So now every time I have a drink, I have this urge to have a cigar."

"You don't inhale, I hope," I said.

She looked, a little grin on her face. "Sometimes."

Without knowing whether it was true or not, I said, "They won't let you smoke a cigar in here."

She appeared to accept that. I looked at her, trying to imagine what she would look like with a big stogie in her mouth. She seemed embarrassed to have brought it up. Suddenly she got a smile on her face. I turned around. Tony was coming through the door, the waitress right behind him. He turned around and talked to her for a second, took the drinks off her tray and started towards our table. He placed the drinks in front of us. "Monsieur, Madame," he said.

"Don't expect a tip," I said.

"This is an added pleasure," he said to Faye. "To what do we owe the honor?"

"I think he was feeling guilty about leaving early again," she said as she nodded towards me.

I was surprised, I didn't think my motives were so transparent. "I just thought she needed to get out of the office for a change as well," I said.

"Is Ken coming?" Tony asked.

"Not unless I call him," she said.

"Well, then, don't call him," said Tony.

By then the waitress had brought Tony's beer. He raised it up to clink glasses in a toast. "To Kate," he said.

I touched his bottle, I was going to say, "To Kate," but my throat thickened and the words wouldn't come out. I was afraid if they did, a gush of emotion would follow. My pain was right on the surface. Both of them noticed. I looked away. They gave me time to regain my composure. I took a big swallow of my scotch. "We're going to start the trial again next Monday morning. You'll have to start making some calls," I said to change the subject.

"No problem," said Tony. "Is there anything new?"

"Not really. Spencer was his old pricky self today. The judge set him straight."

"What an asshole," said Tony. "God I hope we can get rid of that guy someday. Why doesn't somebody run against him? Why don't you run against him?"

"Christ," said Faye, "can you imagine him being a prosecutor? He'd give away the ship."

"That's not true," I said. "I can be hard-nosed if I want to. You know what they say about defense attorneys becoming judges. They're the worst judges to take a defendant in front of because they've heard all the bullshit before . . . they can't be snowed. So I might be a tough prosecutor."

The waitress led another group of people to a table across the room. I motioned to her and ordered another round of drinks. I looked at Tony. "Have you heard anything more on Pam Weber's case?"

"No, I haven't," he said, "but her boss. . ." he hesitated as if he was searching for the name.

"Spokes," I said.

"Yeah, Spokes. There was an article about him in the *Trib* the other day. He's trying to put together a group of investors to get horse racing back at Canterbury Downs. Said something like they had to come up with ten million. I know he's a big shooter, but does he do that well?"

"I think he does," I replied. "But it surprises me he's talking about getting back into horse racing. I remember seeing him on TV several years ago, when they were talking about closing the race track. He was telling the reporter what kind of losses the horse owners would experience if the track closed. One of the biggest problems was they couldn't afford to keep their horses, and nobody wanted to buy them. I remember Spokes mentioned some owners would be shipping their horses to France. Apparently France is a big market for horse meat for human consumption."

"They eat 'em?" asked Faye.

"I guess so."

"How disgusting," she replied, shaking her head in disbelief.

"It's all what you get use to," said Tony.

"Not me," she replied.

"It sounded to me like he lost his ass. I can't imagine why he'd want to get back into it," I said.

"Well, he's back in the thick of things," replied Tony.

"Do you remember what day's paper that was in?" I asked.

Tony thought for a second. "What day was Kate's service?"

"Thursday," I said.

"It was in Thursday morning's paper," replied Tony.

"I don't suppose you kept the paper?" I asked.

"No, I didn't."

"I'd like to read the article," I said.

Faye looked at Tony. "Nothing's happened on the death of that poor girl, huh?"

"No," said Tony. "Did you know her?"

"I had talked to her a couple times over the phone trying to set up that appointment for Bob. She was really pleasant to work with."

The table quieted. By then the restaurant was half full. I could hear little bits of conversation from different tables, laughter, the clinking of dishes. Every so often a thin veil of cigarette smoke would float across the room, drift over Faye's hair in my direction. First I would try to ignore it, then I would give in, take a deep breath, trying to inhale a little.

We were all sipping on our drinks. I suddenly shivered, my mind flashed a picture of Pam Weber. Faye broke the silence again. "Is Kevin's trial going to last all week?" she asked.

"I suppose. Depending upon how long it takes to pick a jury, it could actually go into the next week," I replied.

"Is there any problem with me taking next Friday off?" she asked. "There's talk about snow next week. Ken and the kids are anxious to get the snowmobiles out. We've made reservations at Quadna. We're planning on leaving Friday morning if that's okay."

"God, I hope it doesn't snow that much," said Tony.

"They've already had some snow up north," said Faye. "We don't need much more for snowmobiling. And if it doesn't, well, we'll just have a good weekend to relax."

"That's fine," I said. "I assume there won't be any more crisis."

The waitress came over, and we all decided to order. We sat there for several hours, enjoying the meal and each other's company, just small talk. It was good diversion for me. Faye left about eight thirty, Tony and I stayed for an after-dinner drink.

I knew I was drinking too much. Slowly, during the course of the evening, the feeling crept into me, the realization that I was going to go home to an empty house again. The more I thought about it, the more I drank. Tony protested. It didn't do any good. I just kept ordering.

I don't remember how long we stayed at the bar. I don't remember leaving. I just know the next morning I woke up with cotton mouth, my head pounding, my mind fading in and out of consciousness. I smelled coffee and I smiled. I visioned Kate up and already making coffee. She had done that many times over the years when I had managed to imbibe to excess. Through the tiniest slits, my eyes tried to focus, the light hurt. I was looking for something familiar, a chair, a couch, a picture, anything, any small familiarity to bring me back to reality. I opened my eyes a little further and a sense of fear sent a shiver down my spine. Like a jack-in-the-box, I sprung up, my fists clenched. I felt danger. From behind me, I heard Tony's voice. "The dead has arisen."

My mind was racing, the voice caught me by surprise. I wheeled around, only to see Tony in his boxer shorts, sleeveless t-shirt, a big grin on his face, pouring a cup of coffee. I deflated quickly, my knees weakened, and

I plopped back onto the couch. I let out a deep sigh. "Goddamn," I mumbled.

"What's wrong?" asked Tony.

I sat there speechless, struggling with thoughts and emotions too complex to comprehend.

"Are you okay?" he asked.

I stood up. My legs wobbled. The air in the room was warm, beads of sweat forming just below my eyes. My armpits felt clammy. "How come it's so warm in here?" I asked.

"I like it that way," said Tony. "What happened to you anyway?"

"When I started to wake up, everything seemed so familiar. I smelled the coffee. I pictured Kate standing at the kitchen counter in her bathrobe. I imagined myself getting out of bed, walking up to her, putting my hands on her hips. I could smell her hair. I kissed her gently . . . then reality set in. Suddenly, I had the strongest sense of danger, it was almost overwhelming. I felt the need to protect myself."

I shook my head to clear the cob webs.

"Strange," I said. Tony handed me a mug. I took a sip of the coffee; my head started to clear. Tony sat there silently. He looked at me, I turned away. The picture of Kate in my mind had been so real, the sensation of touching her so complete, that the realization it was just a dream left such a void it tore at me. I wondered if it would ever be any different. How do I learn to cope with such a loss? I was alone in my thoughts.

"Something's terribly wrong with that whole scene, you know," said Tony.

I turned back to face him. "I know," I said.

"Why would she get all dressed up just to commit suicide?" he asked. "I saw her, Bob, she was dressed like she was going somewhere."

"I know," I said. "And why would she lock the door to the house? When I ran to the house to call 911, the door was locked. I didn't think anything of it at the time, but now, now when I think back, why would she do that? Then there's something I didn't discover until days later. The day after the funeral service I went into the garage for the first time and looked through her car. The back seat had several packages, a blouse and a sweater from Daytons. I remembered her trying them on a day or two before her death. She didn't like the colors; she was going to return them. That's where she was going that day. I remember seeing the packages on the counter that morning when I left for court. So she dresses up, takes the packages off the counter, locks the door to the house, gets into her car to leave and then changes her mind and commits suicide—no way in hell."

"But why would anybody want to kill her?" asked Tony.

"Don't you think I've been racking my brain? The only thing that makes sense is some dirtbag I pissed off in the past, some malcontent I represented who ended up in prison and blames me for it—somebody who wants his pound of flesh."

"But why Kate?" asked Tony.

"Just to make me suffer."

"But then why make it look like suicide?" asked Tony. "If it was to get at you, why wouldn't they make it look as gruesome as possible. More importantly, how do you murder somebody with carbon monoxide?"

"Maybe the guy didn't want to tip me off, maybe he wanted to make me suffer but not take any precautions to protect myself. As far as carbon monoxide, there are ways it could be done. He could've drugged her, he could've used chloroform, a number of different things. Maybe it would've shown up on an autopsy. I didn't think about it at the time . . . and I didn't want to do that to Kate anyway."

"Do you have any idea who it might be?" asked Tony.

"I keep going over and over it. There could be dozens of people. I'll have to have Faye do that this week, start going through some of the old files, see who could be violent enough to come up with some plan like this. The only name that pops up is Draper, Scott Draper. This was before your time, but I represented him on a murder case where he literally crushed an old man's skull with his boot. Kicked him to death. One of the meanest sons-of-bitches I ever met. He was eligible for parole about six months ago. He had done a little over seventeen years in prison. The Department of Corrections called me to let me know that there was a potential of him being discharged, wanted to know what my thoughts were. I told the caller exactly that—that he was one of the meanest sons-of-bitches I'd ever met."

"Maybe that got back to him," said Tony.

"I can't imagine the correction agent would be that dumb. I never did hear anything further. Maybe you can check that out for me, Tony, see if he got discharged. And if you get a chance, talk to Faye this week, see what other possibilities may be out there. You don't know where I could buy a gun, do you?"

"You're not thinking about carrying a gun?" asked Tony.

"I've been thinking about it. If there's someone out there trying to get me, well . . ."

"When was the last time you even fired a gun?" he asked.

"Probably thirty years ago."

"You'll probably end up shooting yourself in the foot," said Tony. "You wouldn't use it anyway. Even if the guy was standing in front of you, I can't see you using a gun to blow him away."

"I thought about it a lot. I wonder what I would do. I can't imagine it would be easy to kill somebody . . . even in self-defense. We've both been involved in enough murders, Tony, sometimes cold blooded, calculated, sometimes with such anger it's hard to believe a heart can turn that cold. And then you have killings of happenstance, not planned, but something went wrong, like in Kevin's case. I don't believe it was premeditated. He was in the wrong place at the wrong time."

"But that doesn't answer my question," said Tony. "Could you use a gun if you had to?"

"I suppose if I was convinced it was him or me . . . or if I had to protect someone else, like Carol. But I think it would have to be instantaneous, I couldn't have time to think, see a face. It would make me hesitate, then I'd be lost. I hope I never have to make that decision."

"I'll see what I can do," said Tony. "Something small, something that you can hide away, but yet with enough firepower to knock somebody down if need be."

"Sounds terrible, but I guess that's what we've come to," I said as I got up from the table. "Where's your john?" I asked.

"Down the hall and to the right."

I walked into the bathroom, startled by my face in the mirror. I put both hands on the sink and leaned close. I was a mess. I needed a haircut. I could remember sweating during the night and my hair was matted on both sides of my head, except above my ears where it stood out like little chicken feathers, gray and white streaks. My eye sockets were dark and sunken, my eyes red and puffy, drowning out any hint of their natural color. Stubble covered my chin, giving my face the slightest grayish tinge. The face I looked at was tired and worn. I squinted, and crows feet appeared from both sides of my eyes, little crooked lines. I meant it as a thought, but it came out under my breath, "God, you look terrible." I splashed cold water on my face and looked again, it only accentuated the redness of my eyes. That was the first time the thought crossed my mind: maybe I should end the misery of all this myself—maybe death would be the easiest way out.

By the time I came out, Tony had made some eggs and toast. We sat talking about Kevin's murder case, the witnesses he would have to contact, what sort of time tables we would set. Kate's death never came back up. We had each quietly set an agenda for ourselves and would not bring it up again until we believed we had something definite.

I left Tony's about 10:00 a.m. and stopped at the office. My clothes were disheveled. I hadn't showered or shaved. I could've been a panhandler. Faye laughed in a rather sad way when she saw me. "I knew you were on your way to oblivion when I left," she said. "I told Tony to make sure you got home safely. By the looks of it, you never did get home. Where did you stay? At Tony's?"

I looked at her. It didn't need a reply. She knew I had. "I need a favor," I said. "Tony's going to stop in later this afternoon. I would like you to go through the file index of cases I've handled since you've been here. If you can remember any of them that may have involved somebody who we thought was particularly dangerous, mean, whatever, involved in a murder or an assault, make a list of those, maybe pull some files out."

"What are you looking for?" she asked.

"It was just something Tony and I were talking about."

"It has something to do with Kate, doesn't it?" she said.

"Why would you think that?" I asked.

"It's things that you and Tony have said and what I know—Kate wouldn't kill herself."

It was said more like a question than an exclamation. "Don't get involved, Faye. It's better you don't. Just see what you can find and give it to Tony. I'm taking Kevin's file and going home."

"Are you going to be all right?" she asked.

The question surprised me. "Why?" I said.

"You're in misery. You wouldn't do anything stupid, would you?"

"Like what?" I asked.

"Don't play coy with me, Bob, we've been together too long. I know what's happening to you."

"Don't worry," I said. "I'm okay."

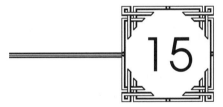

For the next several days I spread my time between office and home. When home, I buried myself in the file, making notes, reviewing the questions I would ask the jurors in voir dire, going through the autopsy report, trying to understand what the doctor was telling me. I visited Kevin several times at the jail. I could tell the pressure was starting to get to him: by Friday he was tense. When I talked to him, he clenched his fists, and I could see his veins, like little mountain ridges, run over the backs of his hands.

Back at the office, I talked to Faye, to see what she had come up with.

"I don't know what you want, Bob," she said. "I've been going through the index, it's such a rogues' gallery. There's been so many reprobates, I don't know where to start. Tony was in yesterday, and I gave him files on a couple of guys, but if I'm right, I think they're both still in prison. I have a couple more files to retrieve today, but, you know, if they were convicted for murder, chances are, they're still in prison."

"It doesn't have to be for murder," I said. "It could be anybody who has some reason to be pissed at me for what happened in their case."

She looked up from the notes on her desk, smiled, and chuckled a little. "That could be quite a list."

I had never quite thought of it that way. I smiled back and in a joking manner said, "I don't need any smart ass remarks from you. We're looking for mean people, somebody who'd wring your neck for a comment like that."

"I'll keep digging," she said. "But, God, you know how depressing it is?"

"I know," I said, "but it's important. I'm having lunch with Tony. Is there anything you want me to tell him?"

"Just tell him I'll keep working on it," she replied.

As I drove out to the Log Lodge to meet Tony for lunch, her comment went through my mind. She was right, it was a rogues' gallery, from petty thieves to murderers and everything in between. There were always some who blamed their attorney. The question was, who would feel such lingering and obsessive anger that he would seek revenge? It was something I couldn't help but think about. I could picture one of my clients lying on his cot at night, in his little eight-by-ten cell, looking at the ceiling, convinced in his own mind that, if it weren't for something I screwed up, he wouldn't be there. He was innocent, and I should've been able to prove it. I believed that after years of doing that, it would be an easy step for one to say: "When I get outta here, I'm gonna to get that son-of-a-bitch." Now I only had to figure out which one went from thought to deed.

The Log Lodge had its typical lunch crowd, construction workers mixed with business men and sales people from the retail shops in the neighborhood. Tony was sitting at our favorite table overlooking the yard and the river. The weather had turned cold; the geese had left. Any place where the water was quiet, the river had frozen. Just a swirling current down the middle stayed open. If this was a typical winter, that would be frozen by Christmas as well. It would be a snowmobile highway by January. Tony didn't see me walk in. He was staring out the window, appeared deep in thought. As I sat down, the waitress followed me over. We each ordered a root beer and the noon special. I could tell from his demeanor something was bothering him. "What's up?" I asked.

He looked at me with a serious tone, said, "You were right about your former client, the murderer. He was paroled two months ago. He did his seventeen and a half years. They have him on paper for another seven and a half. Unfortunately, he's disappeared."

"What do you mean?" I asked.

"I talked to his parole officer," he replied. "You know the sentence for first-degree murder is twenty-five years. He was eligible for parole after seventeen and a half. The parole officer said he was a model prisoner, and they decided to cut him loose. He reported to his officer for the first month and now they haven't seen him."

"I thought they were going to let me know if he got out," I said.

"The officer said he thought you knew. He said he thought somebody from the Department of Corrections had called. What can you tell me about him?" he said.

I shook my head in disbelief. "It was a strange case. He and another kid had been out smoking pot all day, driving around the countryside. They saw this shack back in the woods with piles of cut firewood. They stopped to see if they could buy some. They planned to resell it in town. An old-timer lived there. He told them he would let them fill up their pick-up truck for five bucks. When he told them he thought they had enough, Draper flips out, he took a log and cracked the old man over the head, dragged his body behind the wood pile and kept loading wood. The old man woke up and groaned, and he kicked him in the skull and kept kicking him until he stopped moving. It was pretty awful.

"The cops would've never figured it out, but the kid that was with him got pangs of conscience. Within a couple days he told his sister, who told his mother, who went to the sheriff. The prosecutor gave him a deal to testify against Draper. The first time I walked into his cell, I, honest to God, was afraid he was going to do me next. He was one angry young man. At first he just wanted to plead guilty to first-degree murder. He said his uncle was in prison and had told him it wasn't that bad. I found out later, that same uncle had sexually abused him as a kid. Anyway, I wouldn't let him plead. I told him we had to go to trial. I tried it on the basis of intoxication as a defense, that he was too far under the influence of drugs and alcohol to form the intent for first-degree murder. The jury didn't buy it. Afterwards, one of the jurors told me if he had only hit the old man over the head with a log, they might've bought it. But when he went back and kicked him repeatedly, they thought he knew exactly what he was doing. The decision was right. When it was all done, he wasn't even pissed at me, not the day they sent him off to prison anyway. That came later. He left for prison with a big smile on his face and ten bucks of my money in his pocket to buy cigarettes. It was never appealed, but years later he brought a petition for post-conviction relief, claiming ineffective assistance of counsel. The story I got was apparently he ran into another one of my clients at Stillwater, and the two of them started to compare notes—you see, they were both innocent as far as they were concerned. I guess the other guy convinced him that I was a horseshit attorney and that was the only reason he was sitting in prison. I thought I was going to have to testify at the hearing, but the judge the district brought in denied it, just on the basis of the affidavits. The attorney who represented him at the hearing called me afterwards and told me Draper was one pissed-off dude. I never understood . . . I didn't even ask for my ten bucks back."

Just as I finished, the waitress brought our lunches—a sandwich and tomato soup. We ordered more root beer. Tony opened the cellophane on his crackers and crunched them and dropped them in the soup. As he was about to take a spoonful, he looked at me. "That's got to be our prime suspect at this point," he said. "To get at Kate," he continued, "he would've had to do some planning. He would've had to follow you from your office, find out where you live. I bet he was watching you for a long time. Did you ever notice anybody following you home or any cars out of the ordinary?"

I thought for a moment. "You know, it's getting so built up around there. There was a time I would notice any strange car. Now there's so many new people in the neighborhood, kids visiting, I don't pay any attention."

"If it is him," he said, "how would he have gotten Kate to sit in that car? He would've had to use something, there was no sign of trauma."

"I called Dr. Salk," I said, "the medical examiner. I have a meeting with him this afternoon. He said he would have some free time about three. I'm hoping to find out more."

I took a bite of my fish sandwich. Before I swallowed, I said, "They have no idea where he may be?"

"Nothing," said Tony. "They have a warrant out for his arrest for violation of parole. If they catch him, he goes back for the balance of his term. His history and his attitude tell me he's the one we're looking for. By the way," he said, glancing up from his meal, "I'm gonna pick up your gun this afternoon. If you're gonna be around tomorrow morning, I'll bring it out. I'll show you how you use it. I don't want ya blowing your toes off . . . or something worse."

"Give me a call in the morning," I replied. "If Carol's not home, you can bring it out, and we can try a little target practice in the woods. If she decides to come home, we'll have to do it another day. She would never understand."

Tony's eyes darkened. "Listen," he said, "you may wanna consider getting her a gun as well. Have you ever thought she may be in danger too?"

"All the time. I've told her to be extra careful without really telling her why. I don't want to scare her unnecessarily. I've told her roommate to keep an eye out for anything suspicious, to give me a call if she has any concerns. Until I have something more concrete, I have to be satisfied with that."

"I don't know," said Tony. "I might let her know."

"What, that her mother was murdered by some crazy bastard who may be stalking her? She'd be a basket case in no time."

"I hope you know what you're doing," he said.

We sat in silence finishing our lunch. The waitress brought the bill and I left a twenty dollar bill and stood up. "If you're going to be free around five, I'll meet you back here. I can let you know what Dr. Salk had to say."

"You're getting into a bad habit, Bob."

"Don't worry," I said. "I'm not going to get drunk again."

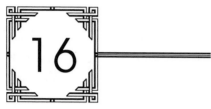

I stopped back at the office on the way to the hospital. Faye had a stack of files on the edge of her desk. "These are the ones I think you ought to look at," she said.

I sat down and picked up the first file. "*State of Minnesota vs. Charles Mullin.*" Aggravated assault and rape. "It wouldn't be him," I said. "He was a mouse of a guy. Besides, he wasn't pissed off at me. I probably saved him about ten years." I picked up the next file. *State of Minnesota vs. Robert Fischer.* Aggravated robbery. I grinned at Faye. "Faye, I won this one, remember?"

"Was he the guy in the mask?" she asked.

"Yeah."

"I wasn't sure," she said. "Besides, I don't know what you're looking for. If it looked like he was charged with a serious offense, I pulled it."

I took the rest of the files, went back to my office and paged through them quickly. None of the names sent any shivers down my spine. I looked at the clock. I had to get going. As I walked past her office, I looked in at Faye. She sat there pouting, obviously disappointed in my response to her hours of digging through dusty files. "I'll look at the files on my desk after I get back from the hospital," I said. "Thanks for your help. If I don't get back in time this afternoon, I probably won't see you for a while. We start jury selection Monday morning. I'm going to go straight to the courthouse."

"Remember, I'll be gone on Friday," she said.

"That's fine," I said. "I'll be tied up for at least a couple weeks."

She smiled at me. "Good luck."

It had been years since I'd been to the St. Cloud Hospital. The lady at the information desk directed me to the elevator and told me to go to the subbasement. I had seen Dr. Salk testify on several previous cases, not as an expert witness on an autopsy, but as the initial examining physician who made the referral to a forensic pathologist. The county medical examiner was an appointed position by the county board, and he had served in that capacity for probably ten years or more. Whenever there was a homicide or a questionable death, he would normally refer the matter to the Hennepin County Medical Examiner's Office in Minneapolis, staffed by a couple of forensic pathologists. In fact, that's what had happened in Kevin's case. The body of the boyfriend was initially seen by Dr. Salk and then transported to Hennepin County for the actual autopsy. The Hennepin County Medical Examiner, Dr. Gordon Mueller, a well-known forensic pathologist, was expected to testify as the state's expert witness in Kevin's case.

I made my way to the subbasement and followed the signs to the morgue at the very end of the hall. The door had a small glass panel, and I looked in. I didn't want to walk in to see some cadaver on the table, the entrails in little dishes, waiting to be weighed and documented. There was a young man in a blue uniform sitting at a table at the far end of the room leaning back casually, reading a magazine. It appeared safe. I knocked on the door, and I startled him. He quickly threw the magazine aside and started towards the door. I took that as an invitation and walked in. "I'm here to see Dr. Salk," I said.

"He called a few minutes ago, said he'd be a little late. You might as well have a seat." He pointed to a wood chair leaning up against the wall.

"I'm sorry about your wife," he said.

The comment caught me by surprise. I turned quickly.

Recognizing my surprise, he said, "I was here when they brought her in. When the doctor told me he was expecting you today, I put it together."

I didn't respond. It appeared he felt a little uncomfortable having brought it up. "I'm just sorry," he said, and he turned and walked back to his desk.

I sat down and looked around the room. At the far end, close to the table where the young man sat, I saw two stainless steel swinging doors, which I assumed led into the actual morgue and autopsy room. The room was clean. There were shelves full of supplies and counters with stainless steel pans. There was a strong medicinal odor.

We sat there not saying a word. The only noise, the rustle of the pages as he returned to his magazine. As if to break the silence, to ease the situation, he looked up from his magazine, "It's been pretty quiet around here," he said, and went back to reading.

To me it seemed like a strange thing to say. By the time a patient makes his way here, I thought, he wouldn't be talking anyhow. I was going to make some comment to that effect, see if I could get a chuckle out of him, when I realized it was stupid. I was about to try to strike up a conversation with the young man when Salk walked in. Probably in his late thirties, the doctor was short, with a boyish face and a bald head. He quickly made it across the room and stretched out his hand. "Mr. Williams, sorry to keep you waiting."

"No problem," I replied. "Your assistant has been keeping me entertained."

The doctor glanced back at the table. "Steve," he said, "they have some specimens up in surgery that they want us to do some testing on. Why don't you go up and see where they're at. If everything's ready, you can bring them down."

He walked out the door and then closed it with a rather forceful bang. "I suspect he would've rather sat around to overhear our conversation," he said. "That would've been a little awkward for you, I suppose. He'll be back shortly, though, so what can I do for you?"

"As I mentioned over the phone, doctor, I'm interested in getting whatever particulars I can regarding my wife's death."

"I did provide the sheriff's office with a summary of my medical report. Did you have an opportunity to see that?"

"Yes, I did.".

"Well that, and the death certificate, is pretty much everything I have."

"I'm more curious as to what may not be on that report, doctor. You talked about the level of carbon monoxide in her blood," I said.

"Yes," he interjected, "the carboxyhemoglobin. When a person is exposed to carbon monoxide, the CO mixes with the hemoglobin in the blood, the oxygen carried to the red blood cells is ousted, and a substance called carboxyhemoglobin is formed; it is a permanent, stable compound carried to the tissues, including the brain, but it's useless. What's happening is the blood no longer carries oxygen to the brain and part of the brain tissue dies."

"I believe your report indicates that in her case, the carboxyhemoglobin was sixty-nine percent."

"That's how we express it," the doctor quickly interjected again, "a percentage of carboxyhemoglobin in the blood. Depending on the percentage, the expected symptoms differ. At that percentage, you can almost always expect coma and death."

"How long would it take?" I asked.

"What is so deadly about carbon monoxide," he continued, "is that it is cumulative. It builds up in the body, and the higher the concentration, the more severe the consequences. I've seen death by carbon monoxide from automobile exhaust before. In a garage, a car can produce a tremendous concentration of carbon monoxide that can cause a loss of consciousness in a very short time. If the car keeps running, and the person keeps breathing, it doesn't take long before they go into a coma. We'll never know what the level of carbon monoxide may have been in the garage, but I would suspect it could've gotten very high. You see, the affinity of hemoglobin for carbon monoxide is roughly 250 times greater than its affinity for oxygen. When the CO concentration is heavy, as it usually is in this setting, you know, in a garage, the process happens very quickly."

"So she may well have been unconscious within minutes?" I asked.

"In all probability," he said.

"Did you do any other toxicology?" I asked.

He looked at me, puzzled. "Just the normal things we look for. Alcohol, drugs, similar things in the system that may show up. Why?" he asked.

"Did you try to make a determination as to the time of death?" I asked.

"To pinpoint an exact time is difficult under the circumstances," he said. "If the car was running and the heater was on, that would affect the body temperature. As soon as the car ran out of gas and shut off, and outside temperatures as cold as they were that day, that would've affected the body temperature. From the color of her skin and the other indications, she was dead for quite a while, sometime late that morning."

"Could you tell whether she had taken any sort of anesthetic? For example, something that might've helped her go to sleep before the carbon monoxide got to a level that would render her unconscious, something like chloroform for example."

"Most of those would require some sort of specific testing," he said. "I wasn't asked to do anything like that. There was no suspicion of any foul play, if that's what you're getting at."

"I'm not sure, doctor. I'm just looking for answers," I replied.

"All I can tell you is," he said, "I didn't see anything out of the ordinary. There was nothing to indicate that she had been through any trauma prior to her death."

"Thank you for your time," I said. "I hope if I have other questions, I can give you a call."

"Feel free," he said. "I hope I have been helpful. I'm really sorry for your loss."

"Thank you," I said.

It was dark as I left the hospital. The doctor only confirmed my own research. I wanted to know it was fast, that she didn't suffer. But what happened before she was placed in the car? Whoever had done it would've had to somehow drug her in the yard, after she had left our home and locked the door. I tried to picture it in my mind. Somebody who was a stranger to her, watching the home, making sure they came up the driveway just as she was going to leave; maybe asking for directions and then quickly grabbing her, using something to anaesthetize her and then placing her in the car, turning on the engine and closing the garage door. I pictured her inhaling the poisonous gas and slowly slipping away. I could feel the warm tears running down my cheek. I reached for the gloves on my seat to wipe them away. "What kind of goddamn animal would do that?" I mumbled.

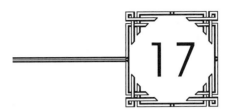

I met Tony at the bar a little after six. We took our usual table. I told him the information I'd gathered at the hospital. Tony ordered a beer, I ordered whiskey soda. I think he could tell I'd been crying.

"What's wrong," he asked.

"I just hope she didn't have to suffer, Tony. I hope the son-of-a-bitch didn't make her suffer. I hope she fought so he had to knock her out right away with whatever drug he had."

"That's the only way it would've worked," he replied. "He had to catch her by surprise, knock her out fast to not have any visible wounds or signs of struggle."

"I agonize over the thought he might've made her suffer . . . you know, that he told her he was going to kill her and made her think about it."

"I would think it was quick, Bob, that's the only way it makes sense."

We sat for a while, neither one making eye contact. For both of us, it was getting harder and harder to talk about it. Finally, Tony broke the silence. "Is Carol coming up this weekend?"

"No, she left a message with Faye. She's got some tests on Monday she has to study for. I suspect she could come home, but all we do is mull this thing over and over—it's probably affecting her schooling."

"Well then, maybe I'll come out tomorrow morning and bring the pistol"

"What kind did you get?" I asked.

"I tapped a friend of mine for a nice little Saturday night special, little snub-nosed .38, something you can hide in your pocket. The only problem with it is, it's no good at any distance. So if you're going to try and hit somebody, they better be looking you in the face."

"Do I have to do anything about registering it? I mean, is it in my name or what?"

"No way," said Tony, "it's clean. I picked it up from a friend who owed me a favor."

"If I get caught with it, I'm not going to get in trouble, am I?"

"I don't know how," he said. "Just tell them you had it for a long time, never took it out of the house, whatever."

I'd known Tony from almost the first day I got to town. He was a sergeant on the police force and was the arresting officer in one of the first burglary cases I handled. Through the years, he had been my adversary on many cases. I had come to respect him, both as a person and an officer. I never caught him in a lie, I never saw him even try to embellish a story. He always told it just the way it was, whether I asked him or the prosecutor asked him. I had given him a hard time in a couple cases, trying to cross him up. He never took it personally. I remember one time he was driving a prisoner back from a court appearance. The man was charged with armed robbery of a liquor store. In the casual conversation going back to the county jail, the defendant admitted that he was one of the guys who robbed the store. Because Tony didn't want to get him in trouble with his co-defendants, he never put the admission in his report, never expecting the matter to come to trial. It did go to trial, and I ended up representing the young man. I asked Tony whether it wasn't the duty of the police officer to document every aspect of the investigation, especially, if a defendant admitted participation in the crime. He acknowledged that it was, but he told the jury why he had not in this case. In closing arguments, I told the jury that they didn't have to believe Tony. If my defendant had made an admission, it would have been documented in the police reports. It wasn't. I made quite a point of it. When the jury went out, Tony and one of the secretaries from the office were sitting in the back. They had listened to my closing argument. As I walked up to them, Tony just laughed, but the young lady looked at me and said, "I don't know how in the hell you could do that, you son-of-a-bitch."

Tony quickly put his hand up and said, "Hey, he's just doing his job, it's nothing personal. Right Bob?"

The jury came back, not guilty. The only way they could have reached that decision was to doubt Tony's testimony. The next time I saw him, it was like it never happened. He understood the process.

There were other cops I'd dealt with over the years who couldn't open their mouths without lying. Most of them had the same attitude as Spencer—the defendants are dirt bags and you use whatever means you can, including stretching the truth, to put them away. There were cops who treated me with disdain. To them I was just a mouthpiece, using every trick to get some guilty bastard off. They didn't understand the process.

Tony and I decided to have dinner. We started to reminisce about some of the old days. It's funny how years later you have a different attitude about events that were ugly at the time. Tony and I had been involved in cases with high publicity, hard fought, filled with tremendous tension and stress. At the time, it was like living in hell; now, we could reflect back and laugh.

"Do you remember that time you screwed me up with that Grand Jury transcript?" Tony asked, laughing a little.

Shortly before Tony had retired, I was defending a young lady charged with murder. Tony had been one of the chief investigators. In his testimony for the prosecutor, he made a mistake, said something different than he had told the grand jury. It wasn't a big issue, but it showed that he was human. My client had changed her statement from one time to the next. One of the issues for the jury to decide was which version of my client's story to believe. I wanted to show that her changes were also just a matter of human error—how the mind recalls things. When I noticed Tony had made a mistake in his testimony in court compared to what he had told the grand jury, I asked him on cross examination, "Mr. O'Donnell, did you read the transcript of your grand jury testimony before you came to court today?"

"Yes I did."

"Do you recall how many times you may have read it?"

"Not specifically."

"Was it more than once?" I asked.

"Yes, it could have been."

"Was it more than three times, for example?"

"Yes, I believe it was."

He ended up testifying that he had read it over probably forty times.

In closing argument, I argued to the jury, how could the State demand that this young lady, who was afraid for her life, recall all of the details exactly or, more importantly, could tell somebody all of the details, without changing some small detail from one telling to the next. Here, a trained police officer, who had read his grand jury testimony over forty times, still came into court and made a mistake.

Tony could tell that I was thinking about it.

"You know, I should have kicked your ass for that. Especially when the jury came back not guilty."

"Yeah, but Tony, that was just a small part of it. I don't think they decided the case based on that little argument."

"It was still a cheap shot," he said with a grin.

That's how Tony and I looked back at our years in court together. There were plenty of times when his investigation was so complete, his testimony so devastating, my client didn't stand a chance in hell. I would get up at closing argument and throw the jury everything but the kitchen sink, hoping that if I couldn't dazzle them with my brilliance, I could baffle them with my bullshit. We both knew that most of the time it didn't work.

I stayed and had dinner with Tony. He cut me off the booze, told the waitress to bring a pot of coffee. He said he wasn't about to baby-sit me all night again. That was fine. For some reason, I wasn't in the mood to drink.

The next morning he showed up about nine o'clock. I had the coffee on. He came in, sat down at the table and put a little package down that clanged hard on the wood. He opened it up with a big grin on his face. "Here's your little beauty."

It was a small revolver, silver, with a white pearl handle.

"Looks awful small. What is it?"

"It's a Smith and Weston 'Chiefs Special', .38 caliber. It's suppose to be small. It's only got a two-and-a-half-inch barrel, so it fits anywhere."

"I don't know," I said, "it's awful small."

"That's the idea. You gonna walk around with some big gun hanging out? This one here you can hide anywhere."

"I'm not going to take it with me," I said.

"Why not?"

"Because I hate guns. How many times have you seen where if a gun hadn't been handy, the outcome would've been something different? You have it on you, you think you have to use it."

"Well I thought you wanted this for your own protection."

"I do. I'm going to keep it here, at home."

"Christ, then I could've brought you a damn shotgun."

"I don't want a shotgun leaning up against my bedstead. How can I hide that? I wanted something small I can hide here, so Carol doesn't see it, so she doesn't get worried."

"Suit yourself," he said. "Sometimes you're a pain in the ass."

"So are you. You going to show me how to use this thing?"

He reached in his coat pocket and brought out a box of shells. "You've handled enough shooting cases, I assume you know how a gun works," he said sarcastically. "You know you put the little shells in here, then you pull this little hammer back, you pull this little trigger, and it goes bang."

"That's what I needed to know," I said. "Let's go see how it works."

"What I've got here is the .38-special load, this is what they call a high velocity semi-jacketed hollow point. Let's see," and he picked up the box, "yeah, this is the 158-gram shells."

"Why do I need hollow point?"

"You wantta make sure that if you hit someone, he goes down."

We walked out behind the barn. I had located a big wooden spool I had heisted from a construction crew laying cable along the country roads. We put it on its side and hung a target. Once set up, Tony had me take about ten paces back.

"This isn't the most accurate gun in the world," he said. "With that short barrel, you have to be kind of close to your target."

He handed it to me, it felt heavy. I held it up, pointed it toward the target.

"I would use both hands if I were you," he said. "Just point it towards the target, pull the hammer back and shoot."

I did as he told me.

"Little shaky, aren't you?"

"I don't know what to expect."

"Well, hold your breath and slowly pull the trigger," he said.

I pointed the barrel towards my target, held my breath and slowly pulled the trigger. The noise and recoil were tremendous. I didn't expect that loud of a bang. When I finally focused on the target again, I didn't see any hole. I looked at Tony.

He was laughing. "You flinched," he said. "Just as the gun was going to go off, you anticipated it, raised it about three inches. From here to the target, that's about three feet. You're never gonna hit anything that way."

Tony took the gun, said he would show me how to do it. In five shots, he hit the target every time. He reloaded and gave it back to me. A half an hour later, after using half the box of ammunition, I was finally hitting the spool. "That's enough, Tony," I said. "I'm getting a headache from the noise, and a side ache from laughing."

"Well, you better hope your target's looking you in the eyeballs or that you can scare 'em to death because you're never gonna to hit anything," Tony said.

Monday morning at quarter to nine, I walked into the courthouse, pushed the button to the elevator and rode the two floors to the courtroom. The doors opened onto a crowded hallway. Court personnel, spectators, jurors, all waiting for Kevin's case. The crowds parted like the Red Sea as I made my way through the hall. Wearing a suit and tie, carrying a briefcase, they obviously assumed I was one of the players in this human drama. I slowly made my way to the back conference room where the deputy was sitting with my client. I walked in, and Kevin sat there in his suit and tie, his face flushed. He cracked an uncomfortable smile and said, "Good morning." He asked nervously, "What's gonna happen today?"

"Just jury selection, again," I said. "Like last time, I expect it'll take a couple days."

"What do you want me to do?" he asked.

"I brought you a pad and pencil. I want you to take notes as I'm questioning each juror, then we'll confer at the end and decide whether we're going to keep the juror or strike them."

I looked at my watch, two minutes to nine. "I suppose we might as well get in," I said.

The deputy took the handcuffs off Kevin, and we walked in the back of the courtroom. Spencer was already sitting at his end of the table. He looked up and nodded.

The judge's clerk was sitting at her corner of the judicial bench. At precisely nine o'clock, the door to the judge's chambers opened. The bailiff rapped the gavel, and everybody stood as the judge made his way to the bench. In some courtrooms, the scene could be quite ceremonious. In this makeshift courtroom, it seemed incongruous. The surroundings didn't seem to comport with the pomp and circumstance afforded a judge. As he sat down, the judge said, "Gentlemen, I assume we're prepared to proceed."

We both indicated we were.

"Madame Clerk," he said, "bring in the prospective jurors."

The courtroom quickly filled, and the process started. The judge had them all raise their hand and give the oath to answer the questions truthfully. He then told them what the case was about, read the indictment and the instructions for the presumption of innocence and reasonable doubt. He then had them return to the jury room and the clerk called one name. That juror, a young lady from Gilman, came back into the courtroom and the clerk motioned her to take the witness seat. It appeared she hadn't expected that, she seemed confused and a little frightened. She looked at the judge the entire time she was attempting to get situated. When she finally sat down, the judge said, "Mr. Williams is going to ask you some questions."

It wasn't until she heard my voice that she looked at me. I said, "Good morning," and it seemed to startle her. I started voir dire, a painful process for everyone concerned.

We spent the next two and a half days picking jurors. A little before three o'clock on Wednesday, the prosecutor and I had accepted our fourteenth juror, the twelve we needed and the two alternates. The panel was made up of seven women and five men and both alternates were men. We had one professional (an accountant), several farmers, a mechanic, laborers, housewives, secretaries. Kevin had his jury of peers. I told Kevin the one we had to convince was the accountant. He appeared the strongest personality on the jury. If we could convince him of Kevin's innocence, he would persuade any juror who held a different opinion. Unfortunately, the opposite was true as well—if he believed Kevin was guilty, he could easily persuade the rest of the jury to follow suit.

The judge took a recess and asked the attorneys to meet in chambers. He invited us to a cup of coffee. As we settled in, he said, "Spencer, you want to make your opening statement this afternoon?"

"I would prefer to wait until tomorrow morning, your honor. I don't have any witnesses lined up for this afternoon, and I would just as soon not break the continuity."

The judge looked at me. "That's fine," I said. "Who do you plan on having on tomorrow?"

"The first officers on the scene, the paramedics, the local medical examiner, the neighbor," Spencer replied.

"What are you talking about, neighbor?" I snapped.

"There's a neighbor next door, an older lady, Mrs. Butkowski. She's gonna testify that she saw Kevin arguing with Josie on numerous occasions, raising his voice and threatening her."

I looked at the judge. "Your honor, I've never heard this stuff before."

Spencer reached for the file on top of the table, gave me an envelope. "Here's your copy of the statement."

"Spencer, what are you doing?" asked the judge.

"Before everybody panics," said Spencer, "look at the date and time on that statement."

I got my copy out. It was taken the night before at approximately 7:30 p.m.

"She said she was afraid to come forward. Josie had told us about her a long time ago, that she had witnessed arguments in the backyard, but she would never talk. Apparently Josie talked to her yesterday and told her how important it was, and she agreed to give a statement. I sent Detective Theisen over there last night. This is what he got."

"Your honor," I said, raising my arms in frustration.

"Take it easy, Bob," he said. "We don't have to make any decisions on that today. Spencer, I don't know, you always manage to do this."

"What? I can't help it if she waited till the last minute to come forward."

"Never mind, Spencer," said the judge. "Just give me a copy of the statement. I want to read it over. I'll call the jury back in and tell them we're going to recess until nine o'clock tomorrow."

Before I left the court that day, I talked to Kevin about the statement. He said he knew the woman, that they had become friends over the months he had been coming to Josie's house. He did acknowledge that he and Josie had had some screaming matches Mrs. Butkowski may have overheard.

"But I read the statement, Kevin. She's going to say that she heard you threaten Josie. She said she heard you say to Josie that if you saw her with another guy, she'd better watch her back. Do you remember saying something like that?"

"We had some ugly fights, Mr. Williams. I may have said something like that in anger, but I didn't mean it. I wouldn't hurt her."

"How about somebody she was shacking up with?" I asked.

He had been sitting there with his head bowed. It quickly snapped up. He was surprised by my comment. "I had no idea she was shacking up with anybody, if that's what you're asking. And no, that wouldn't be enough to get me to do anything either."

I was frustrated, and I was taking it out on Kevin. You prepare for months to try a case, believing you know every intricate detail; then, at the last minute, something is dropped on your lap that may force you to change your entire strategy, and it's something you should have known, and would've known, if your client had been straight with you. So I was a little pissed and it didn't hurt if Kevin knew it.

"It didn't seem important to me, Mr. Williams. They were lovers' spats, nothing more."

"You should've told me," I said. "It's little crap like this that can cause you problems with that jury." I let out a deep sigh. "There's nothing we can do about it now. The judge hasn't decided whether he's going to let her testify or not."

I didn't want him upset all night, so I put my hand on his shoulder and said, "It'll be all right. I'll see ya tomorrow morning."

He gave me a sad little half smile as the deputy put the handcuffs back on him.

I drove back to my office. Faye was just walking out the front door as I pulled up out front. She waited for me to park my car and then followed me back to my office. "How are things going?" she asked.

"We've got our jury picked and testimony begins tomorrow morning."

"How's Kevin holding up?" she asked.

I told her what had happened. "Will the judge let that in?" she asked.

"I suspect he will. It goes to motive, intent, state of mind, that kind of thing."

"I've given Tony a couple more files," she said, "but he said you've pretty much centered in on this Draper character. That was before my time, but we dug the file out of the dungeon. We made the mistake of paging through it before I knew what it was all about. I found the pictures. That poor old man, how could anybody do that?"

"I'll tell you, Faye, it was a combination of booze, drugs, greed and just sheer meanness. When you have somebody who doesn't give a shit about anything or anybody, and they're mean on top of it, that's a combination that can result in just about anything."

"Tony says he's working hard on trying to run him down, but he's disappeared off the face of the earth."

"I doubt it," I said. "Tony's trying to get a recent picture. His parole officer has been cooperating."

She stood up and said, "Well, if you don't mind, I think I'm gonna take off. The boys are excited about going up north this weekend. We're going shopping tonight for some new boots."

"That's right," I said. "I forgot, you won't be here tomorrow. I hope you'll be back by Monday. I don't know where this trial's going, and I might need some help by then."

"We're coming back Sunday afternoon. The kids have to be in school on Monday."

"All right," I said, "have a good time. I'll probably see you Monday after court."

She smiled at me and said, "Good luck," as she walked out the door.

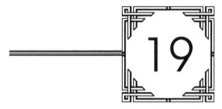

As I said, Judge Morris was a creature of habit. When he had a trial, he wanted to be on the bench at nine o'clock sharp, and he followed that rule religiously. To accommodate him, everybody knew that the jury had to be in the jury box, the lawyers at their table, the clerk at her station. At three minutes to nine the next morning, we were all in the courtroom, everyone exactly where the judge expected us to be. At precisely nine, the bailiff rapped the gavel and the judge walked in from the back door and took his seat. It took me a few minutes to realize something was wrong—there was no court reporter. The judge didn't say a word. He sat there, staring ahead. The jurors stirred a little, looking at each other, not quite sure what was happening. I looked at the prosecutor. He looked at me. He just grinned. Kevin leaned over and whispered, "What's wrong?"

I said, "He doesn't have a court reporter."

The courtroom was too quiet, everyone was looking at us. I indicated he should write anything out. I watched as he wrote on the pad, "What do we do?"

I took the pen and wrote below, "Nothing."

That's exactly what we did, we sat there in total silence. I looked across at the jurors, I think some of them had figured it out. In the back row there were a few whispers back and forth. Finally, at nine fifteen, the door next to the judge's chambers opened, and a red-faced court reporter walked in with her steno machine. She walked behind the witness box and took her seat next to the judge. She looked at the judge as she was setting up the machine. "I'm sorry, your honor. I got caught in traffic."

The judge never acknowledged her. He looked at the prosecutor. "Is the State ready to proceed."

"We are, your honor."

It has to go down as one of the most humiliating things I've ever seen a judge do to any court personnel. I've heard judges yell and cuss at clerks and law clerks; I've seen them treat employees like shit. I've experienced the embarrassment they have felt but nothing compared to how that woman must have felt that morning walking in, knowing the judge had made everybody sit there quietly, like naughty children, waiting for her. I think we all empathized a little with her humiliation.

The prosecutor stood up and took a couple steps to the front of the jury box. "If it would please the court, Mr. Williams, ladies and gentlemen of the jury, good morning. I apologize for the delay. At this point in the trial, I have an opportunity to give you what we call an opening statement, which is a summary of what we intend to prove. You're embarking on a trip and this summary is to be used by you like a road map, to follow from where we are now to where we want to go. I'm gonna tell you a story of love gone bad, of a relationship that turned sour, of a heart that turned killer. We expect the evidence to show that the defendant and a young lady, Josie Klein, met in the spring of 1994, that they started a relationship, that they were, in fact, lovers. Josie will tell you that by late summer of 1994, their relationship was starting to deteriorate. She's gonna tell you that the defendant was putting demands on her time and her affection that were unrealistic, that he was obsessed with her, that he had to know where she was twenty-four hours a day, that he constantly accused her of having affairs, clandestine meetings with men. She's gonna tell you that they had arguments and that he made some threats. It got to the point where she couldn't take it anymore, and she told the defendant she didn't want anything more to do with him. She broke off the relationship, but he wouldn't take no for an answer. He kept sending her cards, flowers, gifts, and when she didn't respond, he made some threats, veiled threats that she'd be sorry."

He paused for a second, walked back to the table, took his glass and had a sip of water. He turned around, picking up his story on his way back. "Then she'll tell you that she met another man, Ronning, and she started another relationship. On a Friday night, he stayed over, and she's gonna be candid with you, they planned a romantic evening. She had made arrangements to have her daughter stay with a friend. She bought some wine for a candlelight dinner. You're also gonna find out that this new friend was married, but Josie understood he was separated. She'll testify that they had dinner, watched television and then fell asleep on the living room floor. She woke up close to two in the morning, and the two of them went upstairs to the bedroom. At that point, she remembered the front door. She wasn't sure if it was locked or not, and she sent Dale down to check. She will tell you that within minutes, she heard voices, loud voices, and she heard the defendant say, 'What the fuck are you doing here.' She's gonna tell you she heard things breaking, a struggle ensuing, and she immediately went to the phone and called 911. You'll hear the tape—she was hysterical. With the phone still off the receiver, she went to the stairs and hollered down, 'Who's ever here, I've called the cops. They're on their way,' and all she heard was the front door slam and a moaning sound. She walked down the stairs, slowly, not sure what she would encounter, and there, on the kitchen floor, she saw her friend moaning, blood gushing from his chest, his eyes rolling back in his head."

I sat there with my head down, scribbling on my notepad like I was taking notes, but I wasn't. I knew what he was going to say, and so far, he hadn't said anything I knew he couldn't prove. From what I could see, Kevin watched him intently as Spencer painted a picture of a cold-blooded killing. From time to time, I would take a glance at the jury; they were glued to every word. Spencer may be a prick, but he knew how to play to a jury, especially if there was a love triangle and a little blood and gore.

He continued for another fifteen minutes or so, outlining what he expected each witness to say. He concluded in a soft and somber tone, "That's my road map, ladies and gentlemen. I know it will lead you to one conclusion, that this was indeed a case of love gone bad."

The night before, I had pondered whether I should give my opening statement right after the prosecutor's or wait until the start of my case. I had decided to wait. The only defense I had was Kevin's testimony. The prosecutor had never heard Kevin's version. He knew we were claiming self-defense, but he didn't know any specifics. To give any opening statement that would have any impact with a jury, I would have to lay out Kevin's testimony. To me, that would only give the prosecutor an opportunity to try and rebut it from the very beginning. It would be a tactical error on my part, I thought. I stood up and looked at the court. "Your honor, I'm going to wait to make my statement."

"That's fine, Mr. Williams," he said, and he nodded towards the prosecutor.

"Your honor," said the prosecutor, "my first witness will be Officer Becker."

The prosecutor spent the rest of the morning going through preliminary witnesses. Officer Becker testified that he was the first officer to arrive. When he got there, the decedent was lying on the kitchen floor, bleeding profusely from an open wound on the left chest. He told the jury how he administered medical assistance until the paramedics got there; that the decedent was alive and awake, mumbling names. He was unable to distinguish any names because of the gurgling sound coming from the decedent's throat.

The next officer to the scene was Meyer. He testified he arrived at the same time as the paramedics, that he helped the paramedics load the decedent into the ambulance and that he came back to take a statement from Josie. He testified that she was hysterical, alternating between screaming and crying, shouting, "You bastard Kevin! How could you do that!" When everything quieted down, he was the one who took photographs of the house, the kitchen where the body laid, the blood on the linoleum, the present for Lisa, and the card sitting on the kitchen table. The prosecutor used Officer Meyer to introduce the audiotape of the 911 call. They played the tape for the jury. Josie was screaming, "There's somebody here! There's somebody here! You have to send help." Then you could hear voices in the background and she said, "It's Kevin! I know it's Kevin!" Then it went silent for a moment until Josie hollered, "I called the cops, they're gonna be here any minute."

The tape had just concluded when the judge looked at the clock, he said, "We'll take our lunch recess. We'll be back at one thirty."

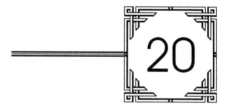

I hated trying cases out of town, especially with Spencer. There was no one to go to lunch with. My defendant went back to jail. Nobody knew what the judge did. We never saw him carry in a lunch. Our suspicion was that he took the time for a nap. I didn't have time to drive back to my office, and I certainly wasn't going to share my hour with Spencer. I normally ended up finding a little café and eating by myself. Today I walked over to Jack's Café. Mary, the judge's court reporter, was sitting there by herself. I looked around, there were no jurors. I asked if I could join her for lunch. She said, "Sure."

Mary and I actually went back years. We had spent many hours together sitting in anterooms, chatting, while we waited for a jury to come back. She was always very circumspect with her opinion, never giving me a hint of what she thought the jury was going to do, unless, of course, I had a real dirtbag for a defendant, someone she had no doubt should be in prison. In that case, she felt free to say, "I hope you lose." When she didn't tell me that, I always assumed it meant I had a small chance.

As I sat down, I smiled and said, "Has the judge ever done that to you before?"

"I've never been late before," she said. "I had to drive home last night to Owatonna. I overslept this morning. I broke every speed limit between there and here and then I was still fifteen minutes late. When I realized I was going to be late, my heart was pounding the last forty-five minutes. You know, Bob, I like him. He's a good judge, but sometimes he can just be a royal asshole." She blushed at her comment.

"If it's any solace," I said, "I think that was a terrible thing to do. I don't know why he has to be that way, so prompt on everything. Maybe it has something to do with toilet training. You know what Spock said."

She laughed a little; it eased the tension, I could tell she felt better.

"Spencer painted a pretty dark picture this morning," she said. "I'm not one to prejudge, as you know," and she winked, "but it seems to me you've got a loser."

"Wait and see."

As we ate, she told me that the judge intended to retire shortly . . . in fact, this might be his last trial. She was already looking for a new judge. She wanted to know if she could put me down as a reference. I told her I'd be happy to give her a reference.

She finished and left a few minutes before me. In a small town, we didn't feel comfortable walking back to the courtroom together, afraid the jurors might feel that there was something sinister going on.

The afternoon pretty much went as I expected. Spencer went through the paramedics and the emergency room doctor. The doctor told us that, at the time the body arrived at the hospital, there was just the slightest pulse. He went through all the medical procedures they used to try to keep the heart going, including the transfusions, but within minutes the heart stopped and all of their efforts to revive it failed. After five minutes, they gave up. I had very few questions.

Spencer stood up. "The state calls Chris Younger."

I heard the back door open and the bailiff hollered out, "Chris."

I could hear his cowboy boots coming down the hall and then soften as he hit the carpet of the courtroom. He looked at Kevin, gave him a slight smile as he walked to the clerk's bench. She administered the oath, and he walked to the witness box, sat down with some authority and quickly scanned the whole courtroom. He was a handsome young man, black curly hair, dark eyes, square jaw. He wore tan cowboy boots, jeans, and a tan suede shirt.

Spencer took him through his background, his prior relationship with Kevin. "Mr. Younger," Spencer continued, "I want to take you to the evening hours of September, 7, 1994. Tell the jury where you were that evening."

"I was at Stubby's Bar in Sauk Rapids."

"Do you recall what time you got there?"

"Early evening, I guess. I don't remember exactly, eight o'clock, someplace in there?"

"Who was with you?"

"My girlfriend Sara, Sara Pendergast."

"Did you meet Mr. Murphy there?"

"He was there, yes."

"Do you know Josie Klein?"

"Yes, I do."

"How do you know her?"

"She went with Kevin for a while. They'd been to the bar together. We went on some dates, trips together, that kinda thing."

"That night at Stubby's Bar, did you have any discussion with the defendant regarding Josie Klein?"

"Yes, I did."

"How did her name come up?"

"I don't remember exactly, I suspect Kevin brought it up."

"Why did her name come up?"

"Well, Kevin, Sara, and I were sitting at a table. We'd had a couple beers. Kevin was feeling a little nostalgic, I guess. He just said he wished she wouldn't have ended their relationship."

"What more was said?"

"There really wasn't much more than that."

"Mr. Younger, I want to remind you, you're under oath. Do you recall giving a statement to Detective Meyer the following day?"

"Yes, I do."

"Have you had a chance to read that statement?"

"Yes, I have."

"I'm going to ask you again, how long did your discussion about Josie Klein continue?"

"I told the cops, and I'll tell you, and it's no secret 'cause I told Kevin many times, I told him to forget that woman. I told him she's just no good. I told him, "You're obsessed and you gotta get over her.'" He stared at Spencer. "You happy now?"

"How did Mr. Murphy respond?"

"He said he knew, but it was tough. He said he missed her a lot."

"Did your girlfriend Sara overhear this?"

"Yes, she did."

"Do you recall about what time you left Stubby's Bar?"

"Right around closing, one o'clock or so."

"How many beers do you think you had that night?"

"I don't know, four or five."

"What about the defendant?"

"Probably less. He didn't drink a lot."

"When you left, what plans, if any, did you have with Mr. Murphy?"

"He was gonna pick something up and then come over to my house. We were gonna sit around and drink a little beer yet. Some other people were coming over."

"Did the defendant show up at your house?"

'No, he didn't."

"When was the next time you saw him?"

"The following morning."

"How did that occur?"

"He called me. He told me something terrible had happened, that he had to talk to me. We made arrangements to meet. I drove out to where he was parked outside of town. When he saw me pull up, he got out of his car.

He was crying. He fell down to his knees bawling. I couldn't imagine what had happened. I finally got him up, calmed him down a little bit. He told me he was standing in the kitchen at Josie's house when some guy came down. They got into a fight."

"What else did he tell you?"

Chris hesitated.

"What else did he tell you?" Spencer repeated with some force.

"He told me he thought he'd cut 'im."

"Did you ask him what he meant?"

"I didn't have to."

"Thank you, Mr. Younger."

I looked at Chris. I knew he was a sympathetic witness. I had to try to bring it out.

"Mr. Younger," I started, "when was the last time that you saw Mr. Murphy and Ms. Klein together?"

"Oh, probably three, four weeks before that night."

"Had you and your girlfriend spent a lot of time with them as a couple?"

"Quite a bit."

"And that was over an extended period of time?"

"Since he first met her, yes."

"How many times were the four of you together?"

"At least weekly, sometimes more."

"And you took some trips together?"

"Yes, we did."

"Did you ever see him get physical with her in an abusive way?"

"Kevin? No way."

"What do you mean by that?" I asked.

"He's not an abusive kinda person."

"That night at Stubby's Bar," I said but hesitated. "Strike that. At anytime since their relationship broke up, since the date of the separation, did Mr. Murphy even bring up the name of Mr. Ronning?"

"No, sir."

"Did Mr. Murphy ever indicate to you that he knew Ms. Klein was going with another guy?"

"He told me he had heard rumors around the bar that she was seeing somebody, but he didn't know who."

"In your conversations with him that night at Stubby's Bar, did he talk about Ms. Klein being with another man that night?"

"Not to me."

"When you all left Stubby's Bar that night at about one a.m., did he tell you he was going over to Ms. Klein's house?"

"No, he said he was gonna pick something up at his house, he'd be back in forty-five minutes or so."

"Were you surprised when he didn't show up?"

"Not really. I figured he just got tired and stayed home."

"When he called you the next morning, did he tell you what happened?"

"No, just that something terrible happened."

"When you drove out to meet him, what did he look like when you first saw him?"

"Terrible. I could tell he'd been bawling his eyes out. His face was red, his eyes were sore, and then when he saw me he just, he just curled over in pain. I didn't know at first what had happened, whether he was sick or what. I thought I was gonna have to take 'im to the hospital."

"How long did it take before he calmed down?"

"God, it was a good ten minutes. I was starting to get worried."

"How long did it take him to tell you what had happened?"

"A long time. He couldn't start telling me without crying, and then he'd have to start all over. I could tell he was really in some kind of pain."

"What did you tell Kevin to do?"

"I told him we had to call the cops. He agreed. We drove to a gas station and phoned, told them we were coming in. I told the officers where we were. They met us on the road."

I figured that was probably as good as I could do. I would leave well enough alone. I was paging through my notes to make sure when suddenly

Chris blurted out, "When he told me, Mr. Williams, I couldn't believe it. He would never be involved with anything like that, he's too gentle."

Spencer jumped to his feet. "Your honor, objection, I ask that be stricken."

"Sustained," the judge said.

I closed my file with a little grin on my face. "I have nothing further."

"Any redirect?" the judge asked.

I glanced over at Spencer. He was furiously paging through his notes. I could tell he wanted to pounce on Chris, but it would have been like walking on a thin sheet of ice, wondering when it was going to give way and he'd plunge into the cold water. It was obvious Chris wanted to help Kevin, any smart attorney would simply leave him alone. Spencer did.

"I have nothing further, your honor."

The judge looked at Chris. "You're excused."

I could tell by Chris' demeanor, his gait as he left the witness box, he was pleased with himself. He thought he'd helped Kevin. He glanced at Kevin as he walked by, put his hand to his side, out of view of the jury, and gave him a thumbs up.

Spencer stood up. "The state will call Sara Pendergast."

Sara came in the door as Chris walked out. They exchanged big smiles. She walked up, took the oath and went to the witness box. She was an attractive young lady, long auburn hair, shoulder length, shapely figure, delicate facial features, hazel eyes. She had a confident air about her. She sat in the witness box and immediately looked at Kevin, and her face softened, not quite a smile but a look of encouragement.

After going through the preliminary questions, Spencer asked, "You were with Mr. Younger on the evening of September 7, 1994, at Stubby's Bar?"

"Yes, I was."

"Did you have a conversation that night at the bar with Mr. Murphy?"

"Yes, I did."

"Was Mr. Younger present during this conversation?"

"Not all of it."

"Did Ms. Klein's name come up in this conversation?"

"Yes, it did."

"Who brought up her name?"

"Kevin did."

"What did he say?"

"It was obvious he was hurting."

"I didn't ask for your impression, Ms. Pendergast, I asked what did he say?"

"He told me he was hurting, that he missed her."

"What did you tell him?"

"I told him to forget her."

"What else?"

"That he was better off without her. I was trying to convince him, I wanted to help him through his pain."

"What else did you tell him?"

She looked at Spencer, blank faced. I knew what he wanted her to say. She'd already said it in a statement to the police, she didn't want to say it here in court. I knew he would force her into it.

"Ms. Pendergast," Spencer continued, "did you know that Ms. Klein was seeing another gentleman?"

"I didn't know it."

"Had you heard that Ms. Klein was seeing another gentlemen?"

"I heard some rumors, yes."

"Did you tell Mr. Murphy that Ms. Klein was seeing another gentleman?"

"I told him that, hoping it would help him get over her."

"So that night, in Stubby's Bar, sometime in the course of the evening, you made the defendant aware that Ms. Klein may be seeing another man, is that what you're telling us?"

"I told him I'd heard rumors, yes."

"Thank you, Ms. Pendergast."

"In the course of that evening, Ms. Pendergast," I started, "did Mr. Murphy indicate he was going to go see Ms. Klein?"

"No, he did not."

"Did he tell you you were right, that he should forget her?"

"Yes, he did."

"Exactly what did he say?"

"He said, 'You're right, I'm gonna just put her out of my mind.'"

"Thank you, Ms. Pendergast. I have nothing further."

Spencer snapped, "Ms. Pendergast, do you recall giving a statement to Mr. Meyer the day following Mr. Ronning's death?"

"Yes, I do."

"Have you had a chance to review that statement before you came to court today?"

"Yes, I did."

"Anywhere in that statement, did you tell Detective Meyer that Mr. Murphy made the comment that he was just gonna forget about Ms. Klein?"

"No, I didn't."

"Why not."

"He didn't ask me."

I could almost hear the air going out of Spencer. She sat there, defiantly. He paged through his notes like he was looking for something special, something he wanted to quiz her on. I knew all he was waiting for was the impact to settle so he could get her off the stand. Without looking up from his notepad, he did just that. "I have nothing further."

The judge looked at me.

"I have nothing further, your honor."

"Thank you, Ms. Pendergast," he said.

She, too, got up and gave Kevin the slightest smile as she walked by.

The speed of the trial caught Spencer by surprise. By three-thirty he told the judge, "Your honor, I've run out of witnesses for today."

"Isn't Ms. Klein here?" the judge asked.

"Yes, she is, but I would only get started with her, and we'd have to recess until tomorrow morning. I hate to take my witnesses out of order. My next scheduled witness is Dr. Mueller, the Hennepin County Medical Examiner. With the court's permission, I would prefer to wait and start with him tomorrow morning."

The judge looked at the jurors. "I would like to keep this moving along for everybody's benefit, but I guess you're going to get out early today. Remember not to talk about this case with anybody and don't read any story about it in the paper."

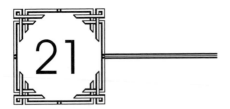

I said goodbye to Kevin and quickly left the courthouse. I was hoping to get back to my office before Faye left. During the course of the prosecutor's examination of a paramedic, my mind wandered to our search for Kate's killer. I thought of another name, another former client who, in his own twisted mind, could believe I was responsible for him going to prison.

As I pulled up to the office, I realized I was too late. Her car was gone. The receptionist, Heidi, told me that she had left early. There was a possibility of snow the following day, and she and her family decided to leave early so they didn't have to worry about fighting slippery roads in the morning.

I went to the index and looked for the files from nine, ten years before. In 1983 or '84, I handled a case of a young man, Larry Wills, who had brutally raped a teenage girl at knifepoint. The prosecution's case rested on the victim's identification of him. Admittedly, it was a weak case for the State, but the jury found him guilty, more, I suspected, because of his attitude than the evidence. In the process of testifying, in response to a question by the prosecutor, he made a comment, something to the effect, "Look at me. I'm so handsome. Why would I have to rape a girl at knifepoint? I can get all the sex I want. The girls throw themselves at me." It caught me totally by surprise.

The victim testified that he had cut her breasts with a knife, just enough to make them bleed, then he sucked the blood. At sentencing, the judge slammed him and gave him twice what the sentence would have been had he not used the knife. According to my calculations, he should have been out about a year.

I never knew whether he was guilty or not. I never asked him. As the deputy slapped the cuffs on him, though, he turned to me. With real anger and contempt in his voice, he said, "You fucked this up, you cocksucker. If I could've afforded a real lawyer, this fuckin' thing would've never happened."

The judge was still on the bench. He hollered, "Deputy, get him out of here!"

Wills looked at the judge. "Yeah, you little prick, I'll get you too." Then he looked at me again. "I'm not through with this. I'm gonna get you, Williams. You fucker. You better keep an eye open at night."

I paged through the file. The State Public Defender's Office had appealed the case. The appeal was based solely on whether there was sufficient evidence for the jury to convict. A court of appeals seldom, if ever, reverses the jury's decision. The court also believed that, given the gratuitous nature of the injuries to the victim, the double sentence was appropriate. I heard that he later petitioned the Federal District Court for Habeas Corpus on the basis of ineffective assistance of counsel. His petition was denied without a hearing.

I had actually forgotten all about him until something said this morning jogged my memory. Even then, when his name popped up, he wasn't high on my list. But the more I thought about his parting words, his anger, the more he inched his way up the list.

I set the file down and paged Tony. He called in about five minutes. I told him I had a file, and I needed to talk to him. We made arrangements to meet at the Log Lodge at six.

Tony was at the bar when I got there. As I sat down, he slid a photograph across the bar. "There's your killer," he said.

I looked at the photograph, it was Scott Draper, taken shortly before his discharge from prison. The seventeen and a half years had not been kind to him. I remembered him as a redhead with bright blue eyes, a reddish complexion. At the trial he had a bright red beard that hid most of his face. In the picture, he had no beard, his eyes were narrow and tired looking. His red hair was streaked with gray and pulled back and tied in a ponytail. His face was heavier, and he wore scars that were either covered by the beard when I knew him or had been picked up in prison.

"You wouldn't think he'd be hard to miss, would you?" said Tony.

"I don't know," I said, "cut the ponytail, clean him up a little, he could be anybody."

"Well, they still don't know anything." said Tony. "They'll let me know if anything changes."

I finished a beer and ordered a second. "My trial's going faster than I expected," I said. "If I'm right, all Spencer has left is Josie and the medical examiner. I can't imagine they'll take more than tomorrow. I might have to have some witnesses by Monday morning. Talk to the couple character witnesses we decided on, tell them to be on call. We'll get a hold of 'em over the weekend and give them the exact time."

"I can do that," he said. "We're suppose to be getting some snow late tonight, going into tomorrow, nothing major. Six, seven inches."

"I don't even care," I said. "I've been so numb for so long, I don't even remember what the weather's been like."

I ordered another beer. I dreaded going home. I couldn't sleep. Carol came home one evening so we could box up Kate's clothes and personal effects and take it to the Goodwill. I know it was silly. I thought if I could remove everything from the house that would remind me of her, it would help, but it didn't. The emptiness only aggravated the situation.

I had taken to using sleeping pills. First, one seemed to help, and then within days, I was waking up at two, three in the morning, unable to go back to sleep, so I graduated to two pills and then to three. A few times, I even considered taking the whole bottle. I thought that would be a pleasant way to go, slowly drift off, never to wake. But then I wondered what if, once I took the pills, I changed my mind, didn't want to die. Could I make it to the hospital in time? What if I would pass out on the highway, crashing into some innocent person?

"Where are you?" asked Tony.

112

I shook my head. I had drifted off. I was staring at the neon "Red Lion" sign behind the bar.

"I'm starting to worry about you," he said. "Faye is concerned too. She told me you haven't been acting right."

"What's right, under the circumstances?" I asked.

"We don't want you doing anything stupid," replied Tony.

"You don't have to worry about me," I said. "I've got a trial to attend to." I reached over and grabbed the file from under my coat. "Here, I dug this out this afternoon. This is another candidate for our rogues' gallery. He threatened both me and the judge when he got put away. According to my calculations, he should've gotten out about a year ago. Why don't you see what you can find out about him."

Tony paged through the file. "I remember this guy," he said. "I busted him once years ago for an assault on a student at the Press Bar. He was a real conceited asshole, God's gift to women."

"That's the guy," I said, "baby-face features, wavy blonde hair."

"Yup," said Tony.

"See what you can find out about him," I said.

"No problem," he replied.

I looked at my watch. "Well, I'm heading home to read the autopsy report again. Dr. Mueller is suppose to be on first thing in the morning."

"You know, if you need someone to talk to, Bob, I'd certainly be willing to come and spend some time."

I grinned, and said, "I appreciate the thought, but I'm not very good company."

"Keep it in mind," he said.

"I will."

On my drive home, I thought about Tony's offer. Through the years, when I had Kate, I never thought much of what Tony did on his own time, what he did for recreation, entertainment, hobbies. He joined Kate and me for dinner a couple times but pretty much stayed to himself. He had been married when he was still on the police force, but she left him a year or two before he retired. She said she didn't get enough attention. Life is strange, I thought. We have a lady, Josie, who complained because she got too much attention and Tony's wife, who complained she didn't get enough.

I hadn't seen Tony with a woman for years, nor did he ever talk about any. I assumed it was part of his private life he wished to keep private. But now I wondered whether he was able to simply put women out of his mind. Was I ever going to be interested in another woman? I had never really thought about it until now. These were all strange thoughts. I couldn't remember the last time I looked at a woman and didn't compare her to Kate. I wondered whether that would now change.

The trip from my house to the Benton County Courthouse took close to an hour. I never minded the time, especially when I was in the middle of a case. It gave me the chance to mull things over in my mind. Today the trip was going to take even a little longer. Tony was right, it had snowed overnight. Nothing major, three or four inches, but enough to make the road slippery. I hated the highway between my office and the courthouse. It was two lanes and heavily traveled by big trucks and farm equipment. It had been the scene of enough fatal accidents to make me cautious on a good day. Just a little snow would compound the risks. I never worried about myself. From the years of traveling the road, I always knew where the slick spots would be. It was the other drivers, especially the trucks, that bothered me.

Today I gave myself a little extra time. I knew, regardless of the weather, the judge would start precisely at nine. I didn't intend to get his ire up.

As I drove, I went over Dr. Mueller's autopsy report in my mind while, at the same time, attempting to gauge how fast I could go on the dry spots and still slow down in plenty of time before I hit the ice. This was not my first encounter with Dr. Mueller. He had been the prosecutor's expert witness in several previous homicide cases I'd handled. A very matter of fact person, he never proffered more than a concise answer to the prosecutor's question. In his middle forties, he was short with thinning reddish hair with a little gray, a stubbly reddish beard and mustache, with blue eyes and slight features. He always seemed out of place on the witness stand, as though he was uncomfortable with the surroundings. He struck me as a person who liked his job, but felt more at home in his morgue, surrounded by his cadavers (nobody to talk back to him), than in the environment of the courtroom.

As the trial progressed, it became apparent to me that Dr. Mueller's testimony would play a crucial role in Kevin's fate. In going over his autopsy report, I kept reflecting back to what my daughter Carol had said, "That wound is awful deep to have been inflicted in an accidental manner." The wound had split the ribs, going entirely through the heart, a little over three inches. The prosecutor told me the doctor would testify that the force needed to inflict such a wound seemed to dispute any claim of accident.

I pulled up to the courthouse at exactly five minutes to nine. As I came to a stop and took my hands off the steering wheel, I could feel the tension leaving my fingers. Between thinking about the cross-examination of Dr. Mueller and wanting to prevent myself from ending up in the ditch—or worse, on the front bumper of a twenty-ton semi—I had glued myself to the steering wheel. I rushed up the steps to find everybody sitting in court, including Kevin. I was right. I knew the judge had driven probably eighty miles from home that morning and regardless of the road conditions, he'd be there on time.

I barely sat down and got my briefcase open when the judge walked in. As everybody settled in, he looked at the prosecutor, "Is the State ready to proceed?"

"We are, your honor," said Spencer, "but we have a slight problem. I was going to call Dr. Mueller, the medical examiner first, but because of the weather, it appears that he has been a little delayed. Rather than wait at this point, I'll call Ms. Josie Klein."

I was surprised. I was prepared for one witness and got hit with another. It called for a change in gears. I slowly turned around to see Josie get up from the back of the courtroom to make her way to the witness box. She had not been to the trial before this. I had purposely sequestered witnesses, requiring that they not be allowed to be present until after they had testified. The trial hadn't picked up many spectators. I noticed on the opposite side of the small seating area was another lady I had not seen before. A plain looking lady, blonde hair, no make-up. She was sitting with the county's victim assistance coordinator. I thought for a second and realized it had to be the victim's wife, Mrs. Ronning. She wanted to see her husband's paramour. She wanted to hear how her husband died. I couldn't imagine why she wanted to put herself through that.

Josie Klein walked up to the clerk's station, raised her right hand and took the oath. She was dressed conservatively, a dark-blue skirt with black shoes with medium heels, a blue sweater with a white silk collar showing. She wore very little make-up, no lipstick. Her face was a pale white, her eyes red and worn, showing lack of sleep. She must have thought about this moment for weeks, for months. Her day in court, having to face Kevin and now finding out she would face her lover's wife as well. Her hand trembled slightly; her voice quivered as she took the oath. She walked slowly to the witness stand and took the chair. She crossed her arms over her stomach and leaned forward, shoulders slumped. She was prepared for anything.

The prosecutor took her through all the preliminary questions, her background, her education, her marriage, her divorce, her daughter, and then got to her first meeting with Kevin. "Tell the jury, please, when you first met Mr. Murphy."

"It was in spring, early spring. I was introduced to him by a mutual friend. He had recently arrived from Colorado. We talked. We found out we had some things in common, and it led to a date."

"You had a relationship with the defendant?"

"Oh, yes," she said quietly. "In fact, he moved in with me the early part of the summer. We had a very close relationship. He was very good for my daughter. They became very close friends, real quickly. He spent a lot of time with her. I thought that was good. She missed her father."

"What do you mean, missed her father?" asked Spencer.

"Her father left quite a few years ago. He's not been in contact, not a dime of support."

"So the defendant filled that void?"

"Yes, he did," she replied.

"At some point did you ask him to move out of your home?"

"Yes, I did."

"When was that?"

"It was July, I believe. It was some time after the Fourth of July."

"Why did you ask him to move?"

"Things started to deteriorate in our relationship. He talked about marriage. I wasn't ready for that. He started making some permanent plans. It led to arguments."

She went quiet, groping for words. Her answers had been slow and staccato, like she was afraid to say what she really wanted to in front of Kevin. I could tell that Spencer was starting to become upset. He wanted to get into the good stuff quickly, and she wasn't getting there fast enough. "You mentioned the Fourth of July," Spencer said. "Is there something significant about the Fourth of July?"

"Yes, there is," she said.

"What?" he asked.

Again, she hesitated.

"Please, Ms. Klein," said the prosecutor, "it's important that we get this out. I can understand that it may be difficult for you. If you need some time, that's fine, but this jury has to know what happened."

She looked up, her face was turning red and blotchy. "We got into an argument. It was probably as much my fault as it was his. We were at a party at the lake. We'd been drinking all day. I guess he thought I was flirting too much with some of the other guys. He confronted me on it, and we got into an argument, and he grabbed me by the arm and pulled me. Somebody else stepped in and told him to cool down. His attitude changed the rest of the day. He was cold, obviously angry. When we got home that night, after we put Lisa to bed, the argument continued." She then looked right at Kevin, inhaled deeply, "And then I saw something I didn't like, a real anger in him, and it scared me."

"How long did this argument continue?" he asked.

117

"Just for a short time, and then I went to bed. I locked myself in the bedroom. He slept downstairs."

"What happened after that?"

"We didn't talk the next morning, he was gone before I got up. But that night, I asked him to move out. He was apologetic. He cried. He said how much he loved me and Lisa."

"What did you say?"

"I told him things had been happening too fast, that I needed my space, that I wasn't ready to think about marriage."

"Did he move out?"

"The next day he did. There wasn't much to move out. He just brought a suitcase. He was very quiet with me when he left. His real good-bye was with Lisa. I could see the tears. I knew it bothered him, but I wasn't gonna change my mind."

"Did you continue to have a relationship with him?"

"Not like it was, not physical. I knew Lisa's feelings for him. I wasn't gonna exclude him from her life. He came over a lot after that to visit with Lisa. I sat and talked to him many times. It always ended up the same, that he wanted me back, that he couldn't understand why I kicked him out, that he couldn't understand how I could keep him out of Lisa's life. He invited us out to dinner a few times, it never ended up being a good scene."

"Do you know where the defendant was living after he moved from your home?"

"He moved into a small apartment on the east side."

"Were you over to his apartment?"

"He invited me over several times."

"When was the last time?"

"Probably a week or so before this incident."

"Did anything happen that night?"

It appeared that she was becoming more comfortable, she appeared more relaxed, her answers coming quicker. "Nothing really happened. He made dinner for me and Lisa. It seemed like he had decided that we were just gonna be friends."

"Did you see Mr. Murphy at all between that time and the night Mr. Ronning was killed?

"Just once," she said.

"Where was that?"

"At my job."

"How did that occur?"

"He came to where I worked and asked to see me. They brought him back. He had a bag in his hand. He opened it and took out a vase with a single rose, and he handed it to me. He said, 'I know you're seeing somebody else. You'll never see me again.'"

"What did you think at that time?" asked Spencer.

"I didn't know what to think. I didn't know if it was a threat or if he'd finally decided that he was just gonna leave me alone."

"Was this the first time that he mentioned that he thought you were seeing somebody else?'

"No," she replied.

"There was another time?"

"Yes, sir."

"When was that?"

"Several weeks earlier. I remember it was a nice warm evening. Lisa and I were sitting on the porch in the back. He dropped by. He was pleasant until Lisa went to bed, and then it turned to the same old thing, 'How can you do this to me after what we meant to each other?' That kind of talk. Then he tried to kiss me, and I pushed him away, and he became angry. He said, 'I know you're fuckin' around with somebody else,' and he just ranted and raved for a few minutes at the top of his lungs. As he walked away, he said something like, 'If I see you with another guy, well, I'd watch my fuckin' back if I was you', and he left. I heard his car squeal away. A couple minutes later my neighbor came over. Mrs. Butkowski, she said . . . ."

I quickly interjected, "Your honor, if she's going to tell us what Mrs. Butkowski said, I would object as hearsay."

The judge looked at the prosecutor. Spencer didn't reply. "Sustained."

"You had a conversation with your neighbor, Mrs. Butkowski?" asked Spencer.

"Yes, I did."

"How long did she stay?"

"Oh, maybe a half an hour or so."

Spencer looked at the notebook on the table in front of him, turned a few pages. He was about to ask a question when the judge said, "This may be a good time to take our morning recess."

As everybody filed out, I leaned over to Kevin, "We have to talk," I said.

The deputy led him to a conference room in the hall. As I walked in, the deputy closed the door behind me. I stood by the window and thought for a moment. Kevin didn't say a word.

From the window, I could see the grade school across the street. The kids came storming through the door for the morning recess. They scattered to different corners of the playground, pushing and screaming as they went. Without taking my eyes off the activity, I said, "Kevin, she paints a pretty bleak picture. That last comment hurts. What're you going to tell the jury?"

"What do you want me to tell 'em?"

I looked at him angrily. "That's a stupid-ass comment."

He recognized my anger. "I'm sorry," he said. "It wasn't as bleak as she paints it. Those were but a few moments in our relationship. I'm gonna tell the jury exactly how I felt, upset, hurt . . . and yes, angry. Angry that she welcomed me into her life and her daughter's life with open arms, seduced me, and then because she didn't like how things were going, wanted to kick my ass out. Yes, I was upset and I was pissed, but I would've never hurt her. She knows that. The way she's portraying it . . . it's, it's just bullshit!"

The room went quiet. I could hear the muffled voices of the kids across the street hollering at each other. I heard the bell ring, the kids scrambling to get in line to walk back into their classrooms.

"You know, Mr. Williams, the one thing she didn't say—you notice she didn't mention anything about shackin' up with me that last night."

I turned my head to look at him. "What're you talking about?"

"The last night that she and Lisa came to dinner at my apartment, we had a little bit too much wine. We put Lisa to bed," and then he got the slightest grin on his face, "and then she made love to me."

"How come you never told me this before?" I said.

"I thought I had," he said.

I thought back. I didn't remember it. He might have, and I just didn't put any significance to it. That was unlikely, though. Chances are he kept it to himself, for whatever reason, or, he just made it up.

The deputy knocked on the door. "We're ready to go," he said.

"Let's see what happens," I said.

As I walked into the courtroom, Spencer pulled me aside. "My doctor's here. I was hoping you'd let me squeeze him in at this point. I'll continue with Josie after he's done."

I thought for a second, concluded it wouldn't hurt me. "That's fine," I said.

I sat down next to Kevin and told him what was going to happen as I watched the jurors parade in and take their seats. Their faces were all expressionless. Nobody acknowledged my glance—nobody looked at Kevin. It was a bad sign, I thought.

As the judge took his seat and nodded towards Spencer, the prosecutor stood up. "Your honor, Dr. Mueller has arrived. So, with Mr. William's permission, he will testify at this point, and I'll continue with Ms. Klein after lunch."

The judge looked at me. "I have no objection," I told him.

He looked back at Spencer. "You may proceed."

"The State calls Dr. David Mueller."

I glanced behind me, the deputy opened the door, and Dr. Mueller walked in. It had been three or four years since I had last seen him. He was a little heavier than I remembered, and he had lost more hair. Now there were just a few long strands across the top and the sides were combed back. He still had his beard and mustache, but it was cropped short and turning gray. His face was bright red as he approached the clerk to take the oath—at least that hadn't changed, I thought. He still didn't want to be in any courtroom.

The prosecutor took him through his background, his education and training. He told the jury that as the Hennepin County Medical Examiner for over fourteen years, he had performed thousands of autopsies. He was a board certified forensic pathologist recognized as an expert in courts all over the country. As he rattled through his credentials, it was obvious, to me at least, that here was a doctor who had testified in hundreds of courts as to the cause and manner of death but never became comfortable in that role.

"Doctor," asked the prosecutor, "did you perform an autopsy on the decedent, Mr. Dale Ronning, in this matter?"

"Yes, I did."

"And in the process of performing that autopsy, doctor, did you take photographs?"

"Yes, I did."

"I believe, with the court's permission," said the prosecutor, "we've already identified and numbered ten of those that you're going to use in your testimony. Do you have those photographs with you?"

"Yes, I do."

Spencer looked at the judge. "Your honor, I believe we already have an agreement with Mr. Williams that these can be admitted."

The judge looked at me. "That's correct, your honor."

"Doctor," continued the prosecutor, "as a result of the autopsy, did you form an opinion to reasonable medical certainty as to the cause of death of Mr. Ronning?"

"Yes, I did."

"And, doctor, what is that opinion?"

"That he died as a result of a stab wound to the left chest area penetrating the heart. He died by exsanquination, which basically means he bled to death."

"Thank you, doctor," said Spencer. "Let's go through this a little bit more thoroughly. Doctor, showing you what's been marked 'Exhibit Number 17,' can you identify that please?"

"Yes, that's the photograph of Mr. Ronning when he arrived at the medical center."

"Doctor," said Spencer, "it appears that he's in just his underwear, his shorts. Is that how he arrived?"

"Yes it is."

"The way he arrived at the medical center was the way they found his body at the scene, is that correct?"

"Yes, that's my understanding."

"What was the first thing you did in performing the autopsy?"

"Well, like I said, I made note of the external injuries to the decedent. In this case, you will notice that the body is stained with a copious amount of blood, from the chest all the way down to his legs. As I indicated, the wound was directly to the heart—the blood would've been gushing into his body cavity and out the wound."

"Doctor, I believe you've read the notes from the medical treatment given to Mr. Ronning by the paramedics at the scene, as well as the emergency room at the St. Cloud Hospital."

"Yes I have."

"And you understand the doctors at the hospital were unable to revive him?"

"That's what the records indicate."

"Doctor, from your experience, in your opinion, how long would a person survive after receiving a wound of that nature?"

"I would expect he would lose consciousness in minutes, probably five minutes, and short of immediate medical attention, death would follow."

"Doctor, showing you what's been marked 'State's Exhibit 18,' can you identify that please?"

"Yes, that's a picture taken of the back of his body. Again, you will note the bruises along the back and several wounds showing where the skin has been broken by an object—some sharp object."

"Doctor, you've seen exhibit Number 7, which has been identified as the buck knife that was found in the home on that night?"

"Yes, I have."

"And you've had an opportunity to examine that knife?"

"Yes, I have."

"And, Doctor, is the blade of that knife consistent with the wound found in the chest of the decedent?"

"Yes, it is, in several ways."

"In what ways, doctor?"

"First, as far as the width of the blade, it's consistent with the width of the wound in the chest. Secondly, the depth of the blade—the blade is three and a half inches, the wound in the chest is slightly over three and a half inches, approximately a quarter inch more."

"How would you explain the difference?"

"It is my opinion that the stab was inflicted with such force that the blade was sunk deeper into the body than the actual length of the blade. For example, if I were to hit myself in the chest here," the doctor took his closed fist and struck himself on the left side of his chest, "you can feel that the pressure of your blow will actually compress your chest a certain distance. That's what happened here, I believe. The blow was of such force that the chest compressed approximately a quarter of an inch, near a quarter of an inch. So the wound, the internal wound, is actually deeper than the length of the blade itself."

"Doctor, as far as the wounds to the back, are they consistent with having been made by the same knife?"

"That's difficult to say," replied the doctor. "The long thin ones here," and he held up the photographs and showed the hairline cut on the back of Ronning, "this one is consistent with having been scraped with the back of that knife, like this," and the doctor demonstrated to the jury how the knife could have been scraped down the back of the victim with the side opposite the blade. "The other contusions look like scratch marks, as if they could've been made with the butt end of the knife, this point here."

Spencer stood up, picked up another photograph from off the table and started to walk towards the witness. In a rather smug voice, he asked, "Doctor, showing you what's been marked 'Exhibit Number 19,' can you identify that please?"

"That's another photograph I took. This one shows the contusion on the top of his skull. You'll notice that I have shaved the hair away, making it visible."

124

Spencer turned around to walk back to the counsel table. He gave me a quick glance. He was making points, and he knew it.

"Doctor, in your profession as a forensic pathologist, certain wounds are identified as what you would term 'defensive wounds'?"

"That's correct."

"And, Doctor, what is meant by 'defensive wounds'?"

"Defensive wounds are wounds that we have found to be consistent with a person attempting to defend themselves. For example, when a knife is used, a common defensive wound would be cuts on the inside of the hand, around the finger where a person may grab a blade to deflect it from his body as somebody was coming at you with the blade out."

"Doctor, in our case today, did you form an opinion to a reasonable medical certainty as to whether any of the wounds on Mr. Ronning were defensive wounds?"

"Yes, I did."

"And doctor, what is your opinion?"

"I believe the wounds to the back of the scalp and the wounds to the back, are defensive wounds, that they were inflicted in the struggle in the course of Mr. Ronning attempting to defend himself."

Spencer turned towards me with a grin, barely perceptible, meant as an unspoken comment: "There, you son-of-a-bitch, take that." He said, "Thank you, doctor. I have nothing further. Your witness."

I slowly paged through my notes for a few seconds, hoping to make the doctor sweat a little, waiting. I finally looked up, scratched my head a little bit. "Doctor, I'm afraid you have me a little confused, maybe you can straighten this out for me."

The doctor nodded his head. "Anyway I can," he replied.

"If I understand correctly, doctor, it is your opinion that the scratch marks on the back and the other contusions are consistent with defensive wounds. That would mean that the person would have to be, in your words, 'protecting himself,' correct?"

"I'm saying they're consistent with that, yes."

"What you're assuming, doctor, is that Mr. Ronning was not the aggressor but rather attempting to protect himself from Mr. Murphy, is that correct?"

"That's my opinion, Mr. Williams. An opinion, I believe, that is supported to a level of reasonable medical certainty, yes."

"Okay, doctor. If you're saying that they're consistent with that scenario, it would be fair to say they may be consistent with another scenario as well."

"That could be the case, yes."

"Say, for example, doctor, that Mr. Ronning and my client are struggling and in the process Mr. Ronning is pushed against a wall. Remember, doctor, he is in just his underwear, and there is no clothing to protect his skin."

"Okay." He looked at me with a sort of blank face.

"Well, doctor, couldn't he have received those wounds in the course of a struggle if he had been pushed up against a wall or a door jam, anything that could've scratched his back or caused a contusion? Wouldn't the wounds be consistent with that scenario as well?"

"I suppose it could be a possibility."

"Or say, for example, doctor, that my client has a leather jacket on with straps and buckles on the sleeves and in the process of the struggle he and Mr. Ronning are wrestling, they are twisting back and forth, wouldn't the wounds that you observed be consistent with the scratch by the buckles on the sleeves?"

The doctor thought for a second, looking pensive, he stared at me. "That's a possibility, I suppose."

"I guess, doctor," I said, "I'm making this more difficult than it has to be. Let me approach it this way, doctor. If you have two people in a physical struggle, a fight, one fully clothed, wearing a leather jacket that would act as some protection, and the other one in just his underwear, and the fight lasts for several minutes, wouldn't it be fair to say that you'd expect the person in just his underwear to have various bruises and contusions as a result of the altercation?"

"It could depend on a number of things," replied the doctor. "Where is this occurring? What's all in the vicinity?"

"Doctor," I interjected, "we're not talking in the abstract, we're talking about this kitchen, this enclosed area where these two people were fighting.

In that scene, would you not expect a person in his underwear to show signs of a struggle?"

"That's possible," he said.

"Doctor, as far as your autopsy, you also sent blood samples to the lab for a toxicology report, is that correct?"

"Yes."

"And I noticed in the autopsy report that it shows the blood alcohol concentration of .08. Now, for the jury's benefit, doctor, we're all familiar with the legal limit of .10, so Mr. Ronning would have been under what the State considers the legal limit for determining under the influence of alcohol."

"Based on that reading, yes."

"The sample on which that was based was taken in the course of the autopsy, is that correct?"

"Yes, it is."

"Doctor, at the time the autopsy was performed, Mr. Ronning had been dead for what, almost twelve hours, correct?"

"That sounds right."

"And would the reading that you obtained from blood taken twelve hours after his death be the same reading you would expect just prior to his death?"

The doctor looked at me a little puzzled. The question was not phrased to his liking. "I think what you're getting to, counsel," he replied, "is whether the blood alcohol reading at the time of death would be the same as at the time of autopsy. I can tell you it's pretty much accepted that autopsy blood taken from intact chambers of the heart within forty-eight hours of death gives a pretty reliable indication of the amount of alcohol consumed prior to death."

"So I'm asking," I replied, "are special precautions taken under these circumstances?"

"I take two samples of blood, one from the chamber of the heart and vitreous humor, or eye fluid, from behind the eye. I believe the literature indicates that a sample from both of those locations would give you an accurate reading of the decedent's blood alcohol concentration as of the time of death."

"Doctor, I believe you already indicated that Mr. Ronning bled profusely."

"Yes he did."

"And I believe you noted that at the hospital they performed a blood transfusion."

"Yes they did."

"Do you know whether the paramedics performed a transfusion as well?"

"It's my understanding, from the records counsel, that the only transfusion given was at the hospital."

"Do you know, doctor, how many units of blood he may have been given?"

"I believe the records accurately reflect that it was two units in the hospital."

"What effect, if any, would that have on his blood alcohol concentration?"

"Well obviously, counsel, each transfusion would have the effect of diluting the blood in his body and lowering the blood alcohol concentration."

"So the .08 reading that you obtained is really a reading after his remaining blood was diluted by two units of transfused blood?"

"That's correct."

"Is there any way for us to determine what his blood alcohol concentration may have been prior to the altercation with my client?"

"None that I know of."

"So realistically, doctor, there's no way of us knowing whether Mr. Ronning's blood alcohol concentration was .10 or .15 or how high it may have been. Is that a fair statement?"

"The only thing I can say for sure was that it was higher than .08, yes."

"Thank you, doctor," I said. "I have nothing further."

The prosecutor stood up and walked to the witness box. "Doctor, showing you again what's been marked as 'Exhibit Number 17,' the photo of the back of Mr. Ronning, in response to some questions by Mr. Williams, you indicated that those wounds could have possibly been consistent with some other scenario."

"That's correct."

"In your opinion, doctor, are those other scenarios possible?"

"I don't believe so."

"In your opinion, what's the difference between possible and probable?"

He sat for a second. "Anything may be possible, but to be probable, there has to be a strong likelihood that it could occur."

Spencer glared across the table at me, gave me a smug look.

"Thank you, doctor, I have nothing further," he said.

"Mr. Williams?" the judge asked.

"I have nothing further," I said.

The judge looked at the clock on the wall. "It's getting close to lunch time. I guess we'll take our noon recess. We'll reconvene at one-thirty.

I talked to Kevin for a few minutes and then found a conference room where I could be alone. I didn't feel like having lunch. I didn't like the way the case was going. It wasn't that the doctor was particularly damaging to our case. I had learned long ago that jurors don't get hung up on expert testimony. They want to know what the defendant is like. Is he capable of doing what the State claims he did? If the jury wanted to believe Kevin was capable of murdering somebody, the doctor had simply given them something to hang their hat on.

I finally closed the file and leaned back, my head against the plasterboard wall. Something was bothering me, and I couldn't put my finger on it. I sat there for close to an hour, my mind rapidly going from one thought to another. No continuity, nothing making sense. It was frightening. It had never happened to me before. I had always remained focused during a trial, knowing exactly where I was headed at all times. This was different. I felt like I was drowning, paddling, kicking my legs, flailing my arms, trying to keep my head above water. I actually felt a sense of desperation, and I didn't know why. I walked into the hall and took out thirty-five cents to buy a cup of machine-made coffee. I put the money in the machine, pushed regular, light whitener, no sugar. I heard the cup fall down. As it filled, I went around the corner to get a drink of water. When I came back, I saw the cup had hit the port at an angle, the coffee had gone down the drain or onto the floor. I figured that was probably a portent of the rest of my day.

I took the cup out of the machine and looked at the bottom, it had managed to catch a couple sips. It looked awful. I walked over to the water fountain, poured it out and filled the cup with water. The whole time I had a sensation that somebody was watching me. I looked towards the elevator. Josie Klein was standing in the hall, watching, with a big grin on her face. I was a little embarrassed, a grown man, kicking a coffee machine. I acknowledged her grin, took my glass of water and headed towards the courtroom. One of the deputies unlocked the door and let me in. I had close to half an hour before the trial would start again. I sat at the counsel table and paged through my file. I couldn't shake the uneasy feeling. In all my years of practice, in the course of a trial, my concentration never left me. I was always prepared for the next witness, confident in what I had to do. This time was different, and I had no idea why. I slid my butt to the end of the chair, stretched out my legs so my head leaned on the backrest. I stared at the ceiling. I pictured Kate standing by the counter in the kitchen, flannel shirt hanging loose on her body, her hair tied up in a bandanna. She turns and looks at me, smiles, her face wind burnt. I lean over to kiss her. She blushes. I can smell her. I can taste her skin. It's invigorating, like an early morning breeze on a spring day. It was so real I could feel my body responding to the emotions.

Suddenly the door behind the judge's bench flies open. Startled to reality, I sit up in the chair. The judge's calendar clerk is surprised. "I'm sorry, Mr. Williams, I didn't know you were in here."

I looked at the clock, it was almost one thirty. Instead of preparing for the next witness, I had spent my time in a fantasy. I realized that was my problem. I wanted Kate back. I wanted my life the way it was. I had taken Kevin's trial as a diversion, and it wasn't working.

The bailiff opened the door to the back of the courtroom, and the people started to file in. I stood up and turned around to see who might be there. Mrs. Ronning came through the door. I could tell she had been crying. Her eyes were red and puffy. She was a little shorter than Josie, slightly built with dishwater-blonde, curly hair. The ordeal of the trial had worn on her, she looked tired and much older than her thirty some years. She caught me staring, and I quickly turned away. I don't think she was there for pity.

Within minutes, everybody was in and settled. The bailiff pounded the gavel and Judge Morris took the bench. He nodded at the prosecutor. "Your honor," said Spencer, "we will recall Josie Klein."

The back door opened and Josie walked in. She had a much more confident air about her than her morning appearance. She took the stand. The judge looked at her. "Ms. Klein, you're still under oath. You may proceed."

"Ms. Klein, if I recall correctly, when we broke this morning, we were at the point of discussing the night when Mr. Ronning was murdered."

I jumped from my seat. "Objection, your honor, we're here to determine whether it was a murder or self-defense."

The judge looked at Spencer. "Sustained. Counsel, you know better than that."

Spencer ignored the comment.

"Ms. Klein, taking you back to the early evening hours of September 7th, where were you?"

"I was at my home."

"And that was here in the city of St. Cloud, Benton County, Minnesota?"

"Yes."

"And was there anyone with you?"

"Yes, Dale Ronning."

"How did you know Mr. Ronning?"

"We had met a few weeks before and had become friends."

"Close friends?" asked Spencer.

She appeared nervous. "Yes."

"In fact, you had a sexual relationship."

She looked down, I assumed to avoid any eye contact with Mrs. Ronning. "Yes," she said.

"And," continued the prosecutor, "did Mr. Ronning indicate to you that he was married?"

"He told me he was separated, that he was in the process of getting a divorce."

I glanced at the jury. I saw some of them looking to the back of the courtroom, obviously trying to see Mrs. Ronning's reaction. I was almost tempted to do so myself. I knew Dale had lied to Josie. To the extent the jury believed that he was just another trucker trying to get laid, it would help Kevin's case. Spencer knew that as well. He was going to get it all in quickly, so the jury would hear it and get over it before he got to the good part of his case.

"Did you ever tell any friends about Mr. Ronning?"

"A couple of my close friends."

"Do you know a Ms. Sara Pendergast?" asked Spencer.

"Yes."

"She's the fiancée of Chris Younger?"

"Yes."

"Did you ever say anything to her about your relationship with Mr. Ronning?"

"About a week or so before this happened, I met her at Stubby's bar. I mentioned to her that I thought my relationship with Kevin was over and that I'd met a new man, but I don't believe I mentioned any name."

"Let's go to that evening, Ms. Klein. What time did Mr. Ronning arrive?"

"He got there about seven o'clock or so."

"Was your daughter home?"

"No, I had made arrangements to have her go to a friend's house."

"Had you had sexual relations with Mr. Ronning prior to that evening?"

132

Again she looked down. "Yes."

"What was planned for that evening?"

"I had planned dinner. He brought a bottle of wine. He was gonna spend the night."

"Was that the first time he stayed at your home?"

"Yes."

"Other than the wine, did you consume any other alcohol that evening?"

"Yes, we did."

"Do you recall what you may have been drinking?"

"Vodka screwdrivers."

"Ms. Klein, why don't you tell us what happened."

"We had some drinks and dinner. We watched television. The last thing I remember watching was David Letterman. I believe he came on about eleven o'clock. Then we fell asleep on the floor. I remember waking up. Dale was sleeping, and I gave him a push and said, 'Let's go to bed.' We got up and went upstairs."

"Do you recall," asked Spencer, "if you left on any lights on the main floor?"

"I believe I left the kitchen light on."

"Why?" asked Spencer.

"It was just a matter of habit. I did it for Lisa in case she got up."

"What do you recall after that?"

"We had just settled into bed, and I thought I heard a car door slam, and I didn't remember whether I had locked the front door or not. I asked Dale to get up and check the door to make sure it was locked."

"Do you recall what he was wearing when he left the room?"

"He was in his shorts, his underwear."

"Go on," said Spencer.

"I heard him go downstairs, and then, within seconds, I heard this voice say, 'What the fuck are you doing here?' Something like that."

"Did you recognize the voice?" asked Spencer.

She looked at Kevin. "I believe it was his voice," and she pointed.

"You mean the defendant, Kevin Murphy?"

"Yes."

"What happened next?"

"I panicked. I had no idea what was going on. I walked to the edge of the stairs and listened. I could tell there was a fight going on. I could hear voices, things breaking. I hollered, 'What's going on? I'm gonna call the cops.' I went back to the bedroom and dialed 911. I told 'em that my ex-boyfriend was here and that he was in a fight. The operator said, 'Stay on the phone. Tell us what's happening. The car's on its way.' Then I walked as far as the cord would go and I hollered, 'I've called the police. They're on their way. You better get out of here.' I didn't hear Kevin's voice again, but I knew it was Kevin. And then it was just quiet, and I heard a moaning sound. I hollered, 'Dale, Dale, are you okay?' Then I slowly made my way down the steps. When I got to the bottom, I looked in the kitchen, and there Dale was, lying on the floor. I remember the blood everywhere, and I heard a car take off. I didn't know what was happening."

Her eyes welled up and her hands were shaking. She put her arms across her chest and bowed her head.

"Do you need a break?" asked Spencer.

"No, no," she said, "I'm okay. I could use some water."

The bailiff quickly grabbed a pitcher and a glass and took it up to her. She reached for the glass, her hand shaking. She took a drink and set it down in front of her. Her arms immediately went back over her chest.

"What happened next?" Spencer asked in a soft voice.

Josie had regained her composure. "I didn't know what to do," she said. "He was lying there, blood gushing from his side. He looked at me, his eyes squinted a little. I didn't know if he was trying to tell me something, then suddenly his eyes rolled back, he was breathing hard. I saw a towel on the counter. I reached for it to help stop the bleeding. Then a police officer came in, and he told me to stand aside. Within moments, I could hear another siren, and the ambulance was there. I don't . . . I don't remember what all happened after that. People were coming in and out. They put him on a stretcher and took him out. I think I could tell . . . I think I knew, he wasn't

134

gonna make it. One of the officers called me later and told me he had died at the hospital."

"Did you stay at your home?" asked Spencer.

"Yes, I did. One of the officers took a statement from me. Then I called a friend, and she came over and stayed with me."

"Do you remember saying anything to the officer who stayed there about Mr. Murphy?"

"Yes, I do. I told him that I knew it was Kevin."

"How did you know that?"

"I heard his voice."

"Ms. Klein, did you ever see the defendant carry a knife with him?"

"All the time."

"Do you know what kind of knife it was?"

"It's called a buck knife."

Spencer got up and walked to the clerk's desk and picked up the knife. "Ms. Klein, I'm showing you what's been marked Exhibit 15. Have you seen this before?"

"That's the kinda knife Kevin carried. He carried it in a little case on his belt."

Spencer turned and looked at me. Content with himself, he said, "Thank you Ms. Klein. I have nothing further. Your witness."

I thought for a second. What did the jury think of this young woman, I wondered. Some of them might have thought her a tramp, but there was nothing about her manner that made you dislike her. I realized that there were no points to be made by giving her a hard time. She had only told them what she saw.

"Ms. Klein," I started, "how long a relationship did you have with Mr. Murphy?"

"I believe I told you, almost a couple months."

"And for a good period of that time, he actually lived at your home, is that correct?"

"Yes."

"So that relationship grew to a sexual relationship, did it not?"

"Yes."

"And I believe you indicated that Mr. Murphy and your daughter formed a close relationship. Isn't that correct?"

"Lisa thought a lot of him. I didn't see anything wrong with that. She needed a man in her life as well."

"When's your daughter's birthday?"

"September 14th"

"Did you and Kevin have plans to take your daughter to the Renaissance Festival on the weekend following her birthday?"

"There was some talk about it. I don't know if I would call it plans."

"In any event, at some point, you told Kevin you weren't going, and you wouldn't let Lisa go. Correct?"

"Like I told you, I wanted Kevin out of my life . . ."

I interrupted, "But even after Kevin moved out, you let him continue to come over and see Lisa. Isn't that correct?"

"Yes, she wanted me to."

"If I recall your testimony, Ms. Klein, you indicated that you met Mr. Ronning two weeks prior to his death. Correct?"

"Yes."

"And this Friday night, the night he died, was the first night he stayed over at your home, is that correct?"

"Yes."

"From the time that Kevin moved out until that night, did you and Lisa ever visit Kevin in his apartment?"

She hesitated. I could tell that she was wondering where I was going. I took a gamble that she wouldn't lie. Before she had a chance to respond, I continued, "Isn't it true, Ms. Klein, that the weekend before, on that Saturday night, you and Lisa were at Mr. Murphy's apartment for dinner?"

I could tell by her face that Kevin had told me the truth. She had been there, and she had sex with him. Her only hesitation was whether she wanted to admit it.

"Lisa spent the afternoon with him. I went to pick her up," she finally said. "Lisa missed him."

"You stayed?"

"Yes."

"Was it an enjoyable evening?" I asked.

"Yes, it was."

"And did you spend the night?"

"You know I did."

"And did you have sex with Mr. Murphy?"

Spencer stood up and with a loud voice said, "Your honor, what's the relevance of this? I object."

"Approach the bench, please," responded the judge.

As we stood before the bench, in front of the court reporter, I whispered, "Your honor, the State has attempted to portray Mr. Murphy as some sort of monster, that after he moved out, he was somehow stalking and harassing her. It certainly seems relevant to me that a week before this happens, she's having sex with him."

Spencer didn't respond.

"I'll let it in but move on," replied the judge.

While returning to the table, I asked, "Did you have sex with him?"

I turned toward her.

With a cold stare, she responded, "Yes, and I regret it."

"When Kevin lived there, did he have a key to your house?"

"Yes, he did."

"When he moved out, did you ask him for the key?"

"Yes, I did."

"Did he give it to you?"

"He gave me *a* key. As far as I knew, it was the only one he had."

"To your knowledge, the night that this occurred, did Mr. Murphy have to use a key to get into your home?"

"I don't know if I locked the door or not. If I did lock it, then he had to use a key."

"Ms. Klein, we've seen photographs taken by the police officers of the kitchen area and the livingroom area where this occurred. Have you seem those photographs?"

"Mr. Spencer showed them to me so that I would be familiar."

"In one of the photographs, on the kitchen counter, is a ballerina music box, isn't that correct?"

"Yes."

"And next to it is a card made out to your daughter, Lisa."

"Yes."

"And those were not there when you went to bed, correct?"

"Yes."

"Now when you look at the photograph of where that item is sitting on the counter—that's at the far end of the kitchen. Isn't that correct?"

"Yes."

"And there's only one exit out of the kitchen, through the living room and out the front door. Is that correct?"

"Yes."

"And to exit the kitchen into the living room, you go through a doorway and to the right hand side of that doorway, up the steps to the upstairs, isn't that correct?"

"Yes."

"And if Kevin is standing at the counter when Mr. Ronning had come down the steps, Mr. Ronning would be in that doorway to the kitchen. Isn't that correct?"

"Yes. I don't know where Kevin was, though."

"I know you don't, Ms. Klein, but I'm just trying to picture this for the jury. All I'm saying is, if Mr. Murphy was standing by the counter at the far end of the kitchen, where that ballerina was found, and if Mr. Ronning was standing in the doorway at the bottom of the steps, wouldn't it be fair to say, Ms. Klein, that if Kevin wanted to exit that kitchen, he would have to get by Mr. Ronning?"

She looked at me. She didn't want to say.

"It's very simple, Ms. Klein. Isn't that the only way out?" I asked.

"If that's where Mr. Murphy was, that would be true."

"Thank you, Ms. Klein. I have nothing further."

"Ms. Klein," said Spencer, "you have no way of telling us where Mr. Murphy was, do you?"

"No, sir."

"Thank you. Your honor," said Spencer, "I only have one more witness. I believe she's here, and there are some things we should discuss. This may be a good time to take a recess."

"We'll take fifteen minutes," said the judge. "I'll see counsel in chambers."

I waited until everybody left, and I looked at Kevin. "That went okay," I said.

"I'm surprised she admitted she slept with me," he said.

"I was too," I replied. "She might've been worried that we would call Lisa if she denied it."

"That should help us, don't you think," he asked.

"Help is a relative term," I said. "For the jury to find in your favor, they're going to have to dislike her and dislike Ronning. What she admitted may help there, but you'll have to convince them that you're worth saving, otherwise it won't make any difference. You're going to have the weekend to think about it." I got up and slapped him on the shoulder and went into the Judge's chambers.

Spencer was already sitting there. "The only witness I have left, your honor, is Mrs. Butkowski."

"Bob," the judge looked at me, "I read the whole statement. Based on the report of the officer, her testimony certainly seems admissible to me. Nobody's trying to pull anything on you. She was apparently afraid to say anything until the last minute."

"I assume you will note my objection for the record, your honor."

"Certainly," he said. "Spencer, do you have anything after her?"

"No, I'll close.

"Well, no sense trying to get anything in from your side today, Bob. We'll start with your case on Monday. How long do you think you're going to take?"

"Well Judge, I only have my defendant, character witnesses, and Chris Younger."

"I saw your list of character witnesses," replied the judge. "I won't let you parade half a dozen or so witnesses in. You better pick out the two or three best ones. So we'll probably get this to the jury by Tuesday or Wednesday. That's good, I'm ready to stay home. I'm tired of that two-lane highway."

I left the Judge's chambers through the back door, exiting into the hallway. As I came around the hallway, I saw Mrs. Ronning sitting on a bench, sobbing, another lady hugging her. The sight pained me. It was senseless. I walked by her quickly, and she didn't look up. Her companion gave me a look and a slight smile.

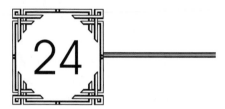

Within minutes, we were all back in the courtroom. As the din quieted down, Spencer stood up. "The State calls Jennifer Butkowski," he said.

The bailiff opened the door, and before he could say anything, a large, matronly lady, probably in her late sixties, walked right by him and made her way to the front bench. She wore a print dress, with large blue and white squares, that accentuated her portly frame. Her gray hair was tied in a tight bun that seemed to pull the loose skin on her face back towards her ears. Her eyes, dark brown, filled the lenses of large-framed glasses that dominated her face. As she sat down in the witness box, she glanced at Kevin and then settled on Spencer.

Spencer went through several minutes of testimony to establish her knowledge of Kevin. "Mrs. Butkowski," he continued, "did you ever hear the defendant, Kevin Murphy, threaten Ms. Klein?"

She looked towards the back of the courtroom, her eyes searching for Josie. "Yes," she said.

"Do you recall when that was?" asked Spencer.

"Not the exact day, but it was several weeks before this terrible incident."

"Do you recall what Mr. Murphy said?"

"Yes," she said.

"And what was it?"

She looked at Kevin, a sympathetic look. "I don't remember the exact words," she said.

It caught Spencer by surprise. "Mrs. Butkowski," he said, "do you recall giving a statement to Deputy Meyer just a short time ago?"

"Yes," she said.

"And, do you recall what you told the deputy?"

"Actually, I don't."

"Have you seen your statement?" he asked.

"I got a copy, but I didn't read it," she said.

"Well, Mrs. Butkowski, if you had an opportunity to read that statement, do you think it would refresh your recollection?"

"Possibly," she said.

"With the court's permission, I'd like to have her read her statement."

The judge looked at me. I shrugged my shoulders. "Go ahead," he said.

The statement was only a page and a half, but she looked at it for the longest time, her eyes moving from one word to the next. She finished and looked up.

"Did that help refresh your memory, Mrs. Butkowski?"

"Probably," she said.

"Do you recall what Kevin said to Ms. Klein?"

"The officer was pretty persistent, you know. I'm not sure those were his exact words or not. They had been sitting in the backyard, and I heard them argue. Their voices got a little loud, and then Kevin got up. As he walked between our houses he hollered at her, something about she should watch her back."

Spencer stood up and with a little anger and frustration in his voice, he said, "Mrs. Butkowski, didn't you tell the deputy that Mr. Murphy said to Josie Klein, 'If I see you with another guy, you better watch your back?' Isn't that what he said?"

Defiantly, she replied, "I told you, I don't remember his exact words."

"I have nothing further," Spencer snapped as he sat down.

I looked at her for a moment wondering if I should even ask her any questions. Something happened here, and I wasn't sure what. It appeared to me that since she had given the statement, she had a change of heart. Maybe it was seeing Kevin again. Now, if it was a question of deciding whether she was going to side with Kevin or with Josie, she was leaning towards Kevin. In the end, I thought, it may be helpful. "Mrs. Butkowski," I said, "how many times did you talk to Mr. Murphy?"

"Oh, dear, many times," she said. "He would come over, sometimes he'd bring Lisa along. He would talk to me for hours. He was the only one who would. I really appreciated it. My children don't come over very often, you see."

"What did you observe about him and Lisa?"

"Oh, dear God, she just adored him."

"I've been over to the site, Mrs. Butkowski. Your house and the Klein home are pretty close, right?"

"Too close. Sometimes it can be embarrassing, what I can hear."

"Other than that evening that the prosecutor asked you about, did you ever overhear any arguments or fights between Mr. Murphy and Ms. Klein?"

"No. I thought they got along fine. I think Kevin was good for her."

"Did you get to meet Mr. Ronning?"

"I knew she had a new male friend. He parked his truck there a couple times and ran to the door, but I never got to meet him."

"Did you hear any of the exchange of words between Mr. Murphy and Mr. Ronning about two in the morning on September 7, 1994?"

"I heard Josie and a man laughing and talking earlier in the evening, but once I went to bed, after the news, I didn't hear anything until the police came."

"Thank you, Mrs. Butkowski, I have nothing further."

Spencer let her be. The judge excused us all until Monday morning. I flew out of the courtroom, eager to get the hell out of there.

I pulled into the Log Lodge a little after six expecting to meet Tony. He was going to give me a run down on the witnesses he lined up for Monday. The parking lot was nearly empty. He wasn't there. I went in and had a seat at the bar and ordered a Manhattan. Jessie, the bartender, set the drink in front of me, and I swished the cherry around for a couple seconds before eating it. I was starting to get worried about myself. I had never been a Manhattan drinker, but I discovered, short of drinking straight shots, it was the quickest way of getting drunk. I hated this time of night, especially Friday nights. It was when I was the loneliest. During the day I could keep my mind occupied with work; by late night, only numbing with alcohol helped. It was the evening hours, the hiatus, I dreaded, and it seemed Manhattans got me through it quicker. It wasn't that I was getting drunk every night. During the week when I knew I had to be in court first thing in the morning and on my toes, I used the booze to help me fall asleep, at least that's what I told myself. On weekends, it went further. I used it to kill the pain.

I finished the first one, and Jessie set another in front of me.

"How's your case going, Mr. Williams?"

"It's just about over," I said. "I guess it's going okay."

"I know Kevin," she said. "I met him at Stubby's last summer. I also saw him there a few times with that Josie lady. They seemed like a nice couple. You wonder what goes wrong."

Jessie was an interesting person. In her middle thirties, she had been bartending on weeknights for as long as I could remember. Her hair was black and long, almost to her waist. Sometimes it was straight, sometimes curled. She had a pretty face with dark, deep-set eyes and high cheekbones. She liked to wear dangling earrings. Her usual attire consisted of jeans, tight jeans, with a white blouse tucked in enough to show the curves of a shapely body. She was married. Her husband would come to the bar once in a while, get slobbering drunk and become verbally abusive. Nobody knew why she put up with him. Over the years, I'd heard a lot of conversations by the men at the bar wondering what she would be like under the sheets. I think some of them probably used her to kick start their libido before they went home.

"I hope you get him off, Mr. Williams," she said.

"So do I," I replied as I glanced around. "Say, Jessie, who's the blonde lady sitting over there?"

She turned to look and then back at me with a big grin. "You don't recognize her either? That happens all the time. That's Vicki Harding."

"Your bullshittin' me," I said.

"No. She had a nose job, and she's bleached her hair."

"God, she looks great," I said.

"She just came back from Jamaica—that's why she's so dark. She's been here a while. She's put down a few. I hope she's all right. She's on the rebound. Her boyfriend dumped her when they got back. I don't know, some fight they had on the beach."

I stared at Vicki for a while.

"Why don't you send her a drink on me," I said.

Jessie smiled at me again. "I'd be a little careful, Mr. Williams. She can be a little loosy-goosy, if you know what I mean, when she's had too much to drink. She starts hanging on guys."

"Jessie," I said, "maybe I need to be hanged on."

"Don't say I didn't warn you," she replied.

She mixed another screwdriver and walked over to Vicki's table and gave it to her as she pointed at me. Vicki raised the glass and smiled. I turned away and starting sipping on my Manhattan. Jessie had her back to me as she was straightening out some bottles on shelves above the back bar. After a couple minutes she turned around, looked across the room and then at me. "I told you so," she said to me under her breath.

I smelled her before I saw her: "Eternity." It was one of my daughter's favorites perfumes. She set her glass down at the bar and pulled a stool out. "Well, Mr. Williams," she said, "to what do I owe the honor. It's not every day a big-shot attorney buys me a drink."

She caught me by surprise. Without thinking, I looked at her nose. She laughed.

"I'm sorry," I said.

"No, that's okay. Everybody does that."

"It looks great," I said.

"Thank you. What are you doing here anyway?" she asked.

"I just finished court a little while ago, and I'm waiting for my investigator. Just having a couple drinks on the way home."

"You know," she said, "I was gone when that terrible thing happened to your wife. Otherwise I would've been at the wake. She always struck me as a wonderful person."

"She was," I said. "And that's okay. We only had a small service."

"Do you mind if I sit and talk to you until your investigator gets here?" she said.

"No, that's fine," I said. "Please do."

I had seen Vicki in the bar many times. She seemed like a fun-loving person, but she was very seldom with the same guy. I think the problem she had was her nose. If you walked up from behind, with her long blonde hair and nice figure, you'd expect this beautiful face, but it wasn't there. Her nose occupied too much of her face. So, I suspect, once the passion to get at that shapely figure wore off, the face was enough to make her boyfriends quickly split. But that was no longer the case. Now her face matched her figure.

We talked for quite a while. She was a secretary at a local insurance agency. She told me she thought she had a lawsuit because one of the insurance agents was constantly making sexual advances. She said he touched her on the breast the week before and then said it was an accident. I told her I knew a woman attorney in town who specialized in sexual harassment cases. I would talk to her about it.

About seven thirty, Jessie told me I had a phone call; it was Tony. He had just gotten back into town. He was willing to still come and talk to me, but I gave him the excuse that I just wanted to get home. We agreed to meet the next morning.

I went back to the bar and asked Vicki if she wanted to have dinner. She eagerly accepted.

The restaurant wasn't that busy, maybe half full. We got a table in the back. I could tell I had already had too much to drink. They say booze causes a loss of self-control, that it allows you to do stupid things and then later use the booze as an excuse. I could tell I was on the verge of doing just that. I was losing my inhibitions. I could tell Vicki was too. Her manner was becoming, I sensed, rather seductive. Before the meal came, she got up to powder her nose. As she walked away from the table, I watched her body as she crossed the room. I wondered to myself, are you really going to try to seduce this woman? I started with no plan of doing so, but during our conversation I would catch myself looking at her, and strange feelings would stir. Her skin was smooth and dark. She had blue eyes, and her lips were painted a bright red. There was a sensuality about her that turned me on.

We finished dinner and went back into the bar and sat at a table. Jessie brought us another round of drinks. She winked at me as she left. By then Vicki's speech was slurred and rambling. She started to talk about her trip to Jamaica. "You know, Mr. Williams, I went with this dink. I even paid for his tickets. We get down there, and the first day all he wants to do is stay in the room. He's hornier than hell. See, he loved my new face. By the third day or so, it wore off a little bit. We met some other couples. We decided we were gonna go to the nude beach. It wasn't really nude. I think it was a con put on by the men. The men still wore their swimming suits, only the women walked around without tops. We met some other couples there and went out that night. We actually had a pretty good time.

"The next day we started early. We were laying out in the sun, drinking all day, those big rum punch drinks in a pineapple with the umbrellas. Everybody just started to tease each other. The guys talked about our breasts. I don't know what happened. My boyfriend left for a few minutes, and when he came back, this other guy was feeling me up. He asked me if they were real or if I had implants. I said, 'Implants, bullshit.' He said, 'Well, let me see for myself,' and I said, 'Go ahead.' Of course, old Bobby goes off his rocker. He almost gets into a fight, doesn't talk to me the rest of the vacation, won't sit on the plane with me on the way back. Traded places with one of the other guys. I didn't give a shit anymore. He was a jerk anyway. They're all jerks, Mr. Williams. I don't know what his problem was. If you have nice breasts, why can't you show 'em? Do you wanna see how tan they are?"

I stared at her face, completely mesmerized by her story, so intently her question didn't quite register. She looked down, the top three buttons of her blouse were already open. She opened several more and exposed her breasts. They were firm and tan. She giggled, "Cute, aren't they?"

I wasn't too drunk to be embarrassed. I quickly glanced around to see if anyone else was looking. She sensed it, and closed her blouse. She reached under the table and put her hand on my leg. "Let's go to my house," she said.

I looked at her. She had a big smile.

"You've got to be kidding," I said.

"No," she said. "I wanna take you home. I wanna show you how nice my breasts are."

"I can't," I said.

"Come on," she said. "I know what you're going through. It'll be good for you. I only live a few blocks away in the River Apartments. You can follow me. I have to go to the ladies room, and we can take off."

I couldn't believe it. I was being propositioned. I hadn't been propositioned my entire life. That's not true, Kate had propositioned me many times. We could be at a party, a dance, anywhere, and she would, totally unexpectedly, walk up and whisper in my ear, "Let's go home." She would smile and take my hand.

But Kate was gone, so why couldn't I make love with Vicki. I wanted to. It would be an escape. For how long, though?

As she started to walk away, I tried to imagine what it would be like lying next to that body, kissing her, feeling her breasts. Once she was out of sight, I walked up to the bar. Jessie had been watching with some interest. I gave her a hundred-dollar bill. "Whatever's left, use to call her a cab," I said. "Tell her I got called away."

She smiled and winked. "Sure, Mr. Williams. You take care of yourself. Tell Kevin I said, 'Hi.' Good luck."

I walked to the car, my steps a little unsteady. I got in. Now, you dumb ass, I thought, how are you gonna get home without getting nabbed?

I started up the car and headed down the long driveway to the highway. Hey, this isn't too bad. I pulled up to the stop sign. A city cop was parked across the intersection facing my direction. I waited, hoping he was going to pull out. He didn't. The son-of-a-bitch is waiting for me to leave, I thought. I gave it a few more moments. I couldn't sit there. I knew he'd be over, wondering what was going on. I put on my right hand blinker and slowly turned onto the highway. He pulled out and was immediately on my tail. All I could think was, I'm a gonner. I have to be twice the legal limit. I watched. There were no flashing lights. He was probably twenty yards behind me. I looked at my speedometer, I was getting near the speed limit of fifty-five. I quickly put the car in cruise control. *Listen,* I thought, *what does he need to stop me? He needs probable cause. I have to do something wrong.* I looked at the fog line and the center white line. *If I stay between the lines and under the speed limit, he can't stop me. I'm driving perfect. If he stops me, the son-of-a-bitch is gonna have to lie. That's what I'll tell the judge. I was driving right between the lines, right at fifty-five, and he had no reason to pull me over. But who's gonna believe me when my test shows I'm stinkin' drunk.* All of this was flashing through my mind as I headed out of town. I watched his headlights in my rearview mirror, waiting for the flashers to come on. Suddenly, in the other direction, a car approached. It shot by going probably seventy miles an hour, never putting on its dims. The flashing lights went on, and I saw the cop make a u-turn and heard the siren as he disappeared out of sight.

All I could think was, how in the hell did I get that lucky? I was living on borrowed time. I knew I couldn't keep drinking the way I was without ending up with some serious consequences. But the truth was, like many of the drunks I had represented over the years, I didn't give a shit. What were they going to do to me? Take away my driver's license, fine me, throw me in jail? That was nothing compared to the pain I felt when I was sober and sitting at home. I don't remember much of the rest of the drive home. I took every back road I could think of. The last couple Manhattans had finally settled in, I was on the edge of consciousness. My car must have been on auto-pilot.

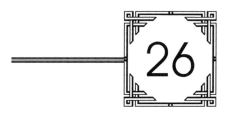

26

Late the next morning, I heard banging on the door. I covered my head, hoping it would go away. I was lying there, covers over my head, when a hand rested on my shoulder and shook me. "Bob, you okay?"

My head snapped up. I threw the covers off in a fighting mood. There stood Tony.

"Easy! Jesus Christ, it's just me," he said.

I took a moment to orientate myself. I was in my own bed. What was he doing there?

"How in the hell did you get in here?" I asked.

"I was pounding on the door, nobody came. I was worried, I came through the basement door, it was open."

"Bullshit, it was open. I locked it myself."

"Go check it. What's your problem anyway?"

"What the hell you doing here?" I asked. I was upset, not with Tony but myself. I had looked at the clock, it was already eleven o'clock. I was hung over. I had a headache, and I had made an ass out of myself the night before. I could well have ended up in jail or detox, and I needed to take it out on somebody. Tony was convenient.

"We were suppose to have a meeting at Jimmy's at nine o'clock, remember? Breakfast. We were gonna talk about witnesses?"

"I was going to call you."

"That's not what you told me last night over the phone."

"Never mind," I said. "Why don't you go make us some coffee. I need a shower."

Fifteen minutes later, I walked out of my bedroom showered, dressed. Tony handed me a cup of coffee on my way through the kitchen and down the basement steps. He was right; the door was unlocked. I remembered distinctly, after the conversations with Tony about somebody looking for me, that I had made sure to lock all the doors. Somehow that door got opened. I looked around the basement. Nothing missing, nothing out of the ordinary. I did the same upstairs. I opened the cabinet by my bed. There was the .38 pistol Tony had bought for me. Maybe I was wrong, I thought, maybe I had missed that door.

Tony and I talked for several hours. I told him how the case was going. He told me who he had lined up for witnesses for Monday morning. He told me he was going to be there early to make sure nobody got lost.

"I don't suppose you've heard anything about Scott Draper?" I asked.

"Nothing. It's like he fell off the face of the earth."

"Don't worry," I said, "he's around. I wonder if he learned any burglary skills while he was in prison."

"Why?" he asked.

"I just wonder how that door got opened."

"Do ya think it was him?"

"Nah. If he'd gotten in, something would be missing. He wouldn't go through all the effort of sneaking into my house just to make sure he could do it."

"How do you know nothing's missing?"

"I did a quick inventory. Anything I thought a thief would take. Nothing. I could've gone out that door and just forgot to lock it, too."

"Have you heard anything from Carol," he asked.

"She hasn't been here since the day we packed up Kate's clothes. I've talked to her on the phone. I don't say anything. I don't want to scare her. She would tell me if she noticed anything. I don't think he's bothering her. She's got another couple weeks of hospital duty, and then she's coming home for a few days over Christmas. I'm hoping we can take off, do something."

"Have you fired that gun since the last time I was out?"

"Actually, no."

"You'd better do it, you'll probably get rusty."

"Tell ya the truth . . . I don't like the noise."

"I better get my ass going," he said. "I've got some things to get done this afternoon."

"Like what?" I asked.

"I've got my own life, you know!"

"I'm not doubting you, but what do you have to do?"

"I don't have to do anything, but there's things I like to do."

"Like what?"

"Reading and writing, for example."

"What do you write?"

"Poems."

"You're kidding me?"

"No."

The room grew silent.

"What's the matter," Tony said, "you have a hard time believing I can write poetry?"

"Matter of fact, I do."

"Why?"

"I always thought poets were kinda sensitive guys . . ."

"You want your ass kicked?" he said.

I held up my arms. "Peace," I said, "I was just kidding. I'd like to see your poetry sometime. Would you let me read some?"

"Not with your attitude."

"I just thought you had to be a sensitive kinda guy to be a poet. I guess I never thought of you as a particularly sensitive kinda guy, if you know what I mean."

"I'm not even going to talk to you about it anymore. Here I thought you'd be one person who'd understand, who I could share some of my work with, and you end up being a smart ass."

I could tell he was serious. I'd hurt his feelings. "I'm sorry," I said. "Really, I am. I'd like to read some of your stuff."

Tony left a couple minutes later. I didn't know if he was still mad at me or not. Suggesting he had to be a pansy was a dumb thing to say, but I guess I just never pictured him as a poetry-writing kind of guy. But then, what did I know?

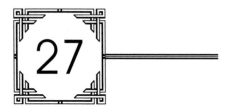

I managed to waste the rest of the day doing nothing. Saturday evening I got out my bottle of whiskey and watched a movie. That had become my Saturday night routine. Sunday morning I couldn't get out of bed until noon. I took Kevin's file out. I would page through the documents and glance at my notes, but it was all perfunctory. I wasn't trying to learn anything, I was trying to make the time go faster.

It was about three-thirty Sunday afternoon when the phone rang. It was Tony. "I've got some terrible news," he said.

My first thought was that one of my witnesses had called and said they couldn't make it.

"What now?" I asked.

"Faye's dead."

I remember my knees got weak; my lower lip quivered. I put the phone down on the counter, brought a chair over and sat down. I picked up the phone, with both hands, Tony was saying, "Bob, Bob, are you there?"

"What're you talking about?" I asked.

"Heidi just called, she was afraid to call you. She heard it from some friends. They say she fell down some stairs at Quadna and broke her neck."

"Broke her neck! Kiss my ass. How could she do that?" I said.

"Bob," he said, "don't holler at me. I don't know."

"Where are you now?" I asked.

"At home."

"Let me make some calls. I'll get right back to you."

I tried Faye's number, the line was busy. I looked up Heidi's. She answered after a couple rings.

"What do you know about this?" I asked.

"Mr. Williams, I'm really sorry."

"Just tell me what you know about it."

"Her friend Jackie called me. She was with them at Quadna. It was late last night, after midnight. They found her at the bottom of some steps barely alive. They rushed her to the hospital. She died early this morning. Isn't it terrible? What about those poor boys? I haven't tried calling. I couldn't imagine talking to Ken."

"You're sure it's true?"

"Mr. Williams, Jackie was bawling, almost hysterical when she told me."

"I'm sorry," I said, "that was a dumb thing to ask."

"What are we gonna to do at the office?" she asked.

"I don't know," I said as I hung up.

That was the least of my concerns. I couldn't believe it. I sat there, dazed. I grabbed the whiskey bottle from the cabinet and poured myself a shot. What the Christ is going on? All of a sudden, everybody around me is falling over dead. I tried Faye's number again, Ken answered.

"Ken, Bob. Tell me what happened?"

"Bob, it's terrible, I don't know what happened."

I could hear him crying, and a lady's voice said, "Who's this?"

"Bob Williams."

"This is Ken's mother. He's unable to speak to you now."

"Is it all right if I come over?"

I could tell she put her hand over the phone, her voice was muffled. Seconds later she came back on, "I don't think that would be very good, Mr. Williams. I'm sure you understand. Ken and the boys . . . well, they can't face anybody just yet."

I told her I understood and hung up. I called Tony back. "We've got to talk," I said. "Why don't we meet at the Lodge?"

"No," he said, "we don't need any booze. Why don't you come to my place, or I'll come out there."

"I'll come in."

I went in to change clothes, and I noticed I hadn't showered or shaved. I went into the shower stall and turned the water on as hot as I could stand. I put my hands on the back wall and leaned my head down and let the water pound off my back. I had fought back my tears, but I finally let them go. I could feel them run down my cheeks, collect below my chin to be washed away. My arms were out straight, my hands flat against the wall, stiff armed. I was afraid to let go, afraid I would collapse to the floor. I stayed that way, trying to regain my composure. I had a clear picture of Faye in my mind walking out of the office on that Thursday night, smiling and saying, "Good luck." I struggled to straighten up and finish my shower. When I got out, I stood by the mirror. My eyes were raw and red. I quickly combed my hair, but I didn't bother shaving. I threw on my clothes and I was out the door.

As I drove in, I couldn't help but wonder. Without knowing what happened, my first thought was, this was also meant to get to me. This was Mr. Draper's way of extending my agony, letting me know that there was more to come. If it was Draper, I had underestimated the extent of his anger, the extent he would go to make me suffer. I wondered if that was what seventeen and a half years in prison, obsessed with revenge, did to a person. But why Faye? She wasn't even around when he got sent to prison. And then, maybe I wasn't right—maybe it was just an accident.

Tony had a pot of coffee on when I arrived. He poured me a cup, and we sat at his kitchen table. "Have you been able to find out anything more?" I asked.

"I know a cop from Grand Rapids," he said. "I put a call in to him. He said he would check with the sheriff's office. Apparently a deputy was there, followed them to the hospital. I gave him my number. I expect a call any minute."

"I don't imagine the Grand Rapids cop knew anything about it."

"He had heard something on the morning news about some lady falling down the steps at Quadna, but he didn't pay any attention."

I took a sip of coffee and I thought about Faye again. I thought about her two boys. She had been telling me what they wanted for Christmas. She hadn't been able to find it in town, and she was going to go to one of the malls in Minneapolis. My eyes started to well up. Tony noticed. "It's getting a little hard to take, isn't it?" he said.

"I can't believe it, Tony," I said, my voice breaking. "How in the hell does that happen? I had a terrible thought driving in, maybe it wasn't an accident, maybe it was Draper."

"I thought of that, too," he said. "He's got to be one sick bastard if he wants to get everybody in your life. Did you call Carol?"

"I did, she's not home. I left a message to have her call. I told her to call here. I don't know," I said, "maybe I'm so paranoid I'm jumping to conclusions. They said it was an accident. We'll just have to wait and see."

"What's gonna happen with the trial?" Tony asked.

"The judge won't consider a mistrial again; we'll have to go ahead. The only thing I'll have to work around will be the funeral. I suppose that'll be Wednesday or Thursday. God, I can't take another funeral, Tony. I'm not sure I can face Ken without becoming a blubbering idiot. What'll I say?"

The phone rang, and Tony answered it. "Yeah," he said, "thanks for calling back."

I could hear a muffled voice talking fast. Tony listened for several minutes. "Thanks Jim," he said. "I appreciate it. I know her boss, the attorney I work for, will want to see the reports and the medical records. Do you think you could get a copy for me and send them down? If there's any costs involved, let me know. Okay? Thanks, Jim."

He put the receiver down and sat back down. "Do you care for more coffee?" he asked.

"Just tell me what happened," I said.

"Well, he talked to the deputy. Apparently there were a bunch of people having a party in a room on the second floor. They'd been out snowmobiling most of the day, taking shots of Schnapps here and there. I guess they had partied pretty hard that night. Have you been to Quadna?" he asked.

"Yeah, years ago."

"Well you know they have those bigger rooms on the second floor with the fireplace and balcony? That apparently was the party room. Faye's room was on the first floor, she was going down to check on the boys. She left, and nobody paid a whole lot of attention for a while. When Ken finally missed her. he went looking and found her at the bottom of the steps. She'd gone out on the balcony, down the wood steps. It had been melting in the afternoon; there was some ice on 'em. Nobody knows what happened. She fell, anyway, broke her neck. She was still alive when they found her, but she died the next morning at the hospital. She couldn't breathe. The hospital did a blood test when she came in. It was .16. That's a pretty high alcohol count for Faye."

I sat in disbelief and shook my head. It sounded like a terrible accident, nothing more. That didn't help the pain, but it eased the lingering guilt I felt in not warning her.

"The deputy said he would try to get a copy of everything and send it to me," Tony finished. "I'm sorry. Now what'll we do?" he asked.

"There's nothing we can do," I said. "I called her home. Apparently Ken doesn't want anybody over. I'll just have to wait until tomorrow night."

Tony and I talked for hours. Around ten, Carol called. I told her what happened. She had never known Faye that well, but she could tell from my voice I was hurting. I told her I would let her know what was happening. As I put the phone back, Tony brought out a bottle of whiskey and poured us each a shot. I quickly gulped it down. It burned all the way.

Tony leaned back in his chair. "You know," he said, "Kate was probably one of the most feminine women I'd ever known. No matter when you saw her, or what she was doing, she always exuded such a sense of femininity . . . and yet she could be tough as nails. She could be so sensitive and yet so practical. I don't know," he said, and he paused, "it's just not fair."

His comments caught me by surprise. I never knew his insight ran that deep. Now I was starting to see, maybe, some of the poet in him. I always saw him, I guess, as the tough cop.

He poured us another shot, this time, we just sipped. He continued, "You couldn't find a nicer person than Faye, she would go out of her way to help anybody. Even during the toughest times at the office, she could manage to bring a smile out of you. She adored those boys of hers, would do anything for them. I don't know how they're ever gonna replace her."

He took another sip of the whiskey. I took the opportunity. "You know," I said, "I've been thinking about things too. Look at all the skuzzy broads we've worked with over the years, the tramps, the druggies, the ones who don't give a shit about anybody, especially their kids. If somebody has to go, why not one of them? You can't tell me that God has any plan, that there's any sort of divine purpose to all this bullshit. That's what the priest is going to give us at Faye's funeral, just wait and see. For once, I might actually stand up and holler out, 'Bullshit.'"

"You won't do that," he said. "What do you think that would do to the family? The only way you can survive this kind of crap is by deluding yourself into believing that it's all part of some divine plan. Like they say, God needed another angel."

We sat like that until the early hours. We didn't get drunk, but we got maudlin. We told Kate and Faye stories until we were in tears. About three a.m., I dragged myself out of the chair and headed home. I didn't even bother trying to go to bed. I made myself a pot of strong coffee, took out Kevin's file and tried to keep my mind off of my new loss. It didn't work very well. Next to Kate, Faye was the only other woman in the world who I felt comfortable with, that I was close to. Now I hoped I wasn't relegated to the Josies of the world.

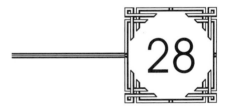

Monday morning I walked into the Benton County Courthouse with red eyes and a black-coffee buzz. Word had obviously spread to the court personnel what had happened to Faye. She had worked with many of them over the years. I was again the object of everybody's pity. People quickly deflected my acknowledgments, like they hadn't heard. Mary, the court reporter, finally came up and said, "Bob, I don't know what I can say. I'm really sorry about Faye. If there's anything I can do to help . . . the judge wants to talk to you and Spencer before we start."

She started to walk away and then turned around. "Are you going to be all right?" she asked. "It looks like it's really been rough on you."

"Mary, I don't understand how, in less than a month, two lovely ladies can be taken. You're right. I'm not good. But I'm gonna get through this crap if it kills me."

She came up to me, wrapped her arms around me and hugged gently. "You'll make it," she said.

As I walked in to the judge's chambers, he reached out his hand. "Condolences, Bob. This is getting difficult to understand, isn't it?"

"It's certainly more than a person should have to take," I said.

"I was telling Spencer," continued the judge, "that if there is some break needed for the funeral, I certainly understand, but he was afraid we weren't going to be able to continue this morning. You're not asking for that, are you?"

I could tell by the tone and manner of the Judge, that it was said more as a judicial order than a question. And frankly, I didn't blame him. "No, your honor," I replied. "I'm not sure of the funeral arrangements, but I expect they'll be Wednesday or Thursday. If we can simply work around that."

"Thank you," he said. "I can't put this off again."

Within minutes, I was standing before the jury. "If it please the court, ladies and gentlemen of the jury, Mr. Prosecutor, it is now my opportunity to give you a brief statement as to what we expect our evidence to show. I can tell you that there's not a great deal of dispute with what the State has set forth. I can tell you that Mr. Murphy's going to take the stand, and he will acknowledge that he made some mistakes, some terrible mistakes in his relationship with Ms. Klein. I think through his testimony, you'll learn a little bit more about this young man, and you'll get a different picture of him than the one portrayed by the State. Mr. Murphy's going to tell you that he did know that Ms. Klein was seeing another man, that he had heard rumors of that through mutual friends, but he had no way of knowing that person would be there on that fateful Saturday morning. He'll tell you that the only reason he went to Ms. Klein's home was to leave a present for Lisa, something he had bought over a month earlier on a trip. And to him it was something precious, something for her to remember him by, something he knew that little Lisa would cherish. That was the only reason he went there. He will tell you what happened when he was confronted by Mr. Ronning, what was going through his mind at the time, the predicament he felt he was in, the danger he felt he was in, and what happened that led up to Mr. Ronning being stabbed. He will tell you that it was not intentional, that the only reason he took out the knife was to protect himself and that Mr. Ronning sustained the fatal wound accidentally."

As the words came out, I watched the juror's faces. After years of doing this, I believed I could tell from their expression where their minds might be. It appeared to me that most were still open; most had not decided on guilt or innocence and wanted to listen to my client. I figured we still had a chance.

"Finally, ladies and gentlemen, we're going to bring in some character witnesses, people who know Kevin, his character, and are willing to come in and tell that to you. And at the end, the judge is going to give you an instruction as to why character witnesses are important. If you recall in the voir dire process, I asked each of you whether you could keep an open mind until you heard all the evidence, the defense as well as the prosecution. You all said you would, and as I now look at you, I know you intend to keep that promise. Thank you."

I turned towards the clerk. "The defense calls Kevin Murphy."

Kevin took the stand, and I took him through all of the preliminary matters as quickly as possible. He told the jury he was basically a handyman, a jack of all trades. Since his return, he had been working for various apartment owners in St. Cloud doing odd jobs, repairing plumbing, things like that. He told the jury he liked the freedom of being able to set his own hours as much as possible.

"Mr. Murphy," I asked, "you were here when Ms. Klein related to the jury how you met and how your relationship started."

He smiled. "I certainly was."

"Was that pretty much as you recall it?" I asked.

"For the most part, yes."

"When did you move into her home?"

"Probably the first part of June or so."

"In your mind, what was the relationship with her like at that time?"

"I thought we had a wonderful relationship. We did a lot of things together. I loved her daughter, Lisa. We got along great. I don't know what to say. I thought things were going good."

"Do you recall her asking you to leave?"

"Yes, I do. It came as a complete surprise. She talked about this argument we had on the Fourth of July. It wasn't an argument. I was just getting concerned about her drinking. She was drinking way too much and way too often. By early afternoon she was already drunk. When I told her to stop, that's when she got mad at me. It had nothing to do with other guys."

"When did she actually ask you to leave her home?"

"It was after that."

"When did you actually move out of her home?"

"It was around August 1st. I had to find an apartment. She gave me a little time to do that. I think my lease started August first."

"Did you have any contact with Ms. Klein after August first?"

"Oh, many times," he said. "I would call Lisa almost daily. She never objected to that. Then I would stop over in the evenings, sometimes on weekends. Once in a while she'd let me take Lisa out."

"What was your understanding of why she wanted to end your relationship?"

"I don't think she ever told me that she wanted to end the relationship. She told me I was doing things too fast, and I know I did talk about marriage, and that upset her. I didn't think she wanted to end the relationship at first, Mr. Williams, I thought she just wanted to have her space, you know, some time to think. At least that's what she told me."

"When is Lisa's birthday?" I asked.

"September fourteenth."

"Was there some discussion about the three of you going to the Renaissance Festival?"

"That had started, I believe, much earlier. I remember seeing a poster at the gas station for the Renaissance Festival, and I remember talking to Josie about going there . See, Lisa mentioned her birthday way back, I don't even remember when, but I remember her telling me it was in September, on September fourteenth. So when I saw the sign, I thought it would be fun to take her to the Renaissance Festival for her birthday. She had never been there. At the time, Josie thought that would be fine."

"There was some testimony regarding a ballerina music box found on the kitchen table. When did you buy that?"

"That was on a biking trip we all took in June. We were on the North Shore, Lake Superior. I found it at a gift shop. Lisa would always make us sit and watch her dance like a ballerina. This was a music box with a ballerina that danced to the music. I was gonna give it to Lisa right away, and then Josie said no, that would spoil her, I should wait 'til her birthday. So I had it at my home."

"Do you know Mrs. Butkowski?" I asked.

"Yes."

"How do you know her?"

"I'd met her even before I'd moved in with Josie. She lived next door by herself. The home was rather close, within feet, so you couldn't go in or out without seeing her in the backyard, in her garden. She seemed to be very lonesome, so I went out of my way to visit with her."

"Do you recall a time when you and Josie may have had an argument in the backyard that she would have overheard?"

"I suspect she may have overheard quite a few things. The homes were so close that if she was in her kitchen with the window open and I was in our kitchen with the window open, we could actually talk across the sidewalk."

"Well I'm asking about a specific occasion when you and Josie were in the backyard and may have gotten into an argument in which your voices were raised."

"I recall that," he said.

"What happened?" I asked.

"I had already moved out. I had been over visiting with Lisa for most of the evening. It was dark out, so it was already late. Lisa had gone to bed. Josie and I were sitting in the backyard talking. Mrs. Butkowski was probably in her backyard or even on her porch. To be honest, Mr. Williams," and he looked at the jury, "I missed Lisa and Josie so bad that I was pleading with Josie to let me move back in. I told her that I loved her so much that I was in anguish. I told her how much I missed her. I basically bared my soul."

"What did she say?"

"She sorta laughed, like she enjoyed making me miserable. She said, 'No way,' just like that, with no feeling whatsoever, just, 'No way.'" Kevin hesitated, and he looked down. He lowered his voice a little and continued. "That's the first time I thought she might be seeing somebody else, and I won't lie to you, I was angry. I was mad that she could dump me and then say, after I had opened my heart to her, 'No way,' with no feeling whatsoever. As I stood up to leave, in my anger, I said something stupid like, 'If you're seeing somebody else, you better watch your back.' I didn't mean anything by it. It was out of frustration, disappointment, heartbreak."

"At some point did you become aware that Ms. Klein was actually seeing another man?"

He looked up, directly at the jury. "I heard rumors from a couple people at the bar. Sara Pendergast told me that she had hooked up with some trucker. She told me not to waste my time on her."

"Mr. Murphy, this incident occurred in the early morning hours of Saturday, September 8, 1994. The previous weekend, did you have an opportunity to see Ms. Klein and Lisa?"

"Yes, I did."

"Under what circumstances?"

"Since we weren't going to the Renaissance Festival, I had called to see if I could pick Lisa up and if I could do something with her. Josie said, 'Fine.' We made arrangements that Josie would pick Lisa up that evening at my apartment. Just on the spur of the moment, I invited Josie for dinner. I didn't think she'd accept, I was surprised when she did. So I had Lisa all afternoon. I took her shopping. We went for a walk in Munsinger Gardens. We had a lot of fun. Then we went grocery shopping so that I could fix dinner for us all. We picked up the groceries and some wine, and I was making dinner when Josie came over. It got late. We were talking. Lisa got tired and fell asleep on the couch. It seemed like everything between me and Josie was

162

patched up. While we were talking, she was enjoying herself. I went and sat next to her, and I leaned over and kissed her. She kissed me back. Before long, we were in bed." He paused, "You know," and he blushed slightly.

"Did she spend the night?" I asked.

"Yes, she did. I made breakfast for them the next morning and, and really, I thought we were gonna get back together."

"What changed those thoughts?" I asked.

"I called her later in the day, and she told me what we did didn't make any difference. As far as she was concerned, it was still over."

"What did you say?"

"I didn't say much at all, but I couldn't believe it. I guess I didn't understand her motive for staying."

"When was the next time you may have had any contact with her?"

"It was Monday or Tuesday of that week that I found out she might be seeing another man. Somebody told me about the trucker. It really bothered me. On Wednesday I decided Josie was right . . . it was over. I bought her a single rose in a vase, took it to her job and gave it to her."

"Did you say anything to her?"

"I don't remember. She said I said something about another man. I may have. I just don't remember. I was really hurtin' when I went over there, and then when I saw her, all the old feelings came back. I remember leaving there very depressed, down."

"Now, Kevin," I said, "I want to take you to the evening hours of Friday night, September seventh. Where were you that evening?"

"I think I got off work around six. Somebody was having a problem with a washing machine in one of the apartments. So I was a little late. I went home and changed clothes, cleaned up and went to Stubby's Bar."

"Do you recall what time you may have gotten there?"

"About eight in the evening, I believe."

"Did you meet anyone there?"

"I had talked to Chris earlier, and he said that he and Sara were gonna be there, so I was planning on meeting them, but they didn't arrive 'til probably nine, nine-thirty."

"In the course of that evening, did you talk to anybody about Ms. Klein?"

"Later that night I talked to Sara. I told her I didn't understand what was going on. She knew that Josie had been over the Saturday night before, that she'd stayed overnight. She told me . . ."

Spencer jumped to his feet. "Your honor, if he's going to testify as far as to what Sara told him, I'm going to object as hearsay."

The judge looked at me. "Well, your honor," I said, "I'm not introducing this statement for the truth, I'm simply having him testify to the conversation as to what was said. I think it's relevant as to his state of mind that evening."

"I'll let it in for that purpose," said the judge.

"Mr. Murphy, to the best of your recollection, what did Sara tell you about Ms. Klein?"

"Well, really all she told me was that she didn't understand what Josie was doing, that she knew she had met this truck driver and had been seeing him. She told me that Josie had considered our relationship over, and she told me to forget about her."

"Did you forget about her?"

Kevin thought for a second. He looked at the back of the courtroom, trying to locate Josie. She had taken a seat in the very last row. He glanced at her, then at me and then looked at the jury. "I'd be lying if I said I did." He started to tear up. "I think it's difficult for anybody to understand how much I loved her." He reached in his back pocket for a handkerchief. He didn't have one. I reached for the box of Kleenex from the counsel table, walked up and placed it in front of him. He took a Kleenex and blew his nose. He took another one and dabbed his eyes. "I'm okay," he said.

As I sat down, I asked, "Kevin, did you know that Ms. Klein had Mr. Ronning over to her home that evening?"

"No, I didn't."

"Did anybody tell you that she was with Mr. Ronning that evening?"

"No, sir."

"Mr. Murphy, what time did you leave Stubby's Bar that night?"

"I was actually there until closing, so I left a little after one o'clock or so."

"From the time you arrived until you left, do you recall what you may have had to drink?"

"I was drinking beer. But you have to remember, I did leave for about an hour from ten to eleven o'clock. A friend of mine called, and he was having trouble getting his car started, so I went over and helped him. I got back to the bar about eleven."

"The question was, Mr. Murphy, do you recall how many drinks you had that evening from eight o'clock until you left at one-fifteen?"

"I believe I had about four or five beers."

"You're positive?"

"Yes."

"Is that more or less than you would usually have on a normal night at the bar?"

"That's about a normal amount."

"Do you recall how you were feeling when you left?"

"Feeling?" he said with a little puzzled look. "Feeling about what?"

"Did you feel the effects of the alcohol?"

"I'll tell ya what the alcohol did, Mr. Williams. I had just enough alcohol to start feeling sorry for myself. I remember just before closing I started to think about all the nights that Josie and I had sat there, and how lucky I felt leaving with her, the anticipation of going home with her. I had enough to drink to think about all that even though I thought I had put it out of my mind. It came back involuntarily, and I felt sorry for myself."

"When you left the bar, did you intend to go to Josie's home?"

"No, I didn't."

"What were you going to do?"

"I was gonna go to Chris' house. They had invited me over. I got in my car with every intention of going over there, and then I started to think about Josie and Lisa. I thought about her birthday. The next day would've been the day we would've taken her to the Renaissance Festival. Then I remembered the present. So like a dummy, I went home and picked it up and headed towards Josie's house. I didn't know what I was gonna do, I wasn't even thinking about it. I didn't know whether she would be up, whether she'd even be home. When I got there, I noticed the light was on in the kitchen. I walked up to the front door. I had the package under my arm. I looked in the window, and I couldn't see any movement. I tried the door and it was open. I figured Josie and Lisa were upstairs in bed. I went in, through the living room, into the kitchen and stood by the counter where the light was. I had a card for Lisa, but I noticed I hadn't signed it. There was a cup of pencils and pens that Josie kept on the cabinet. I took a pen from that and wrote 'Happy Birthday, Lisa. Love, Kevin,' and I left the card and the present. I was about to leave when I heard steps on the stairs. I turned around, and there was a man standing there, a big guy, in just his underwear. I instantly realized what I had done. I had interrupted Josie and her new boyfriend. At least I remember something like that flashing through my mind. Honest, it was a moment of panic. I didn't know what I was gonna do, and then he said, 'What the fuck you doin' in here?' I said, 'Hey man, I'm sorry, I didn't know anybody was here. I was just leaving a present for Lisa.' Then he said something like, 'I know you, you're the prick who's been terrorizing Josie. You can't let her alone, can you? I'm gonna break your fuckin' neck.' And in a second, he grabbed me and threw me back against the wall. I had my back on the counter. I could feel pain shoot down my legs. He knew he had me scared, I could tell. He stood there, a grin on his face. I said, 'Listen man, I just wanna get out of here. Somebody's gonna get hurt.' And he said, 'You fuckin' right, man. You!' and he came at me again and put me in a bear hug. We fell to the floor, we were wrestling around, I could hear things breaking. I know he hit his back on something because I heard him cry out a little bit. I know it was just a matter of moments, but it took everything I had. We broke apart, and he was standing in front of the door, the only door out of the kitchen. By then I could see he was really angry. I thought he was gonna break my neck."

Kevin had been leaning back against the back of the chair in the witness box. As he told how the scene unfolded, with each sentence his body seemed to inch its way forward until he leaned over the railing, his eyes fixed on the jurors.

166

"More in desperation," he continued, "I reached around my back and pulled out the buck knife I carried in a case, and I flipped the blade open. I stood there, shakin', the knife in my right hand, and I said, 'Hey, just let me out.' Then I heard Josie upstairs, 'Whoever's down there, you better get outta here. I just called the cops. They're on their way.' I looked at him and said, 'Man, just let me out.' He said, 'In a fuckin' casket.' I made a dash for the door. He put his arm out to stop me and I remember hitting his arm, and he closed in on me again in that bear hug, and he was squeezing, and we spun around, and we were on the floor, and I heard a groan. His arms . . . they just . . . they just slid off my back, and I was free. I stood up, the knife was still in my hand but he was cut . . . bleeding . . . I couldn't believe it. I let go of the knife, and it fell to the floor. I heard Josie say something again, and I dashed out the door."

During his testimony Kevin appeared to have picked out one juror, an older lady sitting in the front seat, the one closest to the witness box, and he kept eye contact with her, as if he was telling her the story. As he retold the event, his voice became strained. He struggled to finish, and then the tears rolled down his cheeks to collect on his beard. He took off his glasses and reached over for a Kleenex. He wiped his eyes. I tried to look at the juror he had been talking to without being obvious. I could tell she was holding back tears as well. Kevin finally put his glasses back on and looked at me.

"What did you do after that?" I asked.

"I remember driving away, my whole body shaking, terrified. I've never been in a situation like that. I remembered the man's face when I got up, the shock, the bleeding, but I certainly didn't think he was going to die."

"Where did you go?" I asked.

"I drove around. I remember driving out into the country. I ended up on the other side of Avon by Pelican Lake. By then it was getting light out. I had the radio station on. I got the six o'clock news. That's when I heard that the police had been called to Josie's residence and that a man had been stabbed and that he had died at the hospital. I tell ya, I couldn't have felt worse. I just broke down and cried for the longest time. I couldn't believe it. I had never hurt a soul in my life. I had never even been in a fight, and then to find out that this man died. I wondered about him. I wondered where he was from, about his family."

Kevin reached for a Kleenex to dab his eyes. The tears he didn't catch hung precariously on his beard, glistening. I wasn't sure if he was going to proceed, so I broke in. "What did you do after that?"

He turned from me to fix his gaze on the woman juror. "I called my friend Chris Younger, and we agreed to meet. I met him maybe a half an hour later. He asked me what happened, and I told him. I believe I did tell him that I cut the guy. I told him we were in a fight and that I believe I cut the guy. Like he said here, he told me we had to go to the police, that they knew who had done it, that there was no use. He also said that if it was an accident, they would understand. So we went to a gas station, and we called the cops. I told them that I was coming in, but they stopped me before I got there."

"Mr. Murphy," I said, "just so this jury understands, when you left Stubby's that night and headed to Ms. Klein's home, did you have any knowledge that Mr. Ronning was there?"

"No, sir."

"When you saw Mr. Ronning there, when he confronted you in the kitchen, at any time did you form an intent to kill him?"

"Mr. Williams, with God as my witness, it never crossed my mind. I only wanted to get out."

"When the two of you faced off in the kitchen, did he ever offer you the opportunity to leave through the kitchen door?"

"He wouldn't! I've thought about that many times. I never understood. I just wanted to leave, but for some reason he wasn't gonna let me."

"Why do you think he wasn't going to let you?"

"I don't know."

"What was going through your mind before you made that last dash for the door?"

"He said I was gonna get hurt, and I could tell by the look on his face that he meant it. Like I said, I saw an anger there that's hard to explain. As far as I could see, I wasn't gettin' out alive, or at least not without something broken."

"Thank you, Mr. Murphy. I have nothing further."

Spencer barely got to say, "Mr. Murphy," when the judge interrupted and said, "This may be a good time for the morning recess."

It had already gone beyond his normal recess time, and I suspect in deference to me, he had changed his plans, this once.

I watched the jury file out. I could tell Kevin's testimony had an impact on them. They looked somber, nobody glanced either way, intent on keeping their feelings to themselves.

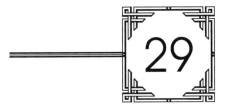

I met Kevin in the conference room. I could tell he was pleased with himself. "How'd it go?" he asked.

"I think it went great. But you know what struck me in your testimony, something I had never thought of before. Why do you think he was so intent on keeping you in that kitchen, and why did he say the things he said? It had to be one of two reasons. Either he had this macho thing about himself, that he was just going to clean your clock because that's who he was, or that, based on something Josie may have told him, he believed you were really dangerous. Do you think she would have told him stories about you?"

"What kind of stories?" he asked.

"Well, he obviously thought you were somehow a threat. I don't know. Say, for example, that she had told him that you had been beating her up or maybe even that you had sexually assaulted her."

"What are you talking about?" he asked.

"Kevin," I said, "for him to stand his ground with you standing there with a knife, when he doesn't know you, has no idea who you are, doesn't make sense. At least it doesn't to me. But say Josie had told him that you were an annoyance, a pain in the ass, physically abusive, that you'd forced her to have sex the weekend before, for example, to give him some reason to be really pissed at you. Then it starts to make some sense. All I'm asking is, is she capable of doing that?"

"I don't know, Mr. Williams," he said. "There's something more to her than I know."

"I doubt we'll ever find out anyway," I said, "but it may be a seed I can plant in the jury's mind."

I looked at my watch. "We better get back in."

Kevin stood by my side until the bailiff rapped the session in order. I motioned him back to the witness stand. As everybody settled in, the judge said, "Mr. Murphy, you're still under oath."

Spencer opened up a notebook, and I glanced over. It appeared that most of the questions he intended to ask were written out with little boxes in front of them.

"Mr. Murphy," he started, "would it be fair to say that you were upset when Ms. Klein asked you to move out?"

"I was upset, yes."

"And you were angry?"

"Hurt, yes."

"And in your own mind, you still loved her. Correct?"

"Very much."

"And you couldn't understand why she was asking you to leave. Correct?"

"No, I couldn't."

"And you've heard some comments made here in court that Miss Klein and other people believed that you were obsessed with her. Do you believe you were obsessed with her?"

"I was in love with her."

"To the point that you wouldn't leave her out of your sight. Isn't that true? To the point you got upset if she even talked to another man in your presence. Isn't that true? To the point that you threatened that, if you ever saw her with another man, she better watch her back. Isn't that true?"

170

I stood up. "Your honor, I ask that the prosecutor let Mr. Murphy answer one question before he proceeds to a new one."

"Fine," Spencer said. "Let's go to the last question. Mr. Murphy, isn't it true that after Ms. Klein asked you to move out, that you were at her home on one evening, that you were angry because she wouldn't let you move back in and that you told her, if you ever saw her with another man, she'd better watch her back? Isn't that what you told her?"

"I believe it was something to that effect."

"And you meant it, didn't you?"

"Not really."

"You heard Sara Pendergast testify, did you not, that she thought you were obsessed with Josie Klein, and you heard Chris Younger testify that he told you that you had to get over her, get her out of your mind?'

"I heard that."

"So people who knew you well believed you were obsessed with Josie, but you do not believe that, is that what you're telling us?"

"I'm not sure what you mean by obsessed."

"That you couldn't get her out of your mind, that you wouldn't let her out of your life. That even though she said your relationship was over, you wouldn't take that for an answer?"

"I wanted her back, yes."

"In fact, you wanted her back so bad that you were willing to kill anyone who appeared to take your place, isn't that true?"

"No, it isn't."

"Lets go to the early morning hours of September 8, 1994. It's your testimony that the only reason you went to the home that night was because you wanted to leave a present for Lisa."

"That was my purpose, yes."

"Prior to that night, you had visited Lisa quite often, isn't that true?"

"Yes."

"And when you visited Lisa, was that at her home or did Josie let you take her out?"

"Like I said, she let me take her out a couple times."

"The truth is, Josie never tried to prevent you from seeing Lisa, did she?"

"Not really."

"So if you had a birthday present for Lisa, there would be nothing preventing you from calling Josie and asking to come over and drop it off or to pick Lisa up. You could've done that, right?"

"I could've done that, yes."

"You had that present for several months before her birthday, correct?"

"Yes."

"And as far as you were concerned, it was a beautiful present. You knew Lisa would enjoy it. Correct?"

"I believe so, yes."

"And part of the fun of giving a present is to see the reaction of the person when they open the present. Wouldn't you say that's fair?"

"I believe so."

"So I suppose you would agree that it would've made more sense for you to simply call Josie and make arrangements to deliver that present to Lisa personally, so you could experience the joy. Don't you think that would make more sense?"

"I suppose it would, but remember, I told Josie the Wednesday before that, that I was never gonna see her again."

"Oh, that's right," said Spencer, "the Wednesday before, when you took her the rose at her job. Let's talk about that for a moment. Do you recall telling Ms. Klein that you knew she was seeing another man and that this was good-bye. You were never going to see her again?"

"That was the purpose for my visit."

"So in your mind, that wasn't a threat, that was just a statement of fact. Is that what you're telling us?"

"Yes, sir."

"So, if Ms. Klein took it as a threat, she was mistaken. Is that what you're telling us?"

"She was mistaken."

"So if that was intended to be your last contact with Ms. Klein, why didn't you bring Lisa's present with you as well?"

"I don't know. I didn't think of it."

"Had you been drinking on Wednesday?"

"No, sir."

"On Wednesday afternoon, cold sober, in a final moment with Ms. Klein, you thought about buying her a rose and saying good-bye, but you didn't think about Lisa. Is that correct?"

"I didn't think of Lisa, no."

"But at two o'clock Saturday morning, after sitting in a bar all night, drinking beer, you thought about Lisa and dropping off her present?"

"I did think of Lisa. If you're asking me was it dumb to go over there, I've already said it was."

"You want us to believe that you didn't know that Mr. Ronning was there. Is that right?"

"I didn't know he was there."

"Didn't you see his car out front?"

"I didn't pay any attention."

"You had to park directly behind it, did you not?"

"I believe so."

"In fact, you had to walk around it to get to the sidewalk, correct?"

"I told you, I didn't pay any attention."

"If it was just a matter of leaving a present, why didn't you leave it on the porch?"

"I was afraid somebody would steal it."

"Did you believe Ms. Klein was home?"

"I knew somebody was home."

"Why didn't you knock on the door and leave it on the porch for them to find?"

"I didn't think of it."

"The reason you didn't think of it, Mr. Murphy is because that wasn't your plan, was it?"

"I don't understand."

"Your plan was to get into that house to see what Ms. Klein was doing, who she was with, and if you were caught, you'd use the present as an excuse. Isn't that what you were thinking?"

"No, sir."

"Based on everything you had heard that night, you knew that another man was there, didn't you?"

"No way."

"And you wanted to find out who it was and confront him. Isn't that the reason you went there?"

"I went there, like I said, to drop off a present."

"When Mr. Ronning confronted you in the kitchen, when he came to the bottom of the steps, the words were said, 'What the fuck are you doing here?' It's your testimony that Mr. Ronning said that. Is that correct?"

"That's what he said."

"But if Ms. Klein testified that it was you who uttered those words, she would be lying?"

"Not lying, just mistaken."

"Mr. Ronning was in just his underwear, a pair of brief shorts. Correct?"

"Yes."

"He had no weapons. Correct?"

"No, sir."

"He didn't grab any weapon. There was nothing in the kitchen he used as a weapon. Correct?"

"No, sir."

"And when he came at you, as you testified, he didn't try to strike you with anything. Correct?"

"He punched me in the face with his fist, but no weapon. No, sir."

"The only injury you sustained was that bruise to the cheek, the one we see on the picture your attorney introduced, is that correct?"

"That was the only visible one, but my ribs ached for days afterwards. He almost crushed me to death."

"Well, let's compare your injuries to Mr. Ronning's. You saw the pictures introduced by Dr. Mueller. Is that correct?"

"Yes, I did."

"You saw the pictures of Mr. Ronning's scalp with the contusions on the top of his head. Correct?"

"Yes, I did."

"You saw the pictures of his back with numerous long scratches. Correct?"

"Yes, I did."

"And you saw the pictures of all the other abrasions and contusions on his body. Correct?"

"Yes."

"And finally you saw the picture of the open wound on his left chest. Correct?"

"Yes, sir."

"And the only visible wound you sustained was the bruise to your cheek. Correct?"

Kevin didn't answer.

"Isn't that correct, Mr. Murphy?"

"You have to remember, we wrestled for a long time. I don't know what all happened when we were rolling around on the floor."

"Well, I want to understand this, Mr. Murphy. You're claiming it's self-defense, yet Mr. Ronning is the one who's all beat up."

"Objection, your honor," I said, "argumentative."

"Never mind," said Spencer. "It doesn't require an answer. Mr. Murphy," he continued, "how long do you believe you and Mr. Ronning fought before you pulled out that knife?"

"I don't know. It was just a matter of minutes."

"And if I understand your testimony correctly, other than the first punch he threw, he never tried to throw another punch at you. Correct?"

"I don't remember, nothing that landed, anyway. I think he wanted to get closer to me, I think . . ."

Spencer interrupted, "Mr. Murphy you've answered the question. So if I understand correctly, Mr. Murphy, at the point you pulled out the knife, Mr. Ronning had hit you once with his fist on your cheek, and he had gotten you in a bear hug and threw you across the kitchen once, and you had wrestled on the floor once. Is that correct?"

"To the best of my memory, yes."

"And you want this jury to believe that at that point, based on what had happened, you were in fear of your own life, and you believed the only thing that you could do was take that knife out and—use it to protect yourself. Correct?"

"It was more than that."

"You're gonna tell us it was the threats, right?"

"Not only the threats, but the way he said them. He told me he was gonna break my neck, and I believed it. I could see it in his face."

"Prior to pulling out that knife, Mr. Murphy, you never made any effort to try and get out the kitchen door. Isn't that correct?"

"I couldn't. He was standing right there."

"And the only time you made an effort was when you heard Josie holler down the steps that she'd called the cops; you knew then you were in trouble. You knew you shouldn't be there. That's when you took the knife out. You wanted to get the hell out of there before the cops came. Isn't that true?"

"No, sir, it isn't."

"Mr. Murphy, let me suggest something. Isn't it true that you knew Ms. Klein was home with her new friend that Friday night?"

"I didn't know that, no."

"Well, when you were dating Ms. Klein, did you typically end up at Stubby's Bar on a Friday night?"

"Quite often."

"Friday night was a night that you and Ms. Klein would go out. Correct?"

"Normally, yes."

"And she had not been coming to Stubby's Bar as often since the two of you had broken up. Correct?"

"She had been there a few times, but, no, I wouldn't call it often."

"And you understood that one of the reasons she did not come to Stubby's as often was because she was trying to avoid you. Correct?"

"I don't know. I don't know what was in her mind."

"And Ms. Pendergast had told you that Friday night, at Stubby's, that Ms. Klein was seeing another man and that you should just forget about her. Isn't that correct?"

"Something to that effect, yes."

"But you had already told us that you did not put her out of your mind, did you?"

"No, I didn't."

"And as you were leaving Stubby's Bar that night, it would be fair to say that your feelings for her were still there. Correct?"

"Yes sir."

"And so you really put two and two together, didn't you Mr. Murphy? If Ms. Klein wasn't at Stubby's, and you knew she was seeing another man, and Friday night was the night that she would go out, when you started toward her house that night, you really expected to see her there with her new male friend, didn't you?"

"I told you, I didn't go there for that purpose. I went there to drop off a present."

"I'm just suggesting maybe you had another motive, Mr. Murphy."

"Well, I didn't."

"So you've told us. But I want to suggest, Mr. Murphy, that was your only motive. I want to suggest that the only reason you went over there was to see who Ms. Klein was going with. Isn't that correct?"

"No, sir."

"And you used the gift as a guise for entering the home. Isn't that correct?"

"No, sir."

"And when you were confronted by Mr. Ronning, in your frustration, anger, and disappointment at being dumped by Ms. Klein, you decided to take it out on this poor guy who had no idea who you were. Isn't that correct?"

"No sir."

"And when you started to fight with him, you realized you weren't gonna get the better of him, so you had to equal the odds. You took out your knife and stabbed him. Isn't that what happened?"

"No, sir."

"Mr. Murphy, if it happened the way you told this jury, in your words, 'accidentally,' why didn't you just stay. Why didn't you try to help this poor man?"

"I don't know. I've thought about that many times. I guess I was just afraid. I knew he wasn't alone, I had heard Josie's voice. I knew she would get him help."

"Actually, Mr. Murphy, you were hoping you could get out and then nobody would even know it was you?"

"No, sir."

The prosecutor looked at his notebook. He had been checking the boxes as he went along. The courtroom grew quiet. Moments later he raised his head, "Mr. Murphy," and Kevin and he stared at each other. Finally Spencer said, "Never mind, I have nothing further."

The judge looked at me. "Mr. Williams?"

Kevin had held up better than I expected. I wanted him off the stand. "I have nothing further, your honor."

The judge looked at the clock. "It's a little early, but we'll take our lunch recess. If I can see the attorneys for a moment."

Spencer and I followed the judge into his chambers. "What do you have left?" he asked.

"All I've got are some character witnesses, your honor."

He turned to Spencer.

"I may call Dr. Mueller in rebuttal."

"For what purpose?"

"I'm not sure," he said. "I want to talk to him over lunch, to tell him what Mr. Murphy testified to and see what he says. At least I want to keep my options open."

"Well, if you're going to do that," said the judge, "you try and get him back here later this afternoon, 'cause I would like to talk about jury instructions, and it looks to me that we can submit this to the jury tomorrow morning. What do you think, Bob?"

"I would just as soon wait until tomorrow to make closing arguments."

"Yeah, I'm not going to put the jury out late in the afternoon," replied the judge.

When I got back to the courtroom, the deputy had already taken Kevin back to the jail. I walked out the back door, and Tony was in the hall. "I have all of the witnesses lined up. I have 'em in a conference room at the end of the hall."

We had picked three people who had worked with Kevin over a period of years who were willing to come in and tell the jury what kind of young man he was. I followed Tony down to the conference room, and I greeted each of them. We spent the next half hour or so going over how I was going to present their testimony. We were done by 12:30 and everybody left for lunch. Tony and I walked over to Jack's Café. After we had ordered, he asked, "How's it going?"

"Kevin really did a nice job," I said. "He embellished his testimony a little bit, he threw in a few things he hadn't told me. But you know, when it was all over, you couldn't help but feel sorry for him. It always amazes me, Tony, that, in the course of a trial, it's like a football game, you can feel momentum shifts, and I felt that during Kevin's testimony. I know some of the jurors were glued to every word. He just came across as a very sincere, honest person. The problem he has is he shouldn't have been there in the first place. The only way the jury is going to acquit him is if they absolutely buy his story that this guy intended to break his neck and that he had no way out. The judge wants to talk about jury instructions this afternoon. I know what he's going to tell them, he'll tell the jury that Kevin had a duty to retreat. It's not like a straight self-defense argument. He put himself in the predicament in the first place. But, Tony, you and I both know, if the jury ends up not liking Ronning, wondering what the hell a guy with a pretty wife like that is doing chasing some floozy here in St. Cloud . . . I know they didn't like Josie. They could just decide to let Kevin go home. All I have to do is give them a reasonable doubt, something they can hang their collective conscience on."

I had been staring across the café as I talked, at a table where a woman had pointed at us as we sat down. She seemed to catch my stare and quickly looked away. I looked at Tony. "Have you heard anything from Ken?" I asked.

"No, I stopped and talked to Heidi on the way out. They're apparently making arrangements today. My guess is the wake will be tomorrow and the funeral Wednesday morning."

"God, I still can't believe it," I said. "How in the hell can things like that happen? I simply don't understand. I hate to think about going to that wake. There's been so much gloom in my life. I can't imagine doing it again."

"I'll go with you," Tony said. "Maybe the two of us can hold each other together."

"You know, Tony, when I'm sitting there in court, my mind will wander off. I can see Kate and Faye and I can feel the emotions welling up and I just have to turn it off. I do anything to take my mind off of it—God it hurts. I just wonder how long this is going to go on. I can remember the number of times I've had clients screaming from their jail cells, 'When am I going to get my fuckin' trial? I wanna get in court. I wanna get this over with.' And I would tell them, 'Look, one of the best allies you've got is time. If you're convicted now, that stricken family is going to be in there screaming to have you hung. They're hurting, and getting even with you is the only thing they're thinking about. Give it a little time. Feelings subside.'" I looked over at him. "To tell you the truth, Tony, most of the time it works. But I don't know, now having felt the loss myself, I can't imagine these feelings are ever going to subside, that I'm ever going to feel different. The last time I was in court before Kate's death, it was on a sentencing of a young man who had killed another guy, drunk driving, and the decedent's sister got up and read a statement about what the loss of her brother meant. And I'll tell you the truth, I had a hard time keeping from openly crying right there in court. Can you imagine what sort of impression that would have had on my client? And when she was telling the judge of her pain, it was all in the abstract. Now I know exactly what she was saying, how she felt . . . I don't think I'll ever get over it. There's a void in my heart that's impossible to fill. They say time heals all wounds . . . God, Tony, I hope so."

Tony had been silently listening. "You're right," he said. "You know, I had to deal with the people who lost a loved one right there, moments after it happened, and I didn't even know the person, but it would just tear me up. No matter how many times I did it, it never got any better. But really, as a matter of survival, I've learned to put up a rough exterior to really hide my feelings. I've had to. Now, sometimes people mistake it for being callous or just that I'm a crusty old fart. But that isn't true. I'm hurting, Bob, maybe not as much as you, but I'm hurting."

We finished lunch and walked back to the courthouse. The afternoon went quickly. I put on the three character witnesses. The most interesting one was the last one. His name was Gene Bikel. He was the president of the Jolly Rodder's Club, a biker's club in central Minnesota. Actually, Mr. Bikel was an upstanding citizen, vice-president of one of the local banks and had been a biker for thirty years. It was Mr. Bikel and Kevin who had put together the bike-a-thon to raise money for the children's floor at the hospital. Of course, he had nothing but good to say of Kevin. All three character witnesses were there for one purpose, to show the jury that you could be a biker without having to be a mean son-of-a-bitch. Unfortunately, for Kevin, that was the popular conception of anybody who drove a motorcycle and wore black leather togs. The character witnesses were to change that. I think it worked.

As. Mr. Bikel left the stand, I told the judge, "The defense rests." The prosecutor stood up. "Your honor, with the court's indulgence, I'd ask for a couple minutes to see if Dr. Mueller has arrived. I do have one rebuttal witness."

I had no idea what Spencer was up to. I had to just wait and see. We sat there, quietly. Within a couple minutes, the bailiff walked back in, Dr. Mueller behind him. The judge motioned him up to the witness box, "You're still under oath, Doctor," and he took the stand.

"Doctor," said Spencer, "assume that I have that knife, Exhibit Number 15, in my hand, my right hand, and assume that Mr. Ronning is standing in front of me, preventing me from walking through a door. And assume further that I want to get out that door, and to do so, I make a dash and in the process, Mr. Ronning puts his left arm up to prevent me from leaving. He grabs me, we spin around and wrestle and fall to the floor. In the process, the knife I have in my right hand enters his body, and he receives the wound that you noted in your autopsy and that you testified to here. Doctor, the question is: Based on that hypothetical I just gave you, as a scenario leading up to the actual infliction of the wound, is that consistent with, or could that produce the wound that you actually found in the body of Mr. Ronning?"

"No, in my opinion, it could not."

"And why not, doctor?"

"If you recall my testimony, the wound in the body has a depth a quarter inch deeper than the length of the blade. As I explained, the only way that can happen is if the knife strikes the body with such force that the flesh is indented. That, it seems to me, would require a conscious effort to strike and to strike with some force, which I do not see happening in the type of struggle you just described."

"Thank you doctor, I have nothing further."

Spencer turned to me again with that shit-eating grin on his face and said, "Your witness."

The doctor's testimony didn't take me by surprise, it was the same thing Carol had told me Thanksgiving weekend. Many times I had tried to picture in my mind how it could have happened consistent with what Kevin told me, what kind of force was needed to produce that kind of wound.

I stood up. "Doctor," I began, "assume I'm Mr. Murphy, and I have the knife in my right hand," and I made a motion as if I was carrying a knife. "And Mr. Ronning is standing in front of me, blocking my exit, and my passage by him requires me to go by his left hand side, do you have that picture, doctor?"

"Yes, I do."

"And in my panic to get out, I rush to the door. Mr. Ronning grabs me with his left arm preventing me from going through the doorway, and he puts his right arm around me and has me in a bear hug. Where is the knife, doctor?"

He thought for a second. "It depends on where your arm is."

"If it's down at my side," I continued, "that's one thing, but if I'm holding it up against my chest anticipating that I'm going to have to throw myself at Mr. Ronning's arm with all my force to get by, it would be up here, wouldn't it?" And I brought my right hand up across my right chest.

"It could be," he said.

"In that event, doctor, the knife would be in approximately the area of the wound to Mr. Ronning's left side, isn't that correct?"

"In that area, yes."

"And assume, doctor, that in the force of the struggle, we fall to the kitchen floor, me on top of Mr. Ronning, his back hits the floor. Wouldn't it be reasonable to opine, that if the point of the blade was against Mr. Ronning's body before the fall, that the blade could've entered the body with that much force and to the depth you found based just on the momentum of the fall without any effort extended by me at all?"

He looked at me, going through the scenario in his mind again, he hesitated.

"Isn't that a reasonable possibility, doctor?"

"I suppose it is."

"In fact, doctor, isn't that as equally consistent with how this wound could've been inflicted as the hypothetical set forth by the prosecutor?"

"I would say it is probably consistent, yes."

"Thank you, doctor."

The judge looked at the prosecutor, "Mr. Moore?"

"I have nothing further."

I could tell Spencer's enthusiasm had been deflated some.

The judge turned to the jury. "Ladies and gentlemen of the jury, both parties have rested. The attorneys and I are going to talk about legal instructions this afternoon and tomorrow morning you'll receive closing arguments and the jury instructions. Then you will start deliberations. I want to let you know that once you start deliberations, you'll be together until a decision is reached, so you should all make whatever arrangements you need to in case you end up staying here overnight. Of course, the county will put you up in a motel. Just to be safe, I would bring a change of clothes along. Anybody have any questions? Okay. I'll see counsel in chambers."

"Well gentlemen," said the judge, "I assume you've had an opportunity to look over my proposed jury instructions, pretty much boiler plate. I did take Spencer's memorandum into consideration. I've added the additional paragraph to the self-defense."

"Your Honor," interjected Spencer, "I really don't believe he's entitled to a self-defense instruction. He wasn't invited over. For all intents and purposes, he's in that house as a burglar, he never got anybody's permission. This guy's standing there in his underwear and the defendant pulls out a knife and ices him. Where's the self-defense?"

"Listen Spencer," said the judge, "we've already argued that point. Everybody agrees that he shouldn't have been there, but once he's confronted by Ronning, then it's a question of whether he acted reasonably under all of the circumstances. I'm going to instruct the jury that because of the situation he put himself into, he had an obligation to try and retreat, to back out of it. He had an obligation to convey that to Ronning. So if the jury believes his testimony, he did that. Then the next question is whether the danger he perceived was reasonable and whether he acted reasonably under the circumstances. That's entirely up to the jury, Spencer. That's what your closing argument can be all about."

"Well, I don't agree," said Spencer.

"Nobody's asking you to agree. This is what I'm going to do."

Spencer sat there shaking his head.

"Bob, how about you?" asked the judge.

"Well, of course, I'd just as soon not have that language in there but I think that's what the law is."

We all sat there paging through the jury instructions one last time. The judge looked at me. "Have you heard anything about the preparations for the funeral of your legal assistant?"

"Nothing definite, but I believe the wake will be tomorrow and the funeral Wednesday morning. I hope that jury doesn't take days to decide this thing. It's going to be hard enough sitting through that funeral without wondering what's going on here."

Spencer chuckled a little. "That's wishful thinking. Shouldn't take that jury more than a couple hours to convict your guy."

I ignored him. "Well, judge, I don't see anything else we would have to add," I said. "If there's nothing further, I think I'll head home."

As I reached the elevator, Tony was sitting on one of the benches. "That was interesting," he said. "I bet Spencer wishes he hadn't brought Mueller all the way back. His big hypothetical kind of bit him in the ass, didn't it?"

184

"I get to thank Carol for that," I said. "She brought that point up a long time ago. I'm going to stop at the office, why don't you stop by?"

It was close to four o'clock when I pulled up to my office. The receptionist, Heidi, was on the phone as we walked in, tears were running down her cheeks, soaking the notepad in front of her. "Oh, Bob is here," she said, "I'll see you tomorrow," and she hung up. "That was Jackie, she was telling me what happened. God, it was just terrible."

"What did she say?" I asked.

"Oh, don't make me repeat it, I don't want to go over it again."

She put her hands over her face, sobbing. I reached for my messages, the top one said Ken had called. I motioned Tony back to my office, picked up the phone and called.

"Thanks for calling back, Bob," he said. "I just wanted to let you know what the arrangements are."

Just as he said that, Tony, who had been paging through the local newspaper, dropped the obituary section in front of me. There, staring at me, was Faye's picture. I read the obituary as I listened to Ken tell me almost the same thing over the phone. The wake was going to be at the Miller Funeral Home starting at one o'clock on Tuesday, with prayer services at 7:00 p.m. The funeral was Wednesday morning at ten at St. Luke's Parish. I looked up at Tony, biting my lower lip, shaking my head. Ken finally stopped. "Ken, I still don't understand what happened. How could that happen?"

"The sheriff thinks she slipped on the top step and fell all the way down. She had a broken neck."

"Did anybody see it?" I asked.

"That balcony runs the length of the whole building," he said. "They talked to all of the other guests. Nobody saw a thing. She was just going to check on the boys. Bob, it was just a spur of the moment thing."

"How are you guys holding up?" I asked.

"It's been awful. The boys don't understand. They cried almost all day Sunday. We had to have a doctor give them a sedative. Today I think they're just stunned. There's been a lot of activity, people trying to console them. My mother's been here since early Sunday morning. You know, Bob, it's terrible. One minute we were a happy family on a weekend break and moments later . . . everything's shattered. There's so much I wanted to say to her at the hospital, but they told me she couldn't hear." His voice started to quiver.

"Listen Ken," I said, "I have to be in court in the morning. There's nothing I can do about it, but Tony and I will be there tomorrow afternoon. If there's anything you need either of us to do, just let us know, please."

"Thanks, Bob," he said. "I know it isn't that far from your own loss." You know what I'm going through."

"Tony," I said as I hung up, "seems to me I can do one of two things, I can go home and work on my closing argument, or we can go to the Lodge and get stinkin' drunk."

"No, Bob, there's a third alternative. We can just go have a drink, and then you can go home and work on your closing argument. Bob, you used to be able to have one or two drinks and then just say goodbye. Now, you have to drink yourself into a stupor every time. That's got to stop. I know you're hurting, but becoming a drunk isn't the answer."

"I know," I said. "I've thought a lot about it myself. I should know better, especially with all the clients I've had over the years who tried to find escape in the bottle. All I need is time, Tony. But you're right, let's go have a drink. I'll tell you what I'm going to tell the jury, and then we'll go home."

"Sounds good to me," he said.

As we walked out, Heidi was still sitting there sobbing. I put my hand on her shoulder. "Why don't you just close it up and go home."

"Can I?" she sobbed.

"Why not?" I replied. "I think we'll just close for the next couple days."

Twenty minutes later, Tony and I were ordering a drink at the Log Lodge. My throat was dry so I ordered a tall beer. When it came, I took a big swallow. "You know what I'd like to have?" I said.

Tony put his beer down. "What?"

"A cigarette."

"Don't even think about it," he said.

"I just saw that lady over there light up and take that first big drag. I've thought about starting a lot lately. It looked so good."

"How long has it been?"

"Six years."

"Look, it would be a big mistake," he said. "You don't need 'em."

"Yeah, but the only reason I quit was because they were telling me I was cutting my life short. Now I don't have anything to live for anyway."

"That's bullshit, and you know it. What about Carol?"

"She's going to be a vet someplace. She'll have her own life, family."

"That's what I mean," said Tony. "You can be part of her family."

We each took another swallow of our beer.

"You know what we ought to do?" he said. "We should look at starting our own business."

"Like what?" I asked.

"Something where we can be outside in the summer, you know, like landscaping or maybe a greenhouse, something like that."

"Yeah, I can see the two of us trying to sell daisies," I said.

"No, think about it," Tony said. "We don't have to make a whole lot of money, just enough to get by on. We'd be our own bosses, let somebody else deal with the scoundrels of this world."

We spent the next hour and a half sipping beer and fantasizing about this great garden shop we could start. We'd start in early spring, in our own greenhouses, grow our own plants, and then bring them out to a roadside stand in the summer and sell them. It wasn't really a plan. I didn't think we were even serious. It was our way of keeping our minds occupied, away from the sadness of the next several days. It's amazing what the human mind will do to get you through.

I was home by eight, sober. I shuffled around the house for a while trying to keep busy. I went out to the sunroom to look at the plants. I flipped on the light. I shook my head, yellow leaves were laying on the floor, plants drooped in every pot. I knew some of them were beyond saving. I imagined that Tony would have second thoughts about having me as a partner in any greenhouse venture. The thought brought a smile to my face. I went about rescuing the plants I could and threw out the rest.

In the back of my mind, I was putting the finishing touches on my closing argument. At ten thirty, I turned on Letterman, took out a yellow pad and in big, bold strokes, made an outline. I finally crawled in bed about midnight knowing I wasn't going to sleep. I left the curtains open, the night was bright. A three-quarter moon bounced off the snow. Somewhere close I could hear the hoot of a barred owl. I had been seeing it most of the fall. The frogs would sit on the tar road after dark, absorbing the leftover heat. The owl had picked a sign post along a curve as a perch. Every night as I approached the curve, I would have to slow down to make sure I didn't hit it as it swooped before my lights. Somewhere in the distance, a great horned owl joined in, the two actually serenaded me to sleep.

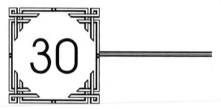

I had a nervous young man on my hands the next morning as I sat down in the conference room.

"What do you think's gonna happen?" he asked.

"Kevin," I said, "everything has gone exactly as I hoped. There've been no surprises. I think the jury likes you. At least they don't dislike you. You did a nice job on your testimony. The character witnesses did nice jobs. All I can do is make my pitch, and we'll see."

"Right," he said. "You know I'm a minister at the jail. We had a little service last night. Everybody was praying for me. I told 'em I just had to put my fate in the hands of God. Whatever happens will be what he wants to happen."

"Well, I'd like to be a little more positive than that," I said as I started towards the courtroom.

There it is again, I thought. Faith. Faith that God has some divine plan in all this, that all we have to do is ask, and he'll intervene. Who knows, I thought, maybe he does. We could certainly use him.

I walked into the courtroom, Kevin trailing behind me. Everybody was already there. The jury in the jury box. I looked at the clock, two minutes to nine. I barely took my chair when the bailiff rapped the gavel. The judge walked in and said, "Good morning." He looked at Spencer, "Mr. Moore, if you're ready."

Spencer stood up, he wore a blue pinstriped suit, white shirt with a dark blue tie. He strolled to the jury box, tall, thin, handsome, in his five-hundred-dollar tailored suit. "If it please the Court, Mr. Williams, ladies and gentlemen of the jury. We've now reached the part of the trial where Mr. Williams and I give to you what we call closing arguments. It's our summation of what we believe the evidence shows. The judge will then give you the law in this matter, the jury instructions, and then you're going to retire to the jury room to deliberate. In my opening statement, I gave you what I called the 'road map,' what I expected the evidence to show, and I believe I led you down that road. I believe the evidence proves exactly what I said it would, that we have a case of love gone bad."

For the next half an hour, Spencer laid out, detail by detail, the events of the whole evening, ending up with Dr. Mueller's testimony and going over each exhibit, bringing to the jury's attention each bruise, scratch, cut and contusion on Mr. Ronning's body.

"Mr. Williams admitted, in his opening statement, that most of what happened that night is not disputed. The defendant admitted he made a mistake, that he shouldn't have been there. He even acknowledged that it was a stupid thing to do. He didn't have anybody's permission to walk in.

"What he wants you to believe, though, and what Mr. Williams is going to argue, is that he never had any intent to cause any problems when he walked into that home. He's going to want you to believe that once Mr. Ronning came down those steps to confront him, that he only wanted to leave, that he pulled that knife out for that one purpose—to get out, and he thinks he's going to get away with it because there's no one to contradict him. See, only two people know what really happened that night and, of course, one of them is dead. So Mr. Murphy believes he can tell us whatever he wants to and there's no one to contradict him. But he's wrong. There is. William Shakespeare wrote, 'Murder, though it have no tongue, will speak.' Even in his silence, Mr. Ronning can tell us what happened. All you have to do is look at the photographs, and there's a stark statement of what Mr. Ronning went through before that defendant decided he was going to finish him off by plunging a knife in his chest. He claims it's self-defense but look at the evidence. Who's beat up? Look at the contusions on the head. Look at the cut marks and scratches on the back. Look at all the bruises. Remember Dr. Mueller's testimony? Those aren't the kind of wounds you could see on somebody you would consider the aggressor. Remember, he called them defensive wounds and for a good reason, Mr. Ronning was trying to defend himself. It wasn't Mr. Ronning's voice that said, 'What the fuck are you doing here?' It was the defendant's. Ms. Klein should certainly recognize his voice. What does that tell us about this defendant's state of mind at that moment? Remember, what did he tell Josie just weeks earlier? 'If I ever see you with another guy, you better watch your back.' What did he tell her that Wednesday night? 'I know you're seeing another guy, you're never going to see me again.' Remember she told you, both in the way he said it and in his manner, she took it as a threat. And then we know that he was obsessed with her. He admits it. He couldn't get her out of his mind. Even that night, at Stubby's Bar, everybody he talks to . . . it's Josie this and Josie that. They can tell him it's over, put her away, but he can't. So that's the state of mind he's in when he drives over there that night. He can tell us that he didn't expect to see somebody over there with her. Think about it, ladies and gentlemen, think about this history of their relationship. Think about what they did on Friday nights. Why, if he knew she was seeing another man, would he assume that she was going to be alone on a Friday night? It doesn't make sense; it doesn't ring true.

"I believe he went home and got that present for Lisa but not for the reason he told you. It was going to be his excuse. See, if he got caught in there, he was going to say, 'Oh, I was just dropping this off.' No, ladies and gentlemen of the jury, don't be taken in by that line. If it was just a matter of giving Lisa a present, think of all the other things he could've done."

Spencer concluded by taking the jury through every charge in the indictment; from first degree felony murder to simple burglary of a dwelling. He told the jury how most of the elements weren't even in dispute. "The only question was," he said again, "one of intent."

190

"You know, ladies and gentlemen, throughout the charges you will hear the word 'intent.' I know the defendant will argue that he never had a criminal intent. But as you know, actions speak louder than words. You have a right to look at everything the defendant did in the weeks preceding that terrible night. You have a right to think about the things he said to Josie and to the other people, then see whether his actions don't belie what he's trying to tell you his intent was. I'm sure when you do that, you'll reach one conclusion: That in his own words, his anger, frustration, disappointment, hurt over being dumped by this young lady, and then seeing another man in his place, he took that knife out with the intent of doing harm, and he followed up on that intent, and Mr. Ronning died as a result of it . . . I ask you to find him guilty of first-degree murder and every charge in that indictment. Thank you."

As he sat down, silence smothered the room. I could hear a slight whimper from the back. I knew it was Mrs. Ronning. Several of the jurors snuck a quick peek to the back of the courtroom.

"Mr. Williams, this may be a good time to take our morning recess," said Judge Morris, and left the bench.

Kevin and I stayed seated. I put my hand on Kevin's. As the jury got up and filed out, as the last one left, he looked at me. "That's gonna be a hard act to follow," he said.

I just sighed. I stood up and turned around. Tony was in the back, he must have slid in quietly during Spencer's closing. He raised his eyebrows at me. I pointed towards the door. Kevin asked the deputy to take him to the bathroom. Tony and I walked into the conference room and closed the door.

"Spencer hasn't lost his charm, has he?" said Tony.

"He may be a prick," I said, "but he's a good attorney. You notice how he stayed away from Josie? He must've gotten the same impression I did. I don't think the jury likes her. Then he stayed away from talking about any poor family being left fatherless."

"Well, he's right," said Tony. "If the jury wants to believe he went over there with malice on his mind, or at least once he saw Mr. Ronning," he hesitated, "but, Bob, I've seen you pull 'em out before. I think you still have a chance on this one."

"I know I do," I said.

"Another interesting thing happened," I said. "There's an accountant on the jury, the guy sitting on the top row, way to the left. After jury selection, I thought he would be our controlling juror, the one to convince."

"Why's that?" asked Tony.

"Just in his answers to questions, his presence, he seemed to be a sort of take-charge person. That's all changed. I've noticed he doesn't even seem to be interested in what's going on. I haven't seen him talking to any of the other jurors. He's a loner. I could be wrong, but I don't see him as foreperson."

"You don't want a strong personality anyway, do you?" asked Tony.

I grinned. "You do if he's on your side," I said, as we made our way back to the courtroom.

Moments later I was standing in front of the jury, a stark contrast, I believed, to Mr. Moore. My suit was wrinkled, I had to button the front to keep them from seeing a stain on my tie. Unfortunately, my appearance had become the least of my concerns. The last time I had looked in the mirror, my eyes were red, my face was tired and worn. I needed a haircut. The hair in my ears had grown out. I tried to shave it with my razor blade and managed to take a big slice out of my ear which I covered with a band-aid. The only good thing I had going for me was that I knew in an hour or so, this one would be put to bed. I tried to get a painful look on my face, which I'm sure wasn't hard. I started out by setting out the responsibility of the jurors, what the law expected them to do; what the judge would tell them they had to do: They had to ignore the indictment, like it wasn't there; they had to rely on the evidence presented here; they had to give Kevin the benefit of the presumption of innocence. They had to put the burden of proof on the State. They had to believe that the State had proved its case beyond a reasonable doubt, and they had to be unanimous in their decision.

As I looked across the jury panel, I lost my train of thought for a second. They were all looking at me intensely, eyes fixed, hanging on every word. They caught me by surprise. It was a little disarming. I quickly looked at my notes to keep from blushing. It didn't work, the blood rushed to my head, and my face flushed. The jurors wanted me to tell them something, something they could grasp onto, to give them some reason to give Kevin a break. All of a sudden it seemed like a tremendous burden.

I gathered my thoughts, looked at the front row and settled on the same juror Kevin had chosen when he testified. I continued, "There's one essential element to this case the prosecutor hasn't talked about: That's Kevin's character. Why is character important? Why do you think we brought character witnesses to this case? I think every one of us tries to lead our lives so that people think well of us. It may not be, and for the most part, never is, a conscious thing. We don't do a good deed and say to ourselves, 'If I do this, this person is really going to think a lot of me.' We do it because that's the kind of person we are. The benefit of it is, and yes, should be, we leave a good impression. We lead our lives never thinking we're going to need those people to tell somebody else about what we did. Then, one day, something terrible happens, and you have to go to those people and say, 'Hey, I need you to come into court for me. I need you to tell this jury what kind of person I am.'

"And the law lets you do that, and why? Because we all believe we act consistent with our character. So, if a person is willing to come in and say to you as jurors, 'Hey, this is a good, honest, truthful person. This is the kind of person he is', you have a right to rely on that. The law even allows the judge to give you an instruction on character. The judge is going to tell you that if in considering all of the evidence, including that of character, you have a reasonable doubt, you have to find the defendant not guilty. What does that tell you? It tells you that character evidence alone can give you that reasonable doubt.

"Ladies and gentlemen of the jury, the prosecutor is right, most of this case is not in dispute. When the judge reads you the charge in this case, the specific counts against Mr. Murphy, you're going to hear a word over and over, 'intent,' and that's what the law requires. To convict, the law requires that Mr. Murphy had a criminal intent. What they call *mens rea*, a guilty mind.

"Ladies and gentlemen of the jury, there is nothing in this young man's life, either in his history, or in his character, which could lead you to believe that he could form such an evil thought and then carry it out with such an evil deed. Think about it, ladies and gentlemen. What do you think it takes to intentionally kill somebody? What kind of person does it take to do that? All I'm saying is that you don't see that in Mr. Murphy.

"If you're like me, you're wondering what's this case all about? How did this terrible thing happen? You have two young men who never met each other, who barely knew the other existed. They meet in a kitchen in the early morning hours, one ends up dead, and the other ends up having to live with it the rest of his life. The prosecutor's right: I'm going to tell you it was self-defense. The judge will give you the instruction, the burden we have to show before we can honestly invoke that. I believe we have.

"The prosecutor wants you to believe that Kevin went to the house with only one purpose, to confront Mr. Ronning. If that's the case, why did he sneak into the house, put the present on the counter, write a note to Lisa? If he wanted to confront Mr. Ronning, why didn't he bang on the door, or better yet, why didn't he just go upstairs to the bedroom? He had lived in the house, he knew his way around.

"He went there exactly for the reason he told you, and he knew it was stupid, and he knew he shouldn't have done it, but he was there. No criminal intent. Kevin turns around, about to leave, and Mr. Ronning steps before him, blocking the only exit from the kitchen. At that point, Ms. Klein hears the words, 'What the fuck are you doing here?' She claims they're Kevin's. Kevin said that Mr. Ronning uttered that statement. I believe it is more reasonable to assume that Mr. Ronning uttered those words, but realistically, it doesn't make any difference. What does Mr. Ronning do? Mr. Ronning looks at Kevin and says, 'You're the one who's been harassing Josie. I'm going to break your fuckin' neck,' and he leaps at him and knocks him across the kitchen, and Kevin sustains the bruise on the cheek. At that point, Kevin has every reason to believe exactly that, that Mr. Ronning is going to break his neck. What does Kevin do? Kevin does exactly what the law requires of him, he looks at Mr. Ronning and says, 'Hey man, I just wanna get out of here before somebody gets hurt.' To end it, all Mr. Ronning has to do is step aside and say, 'Get your ass out of here'. But he doesn't, he said, 'Fuckin'

194

right, somebody's gonna get hurt. You.' And he comes at Kevin again, this time puts him in a bear hug and almost squeezes the life out of him.

"Do you believe Kevin's not afraid at this point? What is he, five-ten, 150 pounds? What is Ronning, six-one, 205 pounds? You saw the picture of him, there wasn't an ounce of fat on that man. That sounds like a cold thing to say, but it's the honest-to-God truth. That's what you have to look at. You have to put yourself in Kevin's place and say, 'What would I do under those circumstances? What would reasonable be for me to believe was in Mr. Ronning's mind?' In doing that, I think you have to take two things into consideration: First, it never seemed to make sense that Mr. Ronning would be that combative with a person he didn't even know, unless he either just had a mean streak in him or that Ms. Klein had told him something about Mr. Murphy, something that would've made him angry. Why else would he use the words, 'You're the one who's been harassing Josie'? Did he want to show his lady that he was going to take care of this little punk, this 'ex,' who had been bugging her? The second thing, what effect did the alcohol he consumed have on his thinking? We don't know what condition he was in when he came down those steps. We know he was .08 after he died—after he had had two transfusions. We know they had been drinking all night. Josie told us, wine and screwdrivers.

"So that is what Kevin is faced with. A man, from his point of view, who was intent on sending him out, in his words, 'in a casket.' Only then does he remember the knife and take it out. Again, he doesn't say, 'I'm going to cut you up.' What he says is, 'Hey man, just let me out of here,' and he makes a dash for the door. We know what happens. We know that wound, that fatal wound could've been inflicted exactly the way Kevin said it was. Not in an intentional, mortal blow, but accidentally, as Mr. Ronning brings Kevin to the floor.

"Look at what we know about him the next morning. The first person he talks to is Chris Younger. Chris tells us he's devastated, on his knees, bawling, and the only thing he remembers is he thinks he cut the guy. What does the cop say, the one who first stopped him? He was crying so hard he was shaking, he was like Jell-O. Does that sound like the hard-boiled killer that the prosecutor tried to portray?

"Ladies and gentlemen, Mr. Murphy didn't come in here and say he was perfect. He acknowledged his errors. He acknowledged his faults. He came across as a simple human being, and he reacted that night the same way any one of us might have reacted believing that our life was in danger. If you believe he acted reasonably, the law excuses what happened. It doesn't require that you find him guilty. I'm asking you to send this young man home. I'm asking you to find him not guilty. Thank you."

I could be wrong, but I thought my lady juror winked as I turned away. I walked back to my chair, glanced to the back. Tony tried to hide a grin. Kevin sat, with his head down. I sat next to him, he reached out his hand.

The next half hour was taken with jury instructions. We all had copies and as the judge read them, I paged through, but I didn't pay much attention. My mind was on a little room with a casket surrounded by flowers with a husband and two little boys standing there, trying to act brave as people paraded by. I truly dreaded the thought of facing that. I often thought if Kate had been there, it would be different. She would know the right things to say. I didn't.

My mind continued to reflect on it as the judge droned on. Finally, I heard him say, "Mr. Wilson and Mr. Simmons, I know you weren't aware, but you were the two alternates, you will not be going back for deliberations with the rest of the jury. I'm sorry to have to inform you of that but we do thank you for your services. I'm sure you can understand."

The two of them got up, looked at each other rather dejectedly. Simmons shrugged his shoulders, slapped the juror next to him and said, "See ya," and they both made their way out. The rest of them left through the hall to the jury room.

The deputy took Kevin in one of the conference rooms, Tony followed us in.

"That went pretty well," Tony said.

Kevin took my hand and shook it vigorously. "Mr. Williams," he said, "thank you. That was terrific. That's exactly what I wanted to say. That's exactly how I felt. Now if the jury wants to find me guilty, it's God's will. How long before they come back, do ya think?"

"Your guess is as good as mine. Based on my experience, it could be hours, it could be days, but I wouldn't be surprised if it goes late."

We said our goodbyes to Kevin, and I talked to the judge's clerk before Tony and I left. I told her I would be at the funeral home all afternoon and all she'd have to do was call and leave a message, and I would be back.

Tony and I made arrangements to meet at a little roadside café just outside of town. We had a little over an hour before we could go to the funeral home. We each ordered a hot beef sandwich, and we sat there, kind of poking at our food. Finally I said, "Are you ready for this?"

He looked up, shook his head. "No."

That's how the next fifteen minutes went, picking at our food, letting out deep sighs, thinking. Tony finally gave up on considering eating. He put his fork down on his plate. "Haven't you had enough of this shit yet?"

I didn't answer.

"Have you thought any more of what I talked about?" he asked.

"What's that?"

"You know, about opening a greenhouse. You and I?"

I laughed. "Tony, I've managed to kill all of Kate's plants, things she's had for twenty-five years. How in the hell can I run a greenhouse?"

"I'll take care of the plants," he said. "You just, you just . . . we'll find something for you to do. You can pull weeds. I'm serious. I'm getting too old to be running down bad guys. There's too many pretty days I spend sitting in a car when I want to be out smelling the grass, pruning my roses. I've done a lot of reading on it. I think this town is just right for a little greenhouse where people actually care, where they can get their questions answered."

I didn't bother answering him. My mind was already miles away. I knew the jury wouldn't be back for hours. It was stressful enough waiting for a jury to come back when nothing else was going on. But here I was, on the way to the funeral parlor to try to console a husband and children, while I wondered whether my client was destined to go to prison for the rest of his life.

With my office closed, there was no sense stopping; nobody was there to take messages anyway. Tony and I pulled into the funeral parking lot, side by side. There were maybe a half a dozen cars there. We walked in and the first people we saw were Ken's parents. Faye had brought them to the office several years before. They walked up, and I gave them my condolences. I introduced Tony. Mrs. Carlson pointed towards the viewing room. "Ken's in there," she said.

I sighed deeply, looked at Tony, ushered him in. We both went through the door, shoulder to shoulder. Some people were already sitting in the chairs. Up front was a row of people, their backs to us, peering at an open casket. Ken was in the middle, wearing a dark suit. Standing to his right, holding each other's hand, were the two boys. They had grown since I had last seen them. They were now eleven and eight. From the back it appeared they both wore identical suits, black. Their light brown hair was neatly combed.

We made our way up, slowly. Ken must have heard our footsteps. He turned around. He broke off the conversation he was having with an older lady, started towards us, the boys followed. As he approached me, his body prevented me from seeing the casket. We reached for each other's hand, my lower lip quivering. I knew I was going to lose it. My eyes watered up. I shook his hand, unable to speak. I had to turn away. He knew what I was doing. He looked at Tony. "I'm glad you could make it," he said, shaking Tony's hand.

I finally regained enough composure to say, "Ken, I'm really sorry," and then I made the mistake of looking at the boys. Two angelic faces with bright blue eyes, sandy hair, their cheeks were red and raw from wiping away the tears. I turned away and brought out my hanky. I looked at Tony, he wasn't faring much better. I would have been all right at that point if I had turned around and walked away but Ken grabbed my left arm and gently tugged me toward the casket. It was flooded with lights, surrounded by red roses. My eyes were so washed in tears that it was like looking through cut crystal. Everything sparkled. As I approached, she slowly came into view. I stopped, stunned. Through my misty eyes, she looked natural, alive. I almost expect- ed her to open her eyes, look towards me and say, "Good morning, Bob."

A pain shot through my entire body. I could feel my knees weaken. I thought I was going to go down. A strong arm went around my waist, Tony held me up. I looked at Ken. "I'm sorry, Ken, I can't," I said and turned. Tony led me to the side door.

"I have to get out," I said, "I need air."

We started towards the door, a group of friends were coming in. They could see what was going on and they slowly parted to let us out.

"Tony," I said, "I can't do it. I don't have the strength left."

"Just take it easy," he said, "you'll be all right."

Tony and I stayed until late afternoon but I never went back into the viewing room. I either stood in the hall or the little anteroom where they had coffee. I know I talked to many people, other legal assistants, court personnel, lawyers, but I don't remember much of what was said. I should've been stronger. I should've been in there, helping.

The main business office of the mortuary was at the end of the hall just as one came in the door. Every so often I would hear the phone ring, and I would jump. I would expect somebody to come running out of the office and ask, "Is there a Mr. Williams here? He has a phone call." The clerk would be calling to say the jury has returned a verdict. I had almost forgotten about my trial, forgotten that twenty miles away, twelve people were also dealing with death. I thought of the contrast, Faye lying in white silk, wearing a baby-blue dress, her hair combed neatly over the sides of her face, much more neatly than I'd ever seen it, her face a painted serene stare, a cosmetic look of death; while twenty miles away, jurors spread out eight-by-ten photographs of a young man covered in blood, his eyes staring coldly ahead, a look of shock on his face, a gaping wound in his side, no effort made to hide the stark reality of death.

A little after five, I called the courthouse. The clerk indicated that the judge wanted me back. He intended to send the bailiff in to talk to the jury, to see whether they wanted to stay later or wished to call it a night and come back the next day. I asked Tony if he would ride along. We were almost halfway there before the silence was broken. "I want to thank you for helping me," I said. "I don't understand why I had to break down like that. I anticipated what it was going to be like. In fact, I pictured in it my mind and yet, when I saw her, I just couldn't help it."

"I know what you mean," he said. "Believe me, I was having just as hard a time."

I looked at him. He was staring ahead, stone faced. That was the exterior he always tried to portray.

Tony and I walked in the side door of the courthouse and took the elevator. As we got out, the court reporter was walking down the hall. She heard the door open and waited. "Well, you've got 'em arguing, Bob," she said. "The bailiff says they're screaming at each other. He can't hear over what, but the voices are getting pretty loud. I thought you'd probably convinced a few of them. Now the question is, who's gonna hold out. Anyway, it doesn't sound like they're gonna get done tonight. I think the judge plans to let 'em go so he can go home. Spencer's already in chambers with him."

I left Tony in the hall talking to Mary, and I walked to the judge's chambers. I knocked on the door and walked in.

"It's a good thing you're here, Bob," the judge said. "I'm going to let the jury go until seven o'clock. If they don't have a decision by then, or don't think they're going to reach one quickly, we'll put them up for the night. It's been a long day, I hate to make them work later than that."

"That's fine, your honor," I said. "You know I'll be at the funeral tomorrow morning so it'll be close to noon before I can get here."

"Well, if they come back before that, we're just going to have to wait."

I stood up and turned around to walk out when I realized Spencer hadn't said a word. He didn't greet me when I walked in, he didn't offer anything to the judge's comments, and he wasn't going to say anything as I walked out. I stopped at the door and turned around. "What's wrong with you?" I asked.

"You've got a weasel for a client," he said. "If he hadn't lied through his teeth, they'd been back hours ago."

"Spencer," the judge said, "take it outside."

Spencer got up, walked past me, nudging me aside. I didn't mind. I knew I had pissed him off.

We waited around until seven. We'd brought a couple newspapers and we sat there in silence. The bailiff came in and said the judge was going to send the jury to the motel. He said that on the judge's instructions he had talked to the forelady and that she had told him there was no way they would reach a verdict tonight. As he left, I turned to Tony. "That's interesting," I said. "Forelady. Not very often you get a woman leading the jury."

"What do you think that means?" he asked.

"I don't know," I said. "There were three or four women on there with pretty strong personalities. If she's on our side, it could make all the difference in the world."

We walked out. I pictured the lady up front, the one I believed winked at me. Could she be the foreperson?

We got back to the funeral home just as the prayer service was ending. Tony and I stood in the back as the priest walked up to the family and blessed them.

The room was packed. I recognized Faye's family, many of her friends, people who had been in and out of the office visiting with her.

As people started to move around, I saw Jackie and her husband leaving through the side door. I took Tony's arm and started out the back. We intercepted her just as she was going out the door. When she saw me, she came up and gave me a hug. "I have to know what happened," I said.

"I have to have a cigarette," she said.

We went outside and stood under the canopy. I watched Jackie light her cigarette, take the first deep drag. It was nostalgic. She inhaled deeply. I watched her mouth, anticipating. Her exhale was like a gentle sigh, slowly a smoky stream escaped through ruby lips, to be whisked away by the cool air. Her husband said, "If she'd just gone down the inside steps . . . there was no reason to go outside."

Jackie looked at him, perturbed, took another drag. "Why do you keep saying that? There was no way to expect that was gonna happen," she said, smoke escaping with each word.

"What do you remember?" I asked.

"We were having a good time, Bob. We'd all had dinner together. About nine o'clock or so, she put the boys in their room. I remember she argued with them a little bit, they wanted to stay up and watch television, but they could only get that one channel, I think it's Duluth. There was some movie on that she didn't think was fit for kids. They had brought some of their books along. I told 'em to read. She kidded them, I remember everybody was laughing when we left. We went upstairs, everybody was up there. There was a fire in the fireplace, nothing out of the ordinary. We just drank, told jokes, laughed. I remember a couple times we got awful warm, and Faye and I went and stood on the balcony. You know, it kind of overlooks the parking lot. There were people coming and going."

"Anybody else come down the balcony while you were there? You know, from another room?"

"Yeah, I think another couple walked by. We didn't really pay a lot of attention. Oh, yeah, they did, that's right. Faye invited them in. I remember the wife said they had had enough for one day. Actually, I remember they were hanging on each other. We both suspected they had something else in mind."

"Had you been up and down those steps yourself?"

"No. The only reason she would've used the steps outside, Bob, is it was shorter. If you went out through the hall, you had to go all the way down the hall, down the steps and then back. If you used the outside steps, you were almost to their room. The keys worked on either side."

"What do you remember next?" I asked.

"A little after midnight, she started towards the door, and I asked her where she was going. She said to check on the boys. I didn't think anything of it. I saw her go out the door, and I saw her shadow walk past the window. Never heard a thing. Of course it was too noisy. Maybe ten, fifteen minutes later, Ken came over and asked me if I knew where she was. I said, 'She took the back way,' and I pointed toward the balcony. He said he was gonna check on her. And then moments later, he came flying through the door, screaming, 'Dial 911—get an ambulance—Faye's hurt!' We all went out, and I could see her lying at the bottom of the steps, and I could tell she was hurt. She was in this awful position, and her head was twisted around."

"So nobody actually heard her fall down the steps?" I asked.

"No, but like I said, it was so noisy, I doubt if anybody could've. Ken was kneeling by her, crying and pleading with her to be okay. He was gonna move her, and I hollered that he couldn't, that there might be something spinal, that she had to stay there until the ambulance came."

"Did you notice anything about her behavior?" asked Tony. "I mean, they did a blood alcohol test, and it was quite high. Did she seem to have trouble talking or walking, I mean was there anything about her behavior that caused you any alarm?"

"Look, Mr. O'Donnell, we'd all been drinking off and on since noon. We drank right through dinner, and there was an open bar upstairs. Nobody was worried about what they were drinking because we weren't going anywhere. If you fell over on the bed right there, that's where they would've left you. So, we weren't feeling any pain, but, to answer your question, no, I wasn't worried about her."

"Did you go to the hospital with her?"

"There was a deputy sheriff that showed up with the ambulance. He let Ken and me ride along. He knew we were in no shape to drive. We didn't get to see her until almost six in the morning. It was awful. It's not a big hospital. It's not like being down in the Twin Cities. The doctor came out and said that she had broken her neck. They couldn't save her. She couldn't breathe. They said she passed away without any pain. Ken and I just hugged each other and cried. The rest of the day was the longest I'd ever spent in my life. We had to go back and tell everybody, tell the boys."

A steady stream of mourners passed as we stood under the canopy. The evening air was cool and damp. We were all getting cold. As Jackie would exhale on her cigarette, a big puffy white cloud would form, a mixture of smoke and hot breath, and settle above her head momentarily until caught in the evening breeze.

"There's nothing more I can tell you, Bob," she said. "I hope I never have to live through something like that again." She looked for a cigarette butt receptacle. Not finding one, she nonchalantly put it at her side and then flipped it behind her. "I've watched Ken all evening," she said. "He's running on pure adrenaline. I suspect he's gonna collapse when this is all over. I think the boys are just numb." She shivered.

"Well, thanks for your help, Jackie. We'll see you at the funeral tomorrow."

Tony and I stood by our cars for a few moments. "It doesn't sound like our friend was involved in anything with her fall," Tony said. "I knew that's why you were quizzing her."

"I know," I said. "It just seemed too coincidental it should happen so shortly after Kate. Well, I don't know about you, but I'm going home and try to get some sleep, even if I have to take a bottle of sleeping pills."

"Don't even . . . ."

"I was just kidding," I said. "Why don't I meet you at the café at nine and we can have coffee and go to the funeral together."

"That's a plan," Tony replied.

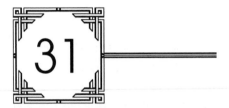

The next morning, a little before nine, I was sitting at the café sipping on my first cup of coffee. I had stopped and picked up the *Minneapolis Tribune*. A heading in the metro section caught my eye, "Local Group to Meet with Commissioner on Reopening Canterbury Downs Race Track."

> A group of investors, headed by well-known Minneapolis Attorney John Spokes, will meet with Racing Commissioner William Turbin on negotiations to reopen the race track this coming season.
>
> Canterbury was closed following the 1992 racing season because of financial problems.
>
> According to Spokes, the proposal calls for some form of partnership between the local investors and the state.
>
> "Even if it's in the form of some tax reductions or other considera-tion," said Spokes, "I believe there's enough interest among the investors I represent to move ahead."
>
> Spokes indicated that he hopes to have a plan in place early enough that the track can be reopened this spring. Spokes said his group is con-fident that they can raise the twenty million dollars the state believes is necessary to consider reopening the track. Spokes is one of the local breeders of thoroughbred horses who compete in the racing program.

I must be practicing the wrong kind of law, I thought. The guy's involved in a multimillion-dollar project, thoroughbred race horses, and I'm representing some poor slob as a court-appointed attorney because he had too many beers to drink and probably got a little horny.

A little after nine, Tony walked in. He plopped a bunch of magazines in front of me. The top one was titled, "Greenhouse Management." It had a banner, "Profits to Be Made in Your Own Backyard." I paged through the magazines. They were all pretty much the same.

"See, I didn't pull it out of my hat," he said. "I've been working on this. You take those along and read 'em. You'll see what I'm talking about."

I promised him I would.

Tony sat down and poured himself a cup of coffee. "You haven't heard anything on our friend Mr. Draper?" I said.

"Nothing," he replied. "When this is all over, I'm calling the corrections officer again. I know they have a warrant out for him. Did you sleep?" he asked.

"No. Did you? It all seems too surreal," I said. "We're standing at a wake for one of the gentlest people I've known, and everybody's so civilized and respectful. At the same time, we're waiting for a jury to return on a case where, with a little civility, one man would be alive, and the other free."

Other than Kate, Tony was the only person I felt comfortable with just sitting, saying nothing. We sipped our coffee in silence. Reluctantly, I looked across the table. "Well, I suppose we might as well get going. It's not going to get any easier," I said.

He nodded, and I got up and paid the bill. We decided to leave his car there. He would ride with me.

"Have you ever been to this church?" I asked.

"No." Tony replied.

"The last time I was there was when Faye got married, about thirteen years ago. It's a beautiful little church, one of those old turn-of-the-century structures, a lot of gothic arches, statues along the sidewalls that stare at you. It has a little side altar to the right with a huge crucifixion scene. Pretty awesome. The cross and the figure of Christ hang at kind of an angle. The reason I remember it so well, it reminded me of the Salvador Dali painting. Have you ever seen that painting, Tony? The Crucifixion?"

"I don't think so." he replied.

"When I was in law school in Washington, I went to the National Gallery of Art. They had a Dali exhibit. It's a great picture. I'll have to show it to you sometime."

"Are you gonna try and call the courthouse in Foley?" asked Tony.

"No, I told the judge yesterday it'd probably be noon before I could get there."

"So you're not going to the actual burial?" he said.

"Oh, God, I forgot all about that," I said. "I think I have to. Ken would probably never forgive me. I'll just call after the service, and if the jury is still out, they'll send them for lunch, and it won't make any difference."

We met the intersection to the old highway just as the big white hearse and funeral cars turned the corner. We waited for them to pass. I could see Ken's car immediately behind the hearse, with the two boys and his parents in the backseat. We pulled in behind the procession and followed them to the church. I pulled into the back part of the parking lot, as far from the church entrance as I could get. I was a coward, and I knew it. I didn't want to confront my emotions.

I had been to a few funerals over the years where death came quickly, a car accident, a heart attack, something unexpected, but nobody close. I had often wondered how families faced with such a tragedy survived. They always seemed so strong and so resigned to their fate. I was amazed at their fortitude. After experiencing it with Kate's death, though, I realized what it really was: By the time I got to the actual wake, I was so crushed emotionally, so sapped of any strength or feeling, that what people saw was an empty shell, an automaton.

Here, the problem was, I realized, that I had never gotten to that point in Faye's death. With everything else going on in my life, the opportunity wasn't there to empty my soul. So every time I was confronted with her death, seeing the casket, the family, it was a new rush. I swelled up, waiting to explode into a blubbering fool, and I didn't want anybody to see me like that.

We sat in the back of the parking lot, silent, watching the cars come in. The funeral director pointed fingers here and there, trying to give some direction to a chaotic scene. Ken came out of the back of the church and walked to the hearse. The funeral director opened the back door, and they pulled the casket out. The pallbearers each took their spot, and as they lifted the casket up on the gurney, Ken placed his hand on it and bowed his head. Within minutes, everybody disappeared through the doors. I looked at Tony, he looked at me. Without saying a word, we got out and walked towards the church.

No matter how hard the clergy try, it's impossible, in my opinion, to make a funeral a celebration of life. As far as I'm concerned, I would concede to a celebration for a person who's ninety and dies in his sleep. Short of that, I don't see a lot to celebrate. And when a young lady, with everything to live for, at the age of thirty-five, dies a senseless death, I can't believe there's some divine plan, something to celebrate.

The next hour went easier than I'd expected. I lost it once at the offertory when a young boy, serving the Mass, walked up to Ken and the two boys. He had a small round face with big brown eyes and brown hair cut in bangs right in the middle of his forehead. He smiled at them, oh, so softly. He said, "Peace," and shook their hands, one by one. I think I really saw peace on Ken's face; I don't know, maybe faith does make a difference.

We stood there as everyone paraded out, the casket slowly rolled by. I stared at it, piercing the mahogany veneer to picture Faye lying inside, cold and still. I grabbed Tony by the arm and said, "Let's get out of here."

We quickly rushed by people standing outside. I'd had enough. I understand there's a purpose to all this, that there must be, as they say, some closure for the family. But for me, that would have to come another day. I took a right out of the church parking lot towards the highway. "Are we going to the burial?" asked Tony.

"If we go, I'm going to watch it from a distance. I have to call the courthouse first and see what's happening."

I pulled into the first gas station and called the District Court. The clerk indicated they had been waiting for my call. The jury had reached a decision about a half an hour before. The judge wanted me there.

32

The drive would be about twenty-five minutes. Neither of us said a word. If the jury had been arguing, in a shouting match before they left last night, I couldn't imagine what they had done to resolve their problems in a mere two and a half hours. I believed it didn't bode well for Mr. Murphy.

As we drove, snowflakes started to fall. My mind was divided, like it was split down the middle, half of it wondered what the jury had done to young Kevin; the other half pictured the hearse pulling up to a snow covered cemetery where a little tent had been erected over a frozen hole in the ground, shrouded in purple drapes.

I thought of seeing Kevin in the hall, the anxiety on his face as he wondered where he would spend the rest of his life.

Then I would see the casket carried from the hearse and placed on the burial site, the priest standing at the head of it. The little server with the bangs stands to his right and hands him the holy water. The priest invites everybody to move in closer and they stand there, in a semi-circle, as he starts his prayers.

In my daydream, I assure Kevin that I think everything's all right, but I tell him we don't know what the jury's done. They didn't have to find you guilty of murder, I tell him; they could've found you guilty of one of the lesser included charges, even a simple burglary. Then the sentencing will be up to the judge. So, whatever you do, if they find you guilty, you accept it calmly, as a gentleman.

I looked at my watch, it was quarter to twelve, another fifteen minutes on the road.

The priest finishes the prayers. He looks up from his missal and closes the book. The little server hands him the holy water. He sprinkles it on the people and the casket as he gives his blessing. "Dear Lord," he says, "into your hands we commend the soul of this young wife and mother, and we ask that you welcome her into the kingdom of heaven."

The bailiff opens the door to the courtroom, and we all rush in. As we sit there, in the quiet, we can hear the muffled sounds of the jurors at the end of the hall. Their speech seems animated, and there is nervous laughter.

The two men who have been standing in the back, behind the priest, step up and start to lower the casket slowly into the ground. Ken walks up with one red rose in his hand and places it on top of the casket and blows a kiss. The two boys follow, then her dad, Ken's parents, each taking a single rose from a vase and placing it on the descending casket. I can see everything as clear as if I were standing right there.

We all sit in the courtroom, the back filled with spectators. Mrs. Ronning is there. I don't see Josie. Kevin's mother and all of his family are seated up front. His father is to the side, in a wheelchair. We sit there, in silence, anticipating the jury walking in.

The remaining mourners give their respects and follow Ken and the boys back to the road. They gather, shaking hands, hugging; hankies being brought to the face, tears wiped before they freeze. The snowflakes gently settle on everybody's head. Ken shouts, making sure everybody knows they're welcome to return to the parish center for dinner put on by the Christian Mothers.

I could feel the road getting slippery. The snow was starting to accumulate. I looked at my speedometer. I was going seventy-five in a fifty-five zone. There was less than a half a mile to town. I took my foot off the gas and coasted to the first stop sign.

The silence was broken when Tony finally said, "What'd ya think's gonna happen?"

"I had a premonition," I said. "And if I'm right, they've found him not guilty."

"What do you mean, premonition?" he asked.

"I don't know. It was the strangest thing. I pictured us sitting in the courtroom waiting for the jury, and I could hear them down the hall talking and laughing. I thought to myself, that doesn't sound like a jury that has just sent a young man to prison. I hope I'm right."

When the door opened to the elevator, Tony and I stepped into an empty hall. I walked passed the clerk's office. There was only one person in there, a young lady who had started several weeks earlier. We turned the corner to the courtroom, and the bailiff opened the door and let us in. The courtroom was filled, but there was no sound. As I stepped in the door, I saw Kevin's dad sitting in the corner in his wheelchair. I quickly scanned the benches, Josie wasn't there. Kevin was sitting at the counsel table by himself with an apprehensive stare—just as I'd imagined. I walked over and put my hand on his shoulder and sat down. Then I heard the muffled sounds from the jury room, and I thought I heard laughter.

The clerk looked at the deputy. "Bring the jury in," she said.

I heard the heels of his cowboy boots as he walked down the hall. Then there was quiet. Minutes later the jurors made their way the thirty feet or so from the jury room to the jury box. I always watched the jury as they walked in. I believed they telegraphed their verdict by the look on their faces. They came in behind me. I waited until they were all seated and, as nonchalantly as possible, I casually turned. Several of the lady jurors made eye contact and smiled. I knew my premonition was right.

The judge walked in, and we all stood. I barely reached my chair again when he started. "Ladies and gentlemen of the jury, I understand you've reached a verdict."

My lady juror stood up. "We have, your honor."

"Would you hand them to the clerk, please?"

The clerk walked over and took the verdict forms. She walked back to the bench and handed them to the judge. He looked at each one without raising his head. Then he looked at the jury, then at me, and said, "Madam clerk will read the verdict."

The clerk reached for the verdicts and stood in her box. She stuttered slightly as she started. "To the charge of murder in the first degree, felony murder, we the jury empanelled in the above entitled matter, find the defendant not guilty."

A sigh of relief went through the back of the courtroom. It was premature, I thought. I knew we had a long way to go. She put the verdict form down and looked at the next one. "To the charge of murder in the second degree, intentional homicide, we find the defendant not guilty."

By now there was hum in the back of the courtroom. She quickly went to the third verdict form. "To the charge of murder in the second degree, felony murder, we find the defendant not guilty."

Kevin's hands went to his face, and he wept. We weren't home free, but he wasn't going to be spending the next ten to twenty years in prison. The rest of the charges were all burglary. By then everybody was anticipating what happened. The clerk quickly read the rest of the verdicts—not guilty, not guilty, not guilty, not guilty.

It was a clean sweep, they were going to let him go home. Kevin quickly wheeled around and made it to the railing where his mother was standing. They hugged, both sobbing. I looked over. His dad wiped tears from his eyes. His sisters were crying, his brothers were crying. I looked at the jury, the forelady had a big smile on her face, others looked to the back of the courtroom, at the pandemonium. Some of them held back their own tears.

In the middle of it all sat Mrs. Ronning, her head down, her hands crossed on her lap, shaking her head in disbelief.

I turned around. Spencer had already slipped out the side door. The judge was gathering some papers off the bench. He nodded at me, smiled, thanked the jurors, turned around and walked into his chambers. The jury started to file out. The forelady looked at me, a satisfied look, a look that said, I hope you're happy with what I did.

A small piece of my mind was still far away in a country field surrounded by people who were also weeping, not in joy, but sadness as a mahogany casket disappeared into the ground. I could feel my lip quiver again. I blinked back the tears. There was a time, not too long ago, when I would have gone back to the office, been greeted by a big smile and hug, congratulations. Faye would want to know every detail. After leaving the office, I would go home and it would all be repeated. I had my own cheering squad.

I looked for Tony. Chris Younger and Sara Pendergast had him in the corner taking turns shaking his hand vigorously. Sara hugged him. He looked at me, almost in desperation, like, "Let's get the hell out of here."

Kevin finally broke away from his family and came up to me, grabbed my hand, squeezed it hard. "I don't know what I can ever do to thank you, Mr. Williams," he said. "I can't believe I can go home."

"Let me tell you something, Kevin. You might be right. There might've been a little divine intervention in this whole thing. The jury certainly didn't have to come to that conclusion. I don't know what happened that night and I have to believe you. But what you've got is a second chance. I know you've got a lot of good in you, and I hope you put it to appropriate use."

"You don't have to worry," he said. "I found God. That's never gonna change. I'm gonna minister to prisoners, help others find the way."

Somehow I knew he would. He was a changed person. I had sensed it months ago. He was a young man looking for his own niche in life and, through this tragedy, had discovered it. I had seen it before. He wasn't the first client I'd had who found God in prison, but I think he was probably the first one I expected to follow his revelation once he left the cell behind.

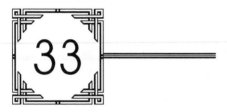

I dropped Tony off. I just wanted to be alone for a while. I started towards the office and changed my mind, taking County Road 75 out of town. Just beyond the last homes, I took a right into the hills and ended up at the entrance to the cemetery. I debated whether I should go in; it beckoned. I slowly took a right hand turn. I followed the winding roads and then I saw it ahead and stopped. There were two trucks, one had a trailer and two men were loading a small backhoe. I drove ahead, slowly. The drivers got in their trucks and left. I parked in the spot they vacated and lowered the window. This was Faye's resting place. In spring a stone would be set, something like: "Faye Carlson, devoted wife and mother." The family would come and visit. This was Faye's memorial. It had been snowing for several hours, big, heavy flakes, filling the foot prints, already hiding any trace of the human intrusion only moments earlier. The only telltale sign was the fresh mound of dirt that was slowly disappearing under a new blanket of white. I thought to myself, Faye would've liked this day. She enjoyed the freshness of a new snow.

Kate and I had talked it over; neither of us wanted a memorial. Carol and I had taken Kate's ashes into the woods and spread them under the trees. I imagined the ashes lying there, warm under the snow, mixing with the humus, lifeblood for next spring's periwinkles. Now, every spring when I saw the little pink-and-blue petals, sometimes appearing even before the snow was gone, I'll think of Kate. That would be her memorial.

I drove back to my office. I wanted some quiet time. I didn't bother turning on any lights. I took a comfortable chair and leaned back, closed my eyes. Within a month, everything had changed. Kate was gone, Faye was gone, the trial was over, I had nothing going for me anymore. Maybe Tony was right, maybe it was a good time to get out. If not for a greenhouse, maybe some other business.

Then I wondered: what are you talking about? You just pulled another one out of a hat. Nobody gave Kevin a chance of walking. There's only one thing you've ever done well in your life, that's representing criminals. You'd be nuts to walk away from it now. The days had taken their toll. Within minutes, I dozed off.

It was past six thirty when I finally woke up. I looked at the clock. I was already an hour late for my meeting with Tony at the Lodge. We had earlier decided to have some semblance of a celebration. When I walked in, he was sitting at the bar, talking to Jessie. She saw me and got a big smile. "The man of the hour," she said. She clapped softly. "I bet ya Kevin's going wild," she said. "I bet Stubby's is roaring tonight. Maybe I'll check it out after work."

A rough voice came from the side. "You aren't going any fuckin' place."

I looked down the bar. Her husband was sitting at the far end, already sloshed. Jessie ignored him. "Hey, puss," he hollered, "I told you, you aren't going any fuckin' place."

Jessie made a motion towards him. Tony stood up. "Let me handle it," he said.

He walked to the end of the bar, hovered over her husband, who had both elbows on the bar barely able to hold his head up. Tony leaned over and whispered something. We couldn't hear. He walked back and sat down. Within moments, Jessie's husband got up and walked by, flipping Tony the bird as he left.

"What did you do?" Jessie asked. "I can never shut him up that quick."

"I just told him, discretion being the better part of valor, he better get his ass out of here before I broke his neck. I didn't say it quite that way, but he got the point."

"I wish he would've decided to take you on," she said. "I'd like to see him get his ass kicked."

I finally said, "Jessie, I know it's none of my business, but why do you put up with him anyway?"

She looked at me. "Mr. Williams, that's the point, it's none of your business. What'll you have?"

I didn't even take it personally. "Well," I said, "I'm in a pissy mood. I'll have a Manhattan and easy on the vermouth. Two cherries, please."

She smiled. "You're the man," she said.

I didn't get drunk. I sipped on that Manhattan for a long time. News of the trial had been on the radio and in the evening paper. People walked by, giving me congratulations. With a quiet meeting of the minds, Tony and I kept the conversation away from Kate and Faye, what we had been through. We were talking about Kevin's trial, when Tony said, "Spencer was right, you know. He didn't have to take that present over there at two o'clock in the morning."

"I know," I said. "I think he really wanted to see Josie. I suspect he was hoping she would invite him up to the bedroom. I think seeing a guy there was a total surprise. But you know, Tony, it doesn't make much difference to me. I think Kevin is really going to do something good with his life. I think he'll make a difference . . . I think we've accomplished something."

"Yeah," Tony said, "I'd hate to think you put a murderer back out on the street," and he looked at me with a big grin. I gave him a dirty look. "Well, it wouldn't be the first time," he added.

"You're a dipshit," I said.

"Well," he replied, "it takes one to know one."

214

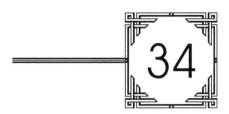

I'd like to say that life got back to normal, but it didn't. Nothing would be normal again without Kate. At the office I pondered whether I could get by without replacing Faye. I hated the idea of starting somebody else fresh, somebody who didn't understand all my idiosyncrasies, somebody who might slap me with a sexual harassment suit if I told a joke I heard at the bar. So I decided to let it ride for a while.

I had been anticipating that Carol would spend the Christmas holidays with me. The previous year, she was able to be home for a little over a week. But she had made arrangements to visit a vet clinic in Chicago, so she was only going to be with me two days, Christmas Eve and Christmas Day. I bought a big balsam fir and set it up in the family room, right in the peak of the cathedral ceiling. It would be, I thought, like old times. We had gotten away from a big tree in recent years. I thought it would be fun again. I had strung it with lights, hundreds of red, blue, and green lights, so at night the spectrums of the color wheel converged and cast an amber rose haze across the room. I didn't put the rest of the decorations on, I left that for Christmas Eve.

Carol arrived about 3:00 p.m. We went for a walk in the woods but it was cold and windy. We didn't last very long. We warmed up with a cup of hot chocolate before we started with the tree. I had the boxes of ornaments lined up on the floor. We gave each other that look, like lets get started, and opened the boxes. I never thought about what sort of effect the Christmas ornaments would have on both of us. Almost every ornament had been hand-picked by Kate. For many years, at every little gift store, every antique shop, every Goodwill or thrift shop we went into, she would look for something unique. She had put together a collection of dozens of bulbs, each with its own history. "Remember this one?" Carol said, and she held up a little porcelain snowy owl. "She found this at the Wildlife Preserve in Wisconsin.

Remember that trip we took to the Helicon Marsh?" Carol remembered where Kate had bought almost every one. It was like reliving everything. It was, I thought, like another memorial.

Carol and I spent the day reminiscing. Christmas was empty without Kate. We decided we were going to bring her back. I got out the boxes of slides from all the trips we had taken. There was Kate and Carol sitting on the rocky ledges overlooking Lake Superior. There was Kate and Carol in a canoe through the swamps of Ding Darling Park. There was Kate and Carol walking the beaches of Captiva Island. It was all Kate and Carol. For a period of over twenty years, since I had first gotten into photography, I had shot thousands of slides documenting the history of our little family.

"You notice, Dad," Carol said, "you're never in the pictures."

"Nobody ever wanted to learn how to use my camera."

"You didn't have to have such a fancy one with all those buttons," she said.

"Then I wouldn't have gotten all these great shots."

"It would've been nice to have some slides of you and Mom."

"I'm in some of the pictures that you took."

"It's not the same," she said.

It was hard to go to sleep that Christmas night. We had spent hours going through the history of my life with Kate. Every picture brought back a memory. I ached to talk to her, to feel her warm body next to mine, to kiss her.

I laid there for hours, drifting in and out of dreams. I'm making love to Kate, and it is so real that when I wake, I cry. My head's on the pillow, my mind in that semi-conscious state where it can be a million miles away, but

I'm still aware that I'm awake, staring into the backside of closed eyelids. My body sensed it first, sort of a sucking of air, like something had been opened quickly. My whole body tensed up. I listened. My eyes snapped open, my head never moving from the pillow. Is there somebody in the basement? I waited. I didn't hear anything. I relaxed, slightly. You're starting to flip out, I concluded. Then I heard it, the creak, on the first step, barely perceptible, oak straining under the weight of a foot. I could feel my pulse quicken, my face flush, my heart pumping. Adrenalin shot though my body. I listened again. Another step, so faint. The open stairway to the bottom level was right outside my bedroom door. I wouldn't be able to see anybody until they reached the top.

Creak, the next step.

My right arm inched its way from under the covers without a sound. My hand reached the knob on the bed stand. I hoped it hadn't snapped shut. I tugged gently. It opened.

Creak, another step.

My hand slid into the night stand, and I felt the pearl handle.

Creak, another step.

I grabbed the pearl handle firmly and pulled my hand out of the drawer and back under the covers. I could feel the barrel of the gun against my chest. I put my finger on the trigger, my thumb on the hammer and I waited.

Creak, another step.

I started to slowly move my body to the edge of the bed. I made not a sound. I peered around the edge of the doorframe. I could see the banister and the top steps. The Christmas tree lights were on. They crossed the entire room and cast a dim light.

Creak, another step.

A head appeared, tinted a strange color from the lights. I couldn't make it out. My body was stiff, rigid, my hand trembled, my mouth so dry I couldn't utter a word if I wanted to. What if it was Draper? He's here, he's going to get not only me but Carol. I know I locked that door. That son-of-a-bitch figured it out. He was here before. I should've listened to Tony.

Creak, another step.

His shoulders appeared. I couldn't tell if it was Draper. There was no ponytail. The hair was short, the body stocky. He had Draper's build.

Creak, another step.

A hand slowly rose to the top of the banister. Half his body was visible. It could be Draper; the facial features looked a little bit like him. I couldn't tell. It had been over seventeen years since I'd seen him. *You're going to have to shoot,* I tell myself. I couldn't. I couldn't just kill somebody. Maybe it was just a burglar. Maybe he was just going to take something and leave. *I can't kill anybody, I know better than that. What if I shoot and miss?* But then, I realized, it wasn't just me. *If he gets me, he's going to get Carol.*

Creak, another step.

He was one step from the top. It was Draper. I knew it was. My mind was racing. *I can't let the creep get away with it. I owe it to Kate, to Carol. I've got to do something.*

I saw his right foot reach the top. He stood there. He turned towards the bedroom. *He's coming in.* There was something in his hand; I saw it flash. I saw the reds, blues, and greens of the Christmas tree reflect. It was a knife or a gun. *Dumb shit, do something. What are you going to do, let him kill you and Carol? You can't let him get to Carol!* I took my hand from under the cover, jump to my feet. He was right outside the door. I didn't even aim, just pointed, bringing the hammer back. I fired. A flash of light, and a tremendous bang echoed through the house. I was momentarily blinded—there were shooting stars, everywhere. When I was able to see, he was no longer there. Maybe I flinched. I was in a panic. *You should've paid attention to what Tony was telling you, you dumb ass. Now what are you going to do?* Then I heard a moan; then a scream. The scream was Carol's. She flipped on the hall light. She stood in the hall screaming. "Dad! Dad!"

I was shaking. I reached the hall in one step, turned and looked. A man was lying on the cream-colored carpet right in front of the Christmas tree, blood gushing from a hole in his chest. I must have hit his heart. I pictured it blasted apart. There was no movement. He was dead. By his shoe lay a switchblade, long and silver.

Carol continued screaming at the top of her lungs. I put the gun down on the table and rushed to her.

"What the hell's going on Dad!" she screamed. "You shot somebody!"

She was hysterical. I put my arms around her. She sobbed violently. "It's okay," I said, "it's okay. He's dead."

All Carol could say is, "Dad, you shot somebody? You shot somebody?" She pulled away. "Who?"

"I think it's somebody I represented many years ago," I said. "I think he wanted to get me."

"Why? Why?" she hollered.

"Stay here," I said. "I'm going to check it out."

She leaned against the wall, her hands over her face, her body shaking violently.

As I reached the end of the hall, I could see the body lying on the livingroom carpet, the hallway light throwing my shadow over his feet. The red, white, blues and greens of the Christmas tree lights send an eerie tint over his face. He was dressed in black, and he wore gloves. I inched closer to see his face. "Goddamn," I said under my breath. It wasn't Draper; it was a black man, somebody I had never seen before. He wore a black knit turtleneck sweater, and the blood was still oozing, crimson, from his chest. I could tell the gun had been so close that the heat of the discharge melted the knit around the wound. I had put it right up to his chest without even knowing it.

The realization that I had just shot somebody, somebody I didn't even know, started to settle in. I looked at his body, the blood had formed a big puddle on the cream carpet. I could hear Carol still screaming, "Dad, Dad!" from the hallway, too petrified to come in.

I knelt down. I was going to close his eyes, and then I realized I shouldn't touch anything. I went back and put my arms around Carol and led her back to her bedroom. "He's dead," I said. "I'm going to call the sheriff."

As I walked out of her room, a terrible thought went over me. What if there were more than one? My steps quickened. I reached and grabbed the gun. I went to the top of the stairs and flipped on the basement light. I stood there, listening. Without taking my eyes off the staircase, I backed up to the wall, grabbed the phone, dialed 911. I told the dispatcher that I had just shot an intruder. I told her I thought there may still be others in the house. She told me to stay right there, on the phone, to talk to her until a deputy got there.

It seemed to take forever. I told her exactly what happened. Every few minutes Carol would holler, "Dad!"

And I would holler, "It's okay. The sheriff's on his way."

I stood by the phone watching the stairway. Several times I stretched the cord of the phone long enough to get around the counter to see if the body had moved. I knew he was dead, but my mind said not to take any chances. Minutes later, for the first time, I had calmed down enough to ask myself, *Who in the hell is this guy?* What was he doing in my house? Why would he want to harm me? I had no doubt he would have killed me and Carol. People don't creep around your house in the middle of the night, in the dark, with a knife in their hand without malicious intent. Then my whole body turned cold. I had just taken a human life, something I had said I didn't think I could ever do—even in self-defense, and yet, when he reached the top of the steps and entered my bedroom and I saw something in his hand, I thought of Carol. All hesitation disappeared. It was simple reflex, the will to survive. I don't even recall whether pulling the trigger was a conscious effort. It was instinct.

I stood there in my shorts and t-shirt, shivering, the adrenalin slowly draining away. It dawned on me that I was only moments away from being one of the victims I had talked about. But for my thoughts of Kate, I would have probably been sound asleep. I would have died in the dark, my throat slit, unable to scream out, the blood soaking the pillow. I shivered.

I saw my camera sitting on the counter. I put down the phone, watching the steps. I don't know why I thought of it, but I quickly grabbed the camera and took a picture. I put the camera aside and picked up the phone.

I heard the sirens on the township road. I told the dispatcher that they were coming up the driveway, and I hung up. I ran to the bedroom and put on some sweat pants and hollered to Carol that the police had arrived. With the sound of the sirens, I figured if anybody was in the basement, they were out the door and into the woods. I went back to Carol's room. She sat on the bed, her arms crossed, leaning over in pain, still trembling.

"Carol," I said, "the cops are here. I don't think you should come out yet."

"Dad," she said, "tell me what's going on."

"I wish I knew," I said. "Somebody broke in. I don't know what he was going to do. I shot him."

"I know you shot him. Where'd you get a gun?"

Through her window, I saw the lights of the patrol cars flashing in the driveway. "Carol, just stay here, I'll be back as fast as I can."

The deputy was already standing in the doorway when I got to the kitchen, his gun drawn. It was Mike Weber. I pointed to the livingroom. He looked. "Jesus Christ, Bob! What happened? Who in the hell is that?"

"He came up the steps, into my room. I thought he was going to kill me. I shot him." I pointed to the gun sitting on the table.

He said, "Don't touch anything."

"I don't know if there's somebody with him or not." I said. "He came up through the basement. He had to open the door. I know it was locked."

He backed up a little and opened the storm door with one hand. "Hey guys, there might still be somebody in the basement. Check it out, take it easy."

I saw two deputies run past the door, around the side of the house to the walkout.

"Stay here," he said, and he made his way to the stairs and slowly descended.

A few minutes later I heard the officers talking. I couldn't make out what was being said. I heard them coming back up the steps. "There's nobody there," he said. "It looks like there's only one set of prints through the snow bank. How in the hell would he have gotten here?"

"I don't know," I said. "Is there a car parked on the road anywhere? Did you see anything?"

"I came in on 390th Street. I didn't see anything. I have to use your phone."

I heard him talk to the sheriff's office, told them they had to send a detective and the medical examiner.

"Is anybody else here?" he asked as he hung up.

"My daughter," I said. "She's back in the bedroom. She's pretty upset. She didn't know what was happening. I'm sure she was sound asleep. The shot must've scared the hell out of her. I'm going to call a friend."

I dialed Tony's number. It rang for a long time. I was sure he was sound asleep. When he finally answered, it was just a mumble.

"Tony," I said, "you're never going to believe what happened. Somebody broke into my house, a black guy I've never seen him before. Tony, I shot him—I killed him. He's here, on the livingroom floor, the deputies are here, Mike Weber."

I heard him say, "Jesus Christ, what else can happen?"

"I don't know what's going to happen. Tony, I need you here. Can you come out."

He said he was already on his way.

The deputy had been looking at the body, kneeling to the side. He looked at me. "I assume the knife was his."

"I saw something reflecting the lights from the Christmas tree in his hand. I didn't know what it was. I thought it was either a knife or a gun."

The deputy walked back to where I was standing. "Is that your .38?" he asked.

"Yeah. I bought it at an auction years ago." I don't know why I said that.

"Is it licensed," he asked.

"No."

"Did you only fire once?"

"Yes."

"What's in there?"

"What do you mean?"

"What kind of shells are you using?"

"It's some new shells I bought. I think they're called hollow points."

"Why would you get those?" he asked.

"What's the point in all this?" I finally said.

"No point, Bob. I'm just asking."

"You're making it sound like I did something wrong."

"I don't know what happened here, Bob. Everything seems to point to what you said, but this is the second time I've been out here to find a dead body. Makes a person wonder, don't ya think?"

"You can wonder all you want," I replied. "All I can tell you is that I have no doubt that he, whoever that is over there, was going to kill me, or if he wasn't going to kill me, it wasn't a social call. If it's okay, I'm going to go take care of my daughter."

By the time I reached the end of the hallway, Carol was coming out of her room. "Carol," I said, "it's okay. Let's go back."

She said, "No, I have to see what happened."

She broke by me and walked to the edge of the livingroom. She stood there, put her hands to her face and said, "Oh, my God, oh, my God. Dad, what did you do? Who is he? What was he doing here?"

She was again on the verge of hysteria.

I went up and put my arm around her shoulder, gently tugging her back. I put my arms around her and hugged her tightly. "Carol, I didn't have any choice."

"I know, Dad. I know. It's just so terrible. I wanna know what's going on."

I wish I knew," I said.

"There's something going on here I don't understand."

Another patrol car pulled up. I led Carol away from the body to a couch in another room. It was still dark in the room. I sat her down, tried to comfort her. Then I walked back to where Deputy Meyer was standing by the counter. The door flew open. It was Detective Lou Jacobs. I'd handled several cases where he'd been the chief investigating officer. He had a reputation for being a tough cop, a good investigator. I thought there were times when he had skirted the line, pulled a few dirty tricks, but for the most part, I trusted him.

He walked over to look at the body. He and Meyer talked for a few minutes. I had started to make coffee by the kitchen counter. He walked back. "The medical examiner and the photographer should be here shortly. Is there someplace we can talk?"

I took him back into the living room, I figured Carol might as well hear everything. I introduced him, and we both sat down. I went through the whole story one more time. He was jotting down notes. Carol would just shake her head.

"You have no idea who this guy is?" he said.

"None."

"I suppose it could be a burglary, but why Christmas night and why night at all? I mean, you're out here in the country, Bob. There's got to be all kinds of opportunities to get into this house during the day, when nobody's here."

"No, this was planned," I said. "Tony O'Donnell came out on a Saturday morning, and I know that basement door had been locked. When I didn't answer his knock, he came in the same door, said it was open. I thought at the time, somebody's been here, opened the door and then left and forgot to lock it again. Nothing was missing in the house, not that I have anything anybody would want to steal anyway."

Just as I finished, I heard Tony's voice in the kitchen. I got up and walked out. The detective and Carol followed. Tony was standing by the body. He looked at me, he knew what happened. He greeted Detective Jacobs like an old friend. I had forgot they had once been on a major crime unit together.

Detective Jacobs looked at Tony. "Well, it seems to me a clear case of self-defense."

More people started coming in the door. The medical examiner kneeled down and looked at the body and then motioned the photographer to start taking pictures. When he was done, Detective Jacobs started to go through his pockets. There was nothing, no identification, not even pocket change.

Carol couldn't stand it. She went back to her room.

Two men came in with a stretcher, placed the body on it and carried it out. I looked at the carpet, it was soaked in blood. The medical attendants had stepped in it and left bloody tracks across the room and out the sliding glass door. There was a stench to it, too; it almost made me throw up. I walked into the other room, found a big old quilt, brought it back and tossed it over the scene.

Tony was talking to Detective Jacobs by the back door. Everybody was clearing out. The detective looked at me. "Why don't you come in tomorrow, Bob. We'll get a formal statement. Just give me a call when you've got time. No hurry."

He was about to open the door when he turned around. "By the way, Bob, I need the gun."

I pointed to the counter. "It's over there," I said.

He took out a little plastic bag, went over, picked it up and dropped it in. "See ya tomorrow," he said as he exited.

Suddenly, it was quiet. "Do you want a cup of coffee?" I asked Tony. "Yeah."

Carol came back out of her bedroom. She gave Tony a hug. "Tony, what's going on?" she asked.

He looked at me. "I think it's time we tell her."

I nodded.

For a long time we sat at the table, and Tony and I recounted our suspicions. How we believed that it was Draper on a binge of revenge who was responsible for Kate's death. Now this. Our dead body wasn't Mr. Draper, but that didn't mean he couldn't be behind it. It could be somebody he met in prison, somebody he hired. After all, there had to be somebody else with him. They didn't find a car, but he hadn't walk the miles from town; somebody dropped him off. We suspected that when the dead man didn't return, or when the driver saw the sheriff's lights, he took off. That could have been Draper.

"That makes sense," I said. "Draper could've conned this poor slob into thinking there was really something here to steal. You know, all you have to do is cut the guy's throat and the house is yours. There's no way they would've known Carol was here."

"I can't believe somebody could do that," said Carol.

"Carol," I said, "you don't understand what kind of animals are out there."

"You know, Dad, you keep using that term, 'animals', 'a bunch of animals'. Believe me, there isn't anything in the animal kingdom that would act like that. Humans are worse than animals."

"It's just a phrase," I said.

"Yeah," she replied, "a bad phrase."

"Well," Tony said, "we're just going to have to see who this guy is. If he comes up with a record, somebody who was in prison with Draper, we'll know it, and then it'll all make some sense."

The sun was coming up. We'd been talking so long, drinking so much coffee, we were all wide awake. I offered to make breakfast. They both gave it thumbs down. We decided to go into Perkins. Carol agreed to postpone her trip to Chicago for a day, or longer, if necessary.

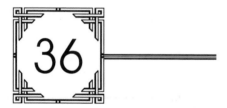

Two o'clock that afternoon, I walked into the Law Enforcement Center in St. Cloud to have a meeting with Detective Jacobs at the sheriff's office. I stood at the reception desk for several minutes and waited. I heard a click at the side door, and he walked out.

"Come on back, Bob," he said.

He led me down the hall to his office. I recognized several other deputies who waved from their desks. He offered me a cup of coffee, which I declined. I could tell he was having a hard time coming up with what he wanted to say. As we both sat down, he said, "We've got a real puzzle on our hands, Bob. The guy comes back 'no means of identification.' We took his prints. No match at the BCA. We wired them to the FBI. It should be a couple days. He had no identification, and his picture doesn't come up matching any mug books, at least nothing we've found so far. He's a real John Doe."

"Let me ask you," I said, "if he'd been in the joint here, you'd have his prints. You'd have a match already?"

"Definitely."

"And there's nothing in the BCA fingerprint bank?"

"Nothing."

"None of the deputies remember seeing any car around there last night?"

"I've talked to them all. That time of the morning, anybody moving, we would've noticed. There was nothing. Whoever dropped him off was gone before we got there. There's nothing we can use to tie him down to anything. The knife was clean, not a print. I talked to the sheriff, Bob. He agrees, we're just gonna write it up as a justifiable homicide. I just have to get your statement to document it for the record. We'll turn it over to the county attorney's office, but I don't see anything happening. By the way, whose gun was that?"

"Mine, why?"

"How long have you had it?"

"For years. I don't even remember." I hesitated, trying to remember what I told Meyer last night. I couldn't. "I think a client gave it to me, for a fee."

"But the shells were new," he said. "And they're a high-velocity hollow points, meant to drop something. I was just curious, Bob, why a gun that's been sitting around for years would be in your bed stand, loaded with powerful hollow point shells, sort of like you were expecting something?"

"There's nothing sinister to it," I said. "After Kate died, I was home alone. I thought I should have something there. I decided to stop at a sport shop on the way home and pick up a box of shells. To tell you the truth, I didn't even know what I was buying. I just knew they had to be .38 caliber. So they were high-velocity, huh?"

He nodded with a smile. He took out his tape recorder, and I gave him a statement.

Fifteen minutes later, I was back at my office, paging Tony. I left a message, "We have to talk. I'll meet you at the Lodge at five."

227

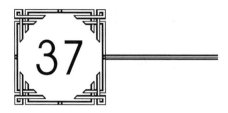

37

"Tony," I said, "I've just been having bad, bad thoughts."

"About what?" he said.

"Detective Jacobs tells me they can't get a make on the dead guy. They're not done, but it's obvious he didn't do any time in any state pen. There's no identification. We don't know how he got there or, more importantly, why he got there. If he's a burglar, what's he doing out in the middle of nowhere? God, my driveway's a quarter mile long. You don't want to be a burglar caught up there with no other way out. He was there for one purpose and one purpose only. And, if he wasn't associated with Draper, who was he working with . . . or for?"

"But Draper's the only suspect that makes sense," Tony said.

"There's another possibility, something that's been in the back of my mind for a while." I hesitated, worried that I would sound like I had flipped out. "Something so bizarre, I've been a little reluctant to bring it up. Now, since last night, though, I've been thinking about it a lot, and it may not be that crazy. Tony look, since August, what's happened: Pam Weber was murdered in Minneapolis, Kate was murdered here. It's made to look like suicide, but we know better. Faye dies, made to look like an accident, but maybe it wasn't. And then a black guy's sent to my house to kill me. I wondered, where's the common thread through all of this? There's only one, Tony, and I believe it relates to a letter I got last summer from a former client of mine. He wanted me to help some government people get seventy-five million dollars out of Nigeria."

Tony had been sipping on a beer, he put it down hard. "What the hell are you talking about?"

"Remember last fall I told you I went to see John Spokes?"

"Yeah," said Tony.

"Pam Weber worked for him."

"Yeah."

"Well," I said, "I received a card from this Matthew, along with a letter signed by a Marshall Umah, who claimed to be the Minister of Finance to the government of Nigeria. Apparently, before the military coup took place in the fall of '93, some government officials had hidden away in a bank seventy-five million dollars skimmed from foreign contractors. The purpose of the letter was to ask me to help them get the money out of the country. Here's the kicker: My fee would have been twenty-five percent, close to nineteen million dollars."

"Jesus Christ," said Tony.

I spent the next fifteen minutes telling him the content of the letter from Dr. Umah, what inquiries I had made in St. Cloud and finally my meeting with Spokes.

"When Kate and I left," I continued, "we had pretty much resigned ourselves to the fact that Spokes was right, it was best forgotten. When I got back, I looked at the federal statutes. Everything Spokes told me was true. There was a host of felony offenses we would've committed by helping them bring the money over. So really, Tony, I put it out of my mind. Even after reading about his legal assistant's murder, it appeared to be just another tragic event in the big city. It was terrible, but I didn't associate it with anything dealing with Spokes or the money. Even with Kate, I had no way of tying it to anything . . . but it's the dead black man, the black man with no identification, no prior life of any kind—then I thought about Spokes. Remember that article you pointed out, the one where he was trying to get back into horse racing? There was another article recently. He's got some investment group, he's going to raise millions of dollars. This letter from Marshall Umah, it said they would take my advice on how to invest the money here in the states."

Tony was engrossed in my story; he didn't say a word. He sipped on his beer and stared straight into my face.

"You know, Tony, he told me to forget about it, and I did. But what if *he* didn't? What if he was desperate? Remember what I told you, that he had those race horses he had to get rid of. As far as I know, he lost tons of money on the whole project. Then all of a sudden he's back, talking about putting in millions of dollars. Where do you think he got the money?"

"You think he would've been involved in murder?" asked Tony. "I mean this guy's got a national reputation. He's a high-powered criminal defense attorney. Christ, last year he was in the paper every day when he was defending some banker on fraud charges involving millions of dollars. He got the crook off, too. Don't you think he made a pile on that?"

"One thing I've learned, Tony, is that it isn't necessarily how many piles come in that count but the number of piles that go out. He could be making millions, but if he's spending tens of millions . . ."

"I just find it hard to believe," Tony replied. "What you're saying is, somehow he took over your deal, helped the Nigerians bring over the seventy-five million. They paid him the twenty-five percent and . . . what? The killings were done to keep everybody quiet?"

"Well look at it, Tony. Pam Weber's the first to go, within weeks. I don't know what happened, but after she's gone, whoever was behind this must've asked himself, who else knows about it? Other than Spokes and his cohorts, it's Kate, because she was with me, then Faye, who I'm not sure what she really did know, but her name was on the fax to Spokes . . . and, of course, me. They get rid of us . . . they're home free."

"But why would they have to go to such lengths . . . to kill?" asked Tony.

"God, you have to remember, these are major federal offenses—twenty, thirty years in prison. More importantly, what if the military government of Nigeria found out about it? What do you think they would do to get Marshall Umah back? Their seventy-five million dollars back? You don't think they have some henchman they can use? Read up on the country. I did, Tony. It's a cut-throat existence over there."

Tony sighed deeply, leaned back in his chair, his fingers tapping the table. He had that habit. Whenever he was nervous, he started drumming out a tune with his fingers. "So, let's assume," he said, "that this guy—your dead body—was the assassin for this group, then we have to try and tie him to all three deaths. Or, even if we could tie him to one, we'd have something to go on. You think he was involved in Faye's death?"

"If I'm right," I said, "it's almost too providential to have happened accidentally. I mean, if they wanted everybody gone, that would've included her. They just can't keep murdering people like they did Pam Weber, at least not around here, that would be too obvious. They'd have to make it look like an accident."

"You're painting a pretty black picture," Tony said.

"Tony, you have to remember what's involved. Seventy-five million dollars. Think what you can hire to have done to protect seventy-five million dollars. Shit, there are people who'll cut your throat for a hundred bucks."

"You may be right," Tony said, with some resignation, "but I really have a hard time believing Spokes had any part of this. I've seen the guy work. With all deference to you, Bob, the guy's slick, as slick as I've seen."

"Mr. Slick," I said, "may also be an accomplice to murder. I can't imagine he'd get his hands dirty, but he had to know what was happening, especially after Pam Weber ended up in the dumpster."

Tony turned his head to stare out the window. He brought his hand to his face and tapped lis lips with his index finger. I remained silent. He let his hand drop to the table and looked at me. "I don't know, Bob. Spokes wouldn't be any part of a murder. If you're right and this black dude that ended up sprawled on your living room floor was responsible for all the deaths, either alone or with someone, I can't imagine that Spokes had any involvement in planning the killings . . ."

I interrupted. "Listen, if I'm right and it's the Nigerians covering their asses by eliminating all potential witnesses, Spokes can't get out of it by saying, 'Hey, I had no idea they were going to start killing people.' He's the one who set the whole scheme in motion by responding to the letter. He was a co-conspirator in bringing the stolen money in and that makes him a co-conspirator in anything they do to cover up their illegal activity. He can't raise ignorance as a defense."

"All I was saying is—"

"I know what you're saying. Why would someone with his reputation risk it all in a scheme like this? Since the thought of his being behind this first crept into my mind, I've asked myself the same thing. Maybe I'm wrong . . . but it's the only scenario that makes any sense."

"Even assuming you're right about the money, I can't see Spokes giving the orders to start whacking people."

"He doesn't have to. It's not much different than Kevin's case. What did Spencer tell the jury in Kevin's case . . . a person's responsible for the reasonably foreseeable consequences of their acts. When you enter a home late at night, uninvited, you might reasonably expect some shit might happen—like getting into a fight with a boyfriend."

Tony's eyes were glued to my face. I could feel the heat rise to my cheeks, perspiration collect around my collar. I could tell Tony was mulling it over. I repeated, "You intend the natural and reasonably foreseeable consequences of your acts, Tony. When you help foreigners bring millions of dollars of stolen money into the country, you should likewise reasonably expect some shit might happen."

"But Kevin walked," Tony said, softly, then paused to let it sink in.

Our eyes remained fixed on each other. I could hear the clinking of dishes and muffled voices in the bar, but it all seemed distant. My mind remained cemented to my thoughts. Spokes walking free was something I had dwelled on quite often since my fist suspicions. Even assuming I could gather enough evidence to tie him to the Nigerians and the money, his first line of defense would be that he took no part in the plotting to kill, or the actual murders, of any witnesses. The whole case would be mired in arguments over the responsibility of co-conspirators for the crimes of others; the right of jurors to infer criminal intent; whether the prosecution could make a showing of the requisite *mens rea* for conviction. All the arguments that defense attorneys like to use to confuse jurors. Spokes was an expert at raising a reasonable doubt. I was afraid there was enough wiggle room for him to squirm out of responsibility. He certainly had the resources to hire himself a good mouthpiece to do just that.

Tony interrupted my thoughts. "How many black guys you think end up skiing at Quadna?" he asked.

"Very few," I replied.

"Then we're on the same track," he said. "If we can put our dead body at Quadna, well . . . I wonder if Detective Jacobs will give me a picture."

"He doesn't have to, I've got one. I took it before they got there."

I took a picture out of my vest pocket, shoved it across the table. "I could've been a little closer, I suppose. I used the flash—a little too contrasty. I'd cut out the blood before I showed it to anybody."

Tony picked it up and looked at it. "I think that should be good enough."

Driving home, I couldn't take my mind off where I thought this was leading. The more I pondered it, the angrier I became. The realization set in that Kate might have been murdered just for money, not because of some vengeful thought to get even with me, a thought borne in anger and frustration from someone spending most of his life in a little cell, blaming his incompetent attorney. In my own weird world of dealing with criminal behavior, I could comprehend that; but to kill three beautiful women, including my Kate, just so he could have his horses, play the big shot—that was beyond comprehension.

I pictured Spokes standing there in his thousand-dollar suit, slicked-back dyed hair, mustache, taking Kate's hand, making her blush. At that point, he'd already looked over all the papers Faye had faxed to him and talked to his hotshot international attorney . . . and, already planned how he was going to keep the money. He so coolly conned me into believing that it would never work, that we'd end up in prison. If I had the lying bastard in front of me, I felt I could ring his neck myself. Money, over frikin' money. I couldn't believe it. I swore he wouldn't get away with it.

Yeah, right. What can I do? I wondered. The whole transaction was surely camouflaged. Maybe the money didn't even make it to any bank in the States. He had all the connections. How would he do it? And more importantly, what could I do about it? I imagined going to the Minneapolis police and saying, "I want Spokes investigated for my wife's murder." They would lock me up for potential mental commitment. I bet he has an alibi, anyway. He was out of the country when Pam was killed. He was probably at a party with the governor the night Faye was killed. He's probably covered every track. I knew I was going to be totally obsessed with this, consumed. That's just me.

When I got home, Carol was packing. She wanted to get away; in fact, she told me she had to get away. Now, with this new line of thought in place, I was less concerned about her safety. Why would Spokes want to get her? She knew nothing about it. I had to make sure it stayed that way.

"What did you find out," she asked.

"They've sent the prints and everything off to the FBI. They're waiting for a positive identification. It could be a day or two. It appears it was just a burglary."

She looked up from her bag, stern faced. "Don't give me that crap, Dad."

"What do you mean?" I asked.

"Who in the hell's going to come out here and burglarize our house Christmas night. I heard you talking this morning. That's bullshit. We both know it. I don't know what's going on, and I don't know why you're trying to con me."

"It's for your own good, Carol."

"You know what, Dad, I believe you. If you were any other person . . ." She hesitated. "Well, I just know I can trust your judgment. That's one of the reasons I'm leaving. It sounds like you and Tony have things to do. I would probably just be in the way."

"You'd never be in the way," I said. "But I agree, you are better off leaving for a while."

I helped her finish packing, and we went into Cold Spring to the Blue Heron for dinner. It was quiet. We sat in a corner overlooking the courtyard. With floodlights off the snow, the Christmas tree lights sparkling, it was a cheery scene, meant to bring joy. It was hard to be happy, though. I had read somewhere that the Christmas holidays produce the highest rate of suicides. I could understand why. You're not supposed to be depressed at Christmas. But here Carol and I sat, blank faces, unable to even crack a smile, wondering what was going on.

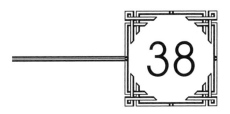

I was in my office the next afternoon when Tony came flying in. He barely nodded at Heidi as he shot by.

"Goddamn, you're not going to be believe this, Bob. The son-of-a-bitch was there, he was at Quadna, the same weekend. The bartender recalls him, said he spoke very little English, or at least piss-poor English. Said he was trying to hit on a couple girls in the bar. At about the time the bartender was gonna try and kick him out, he disappeared. They checked the books for me. He wasn't a guest. They said they wouldn't have had a room for him anyway; they were packed for the weekend."

"How about in town?" I asked.

"I was coming to that," he said. "I checked everywhere from Hill City to Grand Rapids, Sugar Hills. I even went over to Hackensack. Nothing. Nobody saw a black man who couldn't speak English. And believe me, Bob, in those little towns, in the middle of winter, people would've remembered."

"I knew it," I said. "I had a sixth sense. So now what do we do. We know he was there when Faye died, so it wasn't an accident. We can't tie him to Kate, yet, and we can't tie him to Pam Weber. We can't even tie him to Spokes. I mean, think about it, Tony, we have a black man who we think killed three people, with no witnesses, and then he's in my house in the middle of the night, obviously to kill me. What do we tell the cops? You were a detective, what would you do with it?"

"Well," and he hesitated, "I don't know. You're right, I guess, I would have to keep working. I mean, there's nothing to tie him to Spokes. All we have is a hunch, an educated hunch. If we want to prove that this is all about that Nigerian money, you're right, Bob, we really don't have shit."

"I can't let him get away with it, Tony. I have to figure out how he did it. If seventy-five million dollars left Nigeria, there has to be a way of tracing that dough."

"That's out of my league," said Tony. "Maybe they've got it in a Swiss bank, bringing it in in small amounts."

"I don't think so. I can't imagine Marshall Umah and his boys wanting to wait. If I had to guess, they're living high off the hog in New York City someplace where they can hide in a crowd. I remember when I was there, these big white limos would pull up to the hotel—foreign diplomats. I'd see these hookers come out in their miniskirts, wiggle their butts into the limos, and they'd be gone. I tell you, Tony, it would go on for hours. Nobody pays any attention to that shit. Can you imagine one of these guys in New York City with millions in the bank? They're going to screw their brains out."

"You may be right," Tony said. "Christ, there's a million possibilities. You know what I'm gonna do? You know what could nail this down? I'm going to Minneapolis tomorrow and talk to the detective working the Weber case. What if there's a match on the DNA? I know they sent semen samples in on the Weber case for DNA testing. Now if we can get them to send in samples from our black body, and they match, bingo."

"How long would that take?" I asked.

"Depends on how busy they are, but I've heard a minimum of four months, more likely six months to a year."

"They could all be long gone by then, Tony. If they smell anything, if they're spooked because I shot that guy, they're gone. But you're right, that's our best bet."

I leaned back in my chair, looked up at the ceiling. "Maybe I should call Spokes tomorrow, see what sort of reaction I get out of him."

"Don't you even think of such a stupid thing," said Tony. "How do you think he's gonna react? You call him out of the blue, after you just whacked the cutthroat he sent after you, he's gonna know you're onto him. He'll have a whole frickin' army here. Believe me, you'll be up to your ass in switchblades."

He was right. It was a dumb idea. I wasn't thinking. The only way I'm safe is to play dumb. I have to do some research, go back to the books, see how they could bring the money in.

"Tony," I said, "you go ahead, dig into the Weber killing discreetly. I suspect Spokes has got connections in the homicide squad as well. If he finds

236

out somebody's digging around from St. Cloud . . . well, you're right, there's only one logical conclusion."

We left it that way.

I did my research. Every spare hour I could get, I was at the Law Library, or the Municipal Library looking up international finance, banking regulations, money laundering. I got out the federal code, started reading cases. I thought maybe I should go talk to a federal prosecutor, one of the U.S. attorneys. And tell him what? That I thought Spokes was involved in an international money-laundering scheme involving seventy-five million bucks and to keep it quiet he'd left dead bodies all over the state? Of course, they've all tried cases with him. I wondered how long it would take before they'd call the U.S. Marshal to kick my ass out. Mr. Williams, I concluded, you're sucking air.

I didn't hear from Tony for a couple days. This time, when he walked in, I could tell he was depressed. He sat down, a dejected look on his face. "They don't have shit on Weber's case," he said. "The investigation's dead as far as they're concerned unless the DNA turns something up. They don't expect that back for months. The detectives said the lab at the FBI is backed up out the door. This has got a low priority."

"Then, Tony," I said, "we're going to have to work it ourselves. We have to somehow put together a credible case that we can present to the cops. There has to be some way of finding out how that money came in, how it got distributed, where Marshall Umah and his friends are. Wouldn't they need a visa, a passport, something that would have to be registered before they could come into the country?"

"I'd certainly think so," said Tony.

"Who's got access to that kind of information? What if they came in on a diplomatic passport?" I asked.

"See, that stuff's all over my head. I never had to deal with any of that," Tony replied.

"Well, we're going to have to put it together, Tony. I'm not going to let him get away with this. You know, at our meeting Spokes told me if we got caught bringing that money in, it could be twenty years in prison. That was more than enough to scare me away. Now the bastard's got three murders on his hands, and it could've been four or five if he got me and Carol. I don't know how he can live with that. It's not going to happen Tony. I'm not going to let it happen . . . no way."

I had to go back to practicing law, but Spokes, the money, and the murderers remained etched on my mind, nagging at me. During every spare moment I had, I continued with the library research, looking at anything and everything to give me some clue.

I had been appointed on a new case on which I needed Tony's help. A young man had been charged with armed robbery of a local theater. His arrest had been based on two facts: One, that he had a prior criminal record for robbery and, two, the young lady at the front window picked him out from a mug shot. His dad bailed him out of jail at his first appearance, and he ended up in my office, screaming, protesting his innocence. They had the wrong man, he said. He was at a party twenty miles away, with his arm in a sling. There were all kinds of witnesses who could put him there.

"Didn't you tell the cops that?" I asked.

"Damn right, I did."

"Did they check with anybody?"

"Hell, no. As far as they're concerned, I'm guilty. They wanted me to confess. I told 'em to kiss my ass. I guess I pissed 'em off."

"Well, give me the names of the people who were at the party," I said. "We'll send an investigator to see what we can come up with. Seems pretty simple."

I got out the police reports and started paging through. There was the mug shot they used from the previous conviction, the one the young lady had used to identify him. He certainly matched her description: Five-eight, five-nine, hundred and sixty pounds, long dishwater blonde hair hanging over the ears, stringy looking, scruffy face, unshaven, blue eyes, rough complexion. I looked at the picture. Yup, that's my defendant.

On the way home that night, I met Tony at the Lodge. "Here's a list of people Brad wants us to get statements from. He claims they were all at the party, can put him there, as alibi witnesses. Also said he couldn't hold a gun. He had his arm in a sling. I would've thought the cops would've checked that out already."

"I suspect they were just too busy, thought, 'Piss on it,'" said Tony. "He doesn't look like the kind who would generate a whole lot of sympathy, especially with a prior record."

"I don't suppose you've come up with any new ideas on Mr. Spokes?" I asked.

"I talked to Jacobs at the sheriff's office. There's nothing more there, nothing from the FBI. They apparently still got the guy on ice. And, I'm sure the Weber case is still sitting at the bottom of the pile."

"Maybe there's something we can do to spook them into doing something," I said.

"I told you before, Bob, that's stupid. That's the easiest way to get yourself killed."

"Well, I don't have anything on the calendar tomorrow. I think I might go to Minneapolis, the U library, and see what I can find out about this horse racing thing, maybe there's something there we can look at. I've exhausted everything here."

"You know the problem," said Tony, "you're looking at resource material that tells you how to do things legitimately. I can't imagine they have any books that say, 'Here, if you want to beat the federal government, illegally bring money into the States, this is how you do it.' It's like everything else, if you want to catch a thief, you talk to a thief."

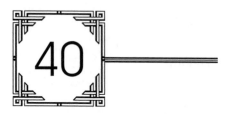

I had told Tony that I was going to the university library to continue my research on money laundering. That was only partly true. I kept thinking of what Tony had said. He was right; from my research, it was clear that a legitimate transfer would have been easy and traceable, but there were a million ways to hide an illegal transfer. What I really wanted to do was find out more about Mr. Spokes. I knew his public persona but very little about his background, how he got his reputation, what people thought of him. I wanted to know why he needed all that money.

It was easier than I expected. *Minneapolis Magazine* had done a cover story on him a little over a year earlier, right after he won his big trial in federal court representing the banker charged with fraud. I dug through the pile, and there it was. Spokes smiled at me from the front cover. He had already dyed his hair. I read the article. Nothing exciting. He had graduated from the University of Minnesota Law School and then spent ten years as an assistant United States attorney. He was known as an aggressive prosecutor, thoroughly prepared, eager. He would take any case assigned and then ask for more. He was lured away from the U.S. Attorney's Office by one of the premiere law firms in Minneapolis to head up a new section representing white-collar criminals. He left the firm several years before over a dispute with one of the senior partners. The dispute, coincidently, the article noted, was over the representation of the banker charged with fraud. At that time, the case was still under investigation by federal bank authorities, and some senior members of the firm believed Spoke's representation caused some conflict of interest in the office. Rather than give up representation, Spokes left the firm—with the client.

The article related that the Justice Department charged the banker, Henry McCann, with fraud involving a scheme where it was alleged that Mr. McCann had falsified documents regarding the development of a commercial piece of property in Bloomington. Mr. McCann was one of three investors attempting to build a multimillion-dollar office complex. The government claimed that the partnership made fraudulent representations to the bank to obtain financing in excess of the reasonable value of the project. The claim was that Mr. McCann had falsified documents to secure the bank financing and had received, or would receive, a kickback in excess of half a million dollars. Mr. Spokes was able to convince the jury that Mr. McCann wasn't the source of the false documents, and that the half million dollar kickback was a figment of the imagination of the government investigators.

Hell of a feat, I thought. But that was his reputation. There was even talk that our Republican senator was considering placing Spokes' name for a nomination to an open position on the federal bench. Word was that apparently Spokes had nixed the idea.

The article indicated that Spokes had spent a small fortune over the years on developing a line of thoroughbred race horses. When the state closed down the race track for poor attendance, he was faced with a decision on how to dispose of a barn full of expensive horses. It was at that time that many of the breeders were shipping their excess stock to France. Spokes and several other breeders bought property off Highway 55, between Minneapolis and Buffalo, and set up a stable to maintain the best of their stock. Spokes was quoted as saying that there were numerous plans before the State Legislature attempting to construct a program that would allow the reopening of the race track. All it would require was a financial commitment from sufficient investors to supplement what the state might be willing to spend.

Spokes was not married. The article talked a little bit about some of the women in his life. He had a reputation as a man about town. His present interest was a Blanche Corcoran, whose main passion was said to be thoroughbred horses. There was a picture of the two of them sitting on the deck at his home overlooking Lake Minnetonka. It wasn't the same blonde I had seen him with so often at seminars.

The article was disturbing, not in its content, but in its impact on me. It made me realize, more than I already had, this wasn't going to be an easy task. I knew, as lawyers like to say, beyond a reasonable doubt, that Mr.

Spokes ended up with the money, and that, if he wasn't involved in the killings, he had to know about them and quietly condone them. If nothing else, he was implicated by his silence. But how could I go public? With what I had, there wasn't a soul I could talk to who would give my story the slightest credence. I had to change that.

I took Tony's advice. I started looking for cases in which the feds had actually prosecuted people for some sort of illegal money laundering scheme. Only a small percentage of the cases ended up being published, those the defendant appealed from his conviction. To my surprise, there were hundreds of them, the vast majority dealing with laundering of drug money. After two hours, I realized this wasn't going to get me anywhere.

I started out of the library intending to go back to St. Cloud, but I changed my mind. I wanted to see how Mr. Spokes really lived. I was going to go to Lake Minnetonka and see what kind of lifestyle his money could support.

As I reached the door, my mind flashed back to Kate and me in the car driving around South Minneapolis. I was hopelessly lost looking for Spokes' office. I heard her voice say, "You could've asked for directions." I reached into the glove compartment to find a map. I had no idea how to get to Spokes' house. I looked for Lake Drive off Beaver Bay, on Lake Minnetonka. There it was, all I had to do was follow Highway 394 out of town and then head south.

The human mind is a funny thing. When it locks in on something, no matter how many times a person tries to drift away, to change focus, it always swings back—involuntarily. At least that's how my mind was working. The traffic was heavy, and the trip took me over forty-five minutes. Whenever I would consciously start my mind down a new avenue, suddenly, bam, there would be Spokes, or Kate, or Faye, or Pam. What had this man done to me? He had spoiled everything. I always had enjoyed driving, listening to public radio, watching the scenery go by, looking for things that piqued my interest—a flock of geese, a doe standing on the roadside munching on the grass laid bare by the hot sun, red-tailed hawks sitting on fenceposts, their eyes scanning the ditches for their next meal. Now none of that mattered. I stared ahead, my mind fixed on one subject—revenge.

I don't think I had ever hated somebody before—I mean really hated. I don't remember ever wanting to get even. Well, maybe with Spencer. But that was different; that was in the courtroom. I was reluctant to acknowledge it to myself, but now I wanted to hurt Spokes, wanted to see him suffer like I was suffering. I wanted the son-of-a-bitch to scream in anguish, to plead for mercy. These were all strange thoughts. Just months earlier, I couldn't, wouldn't have believed my mind was capable of conjuring up such images. Now they came with a rush, one after another, and with each one I thought I felt my spirit rebound ever so slightly. These were dark thoughts. Is that what he has done to me? But what else could I do? I wasn't going to sit still and allow my anguish to turn me into a bitter old man, always regretting that I didn't have the guts to do something.

I pulled onto Lake Drive. It was pretty much what I expected—large mansions, big yards, all overlooking the lake. It was a cloudy day. From the drive, I could look down past the homes, onto the lake, which spread out like a large white expanse, nothing to break the horizon except little clusters of ice fishing houses in an array of colors looking like little gift boxes set about the lake. The clouds hung low and the lake disappeared in the distance, the snow and the white clouds seeming to become one. I found his address and stopped. The property was surrounded by a wrought-iron fence probably eight feet high, the tops looking like spears, intended, I thought, to discourage any attempt to climb over it. Mr. Spokes must be a little paranoid, I concluded, an occupational hazard of the criminal defense attorney. He, too, must wonder whether some disgruntled former client might come looking for him.

An iron gate protected a circle drive passing in front of a spreading two-story mansion. I could tell it was old. It was constructed of limestone that had already turned a mossy, yellowish-green color. I had no idea what the home was worth, I assumed several million. To the side, attached by a breezeway, was a large garage. In front of it was parked what appeared to be a recent vintage Jaguar. There was no sign of activity.

Driving slowly past the house, I could feel the blood rushing from my heart into my head. My temples started to pound. I had never experienced this before, this pure unadulterated anger. I put the car in gear and rolled by.

I could almost feel the disgust on my face. My thoughts were so diabolical they frightened me.

As I pulled back onto the highway, I looked at my watch. A little after three in the afternoon. I drove north until I hit Highway 55, and then I headed west. Fifteen minutes later, I pulled over and parked in front of a sign saying, "Rolling Hills Thoroughbred Stables." The article in the *Minneapolis Magazine* didn't tell me how many partners he had in the venture. I didn't know whether I could get anywhere near the barn, but I was obsessed enough with everything about Mr. Spokes that I was willing to try anything.

I pulled in through the white gate, to the side was a big concrete thoroughbred horse standing on a pedestal. I followed a winding road that started high above the pasture. I could see the stables and the indoor riding arena in the distance. Acres of pasture lay barren under a white blanket unmarred by human or animal tracks. It appeared the horses were all barned. I saw no outside activity at all. I pulled ahead, slowly, hoping I didn't run into anybody I knew, especially John Spokes. The road wound down the hill and ended up in front of the riding arena. To the side was a log building with a sign that said "OFFICE." Behind that, an older home, probably the original farmstead with two cars parked in front of the garage. As I pulled up, the front door of the house opened, and a young lady came out, putting on a jacket. She walked up to the car. "Can I help you?" she asked.

"I'm not sure," I replied. "My name is . . ." and I had to think quick, "Kevin O'Donnell, and I'm interested in looking at some thoroughbred horses. I was at a gas station on Highway 55, and they directed me over here. They indicated you may have some for sale."

"As a matter of fact, I do," she said. "Are you familiar with the thoroughbred line?"

"Well, I have to admit," I said, "my knowledge of thoroughbred horses, any horses, for that matter, is rather limited. But I'm looking more as a present for my daughter. She's graduating from college in the spring, and she loves horses, has all of her life. I know she gets a magazine on thoroughbreds. I've read it a few times. So . . ." I said, kind of throwing up my arms, "you're going to have to help me through this."

She smiled, like she had heard it all before. "Why don't you come into the barn, and I'll show you what we have."

Suddenly I felt comfortable. I'd never been good at conning people, though, I had to admit, I seemed to be doing fine.

I walked into the barn. It was immediately obvious this was a rich man's sport. They could have played football inside that barn. As I stood by the entrance, to my right was a riding arena, to the left was a big concrete apron leading to two main isles with horse stalls on each side. The stall fronts were all in knotty pine with various colored flags and banners hanging in front. As she led me down the aisle, the horses stuck their heads over their stall doors, whinnying. There was a mixture of smells, hay, straw, manure, a medicinal smell—liniment, I thought. The front of some of the stalls were covered with charts showing a history of the breeding—dams and sires going back many generations. Two thirds of the way down the hall, after probably twenty horses, she stopped. "I assumed from your comments," she said, "that you're not necessarily interested in racing stock. These two mares are for sale. They both have great blood lines, both have thrown some nice fillies and colts. There's no racing history here, but they've shown very well in hunting class."

I had no idea what she was talking about.

She looked at me. "They're expensive, though. What price are you interested in? Do you have any idea?"

"Not really," I said. "What sort of range are we talking about?"

She grinned at me. "In this barn?" she said. "There are cheaper horses."

"No." I said. "What would I be looking at here?"

"Anywhere from ten to a hundred grand."

I looked at her, a big grin. "I assume you're talking ten thousand."

I could tell she understood where I was coming from. She just nodded.

"Well, I suppose for a good thoroughbred," I said, "that doesn't seem too outrageous. On the lower end, not out of the realm of possibility. After all, she only graduates from college once."

I looked at the two horses, both had their heads over their stall doors. She had her palm out, feeding a little grain. "This is Pretty Woman," she said. "She's seven. She's had some good training, and she would do well in any sort of show. I think you could probably get her for twenty-five thousand."

She went to the next stall, did the same, the horse nuzzled her hand dropping more grain on the floor than it ate. "This is Bonnie's Princess. She just turned five. She probably needs a little bit more training, but her blood lines are better. You could probably get her for forty thousand."

I walked up, the horse stretched her neck out to get a sniff. I put my hand up. The horse thought I had something to eat. I quickly pulled it back, afraid I was going to lose a few fingers.

The young lady rubbed the horse's forehead. The horse appeared gentle enough.

"If you don't mind, maybe you can show me around a little bit."

"Sure," she said.

We proceeded to follow the aisles up and down the stalls.

As we went, I opened the conversation. "I read an article recently about racing at Canterbury Downs. The article talked about an attorney in Minneapolis, a guy named Spokes, who apparently is trying to put together a group to open racing. Do you have race horses here?" I asked.

"Oh, yes. Mr. Spokes is one of the owners. He has his own area of the barn back here. I'll show you."

We turned the corner and walked to the back. "See the banner there? That starts his stock."

I looked up at a big blue banner hanging across the aisle with white lettering, "Johnny's Stables."

"These are all his horses," she said. "The one over there, staring us down, that's his pride and joy. That's the one he's hoping to get back into racing."

I walked over, the sign on the door said, "Johnny Come Lately."

I tried to ask as casually as possible. "What's this horse worth?"

She was rubbing the horse's nose. "I'd hate to guess," she said, "could be millions. If it wins a few more races, he could make that on just breeding fees."

I looked around, across the aisle into another stall. A horse stared at me with big brown eyes. The sign underneath said, "Blanche's Lady."

"Listen," I said, "I appreciate your time. Do you have any information on the two you showed me, the ones for sale?"

"Yes," she said. "If you want to come to the house, I can give you a little information sheet on both of them."

"You know I hate to spend that kind of money without my daughter seeing the horses. Is it possible for me to bring my daughter back here some time? Maybe she can even ride them."

"I'll give you my card. You can call me anytime. But you have to remember, Mr. . . . . I'm sorry, what's your name again?"

The question caught me by surprise, what did I tell her, I could feel the sweat forming on my brow. It was Kevin something, Kevin what? That's right, O'Donnell.

"O'Donnell," I said, "Kevin O'Donnell."

"Well Mr. O'Donnell, you have to remember, there's a demand for these horses right now, so I wouldn't wait too long."

We walked to the house. She gave me the information sheets on the two mares. I thanked her again for her time and left. Getting into my car, I glanced at the barn. In the back of my mind was the darkest thought: I wonder what Mr. Spokes would feel like if he got a call some morning that Johnny Come Lately was dead?

I pulled into my office a little after five, just as Heidi was leaving. She waved at me from across the street and waited until I got there.

"Tony was here just a few minutes ago," she said. "He said he would meet you at the Lodge about six."

"Anything exciting happen today?" I asked.

"Just the usual," she said. "I think you've got a couple new clients. I left the information on your desk. Have you thought anything more about replacing . . . ."

She let the sentence dangle.

"Actually, I haven't," I said. "I need a little bit more time."

"It's getting a little hectic."

"You'll just have to take care of it as best you can," I replied.

I knew why it was getting hectic, I was ignoring what I was suppose to do. I had a few irate clients looking for things I promised to have done but never got to, I had more important things on my mind. My desk was telltale, it was scattered with files and documents, nothing in any order. Faye had always made sure things were always in the right place. Now things just accumulated. It had gotten to the point where I wasn't even bothering to keep things straight.

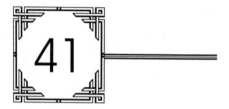

I pulled into the Log Lodge a little after six. Tony was already at the table. I stopped at the bar, Jessie handed me a beer on the way through. As I started towards the table, I noticed Tony's glass was empty. I did a quick about face, and Jessie handed me another beer across the bar.

"Well, who goes first?" Tony asked when I had sat down.

I wasn't necessarily going to tell him what I had done, so I said, "Why don't you."

"Well it seems like our client, Brad, has got some problems with his alibi. I talked to some of the people at the party in Avon. There were a lot of people there, it was an anniversary party. At some point in the evening they brought in some more beer. Guess who helped carry it in? This one gal, Susie, she said that Brad took his arm out of the sling and tossed a case across the floor with no effort. Another guy said the same thing, said he saw Brad take his arm out of the sling several times in the course of the evening— didn't seem to bother him at all. But here's the kicker, nobody can put him there precisely between nine and a little after ten o'clock. You remember, the young lady at the window of the theater said the car pulled up right around nine fifteen, someplace in there."

"So what are you telling me?" I asked. "Our young man's lying?"

"Well, Bob, what do you think? He gave us two reasons why it couldn't be him: First, his arm was in a sling, and he couldn't hold a pistol, and second, he was at this party. Now we find out that he was using the same arm to throw around cases of beer, and he disappears for a little over an hour, just about the time it would take to drive from Avon to St. Cloud, rob the theater, and get back. What do you think?"

I shook my head trying to display my dismay. "You know, you'd think that after all these years I would know better. I thought, here, I finally had a guy I could believe. I just thought it was a matter of the police being too lazy to finish their investigation."

"Where does the case stand?" Tony asked.

"We have a hearing set. I was going to see how strong the young lady's eyewitness identification was. We might have to forget that. We'll see."

"What'd you find out?" he asked.

"Pretty much what I already knew. There's more damn ways to hide that seventy-five million dollars than you can imagine. You know how much dirty money is laundered every year? They estimate close to four hundred billion dollars. Can you imagine that? That's more than most countries' national budgets. Maybe a hundred billion or more of that is laundered right here in the United States. What I found out is, every time the feds try to plug a loophole, the bad guys figure a way around it."

"Well, what do ya think they did with the seventy-five million?" he asked.

"Christ, who knows," I said. "It could've been transferred from one bank to the next all around the world before it finally got here. No way of possibly tracing it. I'll tell ya, Tony, there's a world out there that we know nothing about. You know, if you have the money, and you don't even need that much, there are islands where you can set up your own bank. All you do is buy a bank charter, get the bank set up—you don't even have to be there. You can buy a representative on the island to run your bank. It's called a captive bank. So you know what they're doing?"

Tony was finishing his beer, he took a quick gulp. "What?" he asked.

"They're setting up these offshore banks, and then they come up with fraudulent bills of lading, like an import-export business. Then, all of a sudden, a check appears in your account from this export company, but it's really coming out of this offshore bank. There's no reason why your banker should be suspicious, it looks like a legitimate transaction. So there's no end to what these guys could've done. For all we know, they've got a bank someplace on one of these islands, slowly bringing the money into the states, or it could've been here months ago, divided and spent on things like . . . horses."

"Isn't there some way we can check on it?" Tony said.

"How? How in the hell are we going to do it? Where would we start? I mean, some of these schemes have taken the Feds years to figure out. They've ended up having to use undercover informants, bugs in apartments, double agents. You wouldn't believe the elaborate plans they've had to concoct just to put an end to a simple money laundering scheme. Have you ever heard of smurfing, Tony?"

"I've heard of Smurfs. Aren't they those little blue characters on TV? How did you get onto smurfs?"

"There's an anti-smurfing statute. The government required banks to report any cash transactions in excess of ten thousand dollars. To get around it, drug dealers started recruiting guys to run from bank to bank and deposit just under $10,000 in cash, get a cashier's check. There were so many of these guys running around they became known as smurfs, after the little blue cartoon characters, because they seemed to be everywhere. Anyway, the government made it a crime to structure financial transactions like that, and they called it the anti-smurfing statute."

"It would take a while to clean up seventy-five million," said Tony.

"Yeah, that's too cumbersome. Besides, there's a risk to bringing cash into the country. That's also supposed to be reported—I think anything over five thousand. No, it got deposited in a bank somewhere, somewhere overseas, in the Caribbean, maybe."

By then Tony had turned away. He was looking at his reflection in the window. He was deep in thought, his mind miles away. He finally turned to me, "So what're ya gonna do?" he asked.

"I don't know," I said. "I'm stymied. Somehow I have to get Spokes to commit himself, screw up somewhere, something maybe that would implicate him . . . I don't have the slightest idea how I'm going do that."

"There's got to be something we can do," he said. "Let me put my mind to it."

We decided to have dinner. Our conversation turned to other matters. When I thought I could conveniently slip it in, I said, "By the way, Tony, can you get me another gun?"

He looked up from his meal, his eyes boring into mine. "Why?"

"Why? Just because I need one."

"Can't you get the gun back that you had?"

"They're holding it for the time being. Besides, that gun is burned."

"Why do you need a clean one?" he asked.

"What's your problem?" I asked.

"I don't have any problem, I'm not the one who needs a clean gun. What the hell do you have in mind?"

"Look, they failed once, what's keeping them from trying again. Since Christmas night, I've been sleeping with a meat cleaver under my pillow. Every little sound I hear I jump. I have to double check all the doors at night. I need some added security."

"You don't need a clean gun for that. Like you said, you could buy a shotgun. You're not thinking about doing something stupid, are you?"

"Tony, if it's a bother, forget it. I'll find my own."

"Just cool it," Tony replied. "I'll get it for you, but don't go playing cowboy. You've got to give this a little time. We can put it together."

We finished our meal in silence. We started on a cup of coffee when Tony asked, "When's your hearing in Brad's case?"

"A couple weeks."

"You think I oughta try and talk to anybody else?"

"If you think it'll do any good. I'll get Brad in and see what he has to say." Then I shook my head. "The little prick was trying to con me. You'd think that after all these years I could spot it."

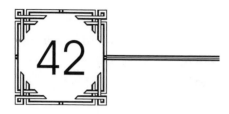

The next several days I spent ruminating. There were times I would sit at my desk for hours trying to conjure up a picture of how Spokes and his Nigerians could have structured their transaction to get the money into the country. Where would be a place to start? Hell, it was useless. What could Tony and I do? I had to do something, though, to get at Spokes. In my lowest moments, when my mind focused on nothing but revenge, I would think of Johnny Come Lately.

Carol called me after her return from Chicago. I told her I was anxious to see her. I was, but I had an ulterior motive. "Are you on the hospital shift this weekend?" I asked.

"I'm on all week, starting Saturday morning."

"I was thinking about visiting on Saturday. If I do, you think you'll have some time for lunch?"

"That would be great. If it's quiet, I can get away and show you around."

We made arrangements that I would be there a little before noon. Kate and I had picked Carol up several times at the vet school. The last time was to go to the State Fair. The campus skirted the fairgrounds, and we had used Carol's parking pass to be within walking distance.

I was a little early when I got there. I decided to visit the Raptor Center. I'd planned on doing that many times before but never found the time. The center had garnered a national reputation for rehabilitation of birds of prey. I had seen a news clip recently where they had brought in a harpy eagle from South America that had been shot in the wing. Unfortunately, it didn't make it. I looked at my watch, I had a little over fifteen minutes. I walked up to the window and stared at the bald eagle. They had a plaque giving his history. He also had been shot in the wing. They had saved the bird's life, but he could not be put back in the wild. He was one of their traveling birds. I slowly made my way through the exhibit. All of the birds had suffered the same fate and were now used for educational purposes. There was a great horned owl, a kestrel, a red-shouldered hawk. I went to the counter and bought Carol a t-shirt with three birds of prey on it: a bald eagle, a golden eagle, and an osprey.

I walked across the street to our designated meeting spot and waited. A few minutes later, Carol came running down the driveway dressed in a hospital frock to give me a flying hug. She grabbed my hand and tugged me towards the building. I could tell she was excited about showing me around.

We walked in the back door. In the first stall stood a big horse. "That's a Belgian," she said. "It came in last night. Colic."

She led me down the hall, saying "hi" to what I assumed were other students scurrying by. She introduced me to one of her professors. Everybody seemed to be in a hurry.

"You're going to love this, Dad. Come on in. I have to show you."

She led me into a room with all kinds of strange contraptions. In the back was a small paddock, she opened the door, lying there on fresh straw was this little horse. It struggled to stand up on wobbly legs. "It's a colt," she said. "It was born last night. The mother died, we're trying to keep it alive. We have to teach it how to eat. The mare belonged to the university. They said I can have the colt. Don't you think we could make a place for it at home?"

She looked at me, her face beaming. How could I say no. "Who's going to take care of it?" I asked.

"I'll come home as much as I can. Once we get it along a little bit, all we'll to have to do is give it grain and a little hay."

I had no idea if she was telling me the truth, but I wasn't going to burst her bubble. I watched the two of them. The baby horse nuzzled her hand, trying to suck on her finger. Carol looked at me. "He's already imprinted," she said. "He thinks I'm his mother. I just fed him, so we can go have lunch."

"How much time do you have?" I asked.

"There's nothing pressing right now. I have my pager. If they need anything, they can just call. We can leave the campus."

She took off her hospital uniform. She wore jeans and a dark blue sweatshirt. She walked over to the colt again, rubbed it on his forehead. Next to the colt, she looked tall. Her hair was cut short, the same color as the horse's mane, flaxen. She turned to look at me, her blue eyes soft, the hurt appeared gone. She had a new purpose in life, somebody who relied on her, something she could pour all of her feelings into. I knew it was good.

Minutes later we pulled into a little café off of Como Avenue. We gave the waitress an order for a bottle of Summit Pale Ale; she had a vegetarian sandwich, I ordered a club. "What happened to the mare?" I asked.

"It was a mess, Dad," she said. "The colt wasn't lying right, her intestines got all turned around. We knew she wasn't going to make it. We took the colt and put her down."

Put her down, what a euphemism, I thought. They killed her, put her out of her misery, they aided nature—they did all of those things, and it's summed up in a simple phrase: "We put her down."

"Have you had to do that before?" I asked. "I mean to other animals?"

"Sure," she said, "that's part of having a hospital. You end up doing it quite often. Sometimes people simply can't afford the kind of operation or veterinary care the animal needs. They pay us to take care of it. Sometimes the animal simply isn't going to survive. You euthanize it."

"What do you use?" I ask.

"There's a number of different drugs."

"How fast acting are they?"

"Some of them are instantaneous. As soon as they hit the heart, it shuts it down, and the animal's dead."

She gave me a strange look. "Not much for dinner conversation, is it?"

"Well it's something you do," I said. "I've been curious. Remember years ago I took one of the dogs to the vet? I did watch the vet, as you say, 'put her down,' and it was almost instantaneous. I was just curious what they used. Is there anything that may take longer than that?"

"Like what?" she asked.

"Well, you know, something that may take hours to act?"

254

"Nothing that I know of," she said. "That doesn't mean there may not be something. I can talk to one of the professors—he's a toxicologist. I assume there's something out there."

I dropped the subject.

"Have you and Tony found anything out?" she asked.

"Nothing."

"Do the cops know who that guy was?"

"No clue."

"What are you guys going to do?" she asked.

"We're still working on it."

"Is there anything I can do to help?" she asked.

"I don't want you involved, Carol. This is a dangerous situation."

"Then it's dangerous for you as well," she said.

"We have it under control."

I amazed myself. I was starting to get pretty proficient at lying.

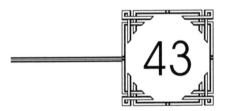

On my drive back to St. Cloud, I started to get this uneasy feeling. In my headlong plunge to the dark side to get even with Mr. Spokes, it appeared I was willing to deceive almost anyone, including Carol, if I believed it suited my purpose. Here I was trying to con her into giving me information on how I could poison a horse. I had reached an all time low. But the truth was, I didn't care. I was on a mission. The end, I believed, justified the means.

I had a plan, and now I had to think it out. I figured it was easy for me to get back to the riding stables and gain access to Johnny Come Lately. All I had to do was call the young lady and ask if I could see the two mares that were for sale again. But then if I poisoned the horse, wouldn't they know it was me? Of course! I didn't give her my real name but now I realized the name I gave her was stupid; Kevin O'Donnell, how long did I think it would take somebody to put that together. Not long I bet. So I had to do one of two things: I had to get into that barn without being seen, nobody knowing I was there, or else, it had to happen in such a way that nobody would suspect that a visitor to the barn was responsible. I wondered if a slow acting drug would work. But wouldn't they detect any drug? I was sure if a horse worth that kind of money fell over dead unexpectedly, they would have to do some testing, like an autopsy, to find out the cause of death. It would be easy to get a toxicology report, and the poison was going to show up. There was only one way I could do it—not being seen. I had decided on what I was going to use, some slow acting drug. Now I had to figure out how I was going to administer it and get the hell out of there.

I waited until I thought it was an appropriate time, when Carol wouldn't get suspicious. It wasn't common for me to run to St. Paul to visit her at the hospital, but I had no other source for the drug. I had called a local vet who had given me the number for a local veterinary supply house, and I was told any drug used to anesthetize or euthanize an animal was sold by prescription only. Based on what Carol had told me, I figured that was true, but I thought it was worth a try. So if I was going to drop the horse with a drug, I would somehow have to get the drug at the vet hospital without anyone knowing.

My life had become a melancholy existence. During the day, I had to force myself to concentrate on my cases. I would get home around seven in the evening and I would have two screwdrivers, make myself a sandwich, usually peanut butter and jelly, sit in a chair and by nine o'clock, I couldn't keep my eyes open. I would crawl into bed, and then, like clockwork, right at 3:30 a.m., my eyes would snap open, and I would spend the next three, four hours just lying there, my mind on one thought. I knew it was crazy. It was as if my mind had set this time aside to plot. And the funny thing was, it was never any different. I never came up with any new schemes, I was locked on one thought: I pictured myself sneaking into the barn, walking to the back, the horse would stick his head over the stall door, and I would rub his nose gently as I took the syringe and injected the deadly poison some-where in his neck. I'd turn around and walk out.

My thoughts would cover every contingency: What if somebody came in? Where would I hide? How would I escape? What if I got caught? What would I tell the police? I realized that my thoughts never went beyond my plans to kill the horse. What was I going to do with Spokes? Killing his horse was hardly getting even, but my mind seemed to resist sinking beyond that point.

Tony was out of town. It had been over a week since I had talked to him. He was investigating an accident case in the Duluth area for a civil attorney. He had called from his motel room a couple times, but we had missed each other. I preferred not to talk to him right then anyway, afraid I would betray my own thoughts.

That weekend I made arrangements to meet with Carol at the hospital again. She was on both Saturday and Sunday. She told me Sunday would be the better day. There would be fewer people there, probably less activity. We'd get more time to visit. From her reaction, it didn't sound like she thought anything about this new desire to come to the hospital. I suppose she thought, with Tony gone, I needed company. She couldn't come home, she wasn't going to leave her little colt.

Carol was right. Sunday afternoon was quiet. There were just a few ani-mals at the hospital—a couple of cows, a couple of sheep, even a pig. All the horses had gone home. There were several other students on duty, but they were back in their rooms with their pagers on. They told Carol she could call if she needed help. Same with the professors. Everybody apparently decided to take advantage of the quiet time and do something else.

Carol met me out front and took me immediately into the hospital. She wanted to show me how much her colt had progressed. I watched as we walked through. I assumed the medicine would be kept, like in a doctor's office, in closed shelves along the wall of the clinic rooms. I could see metal cabinets, some with locks across the front. We walked into the room, and the colt whin-nied. He had grown in the last week—no more wobbly legs. He stood behind the gate, stomping his hoof on the wood floor. Carol walked over and tussled his mane. The colt twisted his head a little to nip at her sleeve. She gently tapped him across the nose. He tossed his head. "He's going to be a beautiful horse," she said. "Have you thought more of what we talked about?"

"Well, if you can make a place for him at home, I have no problem with you bringing him home. I assume it's going to be a while."

"Yeah, he'll have to be here at least until early summer."

"That should work out great," I said.

My eyes slowly scanned the room as we talked. On the far side, above a stainless steel table, I saw a large wall cabinet with glass doors, the shelves lined neatly with little vials. A padlock hung loosely from a hinge, the door open.

"Is this room used for surgery?" I asked.

"Yes," she said. "Mainly large animals."

"What is this for anyway?" and I pointed towards the contraption I had noticed the week before.

"That's for holding larger animals, horses, cows. You walk 'em in, strap 'em so they can't move or kick during examination."

I casually started walking around the room showing an interest in all the charts and pictures hanging on the wall. There were pictures of anatomy of different animals, one showing a cow's four stomachs. I worked my way slowly to the tables and the cabinet. I looked in. "Is this stuff used for anesthesia?" I asked.

"The stuff on the right is, the stuff on the left is medicinal."

I saw what I wanted.

"What do they use Ketamine for?" I asked

"It's an analgesic, it's for large animals. They use it a lot at zoos for anesthetizing gorillas, elephants, animals of that size. It's been around for a long time. I'm surprised you don't recognize the name. Back in the '70s, it's precursor was a popular recreational drug. It's a congener of phencyclidine, PCP. Do you remember that?

"Angel dust," I said. "This is the same as angel dust?"

"Same effect," she said, "it's what's called a dissociative drug. In overdoses, apparently it can cause all kinds of mental problems, induced psychosis with violent, aggressive behavior, it can lead to a stupor and coma."

"I know," I said. "I handled some angel dust cases back in the seventies. It was popular on the college campus. I represented a young man who was so high on it he thought he could walk on fire. Some students were having a bonfire out at Talahi Lodge along the Mississippi. They were lacing marijuana with angel dust. He got so high, he tried walking through the fire. He ended up in the hospital with second and third-degree burns. Then, to add insult to injury, he was charged with possession of a controlled substance. If I remember right, he had a little baggie of it in his jeans. But this looks like liquid."

"I guess you can get in different forms," she said. "Here it's used intramuscularly. Like I said, in a small dose, it produces anesthesia for surgery."

"What affect would an overdose have on a horse?" I asked.

"I don't know, Dad. It would probably go berserk before any physical reaction would set in. I suppose a big enough dose could lead to coma, death."

"How much would you use?" I asked.

She had been playing with her colt. She turned, gave me a strange look. "What are all the questions for?"

"It's an interesting subject."

She grinned. "Well what's in that vial is probably enough for four, five knockdowns. Think about it, Dad, if a guy walked through fire with a little laced on a bud, what would a horse do with five times more than what you need to anaesthize him? I wouldn't want to be anywhere near him."

I walked back over and sat down by Carol. We talked while she sat there, her little colt looking over her shoulder. Every once in a while Carol would reach up and scratch its nose a little, and it would wiggle its upper lip, exposing a row of pearly white teeth. It appeared that they had indeed bonded. I could tell the colt had renewed her spirit. I realized I had been wrong. I thought with the loss of her mother, her enthusiasm had dissipated, but she was using her work, her studies, this little colt, to bring her out of the morass of the loss of her mother. I was happy for her. I, too, had made the attempt to throw myself into my work, hoping it would eventually release me, but for me it wasn't working. My problem was I knew way more than Carol did. I had somebody to blame.

We'd been talking for several hours, a little of everything. She was going to have a week off in March, and we were planning to take a little trip. I wanted to go see the Sand Hill Cranes in Nebraska. She was hoping to go a little further south, somewhere she could sit in the sun and catch up on her reading. I told her I might consider Albuquerque, New Mexico. We could go to Bosque Del Apache, and we'd both get our way—she could sit in the sun, and I could watch the birds.

About two-thirty her beeper went off. She told somebody that she would be there in a few minutes.

"I have to go out front, Dad. They're bringing in a heifer. Sounds like its got a twisted intestine. I have to help get it unloaded into a stall. You can keep Bay Bob company. That's what I'm going to call him, Bay Bob." She tussled his mane and walked out.

I followed her out to the hall. She quickly made it to the end and took a left. I watched for a while to see if there was any other activity. It was quiet.

I walked back to the medicine cabinet and looked through the glass. On the second shelf, to the far right, was a big vial that said " Ketamine." That's what I wanted. I reached in quickly, grabbed it and put it in my coat pocket. I again walked through the door into the hallway, looked both ways. I was safe; nobody there. Even though nobody saw me, my skin was crawling. I could feel little pin pricks all over my body, sweat oozing out. I thought I was safe now, but what if I had gotten caught? What if Carol had seen me put it in my pocket? How would I explain that? I had never stolen anything in my life, never even thought about it, yet here I was, intellectually seducing my daughter to steal drugs to get revenge.

You're going over the edge, I thought, as I tried to control my blood from pounding into my brain. I looked at my hands; they were trembling. I quickly put them in my coat pocket. The little bottle of drugs had sunk to the very bottom. I put my hand around it, it fit nicely in my fist, I knew it was safe there.

I heard footsteps coming down the hall. I tried to compose myself, act normal.

"Dad, I'm afraid I have to break this up," she said. "We've got a real sick cow. I've called for help. I'm really sorry. If you want to stick around, I might be able to get free by dinner."

I didn't dare stick around. I could imagine all kinds of things happening, like taking off my coat and the vial sliding out of the pocket to break on the floor. I was better off getting out of there, quickly.

"No, that's fine," I said. "I've got some work to do, I should really head home."

She walked over to her colt, tapped him on the nose. "You behave yourself," she said. She gave me a hug and raced out the door.

"All you have to do is go to the end of the hall and take the corridor to the left, that'll get you out to the parking lot," she said.

I followed her out. Her young legs left me behind quickly.

As I hit Como Avenue, I was trying to decide which way I should go. One way would take me home, the other way I could get to Highway 55. I decided to visit the stables. The traffic was quiet. I was able to get out of downtown Minneapolis in probably twenty minutes. I pulled into the driveway and stopped. I could see the riding stable, the barns, the parking lot was filled with cars. I pulled closer to get a better look, there was a Jaguar, not a good day for me to visit.

I knew I wasn't going to wait long to do my dirty deed. I had worked up the nerve to do it, wanted to do it, believed I had to do it. I knew if I hesitated, my resolve would fade. My conscious would get the better of me.

I started watching the weather. On Sunday evening news, they were predicting snow Tuesday. The next day I cleared my Tuesday calendar. I wanted to do it at a time when any tracks would be covered. I had already decided all I was going to do was wait until dark, park off the highway someplace safe and walk in. The only thing I had to make sure of was that the main door was not locked.

Monday evening I called the young lady and told her I would be going past the stable and asked if I could stop and look at the horses again. She was very pleasant, said anytime.

261

Tuesday morning, 3:30 a.m., I was lying in my bed going over my strategy for the hundredth time. *Stop worrying,* I thought. *It's no big deal. You just walk in, do your job and leave.*

I left my office a little after noon that day. I had it all planned out; everything looked perfect. The forecast called for snow moving in sometime early evening. I had a little bag on the front seat, the vial of Ketamine inside, and a couple syringes. Brand new needles, nice and sharp. I didn't want to be standing there trying to poke the horse and not be able to break the skin.

It was a little after one-thirty when I pulled up to the stables. I took out the card the young lady had given me, her name was Judy Douglas. I had barely gotten out of the car, and she was standing there.

"Mr. O'Donnell," she said, "looks like you're just in time. I think we're going to get dumped on. I just heard the forecast, they're talking about five, six inches of snow tonight. Well, I've got them all cleaned up for you. Is your daughter going to be here?"

"No, I told her about them, she said anything from this stable would be fine. Apparently, she was out here last summer, but I don't think she talked to you, at least you're not the person she described."

"That could be," she replied. "In the summer we have a lot of help."

As we talked, she led the way to the stable. When we walked in, I noted there was no lock on the door.

She took me directly back to the stalls. She brought Pretty Woman out first. Before she stepped out of the stall onto the concrete walkway, the young lady snapped a lead rope onto the halter, the horse pranced.

"She's ready for some exercise," the young lady said. "If you want to, we can saddle her up. You could take her for a little ride in the arena."

"Lots of luck," I said. "I tried riding a horse once. Ended up on my rump. I don't need any broken bones."

"This horse would never throw you," she said. "A little kid could ride this one. I'll show you."

She led the horse into the arena. She grabbed another strap and placed it on the other side of the halter. She grabbed the mane, and with a quick flip, she was on the horse's back.

262

"I'll show you her moves," she said.

She took the horse out to the middle of the arena and for the next fifteen minutes, I got a little show. She was right, the horse was a perfect lady. She brought the horse back to the railing and slid off the side.

"Pretty impressive," I said.

"Like I told you, Mr. O'Donnell, this horse has had a lot of training. That's the reason for the high price. I wouldn't do this on the other one, Bonnie's Princess. But with a little work, there's no reason why your daughter couldn't do the same on her. But if you want my opinion, this is the best horse you're gonna find for the money. If you wanted to, you could breed this horse. You could actually make some money."

She stood there with the horse on the other side of the fence. I walked a little closer. The horse looked at me, big brown eyes, she had a little white star on the forehead, the forelock and mane dark black. The horse flipped her head a couple times, as if to say, "Yes," agreeing with her handler. She came out of the gate and started to lead the horse back to her stall.

"You mentioned Mr. Spokes last time I was here. Does he have any horses for sale?"

"I don't believe he does," she said. "I think he's trying to keep them all in case the track opens this spring, but his lady friend, Ms. Corcoran, does. I think she'd probably sell Blanche's Lady, but I'm sure that's way more money."

"Maybe I could get a look at her," I said.

"Sure."

She put the mare back in the stall and led me towards Spokes area of the barn. The horse was beautiful, a little taller than the one she had just shown me. It was a dark brown with white stockings and a white star on the forehead, a curly dark brown mane. "How much you think she wants for this one?" I asked.

"I'm sure it would probably be more than fifty grand," she said. "This horse has had a lot of training. It's taken a lot of blue ribbons in shows. The only reason she may think of selling her is because she's devoting more of her time to her other horse, the one over there," and she pointed to Blanche's Princess.

I took the time to look around. I mapped it out in my mind exactly where I would have to come from the main door, down the aisle, so I wasn't fumbling around in the dark.

"Well, I think you've pretty much convinced me," I said. "I think Pretty Woman's the one that would suit her best. I'd hate to put her on a horse that might be dangerous. If something happened, I'd never forgive myself."

"You don't have to worry with her," she said.

"Maybe, if you've got the time, we should go in, and I could try and call my daughter to see if I should make the commitment."

"Sure," she said, "you can use the phone in my house."

"Office not being used?" I asked.

"Nah, there's not enough activity. We just keep the heat at a minimum during the week, save a few bucks. During the winter months when it's slower, I usually just work out of the house."

As I followed her in, I looked up the driveway, towards the barn, then towards the house, imagining where I would go if somebody came out of the door and hollered, "What are you doing there!"

We walked through the front porch and into the house. In the kitchen, she pointed to the phone on the wall, and I walked over and dialed a fictitious number and waited. As I stood there, I looked around. There were drapes over the kitchen window to the yard. If the drapes were drawn, no one could see out.

"Yeah, this is Dad," I said. "I'm at the thoroughbred stable. I think I've picked out the right horse, but I want to talk to you before I do anything more."

I hung up. "Machine. She must be at school," I said. "I'll talk to her tonight, and I'll give you a call."

"That's fine," she said. "I don't expect we'll get any other offers before the weekend. There is somebody coming on Saturday morning who wants to look at her, so if your going to do it, I'd do it quickly."

"Again, I really want to thank you for your help," I said. "It's been fun."

She walked me to the door. I shook her hand and left. As I walked out, I looked for lights. There was a small one on the outside of the porch by the steps and a big yard light right by the garage, one I was sure would cast light to the front of the barn. I made a mental note, I had to stay to the outside.

I got to my car, backed up and pushed the button for the odometer. I drove slowly out the driveway. It was a little over a quarter of a mile to the highway. I took a right and drove a little over a mile, there was no convenient spot to park the car. I did a u-turn and went back west. I found a pull off spot a little more than a block from the driveway, it looked like an access road for farm equipment. My only concern was, if I pulled in, could I get out. I thought I would try it during the day rather than wait until later when it could be a disaster. I pulled past it and backed in off the shoulder of the road. I put the car in forward, my tires spun a little, but I wasn't going to have any trouble getting out. I took a right and headed towards Buffalo. It looked like I was going to have a lot of time to waste. I assumed they would do the horse chores around five, just at dark. That would probably take a couple hours so I would have to wait at least until eight o'clock before I could make my trip into the barn. I looked at my watch, it was only three-thirty. What was I going to do for five hours?

I pulled into Buffalo, past the courthouse, following the road around the lake. I spotted a bar and restaurant with a couple of cars in the parking lot. I pulled in, parked, grabbed a folder out of the backseat and went in. There were a couple of guys sitting at the bar sipping on beer, one lady behind the bar who smiled when I walked in. I looked around. There was a table by the front window. I looked at the bartender. "Do you mind if I sit there?" I asked.

"No," she said, "go ahead. We're done serving lunch, though. We won't have food again until five o'clock unless you want something deep fried."

"No," I said. "That's fine. I just want a beer."

"Anything special?" she asked.

"Whatever you've got on tap."

I took the table, and a few moments later she came over with a large glass of beer. "Miller Genuine," she said.

"Do you mind if I start a tab?"

"No, I just need a name."

"Murphy," I said, "John Murphy."

I took a big swallow of beer and opened my file. I had been accumulating cases and articles I had found on money laundering.

With the tightening of banking regulations in the states, the amount of dirty money generated by illegal activities, and people who just wanted to hide their wealth from the government, off-shore banking was flourishing. In fact, there were companies that, for a modest fee of fifty grand, would help you set up an off-shore bank, all legal. The attraction was that these new banking centers offered customers secrecy, low or no taxes, and fewer regulations. Some of the ads even made it sound exciting: "Ever since the days of the pyramid trade, molasses for rum and slaves, the Caribbean has conjured ideas of incredibly lucrative, if not slightly illegal, stores of wealth." The possibilities were endless, Cayman Islands, Bermuda, Barbados, Bahamas.

When I had called Spokes after hearing of Weber's death, his secretary did tell me he was out of the country. Maybe that's what he was doing, setting it up. That would be just like him, sitting in the Cayman Islands, Bermuda, one of the havens for offshore banking, playing the big shot. Why not? He could do that with millions of dollars. He could have his own captive bank, he could be president, make himself loans. All legitimate.

Maybe they're all in on it. Marshall Umah said he would take advice on investing their share. No safer place than in your own bank. Maybe Umah's his secret partner in the race track—he could certainly con the Nigerians into thinking it was a good investment. I wonder if Matthew's with him. He's probably still the go-between for Spokes and the Nigerians.

About four-thirty, people started to file in, it looked like a working man's bar. It started to get a little noisy. At the end of the bar sat an attractive young woman, probably in her middle thirties. I didn't see her walk in.

She looked to be by herself. She had blonde hair, sort of layered on the sides and back, shoulder length. She wore tight jeans, and her rump fit nicely on the stool. She looked to the side; she had a pretty face. I couldn't tell for sure, but I thought I saw a green sparkle in her eyes. She had a nice smile, white complexion. I watched her for a few moments and then went back to reading.

By six o'clock the bar had pretty much filled up. I had been watching the young lady out of the side of my eye. She had been hitting the beer pretty heavily. At one point she got up to go to the ladies room. I could tell she was getting a little wobbly. She just made it back to her stool when a man came through the crowd. She acknowledged him with a big smile. I recognized the guy. I didn't know his name, but I had seen him in court several times. He was an attorney out of Anoka, probably fifty years old, tall, graying hair, distinguished looking. He walked up beside her, put his arm around her shoulder and pulled her close. She pecked him on the cheek.

I leaned back in my chair to watch for a while. I enjoyed myself trying to figure out what was going on. If I had to guess, this was some sort of clandestine meeting. I didn't take this woman in jeans, sitting at the bar for the last hour or so all by herself, as being his wife. A little hanky-panky I figured.

From my table, I could see the cars pulling off the highway into the parking lot. It had started to snow, little swirls of wind whipped it across the road. I figured I'd have to wait for at least another hour. I sipped on my fourth beer waiting for the waitress who hadn't been over for more than an hour, too busy at the bar. I didn't know whether this attorney would recognize me or not, but I wasn't going to push my luck by going to the bar, I just stayed back in the shadows, watching.

He stood by her side, guzzled his drinks real fast. About seven o'clock or so, he started to nuzzle her on her neck. His right hand slid off her waist, rested on her butt. He gently squeezed her, and she giggled. His hand stayed there, going in little circles, massaging her buttocks. He leaned over, I thought he was going to kiss her on the ear but he whispered something. She leaned back, her gaze met his, she smiled and got up. The hand he had on her rear end raised to her shoulder, steadied her a little and guided her towards the door. They were giving each other ogle eyes as they went by. At that point, I didn't need my imagination anymore. I had a pretty good idea what they had in mind.

I looked at my watch. It was a little after seven. I decided to take my chances. I paid my bill and left.

There was enough traffic on the highway that the snow wasn't building up. It was close to seven-thirty when I pulled into my parking spot. I hesitated for a moment, wondering whether I was going to make it back out. I gunned the car, it moved ahead slowly. I was going to take the chance. I had brought boots and a parka. I sat in the backseat of the car putting on the boots. I took off my top coat, slid on the parka and pulled the hood up. I had a scarf to wrap around my face if needed. I started on my trek. The highway was busy, something I hadn't counted on. For a moment, a little panic set in. What if a highway patrol cop saw my car, pulled over, checked it out, took the license number? Too late to worry about that.

I walked as far off the road as possible without going into the ditch. It was snowing hard enough now that I wasn't sure I was visible from the highway. It only took me a couple minutes to reach the driveway. I almost jogged down the road. As I got to the bottom of the hill, I looked towards the house. The kitchen light was on, the yard light cast a beam over the whole yard. I veered off the road to the left, trying to stay out of the light. The barn looked closed up, quiet. I was right; they had put the horses to bed for the night. I made my way to the side of the barn and followed it out of the cast of the light until I got to the front door. I waited for a couple moments to make sure that there was no activity, no noise. As long as it took me to get the door open, that's how long I was going to be visible, I wanted to make it fast. I pulled the parka hood tighter over my head, gave one last look around and darted towards the door. It opened without any problem, and I was inside. The only light was coming through the glass window of the door, enough to help me get started in the right direction.

I inched my way through the dark. I was scaring the horses. I could hear them tromping in their stalls, wondering, I suspect, what this strange person was doing. There were a few snorts, a whinny here and there as I went by. I hoped we were far enough away from the house that they wouldn't be heard. I remembered where the hay and grain were stored, and I had already made a plan—that's where I'd hide if I heard anybody coming. My eyes adjusted to the dimness of the barn. As I passed the feed stall, I grabbed a handful of oats and filled my pocket. I made my way to the stall of Johnny Come Lately. He was a little rambunctious, kicked at the stall door as I got closer.

I reached in my pocket and filled my palm with oats and stuck my hand over the door. I could just make out his face in the shadows. He was suspicious. He turned his back to me, his rump was standing by the stall door. For a second I thought, just take it out and shoot it in, right there, on the rump and get it over with, but I wasn't sure whether that would do it. I patted him gently on the rump, talked softly. I reached out my hand with the oats. He slowly turned and walked toward the door. He snorted a little and then his upper lip wiggled and went into my palm, nibbling the oats. I could hear him chew. I gave him another handful. By then it appeared I was his newfound friend. He let me put my left hand on his halter and with my right I rubbed his nose. For a few seconds, we just stared at each other. I don't know if he could see me. All I could see was a glint, his two big brown eyes reflecting like little mirrors. He tugged slightly to get me to loosen my hand on his halter. I held him tight. I reached in and got the last of the oats. When he finished, I put my right hand back in my top pocket, felt the syringe. I pulled it out. I had already filled it with the drug, I had used the entire vial. I had no idea what was going to happen.

I put the syringe in the palm of my hand and with my fingers I eased the plastic cap off the needle, pulled it off with my teeth. I put the syringe between my fingers and placed my thumb on the plunger. I stood there ready to jam the needle into his neck. I had pictured it in my mind many times: As the needle entered, my thumb would push the plunger, and it would be done in an instant. Before the horse knew what happened, I would pull it out, drop it in a bag, put it back in my pocket and leave, wondering what agony the horse would go through before it fell over—dead.

I had the syringe in my hand, but my hand wouldn't move. I could feel the horse's hot breath on my face. I could smell the fresh hay he'd just eaten. He would gently flip his head against my arm trying to ease my grip on his halter. I could feel my will dissipate, drain from my body. I took my left hand off his halter, took the plastic cover from between my teeth and placed it over the needle. I slipped the syringe into the bag, back into my pocket.

The horse tossed its head as if happy to be free. I reached in to pat it on the nose. He just flipped my hand out of the way with his head like he knew what my evil intentions had been.

I retraced my steps to the main door, looked through the little window, there was no activity outside. It was now snowing heavier.

I slipped out the door and stayed to the side of the barn until I got out of the cast of the light. The wind had picked up a little, and snow had already filled my earlier tracks. I could feel my heart thump against my chest. My mind raced. What was going through my mind to make me try something so terrible? I just wanted to get out of there.

As I reached the bottom of the driveway, up the windy hill, I started to run. I wanted to fly. By the time I made the first turn in the road, I was out of breath. My head pounded and my side ached. I slowed to a walk, the road was steeper than I thought. The wind blew in my face, and the snow came down so heavy now it was almost a white out. I made the next turn, now every bit of my body ached. I didn't think my legs could carry me another foot. Then I saw headlights turn off the highway onto the driveway. Without the snow, I'm sure the driver would have seen me. I dove for the ditch and rolled down the soft snow. I could feel it flying into my hood, melting on my hot skin, and icy water running down my neck. I lay there as the truck passed, wondering if the driver would notice my tracks. I watched for the red of the tail lights—nothing. As it turned on the next curve, I started to crawl from the ditch, the soft snow disappearing under my feet. I made it back to the road. I was ready to collapse. I walked the rest of the way, slowly, deliberately. At that point, I didn't care any more.

I was hurting, full of shame. Whatever possessed me to think that I could kill that animal? His face flashed through my mind, those big brown eyes. I shook my head and mumbled, "Stupid."

I walked the block from the driveway to my car without seeing anybody. The highway was snowed over, just two tire tracks in both lanes. I got into my car, cold and wet. I had been sweating so heavily under my parka I could feel my clothes cling to my skin. I started the car, stepped on the gas, it inched ahead less than a foot, and then the tires started to spin. I started to rock back and forth. With every effort, I made a few more inches. I turned off my headlights so a car passing by wouldn't wonder if I was in distress and stop. It took me a little over ten minutes to finally get my front tires on the highway. I knew the drive home would be slow. I didn't care. My body needed time to heal . . . so did my mind.

I arrived home close to eleven o'clock. Once I got off the main highway to the county and township roads, with the blowing snow I could barely tell where I was going. I crawled my way through back roads, never sure whether I was on the tar or in the ditch.

I walked into the house totally drained. The tension of the night and then the drive home had stressed me to the limit. I crawled into my bed, and I was out within minutes.

The weather men were wrong. They had predicted five or six inches. When I finally woke in the morning, well after nine o'clock, it was still snowing heavily. I was suppose to be in court at ten. I quickly called my office. Nobody answered. I turned on the radio. Overnight we had received over a foot of snow, and they were predicting another eight or nine inches. Everything was closed down.

I made myself a pot of coffee and sat by the table looking through the patio doors into the backyard. The birds were coming to my feeders, barely visible through the shower of white flakes. They seemed to appear out of the sky like little specks, settle on the feeder and grab a seed, then disappear. Kate and I had spent many hours sitting at this very spot counting the birds, hoping that something new would show up. One morning we had seven male cardinals at the feeder at the same time. I don't think I've ever seen her enjoy anything more than watching them come in from the pine trees, one at a time, cautiously looking around before they settled, to take a seed, staying vigilant, head bobbing in every direction.

I couldn't think of Kate without thinking of Spokes. I had resigned myself to the fact that I was never going to get the authorities to investigate him. There was no one I could turn to for help. I would have to somehow get him to commit himself, maybe tape him in a conversation where he'd implicate himself—something I could use to go to the feds.

The first thing I had to do was figure out a scheme, how I could get him to meet with me. I believed Tony was right. If Spokes knew about the Nigerian and his attempt on my life, which I'm sure he did, any call from me to set up a meeting would be immediately suspicious. There was nobody else I could use. Maybe Tony? But why would he meet with Tony? I had to come up with my own plan.

I suddenly felt a crushing sense of loneliness. In the twenty some years we lived in the country, it wasn't very often we got snowed in—maybe a half dozen times or less—but they were memorable because Kate and I considered them free days. Nothing was planned. We couldn't leave the house. If I hadn't brought a file with me, there wasn't any legal work I could do. So we bummed the days away, reading a book we'd been putting aside; watching the afternoon talk shows, something neither of us ever did—at least I don't think she did. I can even remember one time getting drunk and rolling around in bed all afternoon. Little moments, precious moments, little gems in a person's life, unfortunately taken for granted at the time, moments that make up a lifetime of memories.

How could one person take all of that from me, someone who had no idea what the relationship meant. Who could take a beautiful soul and discard her like so much garbage, without a thought, without a regret . . . simply out of greed? I could feel the tears coming. I closed my eyes to hold them back. It didn't work. I folded my arms on the table, put my head down and sobbed. That's what my life had become: The only time I wasn't wallowing in my own pity was when I was scheming on how to get even.

The snow stopped later in the afternoon. There was no way I was going to get out. The sheer loneliness, being in that large house with all of its memories, by myself, for the whole day, almost drove me crazy. I tried reading, watching television, sleeping—none of it worked. I could picture Kate sitting by the table, watching the birds with a smile on her face, hoping the snow would last for another couple days, hoping we'd be marooned by ourselves on our own little island.

It was noon the next day before I finally got out. I was the last house on the route of the township snow plow. I was so anxious to get out, I followed him down my driveway. I drove into town, but everything was still pretty quiet. When I got to the office, it was like nobody missed me. There were no messages, nobody waiting to talk to me. I think some of my clients had finally given up any hope of getting anything out of me. The only thing I had to do was prepare for my hearing on Friday morning on the photographic lineup of my armed robber. I tried Tony's number; all I got was his answering machine. I left a message that he should get in touch with me as soon as possible. Later that afternoon, he called, and we made arrangements to meet at the Lodge at six.

The bar was packed. All the guys who had been out plowing snow for thirty-six hours straight were in to have a bump or two before they fell into their beds. It was ritual. You could count on it after every snowfall. Sometimes after a few drinks, they'd get into a poker game. I was always amazed at the amount of cash they seemed to carry with them.

I made it through the crowd to my back table. The outside floodlights were on towards the river. The wind had picked up, sending little whirlwinds of loose snow bouncing over the drifts. The waitress came over, and I ordered a screwdriver. I sat there, sipping it, my mind on Mr. Spokes. Tony had said he would work on some plan. I was wondering whether he had come up with anything.

Close to six-thirty, Tony came through the back door. I signaled him to have the waitress bring me another drink. He stuck his head through the little window, hollered out our order and then came and sat across from me at the table.

"So what have you been up to?" he asked.

"What do you think I've been up to?" I replied. "I've been waiting for you to get your butt back here and tell me what you're going to do to help me get Mr. Spokes."

"Well," he said, "that wasn't on the top of my list. I had witnesses to interview on that automobile accident. But I spent a lot of time thinking about it on the way home from Duluth today . . . and to tell you the truth, I'm stuck. We know we aren't gonna get anywhere on how Spokes could have hidden the money without some high-level resources, which neither you nor I have. I can't go to the cops in Hennepin County 'cause I'm not sure that wouldn't get back to him."

The waitress came over and set another screwdriver down in front of me and gave Tony his tap beer. Tony grabbed the salt shaker, shook a little in. We both watched it bubble up. He looked at me, a painful look. "I'm sorry," he said, "I just don't know where to go, what to do. I'm at a dead end."

"It's not your fault," I said. I proceeded to tell him about the article I had read in the *Minneapolis Magazine*. I even told him about my stop to look at Spokes' prize thoroughbred.

"That was kind of dumb," he said. "What if the young lady gives Spokes your name?"

"I didn't give her my real name," I said.

"What name did you use?"

"Actually I used two names, Kevin's and yours. I was Kevin O'Donnell."

"You're a dumb shit," he said. "Now I suppose he's gonna come looking for me."

"There'd be no reason for him to look for anybody. As far as I can tell, he thinks he's the cock of the walk. Big house, fancy car, race horses, some blonde bomber hanging on his shoulder. He's not going to worry about some little pissants like us."

"Well, someone was worried enough to try and bump you off in the first place," he said.

"This isn't getting us anywhere," I replied. "I have to come up with a plan. There's got to be some way. We have to get him out into the open, smoke him out and, by God, I'm going to do it. I'll rot in hell before I'll see that bastard get away with this."

"Well," Tony said, "that's probably where you're going to end up anyway."

"Then I might as well have a reason."

"But, don't go doing anything stupid," said Tony. "At least let me know what you've got planned so I can help you out."

"As I said, Tony, the only thing I can figure is something to flush him out."

"You mentioned something about this Matthew guy who went to school here at the University. Do you have a file on him?"

"It should still be around," I replied. "Why?"

"Well, it sounds to me like, if they came over with the money, he had to come along. He's the one who got in touch with you in the first place, right?"

"Yeah."

"What if he's in the states? Wouldn't that tell us something?"

"But how are you going to find out?" I asked.

"Think about it. If he was a student here, they have to have some papers on him. He'd have a social security number. Maybe he left something with the school. Maybe he's listed with the Alumni Association or sent the school some money."

"I can't believe he'd be that dumb," I said.

"Maybe he wants to play the big shot. Who knows," Tony replied. "I've made cases with thinner leads than that."

"What'll we do?" I asked.

"You have to get me his file from your office. That should have all the information I need."

"You know," I said, "this might be just the dumb luck we need."

"I'll stop in first thing in the morning."

"Talk to Heidi," I said. "I'll be in court on our armed robbery case."

"What did your young man have to say about my investigation?" Tony asked.

"You know what he says? He and his girlfriend found a bedroom and shacked up."

"Did you talk to her?" Tony asked.

"What kind of alibi witness is that going to be? His girlfriend? I mean, nobody else can put him there. Nobody else sees him go into the bedroom with her. Nobody else sees them coming out. I have to face it, Tony, I think the kid's stringing us along."

"Well that's too bad," said Tony. "He's kind of a nice young guy."

"Tony, they're all nice at this point in the game," I said. "That doesn't mean shit anymore. There was a time you could tell the bad guys from the good guys. That's all long gone."

"You're starting to sound like me," said Tony. "I told you it's time to get out."

"Yeah, I guess so. That greenhouse is starting to look better and better."

We had dinner. He started telling me about the case he was investigating in Duluth, an automobile accident that happened north of Duluth, on the highway to Lutsen. A grain truck was coming south; a young mother with her two children in the backseat was headed north. The grain truck lost control on an icy road, crossed over the lane. The mother took the ditch to avoid an accident, but the car rolled over and exploded. All three of them were killed. Tony had been hired to investigate by a personal-injury attorney, Peter Wellon.

When he finished telling me, he looked at me. "Well, old Peter's gonna be making a lot of money," he said. "The driver's employer had a million dollar policy. See, that's where you missed your calling. Instead of representing these crooks, you should've been doing personal-injury work."

"Yeah, I thought about that," I said. "But you're still dealing with everybody's misery. Think about it, Tony. That's all lawyers do—deal with everybody's misery. You know, if you want to be happy at this job, you should just do adoptions."

"You may be right," said Tony, "but at least with personal-injury stuff, you get paid for your misery, not like the crap you have to handle. Look, old

Peter's gonna walk away with probably three hundred thousand dollars or more. I could probably put up with a lot of misery for that."

"The money may be good," I said, "but I'm not sure it'd change a whole hell of a lot."

Tony and I stayed until a little after nine. We made arrangements that he was going to stop at the office on Friday morning to pick up Matthew's file. Now I was really intrigued. What if we come up with something on Matthew? It could change everything.

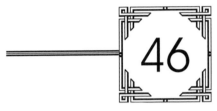

The next morning I was at the Stearns County Courthouse at nine o'clock for the hearing on Brad's case. I had filed a motion to contest the eyewitness identification based on what I thought was a tainted photographic line-up. If the judge agreed, he could exclude the identification made by the young lady of my client from the photographs. My client met me there in the hall.

"The lady's wrong," he said. "It wasn't me. The only reason nobody saw Jeannie and me sneak into the bedroom is because her old boyfriend was there. He would have kicked the shit out of me. Believe me, Mr. Williams, she was all over me. I'd been nuts to pass it up."

"I'll take your word for it," I replied.

"You don't believe me, do you?"

"I'm not getting paid to either believe you or not believe you," I said. "It's up to the state to prove you guilty. I don't have to prove you not guilty."

"That's a horse-shit attitude," he said.

"Maybe you're right," I said, and I was going to add something stupid but had second thoughts and kept my mouth closed.

"What're ya gonna ask her?" he said.

Just as I was about to reply, the assistant county attorney came out of the elevator. He motioned me over. "You're not going to believe this," he said, "your guy didn't do it."

"What're you talking about?" I asked.

"The cops arrested two guys last night about eleven o'clock trying to rob a Tom Thumb Store. They got 'em at gunpoint right outside the building. Scared the hell out of 'em. They took them back to the station. Mirandized them. The dirt bags confessed to five armed robberies in the state, including the theater. Your guy didn't do it, but when you see a photograph of one of these guys, you'll understand why the Paramount employee picked out your client. At first glance, they could be twins."

It took a few seconds for everything to register. "You're not kiddin'?"

"Hell, no," he replied.

"I don't believe it. After twenty-five years of doing this, I finally have an innocent client, I mean one that's really innocent. He told me he didn't do it, and I didn't believe him."

"Well, I hope that teaches you a lesson," he said.

"Yeah, you should talk. How many times have I told you my client is innocent? What have you told me? 'Kiss it.'"

"Well then we both learned something," he replied.

I walked over to Brad with a big smile on my face. He gave me a quizzical look. "What?" he asked.

"They caught the real bad guy," I said.

His face went blank.

"A couple guys tried robbing a Tom Thumb last night, and the cops arrested 'em at gunpoint. They confessed to a number of robberies, including the theater robbery. I should've listened to you, I guess," I said.

His face broke out in a big smile. He clapped his hands. "Yeah, son-of-a-bitch! I can't believe it," he said. "Something finally went right. See, I told you."

"Yeah, I guess I have to apologize."

He stood there shaking his head. "Son-of-a-bitch," he said, time after time. "What's gonna happen?" he finally asked.

"Well, they're dismissing the case. You're done, you're free to go."

"Yeah!" he hollered out again. He put up his hand so I could give him the high five. I slapped it. "See ya," he said, as he turned around and almost ran from the courthouse.

It took a few minutes to walk back to my office. I had a glowing feeling, one of satisfaction, and I really hadn't done a damn thing. In fact, I was convinced he was lying. But there's so few victories in this business, you take credit wherever you can find it.

When I walked into the office, Heidi told me that Tony had picked up the file and was in the conference room. I walked in, he looked up at me, surprised. "You're back early," he said.

"You're not going to believe this," I said, and I told him the whole story.

"You know," he said, "in all my years of detective work, that never happened. I've had guys with alibis before, but they've panned out. If you would've asked me to bet, I would've bet that he was lying."

"Me, too," I said.

"Well, that'll be one for the books," replied Tony. "We probably aren't gonna see that again in our lifetime." He flipped closed the file in front of him. "I got what I need out of here. I'm gonna check at the U. I'll try to be back in an hour or so. If they've got anything on Matthew, it'll be easy to find."

Tony left and I sat in the conference room by myself. I started to wonder if I had jumped to conclusions too soon on Spokes as well? All my legal career I had argued before juries about reasonable doubt, presumption of innocence, and, here, without any concrete evidence at all, I was willing to condemn Spokes and worse yet . . . maybe I'm lucky I didn't complete my plan. What if I was wrong? I would have killed that beautiful animal . . . for what? I told myself, *You ought to practice what you preach. What have you told juries for years? Don't jump to conclusions. Wait until you hear all of the evidence.* I had violated my own cardinal rule.

A little before noon, Heidi told me Tony was on the phone. I picked up the receiver. "Bingo," he said excitedly. "Two months ago he sent a check to the Alumni Fund from guess where?" He didn't let me answer. "Minneapolis. A thousand bucks."

My heart was pounding. "Do you have an address?"

"Yeah, it's one of the fancy motels where they put you up for months at a time. You know, the ones out on 494, where you don't have to rent by the night. It's called the Victorian Inn. But this was back in November. I'd be surprised if he's still there."

"Well you know what you have to do, Tony?" I said.

"I'm on my way."

Now I started to think. Maybe I was right in the first place. Why would Matthew be in Minnesota? Only one reason: They worked out some deal with Spokes, and he continued to act as the go-between. Can you beat dumb luck? I wondered.

For the next couple hours, there was no sense trying to do anything. Thoughts just kept flashing through my mind, one after another. What if Matthew was there? What if Tony located him? Maybe Tony would confront him. Maybe we would get the answers we needed this afternoon, or maybe he's long gone. He'd be stupid to stick around. Of course, he was stupid to send that money to the school in the first place. Pride, I thought. Maybe that's what's going to bring him down. Before we're done, we might just cover all seven deadly sins.

After about an hour and a half, when I expected Tony to be at the motel, every time the phone rang, I jumped. The first five times were false alarms; the sixth time, it was Tony.

I could tell immediately from his voice he was disappointed. "Well, Bob, I can't tell you if he was here or not. The front desk isn't giving me much help at all. I did tip the bellhop fifty bucks. He told me he remembered a black guy with a funny accent here in November. He was here for two weeks and left. He said he pretty much stayed to himself. I can tell from talking to this guy, if there was any action going on he would know about it. He said there were no parties, no hookers, nothing. I showed him a copy of the photograph from the school directory, and he said it could be the same guy, but he wasn't sure. I also showed him a picture of our dead guy. He was sure he'd never seen him."

I sunk back in my chair. I didn't say anything right away. "What do you want to do?" I finally asked.

"There's not much I can do here. I guess I'll head back."

"I have an idea," I said. "Why don't you meet me at the Lodge." I looked at the clock, it was about four-thirty. "I'll meet you there at six."

"If the traffic isn't heavy, I'll be there," he said. "Otherwise, just sit tight."

As I hung up the phone I had already figured out what I was going to do.

When I left the office later that day, I had every intention of telling Tony my plan, but driving out to the Lodge I had second thoughts. What if I was right? What if my plan ended up with me confronting Spokes, and something happened, something I didn't anticipate. Then Tony would be an accessory? If I was willing to go down, I didn't have to take him with me. It was best that I did it by myself. After all, I could be wrong. It could result in nothing.

So when Tony met me at the Lodge, rather than have the conversation I intended to have, I acknowledged defeat. "I don't suppose there's any way we can trace him?" I said.

"I don't know how," he said. "We have to have something to go on. He didn't even use his real name at the motel. There was nobody there registered with the name Matthew, and nothing I would recognize as Nigerian."

"Did you find out how he paid?" I asked.

"In cash."

"Was he driving?" I asked.

"Actually, he was, but it was a rented car. The bellhop didn't remember the make, year, anything. Without some license plate number, I don't know where we would start."

"Didn't the motel ask for the license number?"

"Not with cash, apparently."

"Well, Tony," I said, "it looks like the bastard has us beat."

"I thought you had some idea," Tony said.

"Ah, I gave up on it. It was just stupid. I'll tell you what I'm going to do," I continued. "I'm going to just sit on it for a while, give it a little time. If Spokes was involved in the attempt on me, even if he just knew about it, I'm going to hope that with a little time he'll think I'm not worth the effort. If I watch closely from a distance, maybe he'll slip up someplace."

"That doesn't sound like you," he said.

"It's not what I want to do, but I have other things to think about. I think Carol's going to move back this summer, maybe start a vet practice right here. I can help her. Maybe I'll even think about your proposition. I decided I can do one of two things: I can sit and think about Spokes and waste the rest of my life, or I can move on. For Carol's sake, if nothing else, I have to move on."

Tony appeared to buy it. I turned the conversation to something else and then came back. "By the way," I said, "what about the pistol, were you able to locate one?"

"Matter of fact, I did," he said. "I wasn't sure I was gonna give it to you."

"Why not?" I asked.

"That doesn't need an answer," he said. "You know, you were starting to scare me."

"Well if it causes you some concern, Tony, I can go buy myself one, registered. I guess I just didn't want to do that, but it's no big deal."

"It's fine," he said. "I've got it out in the car. I'll give it to you tonight when we leave."

"What do I owe you?" I asked.

He thought for a second. "Just think about my business proposition. You know it's getting close to spring. If we're gonna do it, we should get going."

"I'll do that," I said. "I really will."

When I walked into the house later that night, I took a little brown bag out of my pocket. Inside was another .38 revolver. I handled the gun, it was also small. On the side it read, ".38 Detective Special." I flipped open the cylinder. Empty. I went back to my cabinet and pulled out the box of ammunition, loaded it with six hollowpoint shells, flipped the cylinder closed and put it back in my overcoat pocket.

I had really sunk to a new low. I wasn't satisfied conning my daughter, now I had done it to the only friend I had left in the world. Everything I told him was bullshit. I had no intention of forgetting about Spokes, putting him on the back burner. Not after what he had done. The fact that Matthew had been in Minneapolis only reinforced my initial conclusion. For a moment, I had almost been conned by my own rhetoric. He wasn't entitled to any presumption of innocence. There wasn't any reasonable doubt. Spokes had the money, and three lovely ladies died because of it.

I wasn't going to do anything over the weekend, I had it all planned out for Monday morning. All weekend I went over it, time after time. I thought it would work, there was no reason why it shouldn't.

Monday morning I drove to Minneapolis. I checked into the Sofitel under a fictitious name. I walked across the street into the lobby of the Radisson South Hotel. I told them I needed to use their fax service. I put a hanky over the phone and called Spokes' office to see if he was in. The secretary said he was in a meeting that would probably last another hour. I asked her for the fax number. I waited about forty-five minutes. I had already typed out a letter on Radisson South stationary dated that day. The letter said:

Dear Mr. Spokes:
It is urgent that I talk to you. Dr. Umah has some doubts on our investment. It requires that you intercede. I would like to meet with you tonight at 7:00 p.m. Radisson South Bar.
Matthew

I put it in the fax machine, dialed the number and then waited to make sure it had been received.

I had no idea if this was going to work. The only thing that made me think it could drag Spokes into the open would be if I was correct, if the Nigerians were going to put part of their new found wealth into his racing venture, the note would seem to put that in jeopardy. If that wouldn't get Spokes to commit himself to come to a meeting, I couldn't imagine what would. Now I just had to waste the day waiting for seven o'clock.

I walked back to the Sofitel and sat in my room trying to imagine what would happen that night. If I was wrong, he wouldn't have the slightest idea who Matthew was and he wouldn't show up. What if he was just busy, though? Or what if he didn't get the fax? If he didn't show up, that didn't mean he wasn't involved. But if he did show up . . . well, that was a whole different story. Then what would I do? I reached for my suit coat. I had my microcassette tape recorder. My plan was to try and get something on tape, some admission, confession, whatever. Something I could take to the police. Something that would make them have to believe me. The more I thought about it, the more I realized I didn't have the slightest idea what was going to happen. If he showed up, I had no idea what I was going to say to him. I was flying by the seat of my pants. It was a desperate effort to get off dead center. For my own sanity, I needed something to happen.

To be on the safe side, I called his office about four-thirty. His secretary said he was with a client. I wasn't going to wait around the Radisson and have him come and see me, unexpectedly, walking through the halls or in the bar someplace. I planned to wait for him to leave his office and then follow his car. If he headed back this way, I knew he was looking for Matthew. If he headed home, an entirely different direction . . . well, then it was back to the drawing board.

Right after hanging up, I left. It took me a little over twenty minutes to get to his office. I pulled off Park Avenue behind the building and looked for his car. I spotted it, parked at a sign that read, "RESERVED ATTORNEY SPOKES." A nice navy-blue Jaguar, license plate number ISU4U. Pretty tacky, I thought.

I pulled back onto Park Avenue. I knew it was one way coming out of the lot. I went to the next intersection and parked on the intersecting road, with a vantage point where I could see a car leaving the lot and taking a right hand turn.

It was starting to get dark. I parked, turned my lights off and listened to "All Things Considered" on Minnesota Public Radio. Close to five-thirty cars started pulling out, but no Jaguar. I waited. I kept looking at the clock. The numbers never seemed to change. I picked up little bits and pieces of the stories on MPR, but my mind wouldn't let me settle on anything. I could feel my body beginning to ache. I was tense, every muscle straining in anticipation. I thought about getting out and stretching, then I thought he might catch me. Better just sit still. I kept trying to imagine what was going to happen if I was right. It was driving me nuts. "Where is he?" I mumbled.

It was almost six-thirty when I saw it. He pulled up to Park Avenue, put his blinker on and made a right hand turn. If he was going to the Radisson, I assumed he would follow Park Avenue out to Lake Street, to Highway 35 South to Bloomington. The traffic was heavy. He waited for an opening and pulled out. He didn't put on his blinker to take a right hand turn, he was going straight. I quickly pulled out right on his tail. I followed him to Lake Street. He put his right-hand blinker on; with the green light, we went. I followed him to Highway 35, and he took a left turn going south. I was right behind him. I kept my headlights right on his tail.

Traffic on 35 South was heavy, bumper-to-bumper, taillights almost as far as I could see. I thought that was to my benefit; he wasn't going to lose me.

I could feel the tension building as we got closer and closer to Bloomington. He could still go straight ahead, out 169 to get home. If he was going to go to the Radisson, he would either follow 35 out to 494 or take Highway 100 South. I still didn't know what was going to happen. I really wanted it to be true. I wanted to know what had happened, why my Kate had to die. If this didn't turn out the way I expected . . . well, I'd be lost. The only thing that had kept me going was my resolve to get to the truth. It still pained me that there were people out there who thought—no, believed—that Kate had committed suicide. That bothered me, really bothered me. If

I could bring it all out in the open, show everybody what really happened, for some reason I thought maybe that would make a difference.

As we got close to the Highway 62 split, traffic picked up. We were going all of twenty-five miles per hour. He stayed to the right on 62. The next question was, would he take 100 South? We finally made it to about forty-five miles per hour. I saw the signs coming up—Highway 100, two miles; Highway 100, three quarters of a mile; next exit, Highway 100. I watched, waited—Christ, his right-hand blinker went on. My blood pressure shot up. I could feel my fingers tighten on the steering wheel. My right hand involuntarily went to my coat pocket. I felt the gun, I guess I needed a sense of assurance. I followed him around the cloverleaf and stayed right on his tail as he inched his way into the traffic on Highway 100. I looked at my clock, ten to seven, he was right on time. I wondered where he was going to look for Matthew. I wasn't going to let him get into the hotel, I was going to stop him right there in the parking lot.

I could see the tower of the Radisson ahead. As we neared the boulevard, I saw him flip on his right-hand signal, and he exited. At that moment, I got giddy. I broke into a laugh, almost a maniacal giggle. I had done it. I couldn't believe it. I never expected it to happen. I was laughing so hard tears were rolling down my cheeks. My hand went down to touch the gun again. I followed him into the parking lot. It was perfect. There was no space close, so he had to follow the driveways until he was almost to the back of the parking lot. He pulled in. I pulled in next to him.

I jumped out of my driver's side, and I was in his front seat—caught him totally by surprise. He looked at me. Then he recognized me.

"Jesus Christ, you scared the shit out of me," he said. "What the hell are you doing here?"

"Mr. Spokes," I said, "it's nice to see you again," a giddy twang to my speech.

"Bob, what the hell's wrong with you?"

"Nothing. Nothing that a little conversation won't take care of. I want to talk to you, Mr. Spokes. I've wanted to talk to you very badly."

He gave me a strange look. "Get the fuck out of my car," he said.

That's all I needed to hear. I brought the gun out, the barrel reflected the lights from the dash. "I've been waiting for this for a long time," I said.

"You out of your fucking mind?" he said. "What's that for? What's this all about?"

I could see a hint of fear come over his face. "Don't shit me, Spokes," I said. "You know what this is all about."

"You're nuts," he replied. "What are you going to do with that?"

"That all depends on you."

"I'm gettin' out of here," he said and he reached for the door.

"I'll blow your goddamn head off," I said.

"Are you nuts or what?" he asked.

"Just back up and take off."

"I'm not going anywhere with you," he said.

"Either you're going to talk to me," I said, "or I'm going to blow your face off, right here."

By then I detected panic in his voice. "Jesus Christ, Bob, what the hell's your problem?"

He wasn't fooling me. I could tell he knew exactly what was happening, how I had gotten him there. He was going to try to bluff me for a while, see what I actually knew. I looked at him, trying to give him the coldest stare possible.

"You know," I said, "I've lost almost everything in this life that counts. Either you're going to cooperate with me or you're going to have one big hole in your head. Do you know what a .38 caliber hollow point will do? You should've seen the guy you sent to my house. I could've put my first through the hole."

"You're nuts," he said, his voice starting to break.

"That may be true," I replied, registering that he hadn't asked, "what guy?" "So, if I were you, I wouldn't screw around with me. I would do exactly what I ask, and what I'm asking you to do is back up and get back out on the highway."

He shifted into reverse, looked behind him, slowly backed out and started to pull out. I wasn't sure whether he had any crazy ideas in mind or not.

"John, I wanna tell you," I said, "if I have any indication that you're going to try and get out of this car, trust me, you'll never make it in one piece. I'll blow you a new asshole."

"I wish I knew what this was all about," he said.

"Don't try and con me. You know exactly what this is about."

"Yeah, you've gone crazy."

"I'm tired of talking. Just drive," I said.

"Where am I going?"

"Back to your office."

He pulled out going north on Highway 100. We retraced the steps back to Park Avenue. The whole time I remained quiet. He'd say dumb things like, "You know you're really in a lot of trouble . . . you know I've got a lot of connections in this town. You hurt me, your ass's in trouble . . . I don't know where in the fuck you get off pulling a gun on me." He would glance over at me. "What the fuck's your problem?" he'd holler.

I looked straight ahead. I couldn't believe how composed I was. I had pictured myself being nervous; instead, it was as if I did this all the time, routinely.

"You know, you're really in trouble," he said. "I don't think this is very fuckin' funny. I'm gonna make sure your ass is thrown in jail . . . you're not gettin' away with this shit." He glanced over at me again. "What the fuck's your problem?" he screamed. "Bob, it's not too late. Let me pull over, and you get out. I'll forget all about this—like it never happened."

I grinned at him.

"What the fuck's your problem?" he hollered again, like a broken record. I attributed it all to a little nervousness.

We pulled up to the parking lot behind the darkened building. "Now what do you want?" he asked.

"Let's go in," I said.

"I'm not going in there with you," he replied.

"Then you're going to die right out here in the goddamn parking lot."

"Bob, what the hell's wrong with you?"

"Give me the key and get your ass out," I said.

He turned the car off, took the key out of the ignition and handed it over. I quickly got out, went around to the driver's side, opened the door. "Let's go," I said.

Slowly he got out and headed towards the building. I followed directly behind, poking him with the gun a couple times just to remind him.

He opened the door with his key. As we stepped in, I said, "Turn off the security alarm."

"What security alarm?" he said.

"Just turn the goddamn thing off!" and I waved the gun at him.

He turned around, went to a little box on the wall and started pushing buttons. I saw the red light go to green. "Lock the door," I said.

I pushed him towards his office. As we walked down the hall, I was amazed at myself; there was no panic in my voice, no fear in my hands. I was as calm as I had ever been. I was thinking clearly. He unlocked his office door, reached in and flipped on the light. I followed him in. "Lock it," I said.

We went through the reception room into his office. "Sit down," I said, and I stood on the side where I could watch his hands. I had been carrying the gun in my right hand. I switched hands and put my right hand in my suit coat pocket to start the tape recorder. Spokes gave me a strange look.

By then I could tell he was getting really frightened. He had lost some of his cockiness. Either he knew why I was there or he figured he had a mad man on his hands.

"I heard about your wife," he said. "I'm really sorry."

"I bet you are. Who'd you hear it from, Matthew?"

"Who's Matthew," he said.

"The guy you went to meet tonight."

"I don't know what you're talking about," he said.

"Really?" I said, as I pointed at his desk. "That's strange. There's Matthew's fax, right there in front of you. I bet it says, 'Meet me at the Radisson, seven o'clock.'"

His hands started to tremble. He reached for the piece of paper on his desk, it fluttered in his fingers. He quickly dropped it. He looked up at me from his chair, a rather plaintive stare.

"That tape recorder in your pocket won't do you any good," he said. "That's pretty amateurish, Bob. What good will it do you if I say something at gunpoint, you threatening to blow my head off? Hey, Detective Moser, it's me, John Spokes, I've got this crazy bastard with a gun at my head, he thinks I'm guilty of something, so if you hear a confession, you can bet it's the truth." He laughed nervously. "Bob, if you read the law, you'd know any confession like that isn't worth shit."

I put the gun back in my left hand, reached in my pocket and pulled out the recorder. I held it up, clicked it off, showed Spokes the light was out. "I'm tired of this bullshit, John, just tell me the goddamn truth," I said. "How could you be involved in this? You of all people?"

He leaned back in the chair, an attempt, I thought, to make me believe he was deep in thought. He sat there, shaking his head back and forth, silent.

"Believe me, Bob," he finally said, "I had nothing to do with it."

"What do you mean you had nothing to do with it? With what?"

"What happened," he said. "I didn't have any choice. You know when you and your wife left that day, Bob, I didn't intend to do anything, and then within a day the shit hit the fan. I had to come up with a lot of money. I took that file out and made a call."

"This was all over money, huh?"

"I needed that money," he said. "I didn't think anybody would get hurt. That wasn't my idea."

"This was all over money?" I asked.

I had never felt so calm in my life. He rambled on. I'm not sure his words even registered with me. He told me how he contacted Matthew, the arrangements that were made. He went to the Carribean to set up the offshore bank account. He made it sound so simple.

"When Matthew came," he continued, "he had some assassin with him, fuckin' animal. They were really paranoid, Bob. They were afraid that if any of this ever got back to the military in power, well, they knew what would happen to them. They weren't willing to take any chances. Then it all started with Pam Weber. She opened her big mouth, how she wanted a cut. I didn't know they were going to kill her, Bob. Really I didn't. I liked Pam, I never would've let them do that to her."

290

I stood there like a statue, the gun pointed right at his chest. Not a muscle moved. I don't think I even blinked. I listened to what Spokes was saying but the words weren't registering. Rather, I looked at his eyes. I was trying to look beyond his eyes, into the recesses of his mind to see if he was really that evil.

"I was as shocked as anybody when they found her body. You know, she's the one who told them that you and Kate were here. She told them about your secretary. What was her name?"

"Faye," I said, "and she wasn't my secretary, she was my assistant."

"Pam's the one who told them all of that. I never would've told them anything."

"You're a goddamn liar," I said. "She didn't have to tell them anything, Matthew already knew. Remember I was the one he contacted."

"Yeah, but they didn't know your wife knew, they didn't know Faye knew anything."

"When did you know what they had planned?" I asked.

"We met after Pam's funeral," he said. "They didn't tell me what they were going to do, but I had some suspicions."

"I bet you did," I said. "They brutally raped and murdered your assistant, and you have some *suspicion* that they may have something in mind for me and my wife."

"I told them, Bob. I told them they couldn't start killing people."

"Is that why they tried to make it look like a suicide and an accident?" I asked.

By then I could see the sweat forming on his face, little beads under his eyes, his forehead. He wiped it to the side with his hand, his dyed hair clinging to his scalp. His nose started to run. He brushed it aside with his finger, wetting his little mustache. His hands shook.

"I have to go to the bathroom," he said.

"You're not going to leave that chair."

I heard a click, and I looked down. Without any thought on my part whatsoever, my thumb had pulled the hammer back on the revolver.

He looked at me, fear in his eyes, beads of sweat running down his forehead. "Please Bob," he said. "I really . . . I really didn't have anything to do with it. All I was going to do was help them bring the money into the country, take my cut. Nobody was suppose to get hurt. I never asked them to hurt anybody, Bob."

"Why Kate?"

"They wanted to get rid of everybody. They didn't want any loose ends."

"Faye didn't even know anything."

"They didn't know that. Bob, I've got some money. I mean, it's not a whole lot, but I can get you more. I've got some money here, and I can cut you in," and he reached for the credenza behind him.

I stepped forward. "Don't move a muscle," I said.

"No," he said, "really Bob. I've got money, I've got some money right here. You can have it. You can take it with you tonight. I can get you more."

He opened the door behind him. I watched him carefully. He brought out an envelope, put it on the desk.

"Here Bob, here. Take this. I'll get you more. There's thirty thousand dollars there," he said.

"To you this is all about money, isn't it?"

"Bob," he said, "I needed it. You don't understand. I had obligations to meet."

The room exploded. It echoed. I saw a flash. When my eyes focused again, Spokes had his hands across his chest, blood gushed through his fingers. He tried to say something, but there was only a gurgling sound. A little stream of blood came out, ran down the left side of his face. His eyes were wide open. He looked at me in disbelief. I watched his eyes, could see life leaving. It was almost like somebody had turned off the lights. One moment there seemed to be something there, the slightest glint; the next moment, blank, nothing.

I looked down at my hand, I still had my finger tight on the trigger, up against the back of the trigger guard. My first thought was, how strange. I don't remember doing that. There was no conscious decision on my part to kill him. I don't recall my brain ever sending a signal to my finger to squeeze. Had he done anything but whine about how he needed the money, it might have been different. I couldn't understand that. For money? I would never understand that.

I eased my grip on the revolver and put it back in my pocket. I wasn't even worried whether anybody else was in the building at that point, whether anybody had heard the shot. I realized that I had set this up for this one purpose. From the moment I knew it was Spokes, I had a suspicion that this is how it would end. I wasn't going to be involved in any long, drawn-out trial, motions being made, stupid-ass lawyer arguments. I knew from the beginning, if counting on the legal process was the only way I could seek justice, I wouldn't let it happen. I wasn't about to give Spokes a chance to walk.

I reached over and took the envelope off the desk, put it into my inside coat pocket. I looked at Spoke's body, he was sprawled out on his chair. By now the blood had soaked his lap. I could tell his bladder had released, the urine mixed with the blood and dripped off the edge of the chair. A lot of good that money's going to do you now, I thought.

I calmly walked to the door, opened it, walked into the hall. I didn't bother to look and see if anybody was out there. When I got into the cool night air, it actually felt good. I walked down the avenue several blocks and then headed east. I walked to the hospital, to the cab stand, opened the back door of the cab, got in and sat down. "Radisson South, please."

As I pulled onto the highway leaving Minneapolis, I was in a cold sweat. I turned on the dome light and looked in the mirror. I was a little taken aback. My face looked hard, old and gray. It's a stranger, I thought; I didn't know who that man was looking at me, a cold-blooded killer. I had never been able to hurt a thing in my life. Years ago there had been a wounded raccoon in our yard. Kate wanted me to put it out of its misery. I knew it was the right thing to do, but as I looked at it, it stared at me with those big round eyes, cowering in the corner, licking wounds inflicted by some other animal. I couldn't do it. I called the neighbor. He dragged it out into the field and shot it. All I heard was the bang. That was sort of the standing joke in the neighborhood for a while—this city slicker who was afraid to shoot a wounded animal. But that's how I had been raised—not to hurt anything. But now, in less than a month, I had killed two human beings. One, of course, in self-defense, for what that was worth. What I had done tonight, however, was with malice aforethought, premeditated, a cold-blooded killing. I possessed, as the law says, the requisite *mens rea*. It frightened me because I didn't feel bad. I should be sick to my stomach. I should be so sick that I couldn't get off the floor, nauseated, vomiting, throwing up until I felt my stomach turn inside out, but I wasn't. I was just stone cold numb with a tremendous sense of relief.

I got home close to midnight. I took out a bottle of wine, poured two glasses, one for me and one for Kate. I went to the sunroom and placed them on the table. There was a nearly full moon, the light bounced off the snow through all the windows, washing the room in a dim white gauzy light. I looked up, I could see a sky full of stars through the skylight. I took my glass and raised it, a toast to the spirit I knew sat across from me. I drank my wine.

I leaned back in my chair, fixed my eyes on one of the stars in the lower right corner of the skylight. I went deep into thought. I kept seeing Spokes' face, his look of disbelief as life oozed out of his chest. I know it's sick, but I had the strangest sense of satisfaction. I wondered if the three ladies knew what I had done. I know Kate never would have approved. She would say something like, "You've condemned your immortal soul to hell." I don't know, maybe I have. But what's left of my life would have been hell if I had not followed through.

I concentrated on the star. It had actually moved, more than a couple inches. I had never been able to sit in one spot that long. A lot of things had changed. I had become no better than some of the clients I'd represented. Maybe I was right. Given the right circumstances, we may all be capable of killing someone. Maybe we all have a dark side to our heart. Lord knows, I'd found mine. But I could rationalize it. I had good reason. It was really Spokes' fault. All I wanted was my Kate back, wanted my life back. He should've just left us alone.

As I stared ahead, the star sailed right out of the window. A while later, I was greeted by a blazing pink sky that turned a deep red as the sun eased its way over the eastern horizon. I could hear the cardinals chirping at the feeders. I sat in wonderment. Life would never be the same.

A little after seven the phone rang, it was Tony. "Where were you last night?" he asked.

"I was right here."

"Don't give me that shit."

"I was. Why?"

"I had on WCCO radio. Guess who was found dead in his office?"

"How in the hell am I suppose to know?"

"Attorney John Spokes."

"No shit," I said. "That's what he gets for fooling around with those Nigerians."

"You didn't have anything to do with it, huh?"

"No way! I was here all night."

"You better hope you were. They already had a quote by the chief of police. He's guaranteed the mayor they're gonna find out who did it."

"Well, I wish them all luck," I said. "What are you doing?"

"Talking to you."

"I know that. Do you have time for a cup of coffee? I mean, I'll come in."

"Sure, where do you wanna meet?"

"How 'bout Jimmy's?" I said. I looked at the clock. "I can be there in twenty minutes."

As I hung up, I had no idea whether he believed me or not, and I didn't care. I suspect he knew, but he wasn't going to say anything. In twenty minutes, he would probably know for sure, anyway. He would only have to look at my face. I'm sure I would telegraph it.

He was already sitting in a booth when I walked into Jimmy's. I sat down and ordered a big breakfast—eggs, hashbrowns, bacon, whole wheat toast. I was hungry. For some reason, I felt like a tremendous burden had been taken off of me.

Tony watched as I sat down, placed my order. He stared at me as I poured my first cup of coffee, steady handed. He smiled, never mentioned Mr. Spokes.

As I waited for the breakfast to be served, I sipped on my coffee. "What do you think it would cost to get us started in your greenhouse business?" I asked.

"Oh, I think we could get a pretty good start with fifteen, twenty thousand dollars. I would start with just two small greenhouses, maybe, seventy-five hundred, eight thousand apiece, enough to get us going on our stock. I've got it all worked out if you want to see the figures."

"No, I trust you," I said.

I reached into my coat pocket, got the envelope out and threw it on the table. He casually picked it up, opened it, his eyes widened. "Where'd you get this?" he asked.

"I've been saving up."

"I bet you have," he said. "When did you make the withdrawal?"

I didn't respond. I just stared out the window, watched the cars go by, deep in thought.

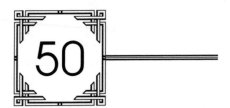

A month later, I closed the doors to my law office. I'd cleaned up all the leftover files. On the only flat piece of land on my farm, Tony and I had built two thirty-by-sixty-foot greenhouses. By the end of April, they were filled with bedding plants we had grown—geraniums, petunias, impatience, snapdragons, some herbs. We had arrangements to sell everything we could grow to one of the garden stores in town. We were already planning our next expansion.

The police are still looking for the killer of Attorney John Spokes. Every once in a while, one of the TV stations will do a news story, sort of an update. Shortly after it happened, Crime Stoppers put up a big reward for information leading to an arrest. The publicity slowly died down, and I haven't heard anything for a long time. I assumed it all got chalked up to just another one of those senseless killings, like poor Pam Weber.

There was a short article in the *Trib* that reported that, with the death of Spokes, some unidentified financial backers of the plan to reopen horse racing at Canterbury Park had pulled out, and it appeared the plan was dead at the state legislature.

Tony and I never brought the subject up until one day when we were working in the greenhouse. Tony told me he had called the homicide detective he knew in Minneapolis and casually brought up Spokes' name. The detective told him they were looking for some guy named Matthew. Spokes apparently had a meeting with him that evening at the Radisson South. The detective told Tony some curious things had occurred. For some months before his death, Spokes had taken an unusual number of trips to Antigua, and his bank balances showed some unexplained large deposits. They had talked to the feds, but it was doubtful they would ever figure it out.

On a nice warm Saturday in early spring, when Carol was home, she, Tony and I went for a walk in the woods. I took them to a sunny hillside and we stopped. I pointed ahead. There were the little blue-and-pink petals of the periwinkle on delicate green stems, poking out of the decaying brown leaves of last fall. Carol and I looked at each other. She reached over and hugged me. I could feel the warm tears as they rolled down my cheeks.

About the Author

Daniel Eller graduated from St. John's University in Collegeville, Minnesota, in 1965, and received his law degree from Georgetown University Law Center in 1969. After graduation, he served as law clerk to Federal Judge Miles Lord on the Federal District Court for Minnesota. He moved back to his home town, St. Cloud, in the fall of 1970 and became District Public Defender in 1977, a position he held until 1990.

As public defender and in his private practice, Eller has tried serious felony cases with state-wide notoriety, including many cases of first-degree murder. He has been recognized by his peers as a Leading Attorney in his field of criminal law and has been selected as a "Super Lawyer" in criminal defense based on research conducted by *Law & Politics*.

Eller continues to practice law in central Minnesota. In his spare time, he is putting the finishing touches on the next novel he intends to publish: In the Interest of Justice.